FLAMES
OF
HERAKLEITOS

BOB LOCK

Screaming Dreams

FIRST EDITION
- 2007 -

Published by
Screaming Dreams

13 Warn's Terrace, Abertysswg, Rhymney
Gwent, NP22 5AG, South Wales, UK

www.screamingdreams.com

ISBN : 978-0-9555185-1-5

Printed in the UK by
Diggory Press Ltd, Three Rivers, Minions,
Liskeard, Cornwall, PL14 5LE, England

Acknowledgements

Many thanks to Youwriteon.com, who are sponsored by The Arts Council of England, for their help in getting this story read by everyone on their site and the subsequent feedback from those readers.

Thanks too for the kind words from the author Neal Asher, author Phil Whitaker and Joanna Devereux, agent for Pollinger Publishers.

To my family and friends for their editing and criticism, another big thank you.

Preface

<u>Herakleitos of Ephesus lived circa 535-475 BC</u>

Herakleitos was a pre-Socratic Greek philosopher whose writings only survive in fragments quoted by other authors.

Disagreeing with Thales, Anaximander, and Pythagoras over the nature of the ultimate substance, he claimed that the nature of everything is change itself.

Herakleitos uses fire as a metaphor rather than his solution to material monism. This led to the belief that change is real, whilst stability illusory. For Herakleitos everything is 'in flux', as exemplified in his famous aphorism 'Panta Rhei': Everything Flows.

Chapter 1

'Everything becomes fire, and from fire everything is born.' –
Herakleitos

'That's one small step for man, one giant leap for mankind.'
The black and white television's picture flickered and James
Fenton took off his slipper and threw it at the screen. It struck
the small set with a satisfying whack and the picture stabilized.
Lucy, his four-year-old daughter tottered over to where it had
fallen and picked it up.

'Good girl, Lucy, bring it back to Daddy,' Fenton said and
craned his neck to look over the child's mass of black curls as
the news repeated Armstrong and Aldrin beginning their
momentous walk across the moon's surface.

The child turned to watch the screen and Fenton sighed,
'Lucy, move out of the way, love. Daddy can't see the
television. Bring it back; there's a good girl.' He struggled to
re-position his body to get a better view but his broken leg
responded with a jolt of pain. 'Shit!' He yelped and clutched at
the plaster-cast covering the limb.

'Daddy said shit!' Lucy exclaimed, pointing the slipper at
him, 'Mommy will shout at you, naughty.'

'Daddy's got a boo boo on his leg, Lucy. That's why Daddy
swore. But you're right, Mommy will shout at Daddy for being
rude,' Fenton conceded. 'Bring the slipper, baby.'

Lucy carried the slipper over to her father and carefully
placed it on the foot that protruded from beneath the plaster-
cast. He'd have to keep the cast on his leg for another six weeks
until the bone, broken by a fall from scaffolding, would be
healed enough for its safe removal.

Fenton hated being confined to the house, let alone the
chair in the living room. He was a tall, rangy man who had

spent most of his life outdoors, participating either in his favourite sport, football, or at work in the construction company. Now, however, he was able to spend more time with his child. Something Emma, his wife, had warned him he did not do enough of. Moreover, she was right and he knew it. Nevertheless, staying at home would not put food on the table.

'Not that I have any choice for the next month and a half anyway,' he said to himself. His stomach burned and he rubbed it with his hand; too much sitting down inevitably led to a bout of indigestion for him.

'Lucy, darling, go get a glass of water for me, please.' He smiled at the child. Dutifully she went into the kitchen and he heard her climb onto her little stool, turn on the tap and fill the plastic beaker with the bunnies on it, her special beaker. As the sound of the tap stopped, Fenton grimaced, a searing pain shot through his stomach and he doubled over in the chair in agony. Grinding his teeth, he looked up and watched Lucy return to the room with the tumbler held in both hands, her full attention on it. She did not want to spill any of the water on the carpet. On reaching his chair, she looked up at him and stopped. He frowned as he saw her eyes open wider as if she was staring at something in the air above his head. Her face became pallid.

'Come on Lucy, Daddy's wait...' his breath was ripped from his chest as he gasped in horror and anguish. An incredible sensation of pain ran through his whole body and he convulsed uncontrollably. An agony unlike any he had ever felt before gripped his lower body so forcefully his bowels evacuated unintentionally. He gripped his midriff with both hands as an ever-mounting sense of burning shot through him. His hands, first becoming warm, felt a huge increase in heat as the temperature of his abdomen soared and the terrifying pain increased. Finally, he screamed as a flare of incandescent flame burst out from his stomach.

Lucy opened her mouth to cry out, but was struck dumb by fear as her father tried to raise himself from the chair. She watched as he staggered to his feet, all thoughts of his broken leg long surpassed by the overwhelming fear and pain, which wracked his body as the fire consumed him. Now that he was standing, she saw the flames hungrily lick their way up his torso to his head. He reached forward as if begging her to help him; his hand, untouched by the fire, extended towards her face. His arm, however, was a conflagration, hissing and spitting as the fat dripped from it to the floor. The child dropped the beaker and reached her left hand out towards her father's and her index finger touched the back of his hand. At that moment Fenton's hand ignited and seared the child's finger to it. Now she screamed, a guttural, animal cry of terror and agony as the heat burnt away her flesh and scorched deep, into the bone. She fell back and her finger snapped off at the lower knuckle.

Fenton toppled to the floor as the roaring of the flames mingled with the keening wail which came from the child who huddled beneath the television set as Armstrong planted the American flag, claiming the moon for all mankind.

Boothby turned over in bed and without thinking; he reached across and felt for her. He opened his eyes and the moment passed, the dreadful pain of loss returned. His wife's side of the bed was empty. Would forever be empty. He looked passed her pillow to the bedside table bearing the photograph of her face; her smiling countenance, so full of health, warmed him and he tried to ward off the image of her emaciated body lying in the hospital bed, the image he knew would forever haunt him. Time heals. If someone ever said that to him again he had promised himself he would scream. Ten months had gone by since his Janet's death, yet the loss was as profound as if it had been only ten hours. Next to the photograph stood a half-empty bottle of cheap vodka and a little brown bottle of tablets. He reached over for the anti-depressant bottle, shook it and realizing it was empty threw it across the room. He was about to pick up the vodka when the phone rang.

'Boothby,' he croaked.

'Christ, you've been drinking again Boothby?' a female voice crooned in his ear.

'Hi Guv'. Drinking? No, just coming down with a cold, I guess.'

'Well take an aspirin; I'm on my way to pick you up. I wouldn't have breakfast if I were you though.'

'Another 'wet one' by the sounds of it then?' he asked, it was their code for a messy murder, and he started rummaging through the cabinet drawer for a Woodbine and found none.

'I wouldn't call it that exactly, but it's not a pretty sight from what I've been told already. You'll see; be with you in ten minutes. Be ready!'

'Yes, Guv',' he replied, put the receiver back on the telephone hook, and threw back the sheets. Swaying slightly he walked over to the bathroom. Shook his head in disgust as he looked at his stubble-covered face and red eyes in the mirror and scratched his square jaw tiredly.

'Ten minutes. No time for a shower, barely enough for a shit and a shave,' he moaned as he picked up the razor.

Laura Murphy curbed the front wheel of her MG pulling up outside Boothby's flat. A street cleaner jumped back in surprise, opened his mouth to remonstrate with her, and left it open as she swung the car door wide, swivelling her long legs around onto the pavement and beamed him a smile.

'Oops, sorry.' She said with a shrug.

'Oh, no problem,' the man replied and remembered to close his mouth whilst he stared at the long-legged brunette dressed in the dark-blue uniform of a Detective Inspector. Its short, cut-away tunic and skirt, accentuated her tall, slim figure as she glided past him and entered the building's foyer.

'Things are certainly looking up in the force,' the cleaner said softly as he took off his cap and scratched the top of his head. 'Modern times.' He said, shrugging and returned the cap to his balding pate.

Murphy's lips curved into a broader smile as she crossed the foyer, her rubber heeled shoes squeaking on the tiled floor. Her position as D.I. had caused many a double take, mostly by men, and she couldn't help but find it amusing. Taking the stairs to the first floor, she walked up to Boothby's door, raised a hand and was about to knock when it opened.

'Morning, Ma'am,' Boothby grinned and walked out.

She looked him up and down; his skin wasn't his usual healthy colour but at least he had shaved. His battered old leather jacket seemed to be in better condition than his face, 'Morning Boothby, looking good.'

'Don't I always?'

'Yeah, right. How you managed to wangle wearing plainclothes I'll never know,' she looked down at her own uniform, 'and I have to go around in this.'

Boothby shook his head, 'Ma'am, you're the first female D.I. to be assigned a male D.S. A bit at a time, you know what The Met's like. Change takes time,' he scrutinised her uniform carefully. 'Anyway, don't tell me that's a regulation uniform. The cut is too good. It almost looks like you've had Mary Quant knock it up for you.'

'You should keep your powers of deduction for our next case, never mind my uniform,' she tugged at her jacket, 'at least it's a better fit than your smelly old jacket. How old is that? Looks older than you, and that's saying something.'

'Smelly old jacket?' he looked annoyed, 'I'll have you know, this is a Schott. If it was good enough for Brando and Dean, then it's good enough for me. It's just a tad worn, just like me. And it's a 1938.'

'Oh, God you were born into the wrong era and country. Now you're James Dean or is it Brando?'

He gave her one of his crooked smiles. 'So what's the fuss? If it's not a 'wet one' then what the hell is it that gets you dragging me out of bed this time of the morning, acting Inspector Murphy?'

'This time of the morning? Boothby, you should have been in the office an hour ago. And if you keep messing things up for me I'll only ever will be 'acting', plus the force will look again at female and male officer partnerships,' retorted Murphy, her dark eyes flashing an ominous warning. His insubordination riled her on times but when asked to pick a male colleague she had not wanted anyone else. However, their partnership was groundbreaking and she knew critical eyes were watching them both. She did not want to be one of the first and perhaps the last D.I. to have a male sergeant.

Boothby glanced at his watch, shook his wrist a few times and put it to his ear. 'Ahh, damn thing has stopped. Sorry Ma'am. It won't happen again, and for your information it's Brando. You been to see him in that new film of his yet? I think it's called 'Burn!''

She shook her head. 'No, but it sounds about right. We're going to see a fire,' then she turned on her heel and walked back to her car with her sergeant in tow.

'From the outside you'd never imagine there'd ever been a fire,' Boothby said as he and Murphy stepped out of her little sports car that was parked half on the pavement and half on the road. He put a fist into the small of his back and groaned, 'Ma'am, a sports car might be okay for a youngster like you, but for a fifty year old copper it's a back breaker.'

She laughed, 'I'll take that as a complement, and you're fifty four, Boothby.'

The only sign that something was not right in the little suburban street of Edwardian terraced houses off Chiswick High Road, near the Gunnersbury station, was the collection of police-cars, an ambulance and fire-tender which practically blocked any possible passage through. Uniformed officers made way for the two detectives and held shocked on-lookers back. Boothby opened the little wrought-iron gate set into the white-painted brick wall, which surrounded the tiny front garden, and stepped to one side to let Murphy through.

'Thanks,' she said, and as she walked up the path to the open door, she rummaged in her suit's pocket and withdrew a handkerchief.

The stench of burnt flesh made Boothby wrinkle his nose but nothing on earth would have made him lose his breakfast, a couple of glasses of vodka, not even the sight of the remains of Fenton's body.

The forensic team was meticulously crawling over everything in the room, like a horde of locusts. Inspector Murphy stepped over the plaster-cast leg of what was once James Fenton and held the small perfumed handkerchief to her nose and mouth. She tapped one of the forensic officers on his shoulder and as he stood up she asked, 'How did it start?' She watched in annoyance as he first looked at Boothby and then returned his attention to her. It was something she knew she had to put up with. Not many had gotten used to seeing a female Inspector, let alone one as young as thirty two.

The man shook his head. 'Damn strangest thing I've seen Inspector, the Fire Brigade found no accelerants, no combustibles and the centre of the fire seems to be around the torso area of the deceased,' he indicated the area with a small, stainless steel scalpel.

She raised her eyebrows, 'No sign of a combustible?' Her annoyance grew as the examiner ignored her.

Boothby hitched up his trousers and crouched down for a closer look. He took a biro from inside his jacket and looked up at the forensic examiner, 'May I?' he pointed at the scorched carpet.

'May as well, there's bugger all left apart from his leg which is still encased in the plaster-cast.'

Boothby picked through the soot and dust, finally uncovering the carpet below. Then he pinched a small portion of the residue between his index finger and thumb and rubbed them together. He stood up and examined the seat and the curtains behind it, then shook his head. 'Strange.'

'Probably S.H.C.' Replied the examiner.

'Spontaneous Human Combustion, yeah I've heard of that,' Boothby replied.

'The first I've actually seen, but I've studied the effects. This is a text-book example,' the examiner explained.

'Rubbish,' laughed Murphy, 'there's never been any proof that spontaneous combustion in humans is possible. This man could've set himself alight with a cigarette for all we know.'

'Not really, Ma'am' the examiner replied with a frown. 'As I said, there's no clue as to what started this, but there certainly wasn't anything used to accelerate it. And it's surprisingly similar to an unsolved case down on the east coast. There they found a young man burned to death in his bed. No damage done to the room and very little done to the bed itself, but his body was destroyed.'

'Like here, look at the carpet, the seat, and the curtains. There's hardly a mark on them, yet the body has been totally consumed, well except for the leg. If I remember correctly, the human body's eighty percent water. To get the damn thing to burn up like that takes some doing. Look, even the bones are powdered.' Boothby held up his smudged figure and thumb for Murphy to inspect. 'I bet this poor bugger burned from the inside out. Okay, there's not been any tangible proof or any witnesses to such an event, but enough cases have arisen throughout the years to suggest S.H.C. is quite possible. Charles Dickens even documented it as far back as the eighteen hundreds. Damn, I'm almost sure he killed off a character in Bleak House with it!'

'Everyone's an expert now, but, actually Boothby, you're wrong on one point there,' the examiner reflected.

'Oh, which one?'

'The witness, there is a witness,' he replied.

'Well, I never heard of one. Which case was it?' asked Boothby.

'Why this one, of course,' the examiner answered.

Chapter 2

Golem

The word 'Golem' can be found in the Bible: Psalm 139:16 uses the word 'gal'mi', meaning 'my unshaped form'. Adam is described in the Talmud as first being made as a golem when his dust was 'kneaded into a shapeless hunk'. Like Adam (whose name literally means 'red (clay)'), all golems are created from mud. To animate a golem one must write one of the names of God on its forehead, place a slip of paper to its forehead, or insert a clay tablet under its tongue. Nevertheless, golems are only figments of a fertile imagination. Well, on our Earth they are.

'One is as ten thousand to me, if he be the best' - Herakleitos

Luther Krell was a mage, and like all of his kind hated being rushed. Yet as he sat in his workshop, he dwelt on the fact that a commission was a commission, and as his reputation was at stake, he had put caution aside and accepted the work. Normally he would have fasted three days for the task required but necessity had made him cut it down to two. The meat was easy to find and he ground the rotting flesh up in the bowl with his mortar. Krell, the golem-creator was nothing if not methodical. The meat he used gradually transformed into a thick, reddish brown paste. The stench permeated his small room, stuck to his clothes, and even seemed to cling to his very skin. It was a good batch, and a good omen. His next golem would be powerful.

Many potential mages, or thaumaturgists as they preferred being called, made animated beings. Thaumaturgy invoked images of miracle-workers or life-givers. However, none had yet discovered *his* method of life-giving. Many thaumaturgists succeeded in creating passable golems, but only Krell's were robust and refined. Not one had been lost in all the time he had been creating them. They had become the pinnacle of animated clay perfection. All-conquering, yet submissive and subservient to their owner. The perfect bodyguards, assassins, or if wanted, common work-horse.

Recently he had seen a creation of his protect its owner from multiple attackers. That incident had led to him being forced to hurry.

'How I hate being rushed,' he sighed as he ruminated on the circumstances that had forced him into the position he now found himself.

It had been when three golems and their handlers burst into the inn. Krell and his customer had been transacting business. Krell was hex-protected but had not taken the precaution of extending the shield to his customer. However, it was hardly necessary. Within seconds of the door being smashed off its hinges and the six assassins rushing towards them it was all over. Sarreg, Krell's customer, had dived beneath the table but Wide, his golem, had moved with incredible speed. The nearest attacker was shattered as Wide's fist tore the hex from within its throat. Then it whirled around smashing the three human handlers with an outstretched arm. The two remaining golems had frozen as their handlers had died leaving Wide to grab each by the neck. He had lifted the stiffened figures towards the ceiling and smashed them together. Pieces of hardened clay and parts of their interior wooden skeletons had flown to the four corners of the room. Customers had to dive for cover as the terracotta shrapnel showered everyone.

Krell nodded in satisfaction as he remembered how Wide had returned to their table and stood frozen, impassive; and how for a moment he had thought there was a flicker of red fire in the hollows which represented the golem's eyes. Krell had walked over to where one of the dismembered clay heads had lain and had prised open its mouth. Poking his fingers in its jaws, he had rummaged around until he had clasped onto something. Withdrawing it, he had stared at the spell-tile. There inscribed into the small plaque of terracotta, along with the golem's command, was the owner's signature. Krell remembered his surprise when he had recognised the golem's owner and how Sarreg had dragged his overweight figure up from beneath the table and dusted himself off with nervous celerity. He had dropped the tile onto the table in front of Sarreg and watched as the man's eyes had become saucer-like with horror.

'Wide will not be enough now, Krell,' Sarreg had whispered, his voice hoarse, his jowls shaking with fear. 'He'll not be enough!'

'You underestimate my work, Sarreg. Hasn't Wide proven enough tonight?'

'Thaumaturgist Krell,' Sarreg had responded, with a nervous clearing of his throat, calling the mage by his title. Krell knew this formality would only lead to a request or petition for something, 'I beg of you a boon.'

Krell had sighed, he could not deny a customer as powerful and as well connected as Sarreg, but he could make certain the man appreciated the fact that he was soon to be obligated to him. A very handy obligation too.

'Speak Minister Sarreg; your request is my command.'

A sly smile had spread across Sarreg's face. He had pushed Krell into a formal response and now a denial of the boon or favour would be beyond him.

'By Lustre's Eve I require a second golem, a golem to dwarf my stalwart Wide.'

Krell remembered how he had gasped, 'That's impossible!'

'You deny me your boon after you have freely given it?'

The room had become hushed. Customers, who had returned to their drinking, paused, tankards frozen in mid-air. Servants who had been sweeping up the remains of the golems gaped and thaumaturgist's assistants who had been extracting 'resources' from the three corpses had turned to look at Krell. One of them was Krell's own man, Davvid, his apprentice in thaumaturgy.

'*I* cannot deny you, Minister, but the forces of legerdemain may well do so,' Krell had explained. 'Never has a golem been created in such a short time span. Lustre's Eve is but four days away. I need three clear days of fasting. I need resources. But most of all, I need a soul.'

'Aye, as you say, Krell, you can't deny me.'

Krell remembered the dropped title, an insult he would never forget. 'You need three days fasting? Well, you have four. You need resources? You have a choice of three. You need a soul? Then you must procure one, my friend,' Sarreg had nodded towards the three corpses and the assistants fussing over them.

In the flickering shadows of his workshop, Krell smiled, as he had smiled that night in the inn, when he had thought, *so be it, the more people think I crop my souls from this world, the better. Nevertheless, time is short.* With a flourish of his cloak, Krell had turned, 'Davvid, I return to my rooms; when you've harvested the resources come immediately there. We've no time to waste.'

Krell recalled how once outside, the immensity of the task had weighed heavily upon him. He had been untroubled by the fasting period, he knew it could be achieved. The resources were available too, but the soul, the soul...

The last reaping had not gone well and he had just recovered from it. Another thing worried him about it too. For the first time ever, someone had seen him.

He dragged himself away from his reverie and the past then put aside all feelings of revenge that he harboured towards Sarreg. For now, he would comply with the request. He was a master-mage and he would fulfil Sarreg's request of a petition, but once accomplished then he would savour the vengeance he could rain down on the fool.

'But first things first,' he muttered as he rose from his workbench. 'It's time to reap.'

The smell of the hospital turned Boothby's stomach more than the acrid smell of Fenton's corpse and he swallowed the saliva that had built up in his mouth.

'You don't look too good,' Murphy said, noting the pale skin and sheen of sweat that had sprung up on Boothby's forehead.

'I hate hospitals. That's all.'

'Look, Boothby, I know this can't be easy for you. Hospitals must be the last sort of place you want to visit.' She thought of how he had to have spent months in one as he sat in silent vigil by his wife's side watching her slowly die. She wanted to say more, but thought better of it. His wife's death had left scars upon the man, not visible, but scars, none the less. She remembered how the first week back in work Boothby had calmly walked up to an armed bank robber and asked for his sawn-off shotgun. She had almost put him on permanent sick leave there and then until he explained that he knew the gun was unloaded. She had demanded an explanation. How did he know? However, he had just smiled at her and winked. She had given him the benefit of the doubt. The gun, it turned out, wasn't loaded.

'You can wait in the foyer if you like. I can take care of this.'

'No, I'm okay, it's just my cold. A touch of fever.'

'I felt a touch of fever too, in Fenton's house,' she said.

'Anybody would be upset in those circumstances, Ma'am.'

She looked at him and stopped. 'Obviously you didn't spot it. Did you?'

Boothby's eyes narrowed, 'Spot what?'

'The condescending way that bloody man spoke to me. First of all I thought he was going to ignore me altogether and just talk to you!'

He shook his head, 'you're talking about the forensic examiner aren't you?'

She sighed, 'Is it always going to be like that?'

'Ma'am, it's the nature of the beast. The boys take the mickey out of me because I have a woman as my boss. I either start banging heads together, escalate things or I just let them get it out of their system. They'll soon shut up when we get a few more cases closed. Especially if we crack a corker like this one. Just ignore them.'

'I suppose so.'

'Pity we weren't together for The Krays' arrest. Nipper Read's a bloody good copper and he went through the same ribbing because he was considered too young at thirty-six to be a D.I. Yet, he got them in the end. That shut up his critics,' Boothby said.

'You know him?'

'Yeah, sort of. He's always been a bit of a loner though. Didn't your boyfriend, Jason, have something to do with the prosecution?'

She screwed her eyes up at him, 'His name's Jensen, and you damn well know it is, and yes, he was on the team that prosecuted them.'

'Sorry, Jensen. Seemed like a nice sort of bloke.'

She nodded and almost in step, they walked down the magnolia painted halls. Murphy's eyes swept over the drawings and paintings done by the children on the ward. Amongst them, The Beatles, in their yellow submarine, sailed over multi-coloured landscapes. By the time they reached the door to the private room in which the tiny form of Lucy Fenton slept, Murphy was subconsciously humming the hit tune from their animation. The door was open and they went in. A tall, bald-headed doctor was standing by the bedside writing a note upon a clipboard, whilst a young nurse, barely out of her teens, smoothed down the sheets on the child's bed. The nurse stood up, adjusted her starched hat and glanced at the two detectives as they approached. Emma Fenton, a small, dark-eyed woman, sat by the bedside holding the sleeping girl's uninjured hand. They had been told Lucy's mother had not left her child's side since being admitted. Murphy and Boothby waited whilst the doctor finished his writing, then as he looked up at them Boothby opened his police warrant card and showed it to him, 'I'm Sergeant Boothby, this is Inspector Murphy. You are?'

'Good afternoon, I'm Doctor Marks, can I help you?'

'That depends, one moment please,' Murphy interrupted and went over to the woman by the bedside.

'I'm deeply sorry for your loss Mrs Fenton. I know this must seem beyond all comprehension, but we must try to establish what happened in your home earlier today.'

Marks raised an eyebrow, 'Are you serious?'

'Doctor Marks, we have to make enquiries. Mr Fenton's death wasn't... wasn't... normal,' Murphy replied and catching Boothby's eyes, she looked towards the door, signalling that a distraction was needed to take the doctor away.

'Doctor Marks, if I might have a word with you in private for a moment?' Boothby gripped Marks by the elbow and steered him towards the door. As the doctor opened his mouth to complain Boothby spoke over him, 'This shouldn't take long, please.' He closed the door to the private room behind him.

The young nurse who had been fussing with the sheets, walked over to a vinyl covered chair, picked up the magazine resting on it and sat down to read. Murphy noted that the girl's eyes seemed more drawn to the scene in the room than the contents of the journal. She pulled up the twin of the nurse's chair and sat down next to Lucy's mother. Murphy watched quietly as the petite, dark-haired woman attempted to control herself. Her face was pale and puffy; mascara streaks mixed with tears on her handkerchief as she dabbed at her reddened eyes.

'What happened? Nobody will explain exactly what happened to my husband and child.' Emma Fenton sobbed quietly.

'We were hoping you and Lucy might be able to tell us that Mrs. Fenton. So far, forensics hasn't been able to throw any light on the circumstances that led up to your husband's death. Can you talk me through what you did this morning?'

Emma Fenton's gaze was drawn back to her child and Murphy waited patiently for her answer, if any answer would be forthcoming. She wondered if it was too soon to put the woman through further interrogation. Then Mrs. Fenton seemed to rally her thoughts and turned her dark eyes on the Detective Inspector.

'I can't think straight and I still don't understand it Inspector. It was just another normal morning for us, nothing odd about it. We were excited about the Apollo 11 touching down during the night, of course. We had breakfast. My husband settled down to watch the television, and I decided to go shopping,' she replied, a wisp of dark hair dropping over her eyes, she moved it back and looked at Murphy again.

'Go on.' Murphy prompted and watched Emma Fenton's bottom lip quiver before she continued.

'Nothing unusual about it at all, well, apart from Jim being home I suppose. He was looking forward to spending more time with Lucy during his convalescence, and of course he wanted to see the repeat of the moon landing. It happened too early for us to watch live and I wasn't really interested in it to be honest. However, being cooped up like that was hard for him, he is…'she paused and drew a long, shuddering breath,

'…was… an outdoors' person. I finished shopping, got home and found…'

Murphy put her arm around the sobbing woman, 'I'm sorry Mrs Fenton. Perhaps it is too early to put you through this, but you have to understand. We've no idea what happened in your home. Any little item that you recall, no matter how small, could prove invaluable to us. That's why I need to ask you these questions, whilst it is all fresh in your mind.'

The woman raised her mascara streaked face, 'Fresh in my mind?' she took in a shuddering breath. 'Do you think I'll ever be able to forget the scene in my front living room?' she shook her head in amazement at the D.I. 'I'll take that image to the grave with me. The sound of my child, screaming the words repeatedly until her voice broke. She hasn't spoken since.'

Murphy's heart seemed to skip a beat. No one had mentioned the girl had spoken. Perhaps it was the break they needed. She took the woman's small hand in her own, 'What words, Mrs Fenton? We were not told that she had said anything.'

'I've been told she was almost catatonic by the time the emergency services came; they think she might never speak again. Her finger, her tiny finger…' Emma Fenton replied.

Murphy patted the woman's shoulder, 'What words?' she continued. 'It could be very important.'

Lucy's mother took a deep breath, 'She kept repeating …the bat…the bat…the bat.'

'The bat?'

'That's all she would say. Over and over again, pointing at the curtains above Jim's chair, the bat…the bat.'

'I don't understand, was there a bat of some sort in the room? A cricket bat perhaps. Do you know what she was referring to?'

'My husband detested cricket; football was Jim's sport,' she replied. 'He loved his football. No Inspector, I can only think she meant the animal. She'd seen one on Peter Scott's 'Look' program and thought it was a bird, Jim explained to her it wasn't. That's the only thing I can think of.' The grief-stricken woman's eyes seemed to cloud over as once again the horror surfaced and threatened to swamp her. She sobbed quietly and turned to look at her daughter again as if seeking confirmation that she was still alive, breathing and within her reach.

'Okay Mrs Fenton, we'll leave the questioning for now. We'll come back in a day or two. Nevertheless, I must warn you, we'll have to speak to Lucy too. Perhaps you could try talking to her when she wakes, gently of course, anything she could tell us…' Mrs Fenton rose and took the Inspector's hand from her shoulder, interrupting her.

'Don't you understand?' She said shaking her head, her dark eyes were no longer looking haunted but blazed with anger, 'My daughter's not sleeping. She's in a coma. The doctors say her brain has taken refuge from the horror that she witnessed this morning by shutting down. She may never wake up, never speak,' slumping back down into the chair, she cradled her head in her hands. The brief moment of anger draining her last reserves. The young nurse stood up and approached Murphy.

'Inspector, I really think you should leave now,' she said blushing.

Murphy nodded, feeling as sterile and antiseptic as the stark room. Too emotional to speak she left with the quiet weeping of Emma Fenton sounding in her ears.

Luther Krell praised his apprentice, Davvid, for his immaculate preparations. The glands the young mage had extracted from the bodies were healthy and soon to be rendered down into the juice he required. Luther had gorged on the first day to replenish his reserves of vitality and the juice had been a welcomed supplement. He knew many thaumaturgists failed to replace the vital fluids and enzymes that a mage's body lost when producing a golem, and many had paid the price.

No legerdemain or sleight of hand could turn a vegetable back in to a revenant again. Returning from the dead is one matter, being alive but with no spark of intelligence, no sense of self, was worse than being one of the things he created, a golem.

The two subsequent days were spent fasting and preparing the spells. The spell-tiles had been fired, their glyphs and instructions neatly incised. The lure paste had rotted well; the stench filled the small house. Soon his neighbours would start giving him black looks again, but they would never dare to grumble. Now as his assistant packed the leather holdall with the necessary equipment and cleaned the workbench Luther Krell sat in a trance-like state, preparing for the reaping to come.

Meanwhile, Davvid sat and waited in silence for his master and mentor's spirit to return to his body. He knew that Luther Krell could exist for days in non-corporeal form, but ultimately he had to return to the body, or the vehicle for his mind would die and his travelling essence would be left, wandering the ether for eternity. The assistant sat crossed legged in front of his master and studied Krell's face and form. Davvid often wondered how old Luther Krell really was. Certainly, no clue could be obtained by looking at the master's face. Yet he had survived for many hundreds of years and his golems survived too. However, the once fair hair of his youth had turned pewter grey and no longer hung shoulder length, but was worn cropped short to just below his ears. His lined face bore no scars or blemishes but carried the pale, delicate features of someone who spent little time relaxing or working beneath the sun. He knew that Luther must have created scores and scores of golems and nearly all of them were still in service. Davvid noted the man's wide and sinewy shoulders, the hard knobbles of bone that protruded from beneath the erubescent cloak, a red as dark as coagulated blood, barely covering the folded wings; wings that Davvid coveted.

One day he too hoped to have enough magical essence within him to form a pair. He held no illusion as to the cost it would entail to extract that essence from within and the toll it would be on his body. It was not simply a matter of growing wings but of actually forcing out the structure from his skeletal frame. He could little afford the cost on the poor stipend that he received from Krell. The money he would need to pay for resources and the replacement juices for his spent essence would be unthinkable for someone of his social standing. During his apprenticeship, Davvid's payment was in knowledge, and was not monetary, but Davvid knew that financial reward would be easy, once he could reap souls for himself. Then the next step would be golem construction. He glanced towards Krell's new construct and once again shook his head in awe. The empty shell of the new golem was huge. Its head almost touching the ceiling of the room; a ceiling that Davvid estimated to be easily eight foot in height. Whereas a normal golem was a poor facsimile of a man with crude form and little detail, this giant was almost a copy of Luther Krell's best creation to date, Sarreg's Wide. Its shoulders were broad, its chest deep and well sculptured. The muscles on its clay arms and legs highly defined. This golem had been much too large to fire in Krell's kiln, probably too large for firing in *anyone's* kiln. Luther Krell had fired the clay construct in situ by using an ancient and long forgotten thaumaturgic hex that no one could witness, not even Davvid. It had been baked within this very room, but no sign of scorching was visible anywhere, a miraculous piece of magical dexterity. This had to be the world's largest. If Krell could pull this off and in such short time, if he could deliver the massive golem to Sarreg on the night of Lustre's Eve, he would carve his name into history for all time.

'You think it cannot be done my young novitiate?' Krell asked, his eyes still closed

Davvid jumped as Krell spoke. 'Master, of course not. Only you, Thaumaturgist Krell, have the power to animate such a construct,' Davvid replied formally, using his master's title and bowing his head.

Krell smiled, he held his apprentice in high regard, and he felt he would be a brilliant reaper and golem-master in time. Perhaps another hundred years or so, he had told him, but not yet, not yet.

He rose from the floor with ease, stretched his long limbs and unfolded the gossamer wings. The light from the unshuttered window behind him shone through their thin membrane, revealing the tiny network of veins that criss-crossed them. Krell was proud of his wings and he smiled inwardly as he flaunted them in front of his novice, the boy could barely keep the avarice from his eyes.

'All's prepared?' Krell asked, knowing full well that Davvid had everything ready.

'Yes master, all is done,' he replied and handed Luther Krell the leather satchel.

Krell nodded and accepted the bag, strapped the belt around his waist and let the holder lie against his thigh. 'I should be back before dawn,' he said as he walked towards the window, 'I'll be exhausted from the soul-reaping. Prepare a broth and the remains of the juice for my return. I'll feast to replace the essence lost from my exertions and then sleep for some hours. Wake me before sundown.'

'As you command, master. I wish you luck with your reaping.'

'Luck has nothing to do with it my novitiate, nothing at all. Preparation is everything, however.'

Davvid inclined his head in deference as Krell stepped through the large window onto the small balcony, and without another word or gesture, soared out into the still air.

The valley appeared on the horizon and Krell breathed more freely. Now he was within reach of his target the mounting anxiety he had been feeling began to subside. Even though he had cast glamours to hide his departure from his apartments he still worried that an enemy or competitor would follow or even try to stop him from reaching his goal. If he did not complete his boon to Sarreg then his reputation would collapse around him; he would struggle to get commissions again. He could afford to retire in luxury but riches were not his motivation in life. He was Thaumaturgist Luther Krell; he lived for his work; without it, he was as good as a *foreverdead*. Krell had died a number of times, but with preparation, he had survived his death and had entered his new host. Nevertheless, should his preparation be incomplete, or should the time come when he did not want to exist anymore, then he would embrace the afterlife open armed and join the ranks of those who went before, the *foreverdead*.

Luther landed some distance away from a small copse, folded his wings and with a small hand movement cast a questing hex for any followers. He was pleased to find none. He strode deeper into the woods. Wiry leather-leaved trees rustled and swayed as he brushed past them, he ignored them, intent on finding his quarry. He raised his head and sniffed the air, he was sure he had detected something. He stopped for a second; closing his eyes, he drew in a long deep breath.

Yes, there it was. The faint aroma of rotting. He cast his head around to the direction from which the stench emanated. With his head held high to capture the slightest nuance of the scent, he walked on. The putrid aroma grew stronger as he approached a small clearing within the copse of leather-leaves.

He entered the arena-like area and stiffened as his foot crushed something brittle beneath him. Looking down, he saw he had stepped upon a dirge's nest. Scowling, he stamped and trampled the fragile construction and its contents beneath his heel then wiped the broken and crushed clutch of eggs from his soft boot. Albumin and parts of dirge foetus marred the lush grass as he cleaned them off.

'Damn birds,' he cursed. 'Sing your funeral song over that!' Knowing that once discovered the area would echo with the animal's strident screeching. Krell despised the raucous little creatures. Satisfied that his boot was clean, he cast around for the source of the pungent aroma and grunted to himself when he spied the plant. A garish floor-hugging growth, which was the colour of decaying flesh. It rested besides the trunk of a dead leather-leaf tree. Its flower, which had petals the size of his hands, was puffy and bloated. The surrounding leaves were dark brown and were almost as big as his torso.

He sat down beside it and watched the centre of the petals stir, excited by the vibration of his movement. A subtle tremor of magical force wafted from the plant as Krell opened his satchel and withdrew a number of items. A small wooden container with an intricate screw fitted top caused the plant to shiver in delight as he placed it on the ground close by. Next, he arranged a number of spell-tiles in order and within easy reach. One tile in particular he checked and rechecked. A filigree of glyphs raced across its surface almost as if they were alive. Even to someone as powerful and as well versed in the thaumaturgic arts as Krell, it still proved to be an hypnotic sight. Tenaciously calming himself, he looked away. Finally, he opened a small leather pouch and withdrew the powdered remains of the golem handlers that Wide had killed. He sprinkled the powder in a rough circle around his position, making sure it encompassed all of the plant and him, and left no gaps.

Krell opened the wooden container and the plant's leaves and petals shook in anticipation. He inserted two fingers, scraped the fetid paste out, and looked at it. The meat had rotted well. There was hardly any difference between the plant's stench and the paste he inserted into his mouth. He wiped his hand on the grass beside him and lay down beside the plant's flower. The growth slowly wrapped him within its leaves and the flower, with ominous care, approached his face and open mouth. The petals parted as the flower head got closer and Krell saw the thick stamen rise, questing and probing from within. The air filled with magic. Krell could feel it rippling through his body, and the closer the stamen got to his mouth the more the reaction of the magic coursed through him like a ravaging flame. Soon he would voyage and then reap.

Something bothered him; it was on the edge of his consciousness and troubling him, an itching on the back of his right hand. The itching turned to a burn as the plant's stamen entered his mouth to try in vain to pollinate the rotted meat. He lifted his hand and looked in wonder at the vision of a child's burnt finger that had sprouted from the back of it. It was then he realised the reaping would not be as he expected.

'Luck has nothing to do with it!' He mumbled and almost choked as laughter billowed up from his chest.

The dirge hen returned to her nest with a maw full of worms and ran in circles around it in frantic panic. Where was her clutch of eggs? The worms fell to the ground as she opened her beak-like mouth and wailed the vibrant call that gave her the genus name – dirge.

The call echoed around the copse, an insidious wail that wormed its way into the very matrix of the flora and fauna. But it could not reach her destroyed, unhatched fledglings and it could not reach Luther Krell who detested it so, and whose mind was no longer upon the same planet. It was now traversing the ether towards perhaps another dimension, at least another planet, he did not know. Her cry did reach another's ears however, someone who had secretly followed Luther.

Davvid crouched in fright as the sound sent shivers down his back.

'Can it be possible that Luther's discovered me following?' He asked himself quietly. Regaining control of his nerves, he stood up and looked at the tile he had sequestered from underneath his mentor's nose. He turned it slightly until the figures upon it aligned. Then he started walking back to where he had left his mount. He was getting closer to Krell's secret.

The hen cried two or three times more before spying the morass upon the trampled grass and then she buried her razor sharp beak-like mouth into it. She wailed once again as the odour of her destroyed brood impinged upon her tiny brain. Then she stopped, another smell titillated her senses, the scent of the destroyer. She poked her hardened tongue into the remains of her children and tasted the scent, drew air over her tongue and up into her nasal cavity where the smell grew stronger and she began to hunt. It did not take long for her to find the spoor, and within minutes she arrived at the hex-circle that Krell had lain down to both contain his reaping and protect his comatose body. The glamour it exuded was sophisticated and complex, meant to fool any hunter from finding him. All they would see would be a large boulder within a deserted opening of a leather-leaf copse. Sophistication was not the forte of a dirge hen however. Normally they were placid creatures, who would steer well clear of any animal other than one of their species, but this hen had transcended the meaning of normal, this hen was enraged and had only one thing on its minute mind... and that was to track the spoor of whatever had destroyed her nest and her unborn chicks.

'Did you really know it was empty?'

'What're you going on about now, Inspector?' Boothby asked, but he knew what she was digging for. Every now and then, when she thought he had mellowed or had let his guard down, she would ask. Three days had gone by since the Fenton fire and she'd asked him the same question once already.

Murphy crunched the gears on the little MG and Boothby winced, wishing again that she would let him drive. She kept him waiting for her answer until she found the gear she was looking for and the car leapt forward. 'You know damn well what I'm on about, when're you going to tell me Boothby?' She glanced at him. 'And what the hell's wrong with this bloody car?'

He raised a hand to his mouth to cover the smile he knew was beginning to appear and then switched on the radio, Marvin Gaye's velvet voice filled the car with '*I heard it through the grapevine*' and he kept time to the beat with his foot.

'I love this song,' he said, trying not to laugh at Murphy's driving. How she had succeeded in passing her driving test he never knew, he glanced down at her long legs, then studied her dark eyes and high cheekbones and took a wild guess.

He composed his face and let out a sigh, 'Off the record?'

'Agreed. Off the record. Just for my ears only, I need to know, Boothby. You owe it to me. I need to know I can trust you with my life. I could once, but since…well you know. You changed, Boothby, after she died.'

Boothby ruminated over her words. Murphy was right, he knew it. He had been hoping the gun *had* been loaded that day. He had been hoping he could have pressured the poor jerk into pulling the trigger and finishing it for him. However, the damn gun had been empty and he had over-powered the potential bank-robber. That resulted in some great publicity for his station and he ended up with a commendation. Murphy had a right to know. Nevertheless, he knew once he told her the truth she would never trust him again. Now she needed the assurance that her trust had not been misplaced. Therefore, he told her.

'How many times are you going to ask?' he shrugged, 'Of course I knew the damn thing was empty. The fool hadn't closed the barrels properly. There was no way in hell there could've been cartridges in it. I would've seen them.' He lied. 'What can I tell you, Guv'? I know I've changed since she died. Forty one is too young to die.' He smiled sadly, 'The boys back at the yard always said I looked more like her father than her husband, but I'm only a dozen or so years older than she was. Janet was everything to me. I know I'm not the same, but you can still depend on me.' His determined look confirmed his statement. 'And there's nothing wrong with the car. Just try using the clutch occasionally. I really wish you'd let me drive, Ma'am.'

Murphy nodded her head and then looked at him again, 'The clutch?'

'Yes, Ma'am, the pedal that you're resting your left foot on?'

'Oh, the clutch. Very funny, and forget about driving, I saw what you did to the last car you were assigned,' she retorted.

'Ma'am, you ever tried to get a V6 Ford Transit to stop when it's full of stolen bank-notes and the driver thinks he's Stirling Moss?' He didn't wait for her answer, 'The only way for me to do it, before he got onto the motorway, was to spin him out on a clear patch of road. The Morris Minor Panda car isn't really a greyhound, more like a tortoise, actually. It was due to be de-commissioned anyway…'

She answered him with a huff and swung the car through the gates of St.Bart's, into the hospital car-park, narrowly missing a sign post warning drivers to take care within its grounds. Above the gate the statue of Henry V111 stood glaring down, hands on hips, as if chastising her driving too.

Boothby shook his head; the sign may as well be in Dutch.

'And stop shaking your head Sergeant!'

'Yes Ma'am,' he replied and gripped the door rest as she skidded to a stop in front of the hospital entrance.

The couple approached the clerk on duty in the hospital's reception and Boothby flipped open his identity card, 'Hello, I'm D.S. Boothby, this is Inspector Murphy.' He nodded in her direction. 'We understand that a young girl, Lucy Fenton has been moved to another room?'

The grey-haired woman examined Boothby's card with care and then looked at her admissions' book, turned a few pages and ran her finger down the long list until it stopped and then tapped the page twice, 'Yes Sergeant, she's in room four on the first floor, poor child.'

'Thank you Ma'am, most helpful.'

They walked towards the stairs as Boothby returned his wallet to the inside pocket of his old leather jacket and adjusted the little lead-filled cosh that he liked to keep for emergencies. Murphy pulled a face and said, 'When are you going to spend some money and throw that heap of shit jacket in the rubbish-bin?'

'Hey, I've told you, this is a classic, I think they started up around 1928.'

'Ha! A classic what though, Boothby?' She screwed her eyes up at him.

The banter continued until they reached the girl's room, 'Well, there's our good Doctor Marks. Looks like he's had a haircut.' Boothby nudged her.

'Christ, don't start, you upset him enough the last time.'

'Me, upset someone? Never,' he replied and put on one of his grins.

'Doctor Marks, it's nice to see you again. You look a little different, is that a new haircut?' Boothby extended his right hand; the Doctor shook it and then patted the few wisps of hair above his ears, 'I pick up on things like that, all part of the job.'

'How's Lucy, Doctor?' Murphy shouldered Boothby to one side.

'Not good I'm afraid. She's regained consciousness but remains unresponsive. I don't think we'll see any improvement for a very long time, if indeed ever. The shock to the little girl's system has simply overwhelmed her, umm...' he paused and seemed reluctant to continue.

'Something else, doctor?' asked Murphy.

'Look, it's about Mrs. Fenton. She's very close to breaking down. Please, don't put her through too much,' he stopped as the handle to Lucy's door moved.

The door opened quietly and Lucy's mother stepped out, 'Hello Inspector, hello Sergeant Boothby.'

'Hello Mrs. Fenton, I want to apologize for pushing you for information three days ago. It was inappropriate of me and I'm sorry,' Murphy said.

'It's okay Inspector. I know now you were only doing it for the best. But I can't see how we can help you, Lucy may be awake but it's as if she's not there anymore. She's gone. I feel as if I've lost her too.'

Murphy put a protective arm around the woman's shoulders and was about to speak when Boothby grabbed her arm and put his fingers to his lips.

'Boothby...' Murphy started to say, but Boothby whispered, 'Quiet!'

The four people froze at his whispered command and listened. Then they heard it; a small sound from within the room, Lucy's voice, repeating one word, 'Bat –bat—bat.'

Boothby swung open the door and gasped, Lucy was sitting up in bed, her pyjamas were smouldering; her face red and dripping with perspiration. Behind and above her, a tenuous shape took form. Murphy gripped Boothby's arm, her fingers dug into the leather of his sleeve and as he tore from her grip, her nails ripped and splintered. He dashed to the bed, pulled the child by the front of her pyjama top towards him, tearing out the intravenous tubes as he did so, and launched the little girl into Murphy's arms as the bat-shaped nightmare reached for her.

Murphy staggered backwards out of the room with the screaming child in her arms as Boothby spun and pulled out the small cosh from his jacket. The bat entity took on more substance as it changed from pursuing the child and enveloped the man.

Boothby swung the cosh but it only connected with air, it was if he was striking at a shadow. Although more defined, the bat-form still had no mass. His old jacket burst into flames and he roared in pain and anger as the touch of the bat burned through his flesh. Realising he would never be able to fight the beast, he turned and staggered towards the doorway. As his head flared into an incandescent torch, he saw Murphy return to the room and he desperately tried to tell her to stop but the unbelievable heat ripped the air from his lungs.

Murphy hit the knob of the extinguisher with her bloodied fist and sent a stream of foam to smother Boothby and splatter across the room, ripping through the shadowy figure that loomed above them like a vast vampire. Boothby crashed to the floor and Murphy played the foam around him and everything possible that she could cover; then she bathed the vampiric shape until she saw it begin to disperse.

The hospital alarm system kicked in adding to the cacophony of sound, the screaming of Murphy, Mrs. Fenton and Lucy. Marks reached into the room and tried to pull Boothby out by his sleeve, but fell back with a handful of burnt leather and charred flesh; he looked aghast at the contents of his hand. Emma Fenton, coming to her senses, scooped Lucy into her arms then ran down the hallway towards the group of orderlies and nurses who were responding to the alarm. The extinguisher spluttering and coughing stopped expelling the white foam and Murphy threw it into the bat's dissipating form. She watched hypnotised as the thing finally wavered, then winked out of existence. A moan from near her feet brought her mind back to Boothby and she knelt down in the foam, amidst the blood and charred remnants of his wracked body.

His right arm was totally consumed to the shoulder, the right side of his face was charred but his eye was intact. The left side of his body was a seared mass of flesh, the left arm was stripped to the bone; Marks had pulled the cooked flesh from it as if stripping a chicken wing. Boothby's left eye had gone; all that remained was a steaming socket. He opened his mouth to speak but she put her fingers to his charred lips, not daring to touch them.

'Don't speak, the emergency team is on its way,' she said and looked at Marks who kneeled by her side and shook his head slightly.

Boothby groaned, his lips cracked and tiny rivers of blood sprang up from them and ran down the side of his face steaming as they dried, 'Is — Lucy — okay?' His voice was a dry whisper, barely audible, his throat burnt raw from the terrific heat.

Murphy nodded, she could not reply, her throat constricted a wail that she felt build up from deep within herself, she dared not open her mouth.

'Good,' he wheezed softly and desperately sucked cool air into his ruined lungs again. Gasping with the exertion, he asked, 'Laura — you — think — my — jacket — can — be — repaired?' Then he died and Laura Murphy knew that beneath his pain-wracked and ravaged face there hid a crooked smile.

The pallbearers gently lowered the coffin into the freshly excavated grave as the vicar concluded the ceremony. One by one, Boothby's friends and colleagues filed past and dropped small handfuls of the cemetery's dark earth into the open grave until the final person, a tall graceful woman stepped forward. She caressed the remains of a tattered and scorched leather jacket that she had been carrying, folded it neatly and dropped it onto the coffin's lid. Then she opened the small, black patent-leather bag slung on her left shoulder, extracted her Inspector's warrant card and dropped that in too, knowing full well she should surrender it along with her resignation, but she cared little about any repercussions. She finally made the sign of the cross, blew a kiss at the open grave and stepped away. She walked a pace or two around the bare earth until she reached a marble headstone that bore the inscription Janet Boothby 1928 – 1968 and rested her hand on the headstone. 'Take good care of him Janet, he missed you so.'

The drayk spat at Davvid as he walked out of the copse and approached it. He clubbed the animal across its scaly snout with the back of his hand. It tried to nip him but the muzzle held its jaws enclosed, and so it spat again. This time Davvid made an intricate sign with his hand and the drayk squealed in pain and took the posture of submission to a pack leader. Davvid swung himself up into the wooden saddle strapped to the creature's back. He pulled the reins with an exaggerated roughness and kicked the beast in the flanks with his heels; the drayk unfolded its leathery wings and flapped aloft. Davvid eyed the wings hungrily; he despised having to use this mode of transport. Drayks were for those who could not afford to extrude their own wings, and to have to ride one was almost a badge of shame for a mage.

Once above the trees again he checked his tile, his quarry was nearer and so he continued following Krell's signature. He had become bolder now. Krell did not know he was following him. His strategy had worked. Over a long period of time he had sequestered various hex-tiles that his master had created, always exhibiting extreme care and caution. Should Luther Krell have discovered the theft then Davvid's life would have been forfeit. He had no illusions that the next golem made by Krell would have carried *his* soul. But his careful plotting had succeeded. None of the tiles were missed, and now he had used Krell's own work against him. Krell would not spot the glamour shield Davvid had cast around himself and the animal, for it was of his own making!

Davvid, laughing at his stroke of genius, spotted a clearing. He had a feeling something was not right. He knew immediately that Krell's work was afoot and his eyes were drawn to a large boulder that wavered slightly as he stared at it. A hand movement from him and the boulder resolved into Krell's supine figure. Davvid coaxed the drayk into landing on the other edge of the copse and dismounted. As he broke cover from the trees, a movement near his master's body made him stiffen.

Panicking again, he wondered if Krell had seen him. Then saw that it was not Krell himself that was moving, but a small animal, hardly bigger than his two hands. It was hopping up his master's legs towards his face. He watched spellbound as he realised it was a dirge hen and stared dumbfounded as the creature wailed in triumph and drove its beak into Krell's eye. His master barely flinched and the dirge hen held its head to one side to study the outcome of its attack. Davvid could not understand why the little creature had behaved so, but all thoughts of its reasoning sped from his mind as he recognised the rarest of flowers that lay next to Krell.

'A Rapture Bud!' he gasped loudly and the dirge hen turned to look at him.

Overcome with euphoria, Davvid cried, 'That is how he does it!' and started to move forward. The dirge hen returned its attention to the prone figure and looked quizzically at the pulsing tube that joined Krell to the plant. It opened its beak, and before Davvid could magic a hex, snipped the stamen in two.

Krell went into spasms. His body thrashed and convulsed, his back arched to an impossible degree as the dirge hen took fright and ran off into the undergrowth. Davvid sprinted towards the terrible form of his master, whose heels were doing their best to reach the back of his neck. The snap of Krell's spine echoed through the small copse like a whip-crack and he fell still. Davvid reached his side and put a hand on his master's chest. There was no movement. Blood covered one side of his face as it oozed from the ruined eye. Davvid took a deep breath, raised the lid on the other eye, and swore, the whole eye was black. Davvid knew this was no ordinary black. It was the endless, infinite black of a lost soul. His master's essence had been torn from his body. The vessel was dead but the soul was alive somewhere in the ether, and would remain so for eternity.

Davvid laughed now, a joyful, relieving laugh. It was all his. He would inherit everything, and he did not even have to do the killing himself! Tears of joy ran down his face as the enormity of what he was to become took hold. He would be the new Master Thaumaturgist. He would have all the riches and respect that went with the title. He knew Krell's secret for capturing the most powerful souls. It was the Rapture Bud's potent magical quality.

He turned his attention to the plant and choked when he saw that it had died. The dirge hen had not only managed to despatch his master but had also killed the plant when it cut through the stamen. The plant that held the secret. The plant that would not flower for another thirty years, and the plant that was the key to him becoming the most powerful man in the world. Killed by a hen! Davvid put his fingers into his hair and pulled out handfuls as he screamed in rage, whilst in the distance a dirge hen answered his call as if mocking him.

Chapter 3

Thirty years later: 1999

And the memories burn

Lucy Fenton opened the Boker knife and drew the little ceramic blade across the back of her forearm with care, bisecting the cicatrise network of raised scar tissue with precision. She had been doing the same for almost thirty years so had achieved a high level of expertise in self-mutilation. A small line of blood followed the track of the blade, ran in a rivulet until reaching the raised walls of previous scars and pooled there for a moment. She inclined her head slightly and lapped at the crimson fluid with her tongue. The touch of the silver stud impaled though it pleased her when it stroked her skin.

She shifted in agitation on the sofa as something hard stuck into her side and she reached her arm around to move the small, but highly potent, fire extinguisher to a better position. She was never without it strapped to her side, and to make fun of her paranoia, or to dare touch her fetish, was to incur her wrath. It was a wrath known by many of those who knew her. Lucy had a temper which would send her into a fit of violence, where any, and all, could suffer. Her knife had tasted other people's blood too when she had prowled the London streets at night just looking for trouble. If she tired of self-inflicted pain, an evening's walk would soon attract the type of street hooligan who would volunteer to provide her with an alternative. Usually they were sorry they ever approached her.

Her apartment was small and had a minimalist feel about it. There was no floor covering, just ceramic tiles with under-floor heating to keep them warm lay beneath her naked feet.

Her sofa was large and the only sitting area in the room. Positioned before it was her plasma television, one of the first produced. She liked new technology. Damaged pixel cells however, dotted it randomly but she hardly cared. There were more interesting things than watching television to do. The ceiling was low and sprouted numerous water sprinklers, far too many for such a small area. A temperature sensor winked a steady and monotonous green eye, forever guarding the room's environment. Any untoward raise in ambient temperature would set it off. The television had suffered enormously until Lucy had achieved the fine balance that the system was now set at.

As she sucked at the small wound again, and waited patiently for the blood to coagulate then scab over, something in the background drew her attention to the television. It was the end of the evening news and the reporting of a late-breaking news item.

A plastic surgeon's dream of a blonde newscaster was explaining the circumstances of a strange fire and Lucy's eyes flicked up to the screen, just in time to see the woman's face grow pale as she described the burnt body of a woman. No pictures of the scene would be shown, due to their horrifying nature.

'Now we go live to our reporter, Holly Harwood, who'll update us on the incident.' The blonde shuffled her script and looked up, 'Hello, Holly, are you there?'

The screen changed to a shadowy street, a young woman with long dark hair, which whipped and swirled around her blanched face came into view. She took her hand away from the side of her head where the in-ear headphone had come loose and said, 'Hello Tanya, yes I'm here, thank you,' the camera panned in closer to her face.

'We are here in a little backstreet in the suburbs of Bristol, where earlier this evening a woman was found burned to death. She lay on the floor of her living room; half a cat stretched out by her side. The top half of the animal was perfect, untouched, but the bottom half, which must have been in the old woman's grip, was charcoal.'

The reporter's voice rang through Lucy's head like an alarm bell, 'Whilst detectives and forensics are carefully collating and taking DNA samples it does seem that this is an inexplicable fire. There's no evidence of arson. The fire's source has not been found. Neither has any accelerant, yet Mrs. Daniel's body has been almost totally consumed by the flames. Flames, I might add that have left the rest of her room intact. Could this possibly be a case of Spontaneous Human Combustion?' she asked, 'This is Holly Harwood handing you back to the studio.'

The sound of fire-engine sirens and the wail of an ambulance filled the room as the camera flashed onto the emergency services departing. The wailing increased, for Lucy had thrown back her head and was screaming in unison, whilst drawing the knife across the material of her jump-suit and into the flesh of her thigh.

Chapter 4

Lustre's Eve Morn

Davvid Krell despised Lustre's Eve. He also despised his name, Krell. The name he inherited along with Luther Krell's fortune and business. What he did not take into consideration was how he would also inherit Krell's obligations. Thirty years had passed since he had returned with Krell's body, thrown across the rump of his drayk, like a game animal he had hunted down. Thirty long years of suffering ridicule by the populous of Marin's Weir, Krell's home township, and by any magus of note anywhere within the known world. Surprise had turned to suspicion as he explained the circumstances of Krell's *foreverdeath*.

Many of Krell's associates — calling them friends would have stretched the truth too far — commented on the strange occurrence of how both of Krell's eyes were ruined. Davvid explained how he had found his master dying, trapped in the thralls of an uncontrollable surge of thaumaturgic force, and how his body had arched like a bow, his eyes blazing with a magical ferocity before bursting.

He left out all mention of the Rapture Bud and the dirge hen. He also failed to mention it was he who destroyed Krell's other eye. The eye that would prove Luther Krell, was not *foreverdead*, but was a lost soul, wandering the ether, eternally searching for a way back. If they had discovered the truth, any claim Davvid would have had on his inheritance would have been negated.

All those years ago Sarreg had not wasted any time in visiting Davvid after receiving the news of Luther Krell's parting. Within the hour, he had battered at the door to Krell's dwelling. His golem, Wide, as usual was at his side; a menacing reminder of Sarreg's power.

'Thaumaturgist Krell.' Sarreg gave a formal bow in front of Davvid as he opened the door to the gross figure.

'Oh, Minister Sarreg. You've heard the news I take it?' Davvid asked, returning the complimentary use of title and inwardly feeling well pleased that the minister had called him Thaumaturgist.

The portly figure rose and smiled, 'Yes I have. Terrible... terrible news.'

'I'm at a loss, Minister. My mentor has left me no instructions as to what I should do in such an event as this.'

'At a loss,' Sarreg looked mockingly at Davvid who wrung his hands behind his back, for he knew he could not put Sarreg off, 'my dear boy... At a loss?'

'Yes sir, I've obligations I know and understand that, but...'

'But nothing... my dear boy. Either you complete your master's boon to me or you forfeit everything. Everything... do you understand?'

Davvid Krell had understood. To not complete a commission, or boon. To not deliver the golem to Sarreg, the evening before midnight's bell, would mean he would lose the lot. Krell's fortune, home, position, but even more valuable than all of these things, he would lose his own life.

'You have until twelve, young Davvid. I expect my golem. Alternatively... I expect you.'

Davvid remembered how he had swallowed noisily, all feelings of well being blown away like smoke and then Sarreg had lumbered away. How Wide had slowly looked down onto his face, two small flames of red shining within the depths of his empty eye sockets. Then, with a swiftness belying the vastness of his bulk, the monster had spun around and walked off after his master.

A frantic search had ensued after Sarreg's departure. Davvid had turned Krell's pockets and satchel inside out, in the hope that his master had already reaped a suitable soul for the giant golem, which kept a statue-like guard whilst he hunted in vain. That is all it would be, a statue, unless Davvid found or reaped a soul for it.

Davvid Krell's thoughts returned to the present as he sat in the darkened room where he had searched in desperation those thirty years past and cursed for letting the painful memories haunt him once more. How those bitter memories burned. He looked up at Tonn and threw the empty bottle of vesper nectar at the vast figure. As it hit and smashed into little pieces the golem flinched, and then slowly started to pick up the fragments.

'That's all you are good for you lumbering fool,' belched Davvid and then lurched to his feet. The golem, which was to be the most powerful in the world, was nothing better than a frightened house cleaner. Nevertheless, no blame could be laid at Luther Krell's feet. It was a panic stricken Davvid who had bought the deformed child from the drunkard mother, and had hurriedly reaped the child's soul. The brain-damaged boy had even walked into the kiln willingly, but the affliction had carried over into the hex-tile and ultimately, into the hulking golem, Tonn.

Davvid had been the laughing stock of Marin's Weir that Lustre's Eve all those years ago, when he had presented Sarreg with the behemoth, which had turned and ran back to the safety of Davvid Krell's room when confronted by Wide. Technically, he had fulfilled his old master's boon, and Sarreg, in a fit of drunken, magnanimous laughter had let him leave with his life, but not his pride, intact. Sometime later Sarreg even sent Davvid an ownership tile so the transference of the burdensome golem would legally revert to him, completing his downfall. No one returned a golem. It was the ultimate insult to a mage, but Davvid had to swallow his bile and accept it.

But one day he would reap more than a soul; one day he would reap revenge, and the day was close. Within a week, it would be Lustre's Eve once more, and his little sentinel within the hidden valley had informed him of how the plant was in flower at last. The three-decade wait was over. Now he could fulfil his destiny at last. He would discover and reveal the secret of the plant.

It pleased him to use the old satchel; a reminder of his one brief day of triumph. It was the day he had fooled them all and had taken up Luther Krell's mantle. However, things did not work out has he planned, but today he would taste the heady flavour of success. Davvid had prepared everything with the greatest care, the rotten meat's stench, which was a smell his neighbours had not noticed for thirty years, had permeated the area for a number of days. His hex-tiles were perfection; the instructions incised within them complicated yet also facile in their tutelage. He was proud of his work; even the ruined Tonn would understand, but if he could supplant the soul that the golem carried with another from the far side of the ether then... Davvid shivered in excitement as his mind raced over the possibilities. One of his hex-tiles, the mate of his sentinel's in the copse, swarmed with animated glyphs.

'Gar, at least *you've* proved to be dependable, my little friend,' he mused.

Davvid knew from the information that the plant had already started to give out vast amounts of thaumaturgic energy. It was time, and he had fasted for four days, one more than necessary, but the gorging of dynamism-giving juices the week beforehand had made him strong. He was confident.

He strode to the window and threw it open, stepped out onto the small balcony and in the warm rays of the morning sun spread his wings and took to the air. The thrill of autonomous flight never failed to captivate him. The cost had been high, but the suffering of the last three decades had at least given him one long-coveted thing, his wings.

The flight to the leather-leaf copse was uneventful. Although he did keep a close watch on the various glamours he had prudently set in place to avoid being followed or detected. When he landed, he sniffed the air. The reek of rotting meat greeted his nostrils and he smiled. His sentinel, a small golem, barely higher than his knee approached and Davvid took the tile from within its mouth. It had allowed it to communicate with the twin tile in his possession and he placed it in the satchel. As he removed another tile from the leather bag and inserted it, the golem stiffened and glared around the small clearing. Davvid did not want to suffer the same fate as Luther Krell; no dirge hen would interfere with this reaping. Although the golem was small, the tile it carried allowed it to do something no other golem had yet been able to do, cast a hex.

'Now, Gar, my small friend, the hunt begins,' Davvid walked over to the plant. He crouched down beside it and smiled as the petals quivered in anticipation. The smell of the rotten meat had already begun to stimulate a vast outpouring of magical excitement. He reached into the satchel and extracted the powder, poured it a circle around him and the plant; he positioned the tiles needed to collect the soul, paying particular attention to one whose glyphs danced and cavorted drawing his eyes deeper and deeper into their dance. He blinked and turned away. The magic was hypnotic here within the augmenting range of the bud. Finally, he unscrewed the little wood container of paste and stretched out on the ground beside the plant, waved a complicated sign in the air, which transformed the patch of ground into the illusion of a large boulder, and scooped the rotten meat into his mouth.

Davvid almost gagged when the bud's stamen thrust itself into his open mouth but the potency of the magical force as it coursed through him a second later ripped any bodily feelings away and he fell through total blackness. Panic rose in him and he screamed, but there was no sound; he tried to look down at his body and found nothing. Somehow, he felt that he was able to turn and look around himself but was unsure if he had actually done so; there were no points of reference. He was alone in a black void, a darkness that had no beginning and had no end. He screamed again. All sense of time left him, his mind raced.

Had he missed something? Did Luther Krell have some other unknown extra, which Davvid had not perceived? Finally, was he trapped in the ether forever?

The answer came as a small glint of light that flashed at the corner of his vision. He looked in its direction and prayed. It sparkled again and hope swelled within him then died again as he realised he had no idea how to move towards the coruscating gem.

He imagined hexing a sign in the void before his face, and saw nothing, no hand, no movement, no hope. The diamond point of light flashed again and madness swept over him. There had to be a way!

He stared at the pinpoint and concentrated; he willed the light to get closer. He dragged at it with the full force of his mind. Leeched onto the one sparkling spot and sucked at it with his whole being, and it moved.

Time passed; he had no inkling of its quantity of passage or the distance he travelled to reach the circle of light that now beckoned like an open door, but he knew he was slowing. The closer he got to the welcoming source of illumination the harder it became to reach. He felt as if any moment he would be pulled back to his starting point; it was if he was stretched out across the void like a tightly pulled string on a musician's lute; drawn to the point of snapping.

Then he reached the doorway and looked in. He smiled as he stepped through with ease and approached the old woman and the cat that she was stroking.

Sergeant Rabbet was impressed as he swung his car in through the gates to the mansion, drove up the tree-lined avenue to the front of the grand old house and parked beside the vintage MG. He switched off the engine and called into the office on his mobile.

He dragged his skinny frame out of the maroon Vauxhall Astra pool car and arched his back, grimacing as it popped. Running a hand through his unruly mop of straw coloured, and straw textured hair, he made a mental note to tear someone off a strip for leaving the police vehicle full of half-eaten, stale sandwiches and then turned an envious eye on to the little MG, which was in pristine condition; obviously restored and well-cared for.

'Want to go for a spin?'

Rabbet jumped and looked up, an attractive older woman was leaning out of an open window on the second floor of the sandstone building. She gave him a flashing smile, 'I'll be right down.'

'Oh... I'm Sergeant...' He started to reply, but she had gone inside and closed the window.

He straightened his tie, coughed into his hand and held it up to his nose, then rummaged in his pocket for a mint as he walked towards the lovingly polished oak front door. He found a warm, soft mint in the bowels of his pocket and quickly unwrapping it, popped it into his mouth. He rolled up the sticky paper and was just about to throw it away when the he heard the latch of the door being opened and quickly thrust the wrapper into his jacket. The door swung ajar with a satisfying creak and Laura Cartwright stepped out to greet him.

'Hello, Sergeant, how do you do? I'm Laura Cartwright,' she said, extending a wrinkled but well manicured hand, although he did notice a malformed nail.

Rabbet withdrew his hand from his pocket and looked at the fluff, which had stuck to the sticky patches on his fingers and frowned.

Laura grabbed his hand and shook it firmly, 'Doesn't matter Sergeant, we can wash in the kitchen, follow me.'

He sighed and shook his head as she beckoned him inside, thinking he had made anything but a great start and had probably failed to instil in her any possibility of his professionalism.

She led him through the beautiful old house until they entered the kitchen, which smelled of warm bread and fresh coffee. His stomach rumbled as his mouth watered.

A stocky, grey-haired man, who was reading a paper and drinking some of the coffee, rose as he entered and smiled at Rabbet.

'Ah, found some skeletons in my wife's past, Inspector?' Asked Laura's husband, Jensen Cartwright.

'Oh, no sir. Not at all.' Rabbet replied, 'Um and it's Sergeant, sir, not Inspector.'

'My apologies, Sergeant. Would you like a cup of coffee?'

'That'd be great, sir. Thank you.'

'Milk and sugar?'

'A little milk and two sugars please,' replied Rabbet.

'Ah ha, another sweet tooth eh?' Laughed Laura as she washed her hands, 'Would you like to?' She nodded towards the wash-basin.

'Thank you, yes.' Rabbet rolled up his sleeves, 'This is a lovely old house.'

'Oh, thank you,' she replied and looked at her husband, 'We love it dearly. It's Georgian and listed grade two which can be troublesome on times, but it's worth it.'

With the niceties over, and the three sitting down at the table, Rabbet began to tell them the reason behind his visit. He explained how when he saw the yard's computer had thrown up Laura's name as the Inspector in charge of the unsolved 1969 S.H.C. case, Rabbet knew he would have to delve deeper. The circumstances, which surrounded Fenton's death when Laura was an Inspector, were remarkably similar to the death of an old woman and her cat, a case that he was investigating. He continued speaking until Laura held up her hand and stopped him.

'Sergeant, I'm afraid I can't help you. That, as you say, was an unsolved crime. It's in the past, and I have no wish to rummage through a very painful period of my life.'

'I understand. If I remember correctly you resigned shortly after the incident, but it is just that...well you did witness something, you and four others, which is unprecedented. But only two witnesses of the event still live, you and the other one who is unfortunately in hospital at the moment and in quite a distressed state.'

Laura clenched her fingers together on the table and Rabbet noticed they were shaking.

'Look, if I thought I could help I would. But what we saw that day beggars belief. You've seen my report. You saw what it did to Fenton. You saw what it did to my colleague. No one believed us then; no one will believe me now. And yes, I did resign after what you call the incident. Boothby was more than just an incident. That case broke me and I lost a good friend. I can't help you Sergeant, don't ask me to.'

Rabbet cleared his throat and nodded, 'I know how it must feel; everyone must've thought you were all insane. Nevertheless, something did happen. You all witnessed it. If it wasn't some sort of mass hysteria then it had to be something else. When you've eliminated the impossible, whatever remains, however improbable... must be the truth.'

'Rabbet, if you think I'm playing Watson to your damn Sherlock Holmes then you'd better leave now before I do something I might regret,' she said standing up from the table, the chair flew back and clattered to the floor.

'That was just a saying, but it does have the merit of truth in it. Mrs. Cartwright, if you won't do it to help me, or the force. Do it to help Conny Flute. She and you are the last ones left who know what happened, but she, unlike you, is infatuated with those events. So much so, I worry for her sanity. If you'd just speak to her. Perhaps it would help. Alternatively, just look over the notes of the recent S.H.C. case. See if you spot anything. We're at a dead end, and a confused woman is at her wit's end.'

'Conny Flute?' She frowned, 'I don't even know a Conny Flute, Sergeant. You have your case files mixed up I'm afraid.'

'Conny Flute?' Interrupted Jensen Cartwright, 'Isn't that the writer of those gory horror stories? Haven't they made a block-busting film based on one of her books? Phoenix Rise or something?'

'Phoenix Rising is the name of it, yes sir.'

'What the hell has that to do with me Rabbet? I told you, I do not know any Conny Flute, and I never, ever, read or watch pulp like that. I've no need to. I saw the real thing,' she said and Rabbet saw the fear in her eyes.

'You do know Conny Flute, Mrs. Cartwright. However, *you* know her as Lucy Fenton; Conny Flute is an anagram of her name. Moreover, if you did happen to know of her books and work, then you'd understand that she's a very mixed up young woman. However, as far as I know, she has never been as out of control as this before.'

'Lucy,' she gasped and pulled the chair back up and slumped into it, suddenly feeling very old and very tired, 'Oh, Lucy…' and the memories welled up in her like a fountain and poured out through her eyes.

Chapter 5

The rabbit and the potato

'Hi Bunny,' the plain-clothes officer said, as Rabbet approached the private room in St.Clare's Hospital on the outskirts of London.

Laura Cartwright gave Rabbet a questioning look.

'Nick-name. Rabbet, they think equals rabbit or bunny rabbit. Bloody fools don't even know what a rabbet is.' He looked skywards as he realised he had sworn, 'Sorry.'

'No problem. Rabbet, it's some sort of woodwork term though isn't it? A groove or channel?' She asked.

'Yes, but these idiots wouldn't know that.' Rabbet glanced at the officer who looked innocently skywards too.

'Almost as bad as what they called me; but only behind my back,' she replied.

Rabbet waited patiently.

'Oh, all right. It was Spud, okay?'

'Spud?' He asked.

'Yes. A Murphy is Irish for a potato; could have been worse though. I think it can also mean some sort of prostitute,' she explained. 'I was one of the first women Detective Inspectors and the first to be assigned a male sergeant. We both took a lot of ribbing.'

'Great team. A rabbit and a potato. I couldn't write something stranger than that.' He smiled.

'Hey we're not a team. I'll speak to Lucy and browse through your paperwork. But that's it. I've been out of the game a long time now, and for chrissakes, I'm too old for this crap anyway.'

'Okay, okay. It's a deal. And look, I haven't thanked you for changing your mind, so… thanks,' he smiled, 'Just see if you can calm her down, then we can pop by the office and I'll give you a copy of all our files, I'll cut it onto a disc. You've got a computer haven't you?'

'Who hasn't nowadays?' She replied.

He nodded and turned. 'Any problems Barker?' Rabbet asked the cop.

'Nope, all quiet. She's settled down now they gave her creepy suit back to her. Oh, and the extinguishers, loads of extinguishers. I think her boyfriend is collecting her soon. She signed herself out already but won't leave alone.'

'Oh well, must be an improvement. Last I heard she was going at someone with a knife.'

'She objected to having the general, said she only agreed to the local anaesthetic.' Barker explained.

'Ok, go get a cuppa. We'll ring you when we're ready to leave,' Rabbet nodded slowly.

'Cheers, Bunny, appreciated.'

'See you later Barker,' replied Rabbet.

'Woof woof,' growled Laura quietly as Barker passed her, and he scowled.

'What did you say to him then?' Asked Rabbet.

'Oh, nothing,' she replied, and then almost silently said, 'Just a little payback.'

Rabbet knocked on the door and entered. Laura took a deep breath, composed herself and followed him in. Lucy Fenton was sitting on the bed, fully dressed. Laura didn't recognise her. She guessed Lucy was about five foot six. She was still a brunette and had a hard athletic build. Laura wondered what sort of regime Lucy put herself through to achieve such a well-honed condition. She certainly seemed to take care of her physique, but then Laura Cartwright noticed the criss-crossing of scars on the girl's arms.

She also noted the abundance of fire extinguishers in the room and a cold shiver ran up her spine.

'Don't fucking start again, Rabbet. I'm okay, right? Just got a little carried away with my hobby,' Lucy said as Rabbet opened his mouth to speak.

'Hobby?' his eyes narrowed. 'You almost lacerated a muscle in your thigh. You're lucky you didn't hit an artery. You threatened the paramedics on the way in. You put a knife to the anaesthetist's throat when you came around, and you tell me you're okay?'

'The bastard knocked me out. I told him no general, a local would have done.'

'A simple enough mistake,' Rabbet replied. 'Not worth killing the guy for.'

'They took my suit too. I NEVER go around without my suit!' She shouted.

'What suit?' Laura asked.

Lucy rolled down the lightweight all-in-one fatigues that she was wearing to show what looked like a silver-lame skin-tight coverall beneath, 'This suit. State-of-the-art. Pyrolite, best there is. You could walk through a petrol fire wearing this,' she pirouetted proudly.

Laura nodded, 'You don't remember me do you Lucy?'

The woman's head flew up in shock, 'What did you call me?'

'I'm Inspector, well, ex-Inspector Murphy. I was with you that day in the hospital. Remember? I sure as hell will never forget it.'

Lucy's eyes glazed over, 'Oh my God,' she whispered and then collapsed onto the bed, curled into a foetal position and started moaning quietly.

Rabbet looked at Laura in astonishment, 'What happened?' He bent down to listen to the young woman and stood up again. 'She's repeating the same word, over and over again.'

'Yes. Bat, I bet my life the word is bat,' answered Laura,

and sat down beside her, wrapping her arms around the young woman.

Davvid's eyes flew open and he retched. The rotten meat splattered out over the plant and it vibrated in ecstasy. The stamen had withdrawn after depositing its thaumaturgic pollen into his mouth, the pollen which had let him transcend his body and send his essence... to where? He did not know but it was like nowhere he had seen before. However, he was certain nothing he witnessed there was of this world. How the plant opened a gateway to another world was beyond his comprehension but the Rapture Bud was known to enhance a mage's capabilities for a short period. Whilst in its thrall-time a person could extend their powers to a higher level, a level that would drop once leaving the plant's vicinity and bondage but a residue would remain. The thaumaturgist would have attained a higher plane, and advancement was always desired.

He struggled to sit up and Gar approached him. 'Gar, all quiet?' A useless question he knew as Gar could not respond, but Davvid had no friends. Gar was his closest companion. The golem stood near and surveyed the area intently, carrying out the script inscribed on its tile. It would protect Davvid Krell from any intrusion. Any intrusion, be it flora, fauna or any stray person who stumbled across their secret spot.

The reap-holder tile glowed and Davvid snatched it up quickly, the tile was hot to the touch and the glyphs looked like fathomless whorls of red smoke, 'THE SOUL!' He shouted, and held the tile up, 'THE SOUL!'

The meeting hall in Marin's Weir was crammed to the eves with revellers. They waited in anticipation for the town bell to strike twelve midnight, when they would welcome in a brand new Lustre Anno. The crowd, including Sarreg, who had now risen to the position of Procurator, wore gaily-coloured costumes and masks. Even some of the golem guards bore brightly coloured hats and accoutrements. Now the people were all hushed as they waited in breathless silence for the first toll. They waited. And they waited.

Suddenly the double-doors burst open; those who were able to sense it felt the work of magic as the large panelled doors crashed against the limit of their hinges. When the shrieks of the women — and some of the more effeminate men — subsided, a lone figure entered the room, his vast wings unfurled and raised above his head and shoulders.

'Good evening, Procurator, fellow magi, ladies and gentlemen. I am sorry I'm late. Or am I?' Asked Davvid Krell.

Sarreg shuffled back but one or two of the higher caste thaumaturgists in the room blustered and stepped forward, their golems, now no longer an object of party gaiety but mindless guardians primed to act should any threat be perceived, moved with them.

'Davvid Krell. What is the meaning of this exhibition? Have you gone mad, young man?' Demanded Thaumaturgist Descar, as his guardian stepped forward a pace.

Davvid bowed, 'Do I not deserve my title, Thaumaturgist Descar? You do me a dishonour sir. Nevertheless, I am agreeable to you rectifying it. If it was done in error.'

Descar laughed, 'It was no error my fine fellow. When you deserve the title I shall eat my golem's tile, sir.' This brought a bout of laughter from the males and titters from behind the fans of the females within the grand room.

'I see, Descar. I do hope you are hungry,' Davvid replied.

Descar's face turned purple at the insult. Not only had the fool ignored his proper title, he had dared to threaten him. Enough was enough and he waved a scrawny hand as he made a sign in the air before him...

... and nothing happened.

Descar spluttered and raised his hand again, but a

movement behind Davvid made him hesitate.

'My, my, Descar, did you just attack me?' Davvid's voice almost purred with contentment. 'Gar will not like that one little bit.' And, as if on cue, the small golem entered the room.

The laughter that roared out of Descar was infectious as the whole room pointed at the figure of the minute golem as it strode past Davvid towards Descar. However, it stopped immediately when Gar signed and Descar rose from the floor and wriggled like a fish on a hook. Descar's golem strode forward and stretched out a large hand to grab Gar around the head, but Davvid flicked a hand as if dismissing a fly from his lacy cuff and the golem froze in an off balance position. Gar kicked it once and it fell onto its side with a crash, shaking all the windows.

'However, I forget, I did ask, am I late Descar? You did not reply. Am I late everyone? Has midnight's bell tolled?' demanded Davvid, but there was no reply.

Descar struggled fruitlessly as he hung suspended, held only by Gar's hex, an unprecedented event, and of the deepest insult possible. A master of the art of legerdemain, bested by a golem.

'But wait; do I hear the first toll?' Asked Davvid and turned towards the door. A massive figure approached the light. It was Tonn, and hanging like a child's toy from one of his enormous fists was the town's heavy bronze bell. Tonn stooped to enter the room then strode towards the centre, raised the bell on high and struck it with his free fist. The room reverberated with the sound and the women screamed and covered their ears.

It was the last straw for the mages and golem handlers within the hall. Hands fluttered as hexes were cast and a number of golems walked purposefully towards Tonn, Gar and Davvid. Gar moved first. He stepped next to Davvid and its clay hands blurred. Descar's body spun and was thrown across the room into the group of his fellow casters who jumped out of the way of his flailing body. One golem had almost reached Davvid who now stood with his arms crossed and a calm smile on his face. Gar stepped into the golem's path. It reached down for Gar clutching the small figure around the throat and attempted to pick it up. It failed and struggled once more as cracks began to appear along its arm, running from the wrist up to the shoulder. Gar watched its efforts in placid tranquillity and then stepped back. The large golem's arm shattered and it stared at the stump projecting from its shoulder in mute amazement as Gar punched it in the groin. A huge crack swiftly spread up its torso and as Gar struck it again it shattered and collapsed to the floor, resembling the fractured shards of a hundred pottery jugs.

In the meantime, four golems had surrounded Tonn who tossed the bell at two of them. They attempted to catch the heavy object but it bowled them over and they slammed to the floor, flailing in a futile attempt to extricate themselves. The other two rushed Tonn and it smashed one into the wall where it fragmented. The other Tonn grasped by the throat and forced open its mouth, tearing off the top of its head as it did so. Tonn pulled out the hex-tile from within, tossed the body aside like a doll, and strode over to Davvid to present the tile to him.

A small hand flourish and Descar floated towards Davvid and dropped to the floor. 'What were we discussing Descar?'

'Thaumaturgist Krell, if I offended you by the slip of my tongue. I...I...'

'I what, Descar?' Davvid asked, leaving out the blustering man's title.

Descar grimaced, 'I apologize and beg your leave, Master Thaumaturgist.'

Davvid smiled, 'But Descar, you haven't eaten yet!'

'I have no appetite, kind sir. But I thank you for your

concern.'

'A snack then… 'Davvid's face darkened, 'Maybe a morsel, do I recall you saying, should I deserve to be called Thaumaturgist Krell then your golem's tile would be a welcome snack?'

Descar winced, 'Yes.'

'Louder.'

'Yes.'

'LOUDER!'

'YES—YES—YES!' cried Descar and Davvid rammed the earthenware tile down his throat.

Procurator Sarreg had the sense to stay at the rear of the hall and observe. He could have thrown Wide into the fight but had decided on prudence, and just watched the affray. He was thankful he had chosen that route as the room was now filled with broken earthenware, all which remained of his companion's golems. He felt behind him, grasped the doorknob to the rear door, and twisted.

Davvid stepped over Descar's body and surveyed the room with glee. Tonn and Gar flanked him and he felt like a king. 'Sarreg, oh… Sarreg. Come out come out from wherever you are,' he laughed and the crowd split like startled sheep as he strode amongst them searching. When the last of the milling flock parted and he spotted Sarreg's wife and daughter he smiled. Then he saw the hall's open rear-door and nodded, 'My ladies, I should have expected him to run. But where can he go?' The two women raised their fans to hide their petrified faces and then fluttered them in nervous fright. Davvid eyed Sarreg's beautiful daughter; he touched her pale cheek with a hand that still bore the spittle and blood from Descar's broken mouth. 'Until later,' he whispered to her, and then pushed past them.

He stepped outside and rose into the night like a giant bat.

Tonn and Gar broke into a trot and followed beneath his flying figure. 'Ready or not Sarreg, here I come!' His voice carried on the still night air and reached the ears of the fleeing Procurator who lumbered towards what he hoped was the safety of his mansion house.

Sarreg burst through his front door with Wide close on his heels. The obese man was red in the face and breathless, but fear was a potent motivator. He slammed the door and shutters closed with a swift hand sign and ran towards the back of the building. The Procurator was no fool. He had many enemies and few friends. Therefore, his house was a fortress. He protected the stonework of its walls with invisible glamour shields, some inscribed within the block work itself, others as a filigree of what looked like decorative scrollwork. Undetectable, to all but the knowing eye of a magic-user. Now he hurried towards his bolthole, a room hewn out of the bedrock on which his mansion stood. All thoughts of his wife and daughter had fled him. He reached the end of a darkened passageway and stood facing a blank wall. Muttering frantically he signed and the wall resolved into a doorway. He signed once more and the stout door open silently. It had no lock and no handle. Sarreg stepped through and Wide followed him; then he closed the door behind himself and descended a flight of stone stairs into the gloom.

Chapter 6

Let us hunt!

To an untrained eye, Sarreg's mansion would have seemed deserted, no signs of life, no guards. Any would-be thief would be sorely tempted, and surely killed, should he be naïve enough to try to break in. The protection built into the walls was not forgiving; anyone attempting to scale them would have been fixed firmly to their surface, and scorched to death. Any window or door that was forced would have resulted in the forcer suffering very much the same consequences.

'Sarreg doesn't believe in giving an enemy a second chance,' Davvid murmured.

However, Davvid Krell read signs extremely well; one of the best had after all, taught him. Davvid glanced at the walls then glanced away quickly, and the after-image on his retinas gave him an idea of its potency. It was extremely strong. The house reeked of magic. The Procurator would not be an easy fish to fry, but fry he would.

He landed a few paces away from the front door and once more looked askew at it. The after-image impressed him. The front door was hex guarded the most. He needed some other means of ingress. A steady pounding of heavy footsteps announced the arrival of Tonn and a few moments later, he was pleased to see Gar appear too.

All three began a circumnavigation of the large building as Davvid looked for a safer way in. At the rear of the mansion, they came across an open cart. It was parked beneath a small stone room that stood high up on two stonewalls, projecting out from the main part of the building; Sarreg's personal privy, and the cart was full of night-soil. He could see a glamour shield surrounding this too, but where the soil fell through a large hole in the high floor above their heads the shielding was at its lowest and Davvid grinned.

He beckoned Gar over to him and he sat down in the long grass. Gar approached as commanded and stood unmoving as Davvid carefully inserted two fingers into the little golem's mouth and withdrew the hex tile with Gar's instructions upon it. Then he delved into a pocket of his cloak and withdrew a small leather pouch that contained a lump of malleable clay. Davvid spread the clay thinly along the back of the tile, being careful not to alter or damage the original instructions incised into the other side. He then extracted a thin stylus made from the finger bone of a drayk. Next, he signed, producing a small, glowing ball of light which hovered near his hand as he began scribing glyphs into the soft clay. With an explicit set of instructions added to Gar's commands, he set the tile on the grass and passed his hand over it slowly. Steam rose from the grass surrounding the tile which then crisped and blackened. After the firing of the tile, he returned it to Gar's mouth and the golem turned and walked towards the night-soil cart.

'Now, little one, time for you to become my key,' Davvid said as he rose up and followed Gar. They both stopped below the opening to Sarreg's privy and Davvid waved a complicated hex. Gar began levitating slightly. Then gathering speed it flew towards the aperture high in the air above them. There was barely enough room for the small golem to get through, but with some scraping which dislodged small stones, and Davvid winced as he guessed what else, then it finally got through.

Once inside, Gar walked away from the outer wall and raised one of its small earthenware hands. It signed an intricate hex in the air before itself and the wall vibrated slightly. Spreading its legs it signed again, this time using both hands and pushed the air as if moving the block-work in the wall. A low rumble sounded and a large block began to move within the matrix of the wall. Gar inched forward as if pushing, its little body quivering under the strain. Unexpectedly the block shot forward and Gar stumbled before catching itself. The block tumbled out from the wall and crashed to the ground below, disintegrating the wooden cart on its way. Davvid stepped back quickly to avoid the flying night soil. He looked up and saw Gar had almost pushed out another block from the wall. There was now enough room for Davvid to enter and join the small golem. Tonn however would have to wait outside. Davvid spread his wings and with the utmost of ease rose towards the opening in the mansion's wall. He reached the break and stepped through. He patted Gar on its clay head and said, 'Well done my small friend,' then realised what Gar was covered in and looked for something to wipe his hand on.

Sarreg shivered, not with the cold, which permeated his secret dungeon, but with the funk that oozed from every pore of his body. Although he was not sure, he had a terrible feeling his perimeter defences were breached. He had a limited knowledge of the thaumaturgist's art, but was not an expert. Therefore, he could not send a questioning hex out to probe for any infiltration. He had to make a grave decision, to stay, wait and fight it out on his own grounds but against a formidable enemy, or to make a run for it now Davvid was inside the house and searching for him. Sarreg decided to run. His confidence in his house's magical defence had waned. Davvid's power was greater than he had first imagined. He had opened the secret door in his dungeon, which led to a low escape tunnel, and finally to a well on the border of his garden. Now he manually tripped a mechanical device and sniggered, 'Let's see if Davvid and his two friends discover that little non-magic trick with their hexes, shall we Wide?' He asked the golem and he patted a large block of masonry, which looked to be part of the ceiling, just in from the doorway to the tunnel.

As Davvid made his way through the house, he deactivated the glamour hexes disguising the various traps with ease. Once or twice, he did stop and think about a particular spell which appeared vastly superior to the others, and he nodded as he recognised his old master's handiwork. 'Nice touch Krell,' he murmured. Then he carefully started to un-weave the hex which would have blasted him with a bolt of pure magical energy, should he had proceeded along the darkened corridor leading towards Sarreg's rear door. Sweat started to break out on his brow and he waved intricate signs in the air. He watched as an arabesque of flowery glyphs appeared on the wall and he carefully manipulated them as they fought to countermand his orders.

Luther Krell had been a grandmaster of the magical arts and Davvid had the utmost respect for the traps and pitfalls, which he had inscribed into his hex-tiles. Finally, the dancing glyphs coalesced and the tile became visible within a scant slit in the wall's mortar. Gingerly he removed it and examined it closely; he was pleased to find he would be able to utilize the magic within it for his own purposes and he carefully stored it within a pocket hidden deep in the folds of his cloak.

'Time to let Tonn join us, eh Gar?' Davvid murmured. He reached the large iron-studded back door to the house and started to work upon its defences. It was easier than he had imagined. No one had thought to secure the door from an attack upon its fortifications from the inside of the house. All of the wards and glamours had been cast to stop anyone from outside breaking in. It proved no match for Davvid's skill as he negated them from the inside and the door swung open to let Tonn stride in.

'Welcome to the party, Tonn. Now my fine friends, it is time to teach Master Sarreg a thing or two about pride,' Davvid grinned at the two impassive faces, one which towered over him like a giant and the other which barely reached to the top of his thigh.

He withdrew a small tile from his cloak and waved a flourish across it and the glyphs swirled in response until they pointed in a certain direction. 'Well, that is where Wide is, and I am willing to bet that is where we find Sarreg.' The tile was another artefact produced by Luther Krell and would seek out any other item manufactured by its maker. 'This is going to be too easy my friends,' he said, 'and I had hoped for much more sport from our dear Procurator. Ahh, they move! Good. Let us hunt!'

The gloomy house threw up some more obstacles in the trio's way, but no more complicated than Davvid had already surpassed. In fact, he was quite disappointed when he arrived at the doorway to Sarreg's basement and he sighed as the pitiful booby-trap upon it crumbled beneath his fluttering hand. Once the magic was removed, Tonn kicked at the massive door and it splintered and fell through into the dark room with a reverberating crash. Davvid knew Sarreg had already left and guessed there was a secret passageway and exit. It did not take him long to discover where.

'I grow weary of this chase,' he said as he removed the magical hex, which had occluded the tunnel down which Sarreg had run. He nodded to Tonn, 'Stop them.'

Tonn stooped so his vast bulk could enter the dank passageway and set off like a hound in pursuit of its prey. However, within a few seconds, there was a terrifying rumble and a cloud of swirling dust spewed out from the tunnel's entrance. Davvid coughed and signed with a rapid waving of his hands. Vortexes formed in the air and swept the dusty cloud away. He stepped cautiously into the gloom. Davvid had gone in about ten paces when he saw the roof-fall and the shattered remains of Tonn beneath it. His anger rose as a storm and he screamed in rage; uncontrolled thaumaturgic energy sloughed off him and rippled along the roof like a roiling cloud of purple smoke.

Wide assisted Sarreg as he climbed out of the old well, a furlong away from his mansion. As he climbed over the lip of the surrounding stone wall, a deep rumble told him his trap had found a victim. A rush of dusty air belched out from the well and for a moment, he thought he heard a voice screaming from within. He turned and ran towards the stables with Wide close on his heels. As he and Wide saddled and mounted his pair of drayks, he noticed a glimmer of purple force waft over the rim of the well. He smiled in contentment.

'I don't give a shit about who's in with her, I'm her fiancé and I want to goddamn know what the fuck is going on.'

The raised voice startled Laura and she stopped patting Lucy to look at the cubicle's door. A moment later, it burst open and a tall, dark-haired man in a long black leather coat stormed into the room with a small nurse attached to his arm. She pulled ineffectively at him, 'Please Mr. Raven, she'll see you all in good time,' she exclaimed as she stumbled and let go of the man.

He turned and looked down at her, 'The bloody name's Raven, not Mr. Raven. Just Raven, how many times do I have to tell you damn morons?'

Rabbet approached the tattooed nemesis and tapped him on the shoulder, 'I'm...' That is all the policeman managed to say before Raven turned quickly and pushed him hard in the chest. Rabbet stumbled backwards, into one of the extinguishers Lucy had demanded be brought with her into the room, and he clattered to the floor.

'Back off man, I don't like people creeping up on me.'

Laura had watched the entrance of the gothic-dressed newcomer and she had taken something from her small handbag and held it concealed in her left hand. She stood and approached the man who looked a good foot taller than she was, 'That wasn't nice Mr. Raven.'

'Listen lady, and listen carefully, the fucking name is…' he bellowed in her face and went to poke her in the shoulder. She grabbed his big hand with her right and with a quick twist and some thumb pressure on its back — between his two middle knuckles — had him collapsing to the floor in pain.

'Hell's teeth woman, leave my damn hand go or I swear I'll smack you across the room,' he shouted and lifted his left hand to show her.

'Oh, well. Time to meet Eric then,' she said.

'Eric?' Raven asked.

'Yes, say hello Eric,' Laura answered and neatly struck Raven across the temple with the small leather cosh. His eyes rolled up into his head and he collapsed into a heap at her feet.

Rabbet extricated himself from the herd of extinguishers he had fallen into and surveyed her handiwork, 'Eric eh?'

'Yes, Eric the Equalizer; belonged to a friend of mine. A handy little insurance policy to have. Should you be at a disadvantage.' She smiled.

The nurse checked Raven over and pronounced him alive but heavily 'sedated' and both Rabbet and Laura laughed. Lucy had stopped moaning and looked at them in shock, for a moment her own worries supplemented by her concern for Raven.

'What've you done to him?' She asked as she slid off the bed and went over to the big man, lying prone and snoring deeply on the floor.

'Oh, he's just…' Rabbet started to say but Laura interrupted him.

'He tripped.'

'Oh, poor baby. He's so protective,' Lucy replied.

'Yes, I can see that, quite impetuous too,' acknowledged Laura.

'He looks out for me, right?' snarled Lucy, 'He may be

impetuous, and some even say he is uncouth and too full of himself, but he's mine. I can trust him.'

'Sorry Lucy, he could have been anybody. He barged his way in here, knocked Bunny, umm... Rabbet over and threatened me. I had to deal with him,' explained Laura.

'Deal with him? He's got a lump the size of a damn egg on his temple, what the hell did you do?'

'Introduced him to Eric,' Laura replied with a wry smile, 'I'm too old to go wrestling with men now, a pity, but there you go.' She smiled and Lucy shook her head, and smiled back.

'I remember you now; well the cosh brought it all back. You saw the bat didn't you?'

'Yes, Lucy. I saw the bat. That's something I'll never forget. It will come with me to the grave.'

'He fought it with that cosh; a brave man. It came for me. I could feel it. It came for me and he saved me.'

'Boothby was a brave guy. And he was my friend; Eric was his, yes,' Laura put the cosh back into her handbag. 'What do you mean, you could feel it?'

'When the *thing* came for my father it appeared behind him; it grabbed him; it...embraced him. He reached out to me, I touched his hand, and I felt it! I can't tell you what I felt. I just do not know, but for a moment, I could sense something. The thing was like another person, another mind. Whatever the creature is I know it isn't human; it's not of this world, but it is so similar to us. I saw things. The creature's mind and its ideas. It was over so quickly but something happened to me in my father's house, which bound me to it. I think it was when my finger touched my father. My finger became as if welded to his hand. It hurt terribly. Later, when I woke up in the hospital I knew the creature was coming again, my finger hurt. And I just knew it was coming.'

'Your finger *hurt*?' Asked Rabbet.

'Yes, this one,' Lucy replied and held up the stub of her

index finger on her left hand. The top two joints were gone and a small red knob of flesh showed above the last knuckle.

Raven groaned and she smoothed back the long black hair from his forehead, 'He's coming round,' she said as she watched him groggily try to sit up.

'Wha... ow, my damn head!' He yelped as he felt the large bump. 'Jeez lady, what the hell did you do that for?'

'I tend to get annoyed really fast nowadays. Must be the menopause,' Laura replied, wishing she were young enough to be still going through it.

Lucy helped him up onto the bed, fussing over him as if he was a small child. Rabbet, Laura and the nurse exchanged glances.

'Mr. Raven,' Rabbet started to say, then as Raven began to glower at him, continued, 'Sorry, Raven. I could arrest you for attacking a police officer, but under the circumstances I am prepared to let it go, if, you can cool down and not disrupt our questioning.'

'He's okay now Rabbet; aren't you?' Replied Lucy, Raven nodded.

'Can you continue Lucy?' Asked Laura as the nurse excused herself and left.

'Yes, but there's not much else I can tell you. Ever since that day I knew whatever it was I saw would come after me again. I've prepared for it as best as I can,' she indicated to the extinguishers and the suit beneath her clothes, 'but if it's enough I can't say.'

'She's told me about it. Fucking thing's haunted her for over thirty years. What the hell do you think you can do about it now?' Raven demanded.

'Shh... calm down Rave, they can't do shit. They know it and I know it. When it comes for me I just have to be ready.'

'How do you know it'll come for you Lucy?' Asked Rabbet,

'It's been more than thirty years. Have you ever seen or felt it again?'

'No, I haven't, but… '

'But what?' He continued.

'But I have a premonition; it's not over. It still wants me and it has started again. You have seen its results, the old woman and her cat. The bat is back.'

Chapter 7

Keep your friends close, but your enemies closer

It was a tight fit, but Rabbet managed to squeeze Raven into the front seat of his car whilst Lucy and Laura took up the rear. Raven was still a little giddy, but pronounced well, and healthy enough to travel by the doctor who examined him in St.Clare's Hospital.

'Lucky you didn't mark his face,' Lucy explained to Laura, 'He would've sued your ass then. His face is one of the things that sell 'Phoenix Rising'. Isn't it lover? Well that, and my damn good writing abilities.'

'Oh, I don't know, Lucy. I think a broken nose would suit him well, don't you?' Laura asked stifling a giggle.

Raven tried to turn around in the front seat and gave up, 'You two are like damn kids. I could have suffered brain damage or something.'

Lucy and Laura looked at each other and burst out laughing, they were still giggling ten minutes later when they arrived at Lucy's street.

'We're here,' Rabbet informed them as he pulled up outside Lucy's apartment building. He got out of the car to open the door, but was too slow. A neatly dressed door attendant in a pseudo-military jacket, complete with medals, beat him to it and opened the door for Lucy.

'Miss Flute, good to see you again. I do hope you're feeling better,' the door attendant asked, tipping his hat as he helped her rise from the car. She hobbled to the pavement and waited for Raven to escape the clutches of the front seat.

'I'm okay now, Bill,' she replied with a smile, 'Knife slipped when I was making a sandwich.'

'Yes, Miss.'

'Crap fucking British cars; built for pox-ridden midgets,' Raven cursed as he finally got himself free.

'Well you could have ordered the limo to come get us Rave. Why didn't you?' asked Lucy.

'Yeah, right. You want to keep a low profile and I turn up in a stretch limo.'

'Sorry, babe. You're right of course.' She took his arm and then led the way inside.

Rabbet was impressed with her apartment, small though it was. He liked the austerity and minimalist style to it; it appealed to him. He was particularly drawn to Lucy's gym.

'Wow this is nice,' he said as he thumped the punch bag, which hung from the ceiling. 'You certainly have a great apartment, and this gym is fantastic. I'm jealous.'

'It's all necessary. I do all my own stunts on the show, and most of them in the film too. I try and keep as fit as I can,' Lucy replied.

'She's too modest,' Raven butted in, 'She's a third Dan in karate and one mean kick-boxer too, and I've got the bruises to prove it.'

'Hey, some of those bruises had nothing to do with my proficiency in martial arts,' Lucy laughed and Raven actually blushed.

She took them into the lounge and told them to make themselves at home. They looked at the one seating area, her couch, and then jockeyed for position on it as she starting brewing a coffee.

Rabbet noted the array of fire-sprinklers set into the ceiling and the excessive amount of fire extinguishers around the room. He shifted uncomfortably on the couch and then slipped a hand behind him and withdrew a small red cylinder, yet another extinguisher. He placed it on the floor near his feet and noted the small, darkened patch of blood on the tiled floor. Now cooked hard onto the ceramic tiles, compliments of the under floor heating. Laura, watching him fidget, nodded when he glanced at her and then at the blood. Lucy returned from the kitchen with a tray of cups and a bubbling percolator. Raven stood up and gave her a hand.

'Okay, who likes it black; who wants milk and who wants sugar?' she asked as she eased herself carefully down onto the floor and crossed her legs into a yoga position and winced slightly as the stitches in her wound pulled.

'Milk and two sugars for me,' replied Rabbet.

'I'll have mine black and one sugar please, Lucy,' Laura answered.

'Okay, coming up. I know how you like yours, sweetie,' she pursed her lips at Raven.

He rolled his eyes, 'Do you have to call me all those stupid fucking names?' He growled, 'Especially when we're in company!'

She laughed and handed the coffee out.

'You certainly don't believe in taking chances, Lucy,' Rabbet said when he had finished the drink.

'How do you mean?'

'Well, the intricate room sensors, the sprinklers, the extinguishers and of course, your suit,' he nodded at each item as he reeled them off.

'Rabbet, if you went through what I went through, then I think you'd probably do the same,' she replied.

'Perhaps I would, but I don't think it'd be of much use though,'

'What makes you think that?' she asked.

'Well, from what we've been able to discover, S.H.C. burns the person from the inside out. Your suit won't protect you from being consumed from the inside will it?'

'Rabbet, have you witnessed somebody burning from S.H.C.?' she glowered at him, an anger gradually building up within her and distorting her pretty face.

'No' he started to reply, but she spoke over him.

'Then shut the fuck up. Ask her, she knows,' Lucy said and looked at Laura.

'Lucy, I can't say what the hell happened that day in the hospital. Boothby ran into your room. I saw what looked like a bat above your bed. It started to put its wings around you, and then reached forward with what looked like a bloody great tongue,' she shivered, 'It was going towards your head. Boothby snatched you up and threw you to me. He tried to strike the thing but couldn't and then the bat reached over and touched him. He burst into flames.'

'There, you've just answered Rabbet's question.'

'How? What did I say?' asked Laura.

'It tried to put its wings around me and touch me with its tongue,' she answered.

'So what?' asked Rabbet, 'I still don't see what you are leading up to?'

'It has to make contact, Rabbet. I saw what it did to my father. Exactly the same as what happened to Boothby, but, it had something in its mouth. A long tube. I can't even say if it was its tongue, but something came from its mouth and touched my father. He burned up before my eyes and the thing… the thing drank his pain. I can't describe it exactly, I'm not even sure what I saw, but it drank, or took something from him.'

'Sweet Jesus,' Raven said, 'you've never told me that before.'

'There's a lot you don't know about me Raven.'

'So, you think the suit will protect you from its embrace?' asked Rabbet.

'I guess I'll find out. I don't think it's finished with me yet,' she answered, rubbing the stubby nub of her knuckle, 'but I'm not going to damn well die easily. This Pyrolite suit's the best there is. I only take it off to shower or change into a fresh one.

There's a hood, which I can pull over my head, and there are mitts just up my sleeves, which will protect my hands. If it comes when I'm here, the sprinkler system will soak the bastard thing. In addition, if I can kick the shit out of it, then I will. Or die trying.'

'I can vouch she never takes it off,' Raven said wistfully.

'What if it comes when you're out, somewhere that isn't prepared like this apartment?' asked Rabbet.

'I'll just have to cope. I always carry that,' she pointed to the state-of-the-art little red cylinder by Rabbet's feet.

'Yes, I've heard of these. I thought they were only military issue though.'

'They are,' she smiled.

'How the hell are you going to fight it Lucy?' Laura asked, 'I saw what it was like when it got Boothby. It was nebulous. He could not hit it. How do you expect to do any damage to it at all?'

'In the hospital it de-materialised before it had become fully formed. When it took my father, it seemed solid. When I touched my father's hand, I felt something. I think whatever it is; it's more like us than we know. Almost human, but not quite. If it is human, or like us, then I can kill it. If it becomes solid then it'll be in for an ass kicking. Once I can get it down, then…' and she flipped her knife up from nowhere and flicked it open, the razor sharp ceramic blade flew out, 'this will cut through anything and heat doesn't do shit to it. It's a Boker, German fighting knife with a ceramic blade.'

'You seem well prepared and confident,' Laura said.

'Don't get me wrong Laura, I might be well prepared, but I'm scared to hell as well,' she trembled, 'I don't know if I can do anything to it, but I have no choice. I'm not going to let it take me like the others,' and she rubbed the scars on her arm. 'I've suffered enough pain for a life-time, it's payback time.'

It took Sarreg almost a full day to reach Fivewinds, the capital city. Both drayks were exhausted but he cared little; they could always be replaced. What he cared about most now was the reception he would receive from the city's mayor, Roget Gorman, the man he was sure had made the attempt on his life all those years ago, back in the tavern. Sarreg at that time was ambitious and had cast a covetous eye upon the mayorship of the city, but events had overtaken him and since Luther Krell's death, he had kept a low profile. Now he hoped that Gorman would not bear any grudges, but he knew that his timing would have to be perfect. He needed many witnesses to be present and he had to ask Gorman formally for assistance.

As daylight faded, he chose a stable on the outskirts of the large city and lodged both of the exhausted drayks there. He paid the stableman well and hired a four-wheeled closed carriage to take him to one of the better hotels within the city. He kept the shutters drawn on the vehicle; he did not want his entry into the city's forum to be pre-announced. Surprise was a major factor when dealing with a man such as Gorman.

The Welcome Breeze Hotel was large and airy, the façade covered in a thick growth of ivy which reached almost to the eves, four stories high. The warming twinkle of the many windows promised him a well-needed rest. He bade the carriage driver to drop Wide off at the rear of the large building and then instructed him to proceed to the main entrance. Sarreg paid the man and disembarked. The major-domo raised an eyebrow when he registered and confirmed that he did not have any baggage. However, the man's air of imperiousness changed to one of fawning when Sarreg presented him with a letter of credit, Sarreg was a very rich man.

'Your best room on the top floor, at the back. I want peace. Your splendid view over the city from the front doesn't interest me. The quiet gardens of the rear will suffice,' he said. 'Accept a small remuneration for your trouble,' and he placed a gold coin in the man's hand.

'Procurator Sarreg, that is not necessary, not necessary at all, sir,' the major-domo blustered but failed to offer the coin back.

'I'm fatigued. I wish to retire. Arrange to send a small repast to my room within the hour and then I wish to remain undisturbed until the morrow. You may awaken me for breakfast at seven,' he instructed.

'Certainly, your honour, it shall be as you desire.' The major-domo clicked his fingers and a young boy in hotel livery led Sarreg up to his rooms.

Once he was sure all was quiet, Sarreg went to one of his windows and stared out into the darkened garden; he opened the window quietly and flourished a sign with his hand. A shadow detached itself from beneath a large tree and Wide stepped forward into the light from the hotel's windows. Sarreg beckoned to him and Wide began to scale the ivy clad structure until he arrived at the open window. Sarreg stood back as Wide entered quietly.

'A pity I didn't have a dozen of you,' Sarreg said ruefully, 'This city would then be mine.'

The following morning, after breakfast, the major-domo had barely enough time to raise his eyebrow once more when Sarreg strolled past the reception desk. Sarreg had Wide in tow and as he passed the desk another coin spiralled through the air and the major-domo caught it deftly and secreted it away in a pocket in one experienced and fluid movement.

Sarreg purchased some new clothes on the way to the forum and sat implacably in the coach until two minutes to nine. The forum convened at nine. He watched as members drifted into the senate. Some he knew, others were strangers to him, but one of the first was Mayor Gorman, flanked by two large golems and their handlers. A small rat-faced young man brought up the rear of the group. He looked around as if expecting something to happen and seemed disappointed when nothing did. They entered through the large bronze doors. Sarreg stepped from the carriage and made his way up the white steps, following in Gorman's footsteps. Wide trailed after him like a faithful dog.

A general hubbub of voices reached his ears as he approached the enormous senate hall and two guards protecting the room looked at him enquiringly as he approached. He drew out his identification and they nodded for him to proceed. They gave Wide a long look but prudently stepped to one side as he followed Sarreg in. Mayor Gorman was in his seat at the head of the senate and members stood or sat in the semi-circle that surrounded him. His two golems and handlers flanked him and the rat-faced man sat at his feet like a pet. Tiers of seating rose high up behind them, all filled with senators.

As Sarreg approached, the general murmur of the members changed to gasps and whispers. Sarreg was known to be envious of the mayor's position and there had been rumours that many years ago the mayor had taken steps towards preventing Sarreg ever attempting to usurp him. Some said Sarreg had even survived an assassination attempt by the mayor. Yet, here he was, in full view of everyone and with a golem at his side! A hush fell over the room.

'Mayor Gorman, it's with great humbleness I come to ask you for a boon,' Sarreg said in a loud voice. Once more, a wave of whispers and gasps spread through the room. Gorman raised a hand and the room fell silent.

'Sarreg, it's been too long since we've seen you within the senate. It's good to see you once more, even though it is because you crave something. What is your boon? Perhaps I can fulfil it for you, we'll see.'

Sarreg's face reddened with anger but he bit his tongue,

Gorman had publicly insulted him three times within the same breath. First, he had not addressed him by his title, secondly he pointed out that Sarreg had only visited the senate because he wanted something, and thirdly to agree conditionally to a boon was deeply insulting. Gorman needed no favours from Sarreg, and although it would seem ill mannered to refuse to grant a boon, it was not to ask the reason for the boon, before acceptance was given. It demonstrated the granter's power over the supplicant and lowered the standing of the latter in everyone's eyes.

'I understand your reticence; I could very well ask a boon from you which you would be unable to supply. But fear not, it's within your power,' Sarreg replied coldly.

Gorman's face hid any umbrage that he felt as he heard Sarreg respond with a carefully worded insult himself.

'I would be unable to supply?' He whispered, 'When the opportunity arises you fat fool, your death shall be supplied, with my greatest happiness.'

Then he spoke out loud, 'Speak man; don't keep us in suspense. What drags you all the way here from Marin's Weir; with nothing but your golem?'

It was then that Sarreg realised that Mayor Gorman already knew of his presence in Fivewinds, Gorman's agents had kept him well informed. He wondered if the mayor knew of Davvid's power but he doubted it. News travelled fast but not even the mayor should have known what had happened on Lustre's Eve.

'There has been an attempted coup at Marin's Weir.' A loud roar swept the room and Gorman raised a hand again, Sarreg continued, 'Lustre's Eve saw an attempt on my life. Many Master Thaumaturgists were attacked and their golems destroyed. I fear for my wife and daughter. We became separated in the affray as I drew the attackers away from our hall. They followed me to my home, which I defended to the last, but all to no avail. It was overcome and I barely escaped with my life.'

Gorman realised he was treading on thin ice. The rule of law had been tried in Marin's Weir. He would have to defend this pompous oaf, but he wondered how much of the truth he had heard from Sarreg's mouth. He would have to delve deeper.

'I'm disturbed to hear your news Procurator Sarreg. I offer you my boon. Name the culprits. They shall be brought before the senate, should what you say be true…'

Sarreg broke into a smile but it froze on his face as Gorman paused and added the last few words… *should what you say be true…* He could not believe the insults this imbecile was raining upon him.

'Your gracious offer overwhelms me, Mayor Gorman. The leader of the group that tried to wrest Marin's Weir away from the true legislation of our dear land is called Davvid Krell.'

Gorman whispered something to the man at his feet and he nodded and rose. He looked greedily at Sarreg's golem and then left the room.

'Fear not my dear Procurator, my servant, Snape, will put the wheels of justice into motion. Davvid Krell will be brought before us to answer for his crimes. In the meantime, my dear fellow, you must come stay with me. The Welcome Breeze will miss your illustrious custom, but I would enjoy your company. I'll not take no for an answer,' announced Gorman and said to himself quietly, 'Keep your friends close, but keep your enemies closer.'

Chapter 8

Every dog has his day

Sarreg wrapped his cloak around himself as he stared out across the misty airdrome. The dew-filled air swirled around him, dampening everything; his woollen leggings were sopping and draining into his leather boots. The air condensed on Wide's body and rolled like sweat down its folded arms to drip off its elbows. The last of Snape's men and golems were boarding the second draykon. They climbed the wooden ladders gingerly, reaching the cradles strapped to the great beast's sides. Each flank of the enormous creature, a species very similar to the lesser drayk, could carry six passengers. It took three handlers to get the creature into the air and to fly in the desired direction. A Master Thaumaturgist sat strapped into a saddle high up on the draykon's neck where he used magical puissance to calm and cajole the beast. Directional handlers sat before each of its vast wings where they urged the beast to turn by the cruder method of persuasion, a sharp goading stick. A group of figures approached Sarreg from out of the writhing mist and Wide stepped forward a pace.

'Your golem is alert,' Snape said as he approached, flanked by a number of golems and their handlers.

'Wide is a fine specimen. I wish I had more of his kind,' replied Sarreg.

'Yes, indeed. I suppose you would, my lord Procurator.' Snape examined Wide closely. He threw back his cloak and withdrew a small tile from a side pocket in his burgundy velvet waistcoat. Before Sarreg could object, he touched the tile to Wide's torso and withdrew it. He glanced at the tile once, raised an eyebrow and returned it to his pocket. 'Good of you to see us off,' he said, then turned on his heel and strode off towards the waiting draykon.

'As if I had a choice,' Sarreg murmured to himself. The two days he had sojourned with Gorman had been a tribulation. Any chance the mayor had to surreptitiously humiliate him he had taken advantage of, and Sarreg had to swallow his bile and not respond. 'Every dog has his day.' And he turned and walked back to his pair of drayks.

The tile shook in Snape's hand. The weather was inclement and the wind that coursed over the draykon's back increased the chill factor in the air, but it was through excitement that Snape's hand shook. The glyphs coruscated briefly, as he signed a hex over them, and then stabilized in a pattern that intrigued him. He had stolen a template of Wide's instructions and makeup. The instructions were, as he would have imagined. Wide was to protect Sarreg from any attack; it could also understand basic hand signals, even some speech. That was a surprise for him, but the biggest surprise was the configuration of the soul. Snape expected to find something other than a normal signature because Wide was far from normal. Nevertheless, what he saw amazed him. The soul that inhabited Sarreg's golem was unlike anything he had ever seen before. It did not look to be a soul reaped from this world.

Luther Krell had been a genius; Snape felt a certain awe as he deciphered the hex glyphs. He wondered how he had reaped such a soul. It was a waste for such a man to foreverdie, his secret lost with him. He was determined to make Wide his own. Mayor Gorman was a generous man to his helpers and a blight on his enemies. Snape counted himself fortunate to be classed as one of Gorman's helpers, if not his right hand man. One way to procure Wide would be the successful outcome of the capture of Davvid Krell and his presentation before the senate. It would be interesting to hear Davvid Krell's side of the Lustre's Eve affair. He wondered if he had learned any secrets from his master before his sudden demise.

The sun rose higher as they flew on. The mist, long since burned away. The monotonous voyage had lulled Snape into sleep and his head nodded and lolled with each beat of the draykon's vast wings, until a sudden jerk brought him around and he realised they had landed. The militia had arrived at Marin's Weir.

They had chosen to touch down in the centre of town. A show of strength often led to no need for conflict. A crowd soon appeared led by a heavily bandaged man with a scarf covering his lower face. They bustled forward to see the grand spectacle. It was not often that the militia were seen in all their glory; disputes were normally rare things and any feuds were carried out clandestinely. It did not take Snape long to find out that Sarreg had exaggerated; there had been no attempted coup. It had been a revenge attack. Sarreg had obviously bitten off more than he could chew. Snape was astonished to hear the reports of a giant golem and even more astonished when the description of Gar reached his ears. A golem that could control magic!

'Impossible!' he blustered, but after seeing the template stolen from Sarreg's golem he *did* begin to wonder.

'Militiaman Snape, it is far from impossible sir. I saw it with mine own eyes. The monstrous thing threw my fellow magi's golems hither and thither. They were like straw in the wind. Then that...that thing of Krell's! That wicked abomination of a thing, propelled me into the air with no trouble at all, sir. I could not believe it possible. I was hung in mid-air for all to see. Then it threw me across the room. I barely escaped with my life sir. Moreover, the final insult was done by the man's own hand.'

Snape looked at the man, took in the bruised face, the heavily bandaged arm, and asked, 'Pray tell me what he did, sir?'

'This Militiaman Snape… this!' and Descar lowered the scarf he had covering his mouth to expose a set of smashed teeth and contused and broken lips.

'Terrible, terrible. To strike a fellow mage like that.'

'He did not strike me sir. He forced me to…'

Snape waited patiently for the man to continue, then finally prompted him, 'Forced you to?'

'He forced me to consume my golem's tile!' Descar sobbed and drew the scarf back around his face.

Snape put a hand to his own mouth, 'A scoundrel. Fear not, the man will be brought to justice,' he answered firmly, although he did feel inclined to laugh at the poor fellow's appearance.

'He has lodged himself in Procurator Sarreg's mansion; the blackguard. He has taken the Procurator's wife and daughter prisoner. I fear to think what's become of them. The man's a scoundrel, as you say sir; a blasted scoundrel.'

'Thank you kind sir. A direction to the Procurator's mansion will see us on our way. The sooner Davvid Krell answers for his wrong doings, the better.' Snape bowed slightly.

'I shall lead you Militiaman Snape. I would wish to see the man's downfall,' Descar replied with clear apprehension, but Snape waved a dismissive hand.

'That will not be possible. It is now a matter for the law; you can't put yourself in harm's way sir. We shall attend to it. Pray give me directions to the house.'

Descar nodded, clearly relieved. He instructed Snape and his militiamen on how best to approach the mansion house and wished them luck as they mounted their beasts and took to the air.

'Woman, this food is cold!' Davvid threw the plate across the room; it missed Denube Sarreg, the Procurator's wife, by inches and smashed against the wall.

Her blood-shot eyes moistened up again and she knelt to pick up the pieces and wipe the food from the wall and floor.

'If you blubber once more, I swear your soul will inhabit my next golem,' he shouted and pushed back his chair then rose from the table. He had been in a foul mood since the loss of Tonn. All his temper he had brought down on the unfortunate heads of Sarreg's wife and pretty, young daughter, whom he had forced into his servitude when Sarreg had escaped.

Tonn would have to be replaced, but Davvid's skill was not as advanced as Luther Krell's and doubts crept into his mind as he formulated the dimensions for Tonn's replacement. He could likely mould and construct another giant but he was unsure as to whether he could fire the clay without the use of a kiln. The magical strength to do so was prodigious and yet Luther Krell had succeeded. Misgivings ate their way through his mind like a worm at an apple's core. It resulted in him bursting into fits of temper and Denube Sarreg paid the cost in one way; her daughter Mari, paid it in another.

He pushed the woman over with his foot as he passed her on the way to the large window and gazed out. The sun was setting and the evening was drawing near. A movement above the trees on the edge of the vast area of lawn in front of the house made him draw in a breath. There were two draykons hovering just above the tree line. He could see that they carried a full compliment of passengers and knew that they were not just ordinary fares out on a sightseeing trip. 'Sarreg has somehow cajoled the Militia into assisting him, it has to be!' Davvid gasped and he spat. He turned quickly and rasped at the woman, 'Take your dress off, NOW!'

She gasped and held a hand to her throat.

'Do not even contemplate that I should desire you. Your daughter serves all my needs. I desire your garment, not your body, woman. Undress now or I'll rip the clothes off your back!' Davvid shouted angrily, and watched as she started to remove the dark-green satin dress. He picked up a sharp knife from the table and pulled the garment out of her hands. 'GAR!' The small golem ran into the room and stood expectantly at his side.

Davvid dropped the dress over Gar's head and knelt down to cut the excess away from the bottom. He used the extra material to gather the dress in at Gar's waist like a belt. Then he snatched up a napkin off the table and made a triangle of it, placed it on Gar's head and fastened it beneath the golem's chin. He stood back, looked at the golem, and smiled.

'Flowers! Find me some flowers woman or your life will be forfeit. Find me flowers!'

Denube raced out of the room in her linen underskirt and top as Davvid pulled Gar towards the window and pointed to the two draykons and their contingency of men and golems. They had decided to land on the lawn and were leaving the protection of the trees. He did not have much time. The woman returned with a bedraggled bunch of flowers clutched in her hands. He ripped them from her and thrust them into the golem's left hand.

'The draykon handlers, strike them my little friend.'

Gar turned quickly and ran down the stairs and Davvid heard the golem open the front door. He stepped onto the small balcony and started to weave a complicated hex in the air in front of him.

Snape surveyed the house from above the tree line and was pleased to see that the defences were minimal, even the poorest mage would overcome them. Perhaps this Davvid Krell is too confident.

He waved the draykon handlers forward and the great beasts proceeded towards the house. As they drew close he was surprised to see the door to the mansion opening and a small child come running out towards them, carrying flowers.

'Sir, there's a little girl running towards us; shall I hover or land? She could be hurt if I land,' shouted the handler on his draykon's neck.

Something was wrong. Snape could not understand why Davvid Krell would send a child out — and then he realised — it was not a child! He started to flourish a hex but the 'child' had stopped and was casting an intricate sign itself. He was too late! It was the golem Gar!

The handler on the draykon next to Snape's screamed and tugged at the harness that held him into his saddle. The bindings were hexed and constricting, strangling him. He lost all concentration and the draykon veered, into Snape's beast. The two collided and their vast wings beat against each other, tearing great rents in their leathery skin. Snape's draykon bellowed in rage and lunged forward to rip into the other's neck with its razor-like beak. Snape hurled the hex at Gar and then clung desperately to the webbing along the flank of his draykon as it started to plunge earthwards.

Gar took the full brunt of Snape's casting and was punched backwards by a burst of reaction. The clothes were ripped from its tiny form and its right arm shattered as it crashed to the ground. Two heavy thuds, intermingled with screams from trapped men and shrieks of rage from the draykons, announced that they had slammed to earth.

As the two beasts continued to fight, Snape managed to crawl away from the wreckage. He put his hand into something warm, wet, and gagged as he realised it was the innards of one of his men, crushed and burst open like a ripe melon beneath the weight of the thrashing draykon. He struggled to his feet and looked around him. There were bodies of men strewn everywhere; some writhing with broken limbs and calling for help; other were still, beyond all salvation. A pitiful few were struggling to their feet and trying to rally their golems to them. Snape twisted around angrily and looked towards the mansion house. There, on a balcony stood the man that had caused it all. Davvid Krell was still waving hexes in the air before him as he goaded the two animals into more rage. Gar was on its back, halfway between the thrashing animals and the house, and Snape nodded in satisfaction as he saw that the little golem was not moving. He looked towards Davvid Krell again then drew a deep breath and started to weave a complicated pattern in the air before him. He was just about to let fly with the hex when he saw a movement behind Davvid and he stopped.

As the two great beasts fell from the sky Davvid fuelled their anger by goading them with his hexes. He saw Gar fly backwards through the air with a terrible force and impact on the ground heavily. Parts of the golem had shattered and he was sure the tile within the golem's mouth had been dislodged, or even damaged. Gar was not moving.

He looked for the instigator of the attack on Gar and spotted a small man attempting to rally the golem handlers. The man turned towards the house and for a moment, it seemed that Davvid's and his eyes locked. Davvid began to form a powerful hex as the leader of the militia did the same. Davvid was a few seconds ahead and knew that his casting would hit first, but a noise behind him made him turn slightly, just in time to see the chair come crashing down on his head.

Nausea and blurred vision returned to Davvid Krell and angry voices made the pain in his head increase. His eyes fluttered open and he stared at the high wooden ceiling above him and realised he was lying on his back upon the table in the room. He turned to look at the window and saw the shattered remains of the chair that had struck him, and frowned. Then he saw Denube Sarreg's smiling face and realised it was she who had struck him. Anger boiled up in him and his instinct was to obliterate her with a hex, but he could not move his hands. He raised his head slightly and saw he was securely bound, hand and foot. The voices became stilled and footsteps approached him from behind.

Gradually the militiamen and their golems surrounded the table. Their faces dark and angry; many were badly bruised; some were still bleeding profusely and held temporary bandages made from sheets and napkins to their wounds. The crowd on his right side parted to let a man through, and Davvid recognised him as the leader who he had almost finished with his hex, before Sarreg's bitch had struck.

'My my, you've caused us some trouble,' the man's voice had a soft, yet cold tone, and Davvid swallowed noisily. The man's face was pinched and rodent-like; his eyes glittered with a fierce temper and Davvid knew that his calm demeanour hid a deep hatred.

'I only defend what is mine. Who are you sir, to come and invade my home like this?'

Snape threw his head back and laughed, 'You have an incredible sense of humour. I hope you manage to retain some of it by the time we've finished with you, Master Davvid Krell.'

'Thaumaturgist Krell, and who might you be?'

'I am Snape. Just, Snape.'

Davvid swallowed again, he had heard of Gerold Snape, and all he had heard was bad. The man was an expert mage and a patron of Mayor Gorman's. Some said he was the mayor's right hand, and could even be more than just his lackey. However, more to the point, everyone said that he was a vicious, power-greedy man who would stop at nothing to advance his thaumaturgic experience.

'Snape, you do yourself an injustice sir. I have heard you are more than a master at the 'arts',' Davvid tried to appeal to Snape's good side, if such a side existed.

He bowed, 'I thank you Master Krell. I do what little I can.'

Davvid's face reddened at the insult again but he calmed

himself, this man must want something or he would already be dead.

'Men, attend to your wounds. Prepare a meal if you would, Madam Sarreg. Send word to the township, you may requisite anything that you wish.'

'All I wish for is justice, Militiaman Snape. Justice for my daughter and myself. This man should hang.'

'All in good time, all in good time,' Snape replied and smiled down at Davvid.

Gradually the room cleared. Men went to bathe and bandage their wounds. Handlers returned to the gardens to begin nursing and soothing the two draykons that had almost fought to the death. In addition, golems began digging pits for the dead. Soon the only two left remaining in the room were Davvid and Snape.

Snape walked around the table, studying the bound man, and Davvid flinched as the strange little man's hands caressed his wings.

'I have long wanted to extrude a pair of wings myself. But I find I just have neither the time nor the resources to do it. I shall have to put both in order and do it though. These are a magnificent pair. You must be proud. The cost I imagine was quite considerable?'

'Yes, both in the monetary sense, and in pain. Extrusion takes a toll on the body.'

'Yes, I know. In fact, so much of a toll that only one pair can ever be extruded from anyone. Well, so I am led to believe. Is it not so?' Snape asked.

Davvid nodded, 'Yes, it is quite impossible to extrude another.'

'Hmm... such a pity. A fine pair of wings like this could never be extruded again. What a loss if something should ever happen to them,' he said as he picked up the knife from the table.

'SNAPE!'

The knife plunged into the soft membrane of Davvid's right wing and Snape dragged it slowly through the tissue leaving a long rent.

'I understand that the flesh does regenerate. The problem lies with the skeleton. Once the bones are destroyed, there is nothing more that can be done. Except perhaps, buy a drayk?' Snape asked and then plunged the knife into Davvid's wing again.

Davvid shrieked in pain and horror, 'What is it you want from me!'

'Ahh... a good question. What — is — it — I — want,' he spat each word out, 'I want to advance my art, Master Krell. I search for advancement, and I think you can help.'

'But... but... you are as skilled in the arts as I am... I cannot teach you anything you do not know!'

The knife plunged again and completed a triangular incision in the wall of Davvid's right wing. Snape lifted the piece of membrane up and examined it as bright red blood dripped onto the floor. 'Exquisite, almost like looking at a network of roads or rivers. Don't you think?' He asked as he held up the piece of wing to the light and studied the criss-crossing of veins within it.

Davvid moaned and it dawned on him that Snape knew his secret, he knew...

'Shall I continue? Perhaps just a small fracture next. On one of the more delicate bones?'

'Tell me what you need to know. I don't understand what it is you want!' Davvid screamed, but he knew what Snape wanted.

The snapping of the small bone on the extremity of Davvid's wing echoed around the room, chased by his howl of agony. Snape held the tip of the wing to the table and then sliced around the broken bone with the knife. He held the long, finger-like bone up to the light coming through the window and nodded. 'Marvellous; air cavities within the bone structure. Strength yet lightness, marvellous. You can still fly, I imagine, but perhaps you will tend to circle to one side a little now?' And he smiled.

Davvid whimpered, 'I'll tell you all you want to know.'

'Yes, you will,' Snape said and withdrew Gar's hex tile from within his cloak, 'Yes, you most certainly will.'

Chapter 9

Everything will be as it once was

'Snape has shown great interest in your golem, Sarreg,' Gorman spoke between shovelling spoonfuls of food into his mouth, and then he belched. 'A trick, Sarreg. Let your golem perform for us all, a trick. I wish to see what makes Snape so envious of your lump of clay,' he said, waving his arm to his guests and they joined in with his demand. The women around the large table started clapping and fluttering their fans nervously whilst the men thumped the table and chanted, 'A TRICK. A TRICK!'

Sarreg fumed quietly to himself and said under his breath, 'So you buffoons want a trick? I will show you a trick. I'll show you Wide's strength.'

He had withstood the worst of Gorman's satire and mockery long enough. Against his better judgement, he motioned a simple sign in front of him and Wide strode purposely forward towards the head of the table and Gorman. Immediately the two golems on either side of it moved protectively into Wide's path but Wide thrust out his powerful hands and gripped each by the throat and lifted them from the floor. They struggled in a futile attempt to free themselves and Sarreg smiled, now you will all see how powerful my golem is, perhaps now you will all respect me! His attention had been on Wide's performance and he noticed Gorman's flourished hex too late; felt his arms pin to his side.

'An attempt on my life is not the sort of trick I imagined, my dear fellow.' Gorman nodded to a group of handlers near the door to his dining room. They sent their golems forward to confront Wide. The large golem turned, still holding Gorman's two bodyguards in his hands.

'Mayor Gorman, it was just a demonstration of Wide's strength!' Sarreg exclaimed, 'Pull your golems back for pity's sake or Wide will defend me!'

Gorman raised an eyebrow, 'Defend you it may, but I have yet to see one golem best ten.'

The words had barely left his lips when Wide crashed the two golems' heads together; one cracked audibly and it repeated the action again. This time the head of the golem in its left hand fragmented and Wide dropped the life-less object to the floor. The other golem in its right hand battered at Wide's head, but to no avail. Then the eight other golems attacked. Wide parried the nearest one and it stumbled past Wide to crash into the wall. It threw the golem in its right hand into the path of the next attacker and they collided and tumbled to the floor. But Wide was outnumbered and the remaining six arriving simultaneously overwhelmed it. Their combined weight dragged the huge golem to the ground. Gorman and a number of his henchmen cast intricate hexes and Wide ceased struggling.

'A formidable golem indeed Sarreg. I can see why Snape would like me to gift it to him,' Gorman said and he walked over to where Wide lay motionless on the floor. He stooped and prised open the large golem's mouth and withdrew the tile from within.

Gorman studied it for a moment in puzzlement and then carelessly dropped it onto the table. He waved the handlers away, 'It is safe now. Call them off.' Then he freed Sarreg from his invisible bonds.

'Mayor Gorman, you cannot intend to take Wide from me? On what grounds? It was merely a demonstration. You asked for it yourself. Sir, it goes beyond the law to confiscate a person's golem without warrant!'

'Of course. You're right, Sarreg. I wouldn't even consider taking Wide from you. However, as you most obviously can't control such a beast I find it my duty to protect the citizens from further harm. I'll exchange your golem for one, which you should find a little easier to master.' Gorman raised a hand, the handlers near the door parted, and a strange golem limped into the room. It had to be one of the oldest creatures that Sarreg had ever seen. Its brown earthenware body was striated with cracks and full of chips. One foot was badly damaged and the golem faltered in its stride to compensate for the defect. 'Sarreg, meet Plain. Plain this is Sarreg, your new master.' Gorman introduced the two and the golem raised a hand as if to shake Sarreg's.

The hand was crude; it resembled a mitten with all the fingers joined into one. It was nothing but a basic pad and a thumb. Sarreg's outrage brimmed over. He had fallen into a trap. He had let Gorman wear him down, and his constant taunting had finally made him do a reckless thing, 'This is intolerable; you insult me sir.' He slapped the golem's proffered hand away and it almost stumbled and fell.

'Sarreg, don't goad me into adhering to the letter of the law. You set your golem upon me. I merely asked for a trick and you respond with an assassination attempt. All witnessed the act. I could have your life for that. Heed this warning well. Accept your place; you are now no longer my guest. However, you may remain as a steward within my household, and as such will still be under my protection. On the other hand, you may leave. Return to Marin's Weir if you should wish. Whether the outlaw Davvid has been apprehended, yet I do not know. It will be a risk you will have to take if you decide to go back. You may take Plain with you for protection; I trust you can control him a little better than your last charge. It is a fair exchange under the circumstances. Don't you agree?' Guffaws and sniggers spread around the room as Gorman twisted his knife of caustic wit further into the Procurator.

Sarreg folded his arms across his chest, his hands within

the folds of his cloak, and moved closer to Gorman's table. The golem bodyguards shifted slightly, but Gorman raised a hand to stop them. He was interested in what Sarreg would do and felt no fear.

The Procurator reached the table and slammed both hands down on it with force; the plates and cutlery rattled, a glass or two fell and spilled wine across the white tablecloth. 'I shall return to Marin's Weir in the morning. Your gracious assistance has been recognised. I look forward to repaying it; ten fold.' Then he backed away a pace, bowed and stormed out of the room. Following him was the limping golem and the laughter of Gorman's guests, which echoed through the hallway behind him.

He reached his room and kicked the door open, it swung back violently and crashed back into the wall causing small pieces of plaster to shower down upon him, but Sarreg was past caring about such trivialities. All that was on his mind was revenge, and the key to that revenge was hidden within his cloak. Plain stumbled through the doorway and dutifully closed the door behind itself. As it turned to face its new master, Sarreg gripped the golem firmly around the jaws and prised its mouth open. The hex tile within was cobwebbed and dirty. It probably had not been removed for centuries. Sarreg tore it out and threw it to the floor where is fractured into two pieces. He stamped on it and then ground his heel into the tile, crushing it into even more fragments. A writhing spiral of what looked like smoke arose from it and dissipated; whether or not it was the soul captured within, he did not know and did not care. The golem rocked unsteadily and went rigid. Sarreg leaned it carefully against the wall and withdrew something from his cloak's pocket. It was a hex tile, the one that had been on the table in front of Gorman; it was Wide's hex tile.

When Sarreg had crashed his hands on the table he had palmed Wide's tile into his cloak and replaced it with another, a blank which was in his pocket. He always carried a spare tile should further instructions be needed he could write them upon the blank and add the tile to whichever golem he controlled.

He held Wide's tile reverently in his hand and then placed it into Plain's mouth and closed the jaws. The old golem shivered slightly and then pushed itself away from the wall and stood erect.

'Welcome back Wide. Don't worry about your present body. It's a temporary thing. First we shall have our revenge and then your body will be restored to you.' As if in reply the two dark pits that represented the golem's eyes flashed red momentarily and Sarreg smiled. Wide had returned.

Snape and Davvid had fasted for three days; in Snape's case it was voluntary, and in Davvid's case he had no choice. Snape had tethered him in the dungeons below Sarreg's house and after continuing his questioning had ultimately wrenched the secret of the Rapture Bud from him. He doubted if Davvid would ever be able to use his wings again.

Not that it mattered to Snape, for once Davvid had taken him to the plant's location his usefulness would be over. The fewer people that knew about the Rapture Bud's effects the better, was Snape's opinion, as he filled the small wooden container with the meat paste.

The smell of the rotting meat permeated everything. It filled the room even though the window was open. It clung to his clothes; it seemed to impregnate into his very skin. The odour reviled him, but it was unavoidable. He would reap his first off-world soul soon, and Davvid Krell would suffer a serious accident; in fact, it would be fatal.

There was a knock at the door. Snape hurriedly screwed the wooden lid onto the container and washed his hands in the bowl of water next to him.

'Come,' he said as he dried his hands but noted that they still stank of the meat. His nose wrinkled in disgust.

Denube and Mari Sarreg entered and fluttered their scented fans beneath their noses,

'Militiaman Snape, what is that terrible odour?' exclaimed Denube.

'Vile experiments Davvid Krell has left brewing my dear lady. I am disarming them now as we speak,' said Snape as he waved his hand over the table, encompassing the various pots, test-tubes and other paraphernalia which he had been working with.

'I trust you two ladies are fully recovered from your ordeal?' He noted the blush that flew across Mari's face. A pleasant young woman. Davvid Krell had good taste; Snape smiled and moistened his lips.

'We thank you, Militiaman Snape. We're quite recovered now. Although my Mari is still upset from...from Krell's advances. How she fought him off and kept her dignity is heartening. Her father will be proud of her.'

Snape raised his eyebrows slightly; he had heard quite a different story.

'As we are both recovered I would like to request that we may join my dear husband in the city. Some time away from the house will do us good. You may stay here as long as you like, my dear sir. *You* will always be welcome in our home.'

Snape inclined his head slightly, 'Your offer is generous Madam Sarreg, and I thank you. My men will escort you to the city. The draykons have both recovered well enough for flight. I'll stay a day or two longer. There are still many things that I have to investigate. On concluding my enquiries, I'll return with the rest of my men and Davvid Krell. He will stand trial before the senate, but the verdict can be none other than death by hanging. His crimes against your husband and your good selves will be paid for.' He was surprised when Mari gasped quietly then coughed as if to mask the noise and fluttered her fan.

'That would be lovely; we shall be in the city quicker than I thought. You are most kind sir. My husband will be extremely pleased; he rewards those who assist the family.' She smiled and curtsied.

Snape grinned widely, wanting to say, your husband will reward me, but I doubt he will be pleased. However, he did reply, 'My pleasure, ladies.' Then he beckoned a militiaman forward. 'Return to the city this evening. You are to transport Procurator Sarreg's wife and daughter to Mayor Gorman's residence. Take the handlers who have been injured and leave two with me and their golems.' Snape ordered his next-in-command, a lanky young man, eager to please, and easily manipulated.

'Yes, sir. Will two handlers and their golems be enough protection for you sir?' he asked.

'Dainman, your concern is noted and appreciated, but there is no need to worry. Davvid will return with me on the morrow. He can't cast or hurt me in anyway. All that remains now is for me to make safe this house and his apartments in town. Once I am satisfied that all is well in Marin's Weir I shall return with Davvid Krell. Mayor Gorman I'm sure is eagerly awaiting his appearance. The trial will be a thing to witness. I can't remember the last time a thaumaturgist was put on trial, found guilty and hanged. It should prove quite a spectacle.'

Dainman bowed slightly, 'As you say, sir. I look forward to your return.'

Snape waved a hand to dismiss him and the young man left the room.

Dainman collected his few things, then went to the women's room, and knocked on the door; a voice bade him enter. He opened the door and went in. Denube Sarreg was struggling to close an enormous travel-chest and looked up at him, 'Ahh… just in time young man, come and sit on this.'

He opened his mouth to reply but was too slow, she continued, 'That dizzy girl of mine; where has she wandered off to now? I told her we were leaving soon and she should be ready, and now where has she gone?' She beckoned him to sit on the chest's lid and he dutifully did so. With some effort, they managed to close and secure the lid and then Dainman had his golem lift the travel-chest up and carry it out to the draykon.

'Where is that child!' she asked him.

'Madam, I shall go look for her. If you would proceed to the garden, I would be most obliged. We shall be leaving as soon as your daughter is found.'

A rustling noise woke Davvid and he sat up straighter against the damp wall, he imagined it was rats again, if only he had a hand free then at least he could eat. Then he realised it was someone trying the door to the darkened cellar room. He shook in fear. Snape had come to extract more information from him. His tattered wings folded in on themselves tightly, almost as if he was trying to re-incorporate them into his body once again. A line of flickering light appeared around the edge of the door as it slowly opened and he saw a figure enter carrying a candle.

It was Mari, and in her other hand she carried a knife; the candle's light gleamed on its blade and he let out a whimper. She moved swiftly across the room and set the candle down by his knees, then brought the knife up. He pulled away from her as she grabbed his shirt collar and pulled him towards her. She pressed her lips to his and kissed him fiercely and he felt her hand with the knife slip up behind his back.

'Mari, I'm sorry. I used you, I'm so sorry,' Davvid said and closed his eyes waiting for the blade to find his life.

She slashed quickly, the bonds holding his hands to the

wall were cut through, and he was free. He opened his eyes in astonishment and she kissed him again, he put his blood-caked hands on her shoulder and pushed her back gently.

'Why Mari? Why?'

'I want to be free Davvid. All my life my parents have kept me like a bird in a gilded cage. You are the first man I have ever known,' she blushed coyly, 'You showed me what life can be like, and I liked it. I will free you now but I want to come with you. Take me with you, please Davvid, please!'

'Where can we go? Your father will not rest until he has the both of us caught. That is if we manage to get out of the house. Once Snape sees I have gone he will hunt me down and then kill me. Mari, I cannot do anything for you. I am a dead man.'

'I have money Davvid, we can go anywhere, and we can start anew.'

'Listen Mari. I am a thaumaturgist; I live and breathe my art. No one will employ me. I can't live on your money, I can't. You should leave. If I escape and can start again somewhere I'll send for you. This way no one will know you released me. If I am caught then only I will pay the price, you will not.' He gripped her shoulders again and she pressed her head against his chest, sobbing.

Davvid stood up and winced in pain.

'What has Snape done to you!' she gasped as she saw his ruined wings and the dried blood that stained the back of his shirt.

'Perhaps what I deserved, Mari. Perhaps what I deserved.'

'I'll beg my father to forgive you, Davvid, I promise. Please be careful.' She touched his cheek gently and he kissed her hand.

'Go…' he whispered.

Mari gave him the knife and then looked around the door warily, beckoning him to follow. She returned to her mother's chamber and Davvid crept towards the main room of the house where Snape had tortured him.

'Come girl, we must go down to the garden. Our passage to the city awaits us,' Denube wagged her finger at Mari, 'Have you been crying again? Your father will see we get justice my child.'

Mari dabbed her eyes with her handkerchief and shook her head. They could never understand what she felt, never. She followed her mother out of the house and across the garden to the awaiting draykon. She turned back once and gazed up at her home before climbing on the beast's side to take her seat, and her mother patted her hand softly, 'There there, you'll be back soon enough. We will shop and have a peaceful holiday in Fivewinds. Then when we return to Marin's Weir, Davvid Krell will have paid for his crimes, and we can carry on as if it had never happened. Everything will be as it once was.'

Mari bawled in frustration, put her head between her hands as the draykon flapped its gigantic wings and soared into the air, up over the roof of Sarreg's mansion and out into the evening sky, towards the great capital city of Fivewinds.

Back in the mansion house, Davvid pushed the door to main room open and breathed a sigh of relief. It was empty. He sneaked in quietly and surveyed the table looking for clues. Snape had prepared the paste; he was going to try reaping a soul from the other world. Davvid was sure of it now. The remains of hex tiles and the pestle and mortar, which contained dried remnants of the rotten meat, confirmed it all. However, Snape only knew an approximation of the Rapture Bud's location. Davvid was sure Snape would force him to accompany him to the site. It was there that Snape would kill him. It was what Davvid would do if the situation were reversed. He did not believe he could escape the house safely; it was probably well guarded and Snape was as good a mage as Davvid had seen. His glamour hexes were well placed. Davvid caught glimmers of them from the corner of his eye.

There had to be another way; somehow, he had to be prepared for Snape's attack. His eyes fell upon a blanketed form in a corner of the room and he recognised the foot that protruded from beneath it. It was Gar.

Davvid drew back the blanket and cursed silently. Gar had received extreme damage. One arm had been completely smashed. Nothing remained; it was severed at the shoulder. There was damage to the golem's head, which had a piece about the size of Davvid's hand missing from the upper skull. If Gar had been a human then his brain would have shown through the opening; as it was all that Davvid could see was Gar's hex tile which had been broken into two halves. They were separated and he took them out carefully. He examined them and was relieved to find that none of the glyphs had been damaged. The crack ran through the script without dissecting anything important. The captured soul writhed dreamily within the tile and Davvid fitted the two halves together with the utmost care. He put the tile down on the floor and with the finest casting possible joined the two halves together with a delicate motion of his hands. He inspected the tile once more and then placed it into the little golem's mouth. A second or two passed. Then Gar struggled upright and Davvid did something he never imagined himself capable of, he embraced the small figure.

He took some cushions from nearby chairs and a couch, and placed them on the floor where Gar's body had lain. Then he covered them with the blanket.

'Follow me my little friend,' he said, and they both quietly left the room. Davvid led the golem back down into the bowels of the house and into his dungeon room where he had been held captive. He sat Gar down in front of him and spent a number of minutes instructing him both verbally and with hand flourishes.

Then he motioned Gar to the blocked tunnel that led to the

well. Davvid stared deep into the tunnel; he opened and closed his eyes rapidly and was relieved to see that it was not glamour hexed. Snape had miscalculated; he had not discovered the secret way out of the building.

'Go, and don't stop for anything, Gar. You must be in position for tomorrow. Run like the wind my little friend. My life depends on you now.'

The golem scrambled over the rock fall, squeezed through a narrow aperture, and then was gone. Davvid returned to the iron ring set into the wall. He slipped the knife into his boot and tied one of his hands behind his back. He motioned a sign upon the other rope and it twisted like a snake. It made a loop and hovered in the air before him; the loop grew smaller and smaller as the rope tightened. He turned his back to it and looking over his shoulder, he slipped his free hand within the closing circle. Davvid winced as the rope bit down onto his wrist. Then he sat back down on the floor and waited.

Chapter 10

Politics, a dangerous business

It took a vast amount of patience on Sarreg's part to sit quietly. He waited until Gorman's household gradually dispersed to their various rooms and settled down for the night.

The party had continued raucously for some hours after he had left. Occasionally a burst of laughter would waft up from the windows in the courtyard below. They spilled light out from the main room into the darkness. That laughter stung Sarreg like an angry wasp each time it found its way up and infiltrated into his shuttered room on the second floor.

It was impossible to say if the laughter had anything to do with his humiliation earlier that evening, but to Sarreg every roar, every peal of merriment that reached his ears was like scratching a sore that refused to heal over; it festered and grew.

As the house finally fell quiet, and he heard the last of the doors close, he smiled in the darkness of his room, 'Soon the only laughter to be heard in this house will be mine.'

Mayor Gorman stumbled into bed. His fat wife cursed as he rolled into her and her nightcap fell over her eyes, 'Roget, you have drunk much too much this evening, and what you did to that poor man…'

'What I did to that poor man!' He interrupted her and belched, 'That poor man, my dear Henrietta, has wanted my position for a great many years. I missed the chance to kill him once, but now I have succeeded in doing very much the same. He may not be dead but he is powerless.'

'Roget, why you have to humiliate him like that I just don't understand.'

'Of course you don't understand my dear. It is politics and

you are a woman; the two do not mix,' he gave her a peck on the cheek, 'and now off to sleep my cherub. Tomorrow will be a busy day. I have stripped Sarreg of his dignity and his precious golem; tomorrow I shall strip him of his house and fortune.'

He blew out the lamp on his bedside cabinet and snuggled down between the clean white sheets. As he drifted off to sleep, he felt something niggling at his mind but he could not think of what it was. Something he had just said to his wife; he was sure. He tried to capture the nebulous thought but the wine and food took its toll and his heavy eyelids closed; within minutes, he was snoring loudly.

His wife huffed and turned on her side. Men, as long as they have their wine, women and politics they are happy.

She listened to Gorman's wheezing snore, and then reached under her pillow for the little packet of laudanum. She opened it carefully so that it would not rustle. She licked the tip of her little finger and dipped it into the powder. Then she returned the finger to her mouth and sucked at it greedily. Henrietta returned the rest of the opiate to the safety of her pillow and started counting the number of Gorman's noisy breaths as if she was counting sheep. By the time she had reached two hundred and ten she had dropped off too. The couple snorted and snuffled, a nocturnal duet, which echoed around the bedroom and seeped passed their doorway out into the hall. The two golems on sentry duty either side of the door were not effected in the least as they stood staring expressionlessly at the blank wall in front of them.

An hour later and the scene was the same. Golems had no need to fidget, change position for comfort's sake, or leave their post to urinate. They were statues until an event would stimulate them into animation. The arrival of Plain, limping down the corridor towards them, head bowed and hands behind his back, made both figures turn in unison. Golems should not have any sense of superiority. They had no feelings. Perhaps to call them soul-less would, in one way, be incorrect. However, to imagine them with feelings would make any thaumaturgist or golem handler cry with laughter. They were animated lumps of clay, sculpted caricatures of men. They had the form of a man, a head upon two shoulders, leading to a pair of arms with hands. A torso, which had legs, and finally, feet. Some were more detailed than others were, but more often than not, they were large earthenware sculptures that moved. That is all, emotionless. Nevertheless, upon the arrival of the limping form of Plain, in the deserted corridor, one could question whether all that was known about golems was true. Did they truly have no feelings? For both guards seemed to exude an air of distain and supremacy as the old golem approached. It was a well-known figure in Gorman's household. Plain had probably outlived every living thing under the house's large roof, but was scorned by all. It was old and damaged. The two golems ignored the shuffling figure and returned to staring at the wall in front of them.

Plain shuffled along quietly until it reached the two guards, and then stopped. The two large golems ignored it; why should they take notice of the old golem? Its presence was well known within the building.

They ignored it. Until Plain whipped the leg of a chair, it and Sarreg had dismantled, around in a vicious arc. It crashed into the nearest golem's knee with devastating results. The whole leg flew apart and the golem crashed to the floor. Plain crushed its skull with another terrifying blow. The next golem lashed out at the smaller figure and caught it a glancing blow, but Plain shrugged it off and the oak chair leg struck again in an upward thrust into the crotch of the golem. A look that an observer would probably describe as surprise seemed to pass across the large figure's rudimentary face. An enormous crack appeared from its crotch area and ran up its torso to the throat.

Plain dropped the chair leg, inserted its stubby, paddle-like hands into the crack, and forced it apart. The golem broke into two halves and Plain followed the side with the head attached to down to the floor. Then with a crunching punch, he cracked its head wide open.

The whole attack had lasted seconds and the noise, although loud, had been extremely brief. Plain waited silently in the darkness until a shadowy figure appeared from around the corner, from the same corner that the limping golem had arrived.

Sarreg peered into the dark corridor, two flashes of red gleamed for a moment, and he almost laughed aloud. He crept forward as silently as his fat bulk would allow until something splintered and cracked beneath his leather boots. It was the remains of Plain's two adversaries.

'It won't be long now Wide, you shall have your own body back soon,' he whispered, and slowly turned the doorknob to Gorman's room.

He did not need to worry; the two occupants of the room were sound asleep and their snores resounded off the walls. Sarreg wondered how either of them could sleep with such a noise, but as he approached the bed, he realised that Gorman's sleep was induced by a drunken stupor. He could smell the stale wine wafting up from him with each exhalation. He sneaked around to Gorman's wife and noted that she too was sleeping exceedingly profoundly, and then in the moonlight that illuminated her face he saw a trace of white powder upon her lips.

'So that is how you escape the tedious life you have to put up with. The womanizing and machinations of your husband has pushed you into the arms of another, but not a man, but a drug, opium, most likely.' He whispered.

Sarreg signed for Wide, who now inhabited Plain's shell, to step forward to Gorman's side of the bed. When the golem was positioned, Sarreg weaved a hex over the sleeping form of Henrietta Gorman. She stirred slightly and started to snore again. He poked her roughly with his fingers and she snorted. He poked her again and her eyes opened blearily. She opened her mouth to speak but no sound came out. Nothing would escape through the invisible gag that bound her. Her eyes grew large and white with terror as she saw who stood above her, but she was unable to move or scream. Sarreg put one finger to his lips and whispered; 'Shh…' as if there was a possibility of her making a noise, he knew very well that she could not. Satisfied that she was bound securely in his hex, he moved around to Mayor Gorman's side of the bed, and almost did a little dance in anticipation.

'Every dog has his day, my dear Mayor. Today this mongrel will mark his new territory,' he said quietly but Gorman just snored on.

Sarreg nodded to Wide and the golem reached forward, put his rough, and clumsily made hand around the mayor's throat. Still he did not awaken and then Sarreg unbuttoned the front of his woollen trousers and extracted his penis. He glanced over at Henrietta Gorman who was now sweating profusely and whose look of terror almost made him feel sorry for her… almost. 'He sleeps soundly; perhaps a refreshing shower will awaken him?'

Gorman was riding a white stallion in pursuit of a nubile young wench who was running away from him coyly. She was on foot and so he quickly ran her down. She fell panting into the long grass and he dismounted his horse and slapped its flanks. It whinnied and ran off whilst he stretched out beside the beautiful creature on the ground. He leaned over her and examined her flawless face, and then he lowered his head and kissed her passionately on her full, ruby lips. She wriggled beneath him and he realised she was not pushing him away;

she wanted him to lie beneath her. He smiled as he lay down in the warm-smelling grass and she straddled him. Her hair fell free and started tickling his face. He brushed it way and yet it still tickled him, it felt wet and he started having trouble breathing. He tried to brush her hair away and found it was getting harder to move. Was it her, or was it raining? He was puzzled; he tried to move again, and could not. Yes, it had to be rain; he felt it pouring on his face now... and then Mayor Gorman awoke.

He spluttered and gulped as a salty liquid ran into his mouth; he tried to swallow but something restricted his throat and he could barely breathe let alone swallow. It was a nightmare! It had to be a nightmare; any moment now, he would wake up. Then his vision came into focus and he realised that Plain, his wretched old golem was standing above him, and had one of its hands around his throat. The other hand was on his chest and was holding him down in the bed. He tried to scream but the little air he had in his lungs could not escape. The darkness of the room started to have small pinpricks of white and red flashes as he realised that he was slowly suffocating. He managed to move his head slightly as a last burst of warm rain fell upon his face and he saw Sarreg. The man was urinating upon him!

'Good morning Mayor Gorman. Nice of you to join us. No please, don't get up!' Sarreg said softly. He buttoned up his trousers and breathed a sigh of satisfaction.

'Ahh, that's much better. I thought I would let you have your wine back. Quite an inferior vintage I fancied.'

Gorman's faced turned purple, before long it would turn black, but not quite yet. Sarreg wanted the man to see the end coming and it wouldn't do if he passed out. He lit the lamp on the bedside cabinet and opened the little drawer. He rummaged through its contents and sighed once again. 'Gorman, where do you keep writing material?'

The mayor's mouth moved silently, so Sarreg put a restraining arm on the golem's hand. 'Ease off a little now, Wide. We don't want to crush the poor fellow's wind pipe do we?' The golem relaxed its grip a little on the mayor's throat and he took in a ragged breath of air. 'There now, is that better?'

'What… how?' Gorman spluttered as he looked at Sarreg and then the golem and then back to Sarreg again.

'Yes it must be confusing for you, mustn't it?' said Sarreg, 'This is not your golem, Plain. It is my golem, Wide and it is quite put out by you, my dear mayor. Wide much prefers its own body. I do not think it likes you somehow. But I digress, where is your writing material?'

Gorman was astounded; he turned to wake his wife and saw that she had been following the proceedings, but was frozen stiff. A glimmer of a hex showed around her and he realised that Sarreg had bound her in her sleep. She could not have raised the alarm, but the bodyguards… he looked towards the door.

'I see you are wondering where your two golems are. Unfortunately they met with a little accident. As I said, Wide is not in the best of temper at the moment.' And as if to confirm Sarreg's statement, the golem's eyes flickered with a red flame and Gorman pulled back from it in horror.

'Does it understand what you say?'

'Of course, why do you think your snivelling wretch, Snape, wants to get his filthy hands on my Wide? Luther Krell's golems are unique. No other thaumaturgist has been able to manufacture them up to the standards of his. Until Davvid Krell of course, and he is next on my list. Once I am finished with you. Now sir, for the last time, where do you keep your writing accoutrements?'

'In the desk,' Gorman replied and nodded towards a heavily carved and ornate desk, which had a brown leather and oak chair before it.

'Good, now stand up carefully and go to it. You have to write a little letter.'

Wide pulled Gorman up from the bed by his throat and dragged him to the desk. Sarreg joined them there and lit another lamp with a taper from their bedside one. The sky was beginning to lighten, however, and Sarreg wanted to finish his business before the household awoke. He opened one of the drawers and pulled out a sheaf of papers. The he found a quill and thrust it into Gorman's hand.

'Write -- *I, Mayor Gorman, do hereby relinquish my position as Mayor of Fivewinds. The weight of responsibility has become far too much for me to bear. My wife and I, during the term of my office, have grown apart. It is time that we make amends and be together again. Therefore, from henceforth, I declare that I am no longer mayor of our great city. The senate will have to decide on another to take my place. In the past, I have been known to chide and ridicule Procurator Sarreg, but there was a reason. It was a test of the man's temperament and I am pleased to say that he has shown himself to be a courageous and honourable man. Many might think that we were enemies. That is not so. I hold him in the highest regard. He has begged me not to take the course of action I have laid out for my wife and myself but I grow weary of politics. For now, I have temporarily made Procurator Sarreg substitute mayor. This is until the senate can sit in its entirety and hold an election to choose a person worthy of taking over the position. However, I cannot recommend Procurator Sarreg highly enough. You would do well to remember this. A warm goodbye to you all, Henrietta and I now leave for a more tranquil place --* And sign and date it!' growled Sarreg, he nodded to Wide who closed both hands around the mayor's throat and squeezed firmly. The mayor struggled briefly then with a shaking hand took up the quill, dipped it in the small pot of ink and began to write.

Sarreg watched Gorman write and a warm glow of satisfaction spread over him. All was going well. Soon he would have the power to do whatever he wanted. He had always held an envious longing for the mayorship of Fivewinds. Once he had come very close to achieving it too. However, Gorman had thwarted him. Now it was finally within his grasp. Next on the agenda would be Davvid Krell and perhaps Jerold Snape. Snape was a dangerous man and his loyalty to Gorman could present a problem. He would be dealt with too.

He snatched up Gorman's finished letter of resignation and read it carefully. Then he placed it on the desk and shook the sand shaker over it, and blew the sand off. The ink was dry. The deed was almost done.

'You'll never get away with this; you know that, don't you?' gasped Gorman through wheezing gulps of breath, 'That paper will be worthless when I denounce you. Stop this charade now and I will let you leave. You can return to Marin's Weir. You can even take your damned golem back with you and nothing will be mentioned of tonight.'

'You are right, of course my dear mayor. This paper is worthless whilst you are around to contest it. But should you not be around?' Sarreg replied and tilted his head quizzically.

'You are a fool if you think I will go into banishment!'

'Oh, I wasn't thinking of banishment my dear fellow. Something far more secure than banishment.' Then Sarreg strode over to the large bed and pulled one of the thick cords that held the drapes back from around it. He threw it over the high beam that ran around the top of the bed and hexed a sign across one end of it. The cord snaked, writhed, and made itself into a hangman's noose as Gorman let out a gasp.

'Sarreg!'

Sarreg flourished another sign and Wide closed his hands tighter around the mayor's throat. His face turned red and his eyes bulged in fear. Sarreg tied off the other end of the cord to a vertical post that stood on each of the four corners of the bed and then pulled the leather chair over. He placed the chair beneath the noose and nodded to Wide. The golem lifted the struggling and kicking mayor into the air until his toes barely touched the floor, but Plain's body was too short, if Wide had been in his own shell then Gorman would have been easily lifted three feet off the floor. However, as it was he managed to keep his toes touching the ground. Sarreg sighed and looked around. He spotted something on a table near the desk and smiled. He picked up the large book and carried it over to Wide, 'There, a little literature has never killed anybody...yet.'

Wide stepped up onto the book and raised Gorman off the floor by about two inches. It was enough. The mayor kicked in vain as his face turned from red to purple. Sarreg looked on emotionlessly; he thought he would have felt pleasure at seeing his enemy's final moments but all he felt was a sense of relief. 'Almost done,' he murmured to himself as Gorman's swollen tongue protruded from his open mouth and his eyes rolled up into his head. Between them, they heaved Gorman's body up onto the bed and raised his head into the noose. Then Sarreg move the chair away slightly and placed it on its side on the floor, as if it had been kicked over. He stood back and surveyed the scene.

Gorman's body swung slowly from the thick cord; the chair lay fallen on the floor. 'Yes, that looks very good, very good indeed,' he said, and then he turned his gaze on the helpless Henrietta Gorman.

'It's so sad how work can break up a happy home isn't it?' he asked her quietly, as she stared petrified into his face. 'How many times have we heard of the terrible toll that it can inflict on family life? Husbands committing suicide, leaving their poor loved-ones to cope on their own. Alternatively, even worse, husbands murdering their family first, and then committing suicide. Terrible, terrible. What do you think happened here?

'Did he quietly sneak away from your side in the night and

write his note. Then when you were asleep, the poor man hung himself? Do you think that is what happened?' He asked her.

She nodded desperately.

'Yes, it does seem that way doesn't it?' he replied.

Henrietta Gorman breathed out a sigh of relief and closed her eyes. She did not see Sarreg bring the wooden chair leg from behind his back and swing it down mercilessly onto her unprotected face. One savage blow was all it took.

'Yes, it would seem like that. Nevertheless, why would he spare you? He went berserk; he destroyed his own golems. You would have woken. You would have raised the alarm, or tried to stop him. No, it just would not do. He killed you my dear. In a fit of frenzy, he killed you, and then took his own life. Ahh…politics, such a dangerous business.'

Snape was like a child; the anticipation of the day's events almost had him hopping up and down as if with the need to urinate. He wanted to shout and caper about like a fool but he composed himself and prepared the equipment needed to summon the souls from another world. The leather bag was ready; it contained the tiles he had prepared and a copious amount of the vile-smelling paste. He had already made excuses to his remaining men, and now he was going to find out where Davvid Krell's secret place was. A Rapture Bud; he was actually going to bathe in the magical puissance of a Rapture Bud. Even more, he was going to harness that power as only two other men had ever done, and transcend this world to find another. He was going to reap souls that would make him an army of golems more powerful than ever before. He, Jerold Snape, was going to be ruler of all.

He swung open the door of the main room he had been using as a laboratory in Sarreg's mansion and was pleased to find the corridor outside deserted. He had sent his men on a fool's errand into Marin's Weir. He had instructed them to search for non-existent, empty golem shells, which Davvid had supposedly constructed. He only wished that there were an abundance of readymade shells for the souls to inhabit, but unfortunately, there were not. However, that was the least of his worries. He was quite capable of constructing the golems for himself. His main worry was Davvid Krell. There was no doubt that the man was a very capable mage. Only fortune had saved Snape from a disaster when they had arrived and attacked the house the week before. If Sarreg's wife had not knocked out Davvid then perhaps the whole expedition would have been destroyed. A full compliment of militia and their golems, destroyed by one man and his little golem. A little golem that was inhabited by a powerful soul however; a little golem that had been able to cast! He looked back into the room for a moment at the blanket that covered Gar, and thought about removing the tile from within the creature's mouth. But time was passing and he wanted to get to the plant, and taste its power. He closed the door firmly and made his way down to the dungeons.

Davvid was extremely weak. The enforced fasting, along with the lack of water, added to the toll taken out of his body by Snape's torture. His wings had stopped bleeding but he had lost a substantial amount of blood. His head spun and he thought he saw a light in front of him. It *was* a light; the door to the dungeon room swung open and Snape cautiously entered. He was alone, no handlers, no other mages, not even a golem protector. Davvid felt a small spark of hope.

'You look terrible. A bit of fresh air will do you the world of good. A chance to stretch your wings. Oh, but you can't. Can you?' sneered Snape. How he despised the man. Still, one day soon, he would have a pair of wings too, and Davvid Krell would no longer have a need for his. He would be dead.

'Water, for pity's sake, I need water.' Davvid croaked.

'Yes, of course. How remise of me. I haven't given you any water have I?' and Snape reached into the corridor for a large wooden pail. He raised it up over Davvid and poured the icy water over him. Davvid held his face up to the torrent and gulped the liquid down greedily. The deluge was over all too soon though, and he shook his head to get the wet hair from his face.

'Thank you,' he said and swore silently beneath his breath.

'Stand up. That was to flush the stench off you. You smell worse than the concoction of meat you instructed me to prepare. Master Krell, if what you have told me is some sort of trick, then be prepared to have your wings ripped from your back. You can then eat them.'

'It's no trick. I have told you everything. All you need to know is where the bud can be found. But for that you'll have to follow me. I can't instruct you on its location. I have to take you there.'

'Yes, so you say. Well, I shall unbind you now so that you may prepare yourself. Be warned, I am protected. Oh, you do not see a golem guard. However, I am protected all the same. Cross me now Davvid and you will wish that I had killed you on that table upstairs. Do I make myself very clear?'

Davvid shook the hair out of his eyes again and blinked rapidly; he could see the glamour hexes that surrounded Snape now. They were plentiful and intricately woven. To break through them would take more than he could possibly summon in the state he was in now. He had no choice for the moment but to go along with Snape's wishes. He would hope for an opportunity at the plant's location. If things went well Snape would have a little surprise waiting for him there.

'Yes most clear. You have nothing to fear from me. I am done. All I want is to be free. I will leave this place forever; you will never see me again. I promise. When you free me, you'll never see me again.'

Snape nodded and hexed a sign over the ropes; they uncurled and un-knotted like a pair of writhing vipers.

'Agreed, once this day is over you will be a free man. And I will not want to see you again,' he said, and imagined how Davvid's rotting corpse will make good fertilizer for the Rapture Bud.

He threw a bundle of clothes onto the floor at Davvid's feet, 'Wear these. They are clean.'

Davvid stripped off his shirt, wincing as he manoeuvred it over his wings. He pulled on the clean, white linen one that was in the bundle, and then the small leather waistcoat.

His boots were covered in congealed blood, all of it his own, and he struggled to pull them off. The new ones were slightly bigger than his usual size, but he was grateful for a fresh pair. Finally he shrugged the dark cloak over the top, threaded his tattered wings through the apertures, and he was ready.

'Put out your hands,' Snape ordered and Davvid obeyed.

The ropes re-fastened themselves around his wrists then crawled around his waist to meet itself once again at his middle. It pulled tight and knotted itself above his stomach, binding his hands closely to his chest.

'I think we are ready,' said Snape and led the way out of the dungeon. They walked up to the back of the house where two drayks were waiting for them, tethered firmly to great iron hoops set into the wall.

Davvid had to be helped into the saddle of his drayk and it arched its neck to snap at him. He caught it a glancing blow with his boot and it almost bucked him out of the saddle. Snape flourished a sign and the beast yelped and cowed down before him. Then he went over to his own mount and jumped into the saddle.

'Lead the way Davvid,' he said and pulled the drayk into the air with its reins.

Both animals rose steadily and wheeled once around the house. Then Davvid kicked the flanks of his mount. The animal started to beat its wings steadily and fly towards the secret location of the Rapture Bud, and the last place Davvid would ever see if his rapidly made plan should fail.

They circled the opening in the woods a number of times whilst Snape checked and re-checked to see if they had been followed or if anything below them was amiss. When he was satisfied, he instructed Davvid to land, and then swooped down beside him. They tethered the two drayks to a tree and Snape reached into a saddlebag to extract two haunches of bloody meat. He threw them down onto the grass in front of the animals and they pounced on them and started eating. Then Snape threw the leather bag with all of his equipment over his shoulder and told Davvid to show him the plant.

A brief walk took them to the mound and the Rapture Bud. Snape could feel the magical force in the air, and as he approached the plant with awe, the energy increased.

'Unbelievable. Can you feel it?' he asked, and goggled at the bud in amazement.

'Yes it's extremely powerful. When you meld with it, the feeling is euphoric,' Davvid replied, and carefully looked around the area, trying not to let Snape see what he was doing.

Snape was engrossed with the plant. He reached forwards and gently caressed the petals; the smell was disgusting and overwhelming. He vomited but nothing came up, just sickly bile, his stomach was empty from the fasting.

'It tries to pollinate you when you put the meat in your mouth?' he asked Davvid.

'Yes, the stamen carries a thaumaturgic charge that opens a rift through which you fall. I can't explain what it is like. You must experience it for yourself. When you see a light in the ether go through. If you see a soul that you can reap, you reach out. The stamen acts as a conduit, and when it touches the victim, it draws the soul away and into our world. The victim burns.' Davvid replied.

'Show me.'

Davvid nodded and stretched out besides the plant. Snape undid his bag and placed a number of the tiles around him, and then brought out the wooden jar of paste. The plant shivered in anticipation.

'The plant senses it!' he exclaimed.

'Yes, the magical reaction is increasing; do you feel it?'

'Yes, it's incredible. Sweet, enticing,' replied Snape softly.

Davvid unscrewed the top and opened the jar. He scooped out two fingers full, put them into his mouth, and inclined near the plant. Snape watched in fascination as the plant slowly dropped its flower towards Davvid's head and the stamen began to appear. Davvid's eyes fluttered and his arms and legs stiffened as the stamen entered his mouth and Snape knew that his spirit had left his body.

Perhaps twenty minutes passed before Snape saw a change in Davvid. His body quivered slightly and the stamen within his mouth expanded and contracted as if something was flowing through it. Thaumaturgic energy hazed over them and Snape's hair began to stand on end. A crackle of discharge flashed through Davvid, the stamen and the surrounding tiles. Snape gasped as the soul tile glowed purple briefly. He drew closer to it and put a shaking hand to his mouth. The tile contained a soul. Davvid had been successful in his reaping. He sat back on his haunches and debated whether to kill Davvid Krell now, or wait until later. The ether an unknown area to Snape, and should something befall his voyage there perhaps it would be good to have someone to aid him on his return. He felt unsure. Davvid was weak, the reaping would weaken him still, and Snape's protection hexes were powerful. He decided to wait and kill him when he had captured his own soul from the other world.

Davvid shivered and opened his eyes. He could barely raise himself from his position next to the plant. The remains of the paste he spat upon the floor and he almost vomited. His gaze fell upon the tile and he nodded in satisfaction; the reaping had gone well. He looked around furtively whilst Snape prepared his own tiles and cursed silently.

'Move to that tree-stump,' Snape indicated a broken stump, a tree long since dead, blasted by lightning or perhaps even thaumaturgic vitality from the plant. He obeyed and crawled up to it. 'Sit with your back against it.'

'There is no need for this. I am too weak to cast a hex, and you are well protected.'

'That may be so. But you are still strong enough to strangle me when I am out of my body,' smiled Snape and he hexed a rope around Davvid and the tree, pulling it tightly against his chest.

Satisfied that Davvid could not move, Snape positioned himself next to the plant and opened the jar. The bud responded to the stimulus yet again and he forced the rancid meat into his mouth. The smell and taste almost choked him, but the potency that started to invade his body took all sense of revulsion away; he was enraptured. As the stamen entered his mouth, he felt his mind take flight and drop into a bottomless crevasse of the utmost black. He screamed in panic but no sound escaped from his lips as he plunged into the ether between the two worlds.

Chapter 11

'Phoenix Rising'

Raven pushed back his long leather coat, which was covering the katana on his left hip. The handle protruded forward and he rested his right hand lovingly upon it. It was his favoured weapon; perhaps some would say it was a little short for its purpose and the longer tachi would have been more suitable, but Raven would disagree.

The katana suited him, it hid beneath his coat like a viper ready to strike, he could almost feel the blade whispering to him, draw me, release me, feed me...

He moved the substantial wooden door before him with his foot; it swung open on rusted hinges. He kept to one side so that his large frame would not present a target in the open doorway and waited for his eyes to accustom themselves to the gloom within. He felt the sword call to him again and he slowly obeyed; the silver-coated blade hissed out from its sheath, almost glowing in the moonlight.

In one flowing move, he stepped into the room, sweeping the blade around to his right in a wide arc. He felt a momentary resistance and then heard a satisfying thump as a head plummeted from the shadows. It rolled along the floor into the swathe of moonlight from the doorway and towards his feet. A louder crash informed him that the body had just tumbled to the ground too. He spun to his left as a banshee wail preceded a further attack and two zombie-like figures rushed out of the darkness towards him. The first fell to a diagonal blow that tore through its left shoulder blade, dissecting the torso and exiting just above the right hip. As the attacker fell into two pieces, the next one crashed into him and they tumbled to the floor. His katana flew from his hand as he tried to protect himself and roll away. The second attacker was every bit as powerful as Raven and crashed a blow into his face; he rolled with the punch and struggled to gain his feet, but a third figure leapt out of the darkness towards him and under the weight of the two he collapsed to the floor. He saw the katana just out of reach and stretched towards it. Another couple of inches and he could grasp it, but the two aggressors pummelled at him and he raised his hands to protect himself. One spattered him with saliva as it bared its yellow teeth and lunged at his throat.

'Enjoying yourself?' a female voice caused all three to look up. There in the doorway was the lithe figure of Phoenix Rising, she was clad from head to toe in a leather suit and she leaned against the doorframe nonchalantly as Raven fought against becoming one of the living-dead himself.

'Phoenix, I could use a little hand here, when you have time!'

She stepped forward and did a neat snap-kick, which caught one of the attackers full in the face; he clasped his broken nose and spluttered, 'Holy shit Miss Flute, you've broken my damn nose!'

'Cut! Cut, cut...' The room filled with a harsh light and Lucy bent down and looked at the man she had kicked.

'Oh hell, sorry Chuck, this set is so bloody dark; I must have stepped in too far before kicking.'

The director of 'Phoenix Rising' pushed through the crowd of make-up people, lighting experts, camera operators and actors who had gathered around the little tableau of Raven and the stuntmen and said, 'Why didn't you stop at the mark, Miss Flute?'

'Because the room is too fucking dark!' she snarled and spun around; he backed away with his hands held protectively in front of him. 'I told you it needs a little more lighting, but no. It is more atmospheric as it is; yeah right, and Chuck has a broken nose now, Ridley. You and your damn atmosphere!'

Ridley Scott backed into the wall behind him, 'Listen, it was an accident. Chuck's a stuntman. A broken nose is nothing; it's all part of the job for him. He will be back on the lot in a few hours, once they have set it. Doesn't matter about the bruising, it will just add some realism to his make-up.'

She looked at him and breathed out slowly, 'Yes, you're right. It was just an accident; sorry I exploded like that. Nevertheless, I do not like to miscalculate. And now Chuck's got another damn scar just because of me.' She reached a hand down and Chuck Reager grasped it and pulled himself up.

'No problems Miss Flute; it will all go in my autobiography. Hey, did I ever show you the scar Stallone gave me?' he asked enthusiastically.

She shot him a warning glance and then looked at Raven who was getting to his feet, 'No I don't think you did, and from what I hear of its location I don't think I want to see it either.'

'Oh, of course, umm… sorry Miss Flute.' He said nasally whilst stemming the flow of blood by pinching his nose.

'Okay, get off to the doc's. I'm going to call it a wrap for today anyway. I've had enough for one day and now this just puts the lid on it for me. Anything to add Ridley?' she turned slowly and looked at the director.

'Ah… no. I suppose you are right; the light has gone now anyway. Okay people it's a wrap. I just wonder how that scene went. We got it all in the can anyway; looks good, realistic.' Scott replied.

Raven picked up the hard, rubber katana and re-sheathed it. 'Should be fucking realistic, this isn't tomato sauce,' he said as he wiped Chuck's blood from his black leather coat.

'Don't worry, accidents happen, man,' said Reager as he left the set.

'Yeah, tell it to my bastard tailor; this coat cost a damn small fortune,' Raven replied to his back.

'Come on you oaf, let's get home before I'm tempted to break your nose too,' Lucy said in exasperation.

Raven spun around and withdrew the katana in one swift movement, 'You feeling lucky, bitch?'

'You really want me to kick your bloody ass in front of all these guys?' She asked and cocked her head to one side.

Raven looked around sheepishly and put the katana away, 'Okay… I can see you are stressed. I'll let you off this time.'

'Yeah, right…' she said and grabbed him by the arm and they left.

Lucy and Raven picked up a Chinese takeaway on their way back to her apartment. The limo wafted an oriental aroma out into the night as they opened the doors and strode towards the entrance to her building. A figure detached itself from the darkened wall and Raven automatically reached for the katana. Lucy looked at him and rolled her eyes as the figure materialised into the form of Rabbet.

'Hi you two,' he said cheerfully and sniffed the air, 'Mmm, smells like one of Mr.Wong's specials. My favourite.'

'Hi yourself, Rabbet,' replied Raven and slid the rubber katana back into the sheath. 'What?' he asked Lucy, as she sniggered softly.

'Nothing, nothing at all,' she said to Raven and then turned to Rabbet, 'Let me guess. Something's happened again hasn't it?'

'Yes, I'm afraid it has. Can we speak upstairs?'

'Yes, I guess so. I suppose you want some Chinese too?'

'That's awfully kind of you. Only if you have enough to spare, of course.'

'Yes, no problem,' she smiled, 'Raven doesn't mind sharing.'

Rabbet waited until the meal was over before he explained the news in depth.

'It was in The States, a forty year old school teacher. They found his body in the cloakroom. Usual thing almost all his body consumed apart from an arm this time. Nothing else around him damaged; no witnesses, no clues, nothing. The cops there are as baffled as we were with our S.H.C. cases. Did you feel anything? You know…' He pointed to the stub of her finger.

'Didn't feel a thing Rabbet, doesn't mean anything though. Only time I have felt something is on the occasions that the bat came for me. I don't believe there is any relationship between me and the other S.H.C. cases. Perhaps I'll only feel it when it comes for me again.'

'You could be right. I'm a pain in the ass, I know, but you're the only person ever to survive an 'attack' like this. Thanks to you, we can really call it an attack. Your case is unique, not only did you survive but you had witnesses as well.'

'It's okay Rabbet. If I can help, I will, but I do not think it will make any difference. As I've told you, the feeling I got was that the thing wasn't from our world. Something similar to our world yes, but not quite right. I have even started studying theories about parallel dimensions and all that crap. I've spent hours trawling the web for information on it but most of the stuff is crack-pot lunacy or pseudo-religious tripe,' she sighed and unconsciously rubbed the scars along the back of her arm.

'Look Rabbet, she's had a rough day on the set. I think she can do without dragging all this shit up tonight. Do you mind?' Raven said standing up and walking to the door.

'Oh… sorry. As I said, I'm a pain in the ass. Listen, just give me a ring if something comes to mind, or… well you know. If you have a 'feeling'.' He made little quotation signs in the air.

Lucy nodded, 'Yes, of course. Thanks Rabbet, goodnight.'

Raven closed the door behind the detective and returned to the sofa.

'Want me to stay tonight?'

'No Rave, I'm okay, just a little stressed. You know.'

'Yes, I know babe. That is why I think I should stay. At least if I'm here you have me to stop you cutting yourself,' he said and ran his large hand across the network of scars that covered her arms.

'It's a release Rave. I can't explain it, the pain gives me release from the anger that I feel.'

'Lucy, you were a child. There was nothing you could do to save your father. Cutting yourself is no way to respect his memory.'

She looked up at him and smiled, 'Rave, you're a big softy beneath that entire gothic exterior aren't you?'

He cupped her face in his hands and kissed her gently; she wound her fingers into his long hair and her tongue slipped into his mouth. Raven collected her up into his arms and carried her to the bedroom.

Snape tried to find his way back to his body, but blackness, far deeper than he ever imagined, surrounded him. He felt a connection to his corporeal form but did not have the slightest idea how to draw himself back to it. He looked around the darkness for some sign or direction. He did not even know if he was really turning his head, if his eyes were actually seeing anything. It had to be his psyche, liberated from his earthly body, which was travelling through the ether. The conduit back to his prone form, lying next to the plant, was the stamen that attached him to it like an umbilical cord. He shivered, or imagined he shivered. If that umbilical cord was severed he would be lost forever in the darkness. His body would die and decay, but his mind would remain wandering the void for eternity. He wanted to wail again but knew it was useless; there was no one to hear him, no one to see him, no one to help him. Snape surrendered to his situation and within minutes realised that something was ahead of him, far, far into the distance something glimmered.

He tried to reach for it but had no idea if he had actually moved, but the glimmer seemed to change position slightly. Yes! It was moving! The doorway to the other world, it had to be! He stretched his mind out towards the scintillating spot in the vast expanse of black. Slowly it drew closer and Snape's excitement expanded with it.

Snape began to wonder if he was moving towards the strange anomaly in the ether or if it was moving towards him. He had no points of reference to give him an idea of speed or distance but he felt that the area before him was drawing closer, and at an increasing speed. The closer it came the more he realised that it was not as Davvid had described; this did not resemble the description of the doorway into the other realm. This was a pulsating ball of vehemence that now slowly began to circle him. It moved in an almost predatory fashion, as if it was weighing him up, examining him. Snape flailed and tried to pull away, but his mind was not prepared for its journey through the ether; he hung in the void like a sailing ship without a wind to fill its sails.

Suddenly the ball of puissance stopped, it drew itself tighter and tighter and then launched itself at Snape with an incredible burst of speed. He opened his mouth to scream and the ferocity was upon him. A brief moment of clarity flew through his mind before his psyche dissipated into the ether, fragmented into millions upon millions of parts. It would be impossible for them to find their way back together again, and would never return to Jerold Snape's body. The two words that flashed through his mind before his psyche was ripped apart were... Luther Krell.

Davvid struggled against his bonds but found it a fruitless waste of time, Snape's hex was much too strong for him.

Perhaps if he were in better health, he would break them, he would break them, and then he would break Snape's neck.

He stopped testing the rope's strength with both his wrists and his mind and relaxed. The ardour of the plant's emanations augmented his thaumaturgic flow but he was both physically and mentally exhausted.

'GAR WHERE ARE YOU!' he put his head back and howled. If the little golem had failed to get to the hidden glade then Davvid was a dead man. As soon as Snape returned safely and possibly with a captured soul, he knew his life would be forfeit. Snape would have no further use for him; he only hoped his death would come quickly. He shivered involuntarily at the thought of further torture and bowed his head. A low moan made him look up and he saw Snape's body contort, his arms and legs thrashed as if he was trying to swim or run. Then within a few seconds, it was over and Snape became as rigid as a pole. Davvid's eyes narrowed as he contemplated what was happening to Snape's mind, the mind that was traversing the ether between worlds, the mind that already held the decision of Davvid's fate within it. Snape sighed, an almost peaceful sound escaped his lips, and his body relaxed. Whatever it was, it was over now, Davvid wondered if his torturer had perhaps experienced trouble with his first reaping.

A hand clamped down onto Davvid's shoulder and he yelped in surprise then turned his head. Gar stood silently at his side and Davvid almost wept, 'Gar, my little friend, you finally found me.'

The small golem had force-marched all the way from Sarreg's mansion non-stop to the glade and was filthy. Mud streaked his brown body, numerous cracks and chips showed where he had fallen or taken damage from wild animals. Nevertheless, he had arrived, and Davvid now saw a small glimmer of hope. Gar could free him, and then he would deal with Jerold Snape.

'Gar, the ropes. Hex them off me if you can,' he instructed the golem and looked down at the thick ropes binding him to the tree. Gar raised its remaining hand and gestured a quick hex over them. Davvid felt the rope begin to move but it was not enough. 'Again, Gar, again!' The little golem repeated the movement and the ropes began to un-knot themselves with sinuous grace. In no time at all they came free and Davvid put one hand onto Gar's shoulder and levered himself off the ground. He stood unsteadily as he waited for his head to clear.

'We have to kill Snape now, whilst he is removed from his body. I fear if he returns before we do kill him, then he will be too strong for either of us to overcome,' he explained to Gar, but was also explaining the situation to himself. He tried to hex a suffocating force of energy over the face of Snape, but failed miserably, he was too weak. He instructed Gar to do the same, and the golem waved a sign in the air, but nothing happened. Snape's protection was too strong. Davvid looked around for a weapon and spied a fallen branch. He staggered over to it and almost fell as he bent down to retrieve the makeshift weapon. He hefted it in both hands and nodded. Now he could deal out some retribution, he approached the supine form of Jerold Snape.

He was almost within striking distance when an invisible barrier almost caused him to crash to the ground. Snape had hexed a protective wall and Davvid had failed to see it. He beckoned to Gar and the little golem trotted to his side.

'Smash down this hex Gar. I am too weak to do so myself. Smash it down. We have precious little time!'

Davvid turned back to face Snape's still form and noticed how the stamen protruding from his mouth was pulsating. Snape had made contact with a soul; the reaping had begun!

'Quickly Gar, quickly!'

The golem hexed furiously in the air before him and

Davvid felt the resistance of the wall weaken; he pushed against it and suddenly he was through. He stepped up to Snape's head and raised the large branch up high. He was just about to bring it crashing down on the man's skull when Snape's eyes flew open and Davvid found he could no longer move a muscle.

Lucy watched Raven's chest rise and fall as he snored softly in bed bedside her. She carefully pulled the satin sheet back from her side and stepped quietly out of bed.

Their clothes laid in a trail from the living room and she padded softly over the floor and collected them. She picked up her Pyrolite suit and sighed.

Will I ever be free of you? She thought.

Lucy walked into the bathroom, threw the clothes into the wicker washing-basket, and switched on the power-shower. Within seconds, it was up to temperature and she stepped in and let the hot water wash away the stresses of the day. The hissing of the water on the tiles; the pinpricks of the deluge gradually relaxed her, and covered the incessant beeping that came from the living room. The beeping of the room's automated fire control system, which warned that a rise in the ambient temperature had been detected; a rise that was not due to the steam that crept out from beneath the bathroom door but from a shadowy cloud that was taking form in the centre of Lucy's living room.

Raven groaned and turned over to switch off his alarm clock. His eyes flicked open; I don't have an alarm clock! Then he remembered he was in Lucy's bed. She doesn't have an alarm clock; what the hell?

He sat up in bed and heard her switch off the shower; she was in the bathroom, but the beeping was coming from elsewhere. He flung back the sheet and crept over to the bedroom door. He opened it carefully and looked out into the little corridor. The light was on in the bathroom, it filtered out from beneath the door and he saw Lucy's shadow move across it as she dried herself. He cocked his head to one side and listened carefully. The sound was coming from the living room, and even though the flat's central heating meant that it was relatively warm, he shivered as he finally recognised the sound. It was the fire alarm system; something had raised the temperature in the flat. It was a stage one warning. If the rapidity of the beep increased then the sprinklers would trigger. It would mean that the flat was on fire, or... he did not want to think of the other reason. He pushed open the door to the living room with his foot and avoided framing his naked body in the doorway. Suddenly he realised that this was no film set, and he was not an all-powerful zombie hunter, but he had to crane his head around into the room to look... he just had to...

Chapter 12

Across the void

The bathroom was steam-filled and Lucy set the power-shower to cold; the shock invigorated her and dispersed the clouds of vapour, condensing it on the walls and on the mirror. She stepped out of the shower, leaving it running to cool down the room and stepped over to the towel rail. The large towel was warm and inviting and she luxuriated in its embrace as she dried her hair and body.

Lucy threw the damp towel onto the rail and slipped into her fresh underclothes. She opened the tall bathroom cupboard, took down a clean Pyrolite suit, stepped into it, and then pulled on clean fatigues. She was just about to dry her hair when the stubby remnant of her finger, which was burnt off all those years before, started tingling and she froze.

'It's time,' she whispered to herself, scooped up the contents of her previous coverall's pockets, and dropped them into the pocket of her fresh one, 'Raven!' She shouted a warning to him.

Lucy threw the door open, just as a bellowing voice reached her ears, Raven's voice. He was in the living-room and the sensor system was bleeping frantically.

How didn't I hear it sooner! She thought, *damn shower!*

She raced down the hallway and into the room. Raven was thrashing at a cloudy form that was taking shape in its centre. No matter how hard he punched or tried to grab the apparition nothing happened; his hands were going through it as if it was smoke.

'Get away from it now!' she cried and he turned, 'Before it fully materializes! Raven, get the hell away from it NOW!'

He turned to protest and the shadowy figure flickered into

a solid form. As Raven opened his mouth to speak Lucy realized it wasn't the bat shape that she had been expecting. It was a man, a man with a gross, pulsating tongue and he was now stepping forward. He stepped forward and placed the tongue on Raven's shoulder.

Raven's eyes bulged and a terrible scream tore from his throat. Lucy hurtled towards him and leapt into the air with one leg outstretched, the other tucked under her. She struck the attacker full in the chest and he crashed backwards with Raven almost falling on top of him. Suddenly the smell of burning flesh assailed her nostrils and Raven's arm burst into flames. The fire-detection system immediately cut in and the sprinkler units poured a torrent of water into the room, dousing the fire and causing a great cloud of steam to momentarily block her vision. The intruder was smaller than Raven but slightly larger than her and as he scrambled to his feet she saw he was beginning to dissipate. She sprung up from the floor like a wild cat and grabbed the man's vile tongue with her Pyrolite-gloved hand. The Pyrolite protected her and she smiled as the man's eyes goggled in fear whilst she brought her fist back and said, 'This one's for my father.'

The blow never landed, as her fist blurred towards his face, Lucy's world turned black and inside out, she felt she was falling forward. She wailed silently as a wave of nausea swept over her and she felt herself tumble through the darkness. Her grip was still on the man's tongue but only her sense of touch told her that it was so. She felt she had gone blind until she turned her head and saw a frame of light begin to dwindle into the void behind her. She cried out again as she realised she was looking into the living room of her apartment which was now accelerating away from her, and then suddenly it was gone.

Davvid knew he was too late; Snape had returned to his body and had blocked the blow. He watched in horror as the man spat out the stamen and signed frantically; Davvid's time was at an end.

'Novitiate! Strike her quickly, before she recovers! Strike her!' Snape cried, as a smoky form began to take shape on the ground next to him.

Davvid felt his arm being released and he hesitated, Novitiate? Suddenly an alarming thought flashed through his mind. He watched amazed as the figure next to Snape took on a solid form, then he realised it was a strangely garbed woman. She was holding onto the plant's stamen and screaming. Davvid made a decision; he brought the branch hurtling down and struck Lucy a cruel blow across the side of her head. She made a slight gasp and slumped into unconsciousness as the stamen, released from her immobile hand, writhed back into the flower.

'Well done my young friend, well done.' Snape took in great gulps of air and rose slowly to his feet.

Davvid held the branch before him in a defensive posture and Snape looked at him quizzically.

'Of course! You will not recognize me, my young novitiate!' Snape laughed.

Davvid lowered the branch, 'Master?'

'Yes, Davvid! It is I! Your master. Luther Krell, I have come back from the void!'

Shaking his head in disbelief Davvid dropped the branch and grabbed Luther Krell's shoulders, 'How? Master, you were trapped in the ether. How?'

'I've waited for an opportunity and it came for me today. I have seen glimmers in the void on occasion but I had never been able to get close enough to understand what they were. However, through practise and time I became adept at 'swimming' through the ether and finally I per-chanced upon a mind that was traversing the void. I overcame that mind and now I inhabit the host body. The man Snape will not need it again my young friend.'

Slowly Davvid began to understand. What is more, he began to realise that Luther Krell had no idea how he had come to be trapped in the ether in the first place.

He thought carefully and then answered, 'When you did not return, my master, I searched for you and followed your glamour trail. It was difficult to follow but you had taught me well. I arrived at the glade and found your body. An animal had destroyed the Rapture Bud. I think it was a dirge-hen, but I can't be certain. You were terribly mutilated. I thought… we all thought, you were *foreverdead*.'

'A dirge-hen,' mused Luther Krell, 'Quite possible, I destroyed a nest just before entering the ether. I once said 'Luck has nothing to do with it' my friend. It seems luck wanted to prove me wrong. How many years have I been 'away'?'

'It's been over thirty years, master.'

'Thirty years…' sighed Luther Krell, shaking his head, 'It could have been hundreds; time means nothing in the void. I didn't know how long I was in there. I can't believe I held onto my sanity. The only hope I had was that someone else would discover the secret of the plant, and use it. I knew I could finally overcome a mind travelling the void… but who would it be? I thought it would be you my boy. I'm glad that it wasn't.'

'Thank you, master. I have travelled the ether too. But I have made many enemies by doing so,' Davvid waved his hand up and down over Luther's body, 'This man for one. His name is…was Snape. He was in the pay of the Mayor of Fivewinds. Snape brutalized me until I gave up the plant's secrets.' He turned and showed the damaged wings to his master.

Luther Krell winced, 'His 'departure' rests easier with me now, Davvid. Your wings will heal. I will see to it. You inherited my estate?'

'Yes…master. I did not ever imagine tha…' Davvid tried to explain but Luther Krell held up a hand to stop him.

'It doesn't matter my friend. You have no need to explain to me. It is only fitting and lawful you should have taken over from me when I was gone. You are now a true Master Thaumaturgist and I bow to you, Davvid…Davvid?'

'Davvid Krell, sire. I hope you don't mind.'

'Mind my boy? Mind? Nay it is an honour. Now I must stop calling you novitiate, you are no longer a novice, and you must stop calling me master. My name is Luther Krell. We are equals. You must call me Luther.'

Davvid smiled, 'Luther.'

'What of our dear Minister Sarreg? Does he still terrorize Marin's Weir with his fat behind and thin brain?' asked Luther.

'Sarreg is now Procurator Sarreg and is the reason behind all of my problems, Luther. He is still as obnoxious as before, perhaps even more so now.'

'Then something will have to be done about that. Don't you agree?'

'Yes, mast… Luther. It is high time Sarreg paid for what he has done, to both of us.'

'All in good time,' nodded Luther and then he looked down at the unconscious form of Lucy, 'First we have smaller fish to fry. This creature has haunted me since a reaping a long, long time ago. She was but a child; now I see she has grown, but still her soul called to me when I captured Snape's body. Once again, I was denied it. I was unable to appear next to her, she was in a room where rain pours from the ceiling. I materialised as close to her as possible and was confronted by a giant of a man. He burns now from my touch but the reaping was interrupted once more by her!' Luther glanced down angrily at Lucy and struck her once with his boot, 'Providence shines upon her; but now it seems not only will I have her soul but also her whole body.'

'Why would her soul call to you?'

'A part of her was consumed by the bud's power; it made a conduit between her and the bud. Whenever I entered the ether again that conduit drew me to her,' explained Luther, 'But we have no time to waste, Davvid. We must get her back to my... no, your apartments. Do you have transport? I presume you didn't get here with those.' He indicated to the damaged wings on Davvid's back.

'Yes, two drayks within the cover of the trees. Luther, do you mean she is from the other world?'

'Yes, Davvid. Somehow, she was torn from her world and returned here with me. It raises interesting possibilities. For us, that is. For her though there can be only one possibility. The fourth reaping of her soul will be done at my leisure and pleasure. Come let us return to Marin's Weir, we still have much to discuss.'

Davvid nodded and called Gar to his side, Luther Krell raised an eyebrow when confronted by the little golem but Davvid decided to keep some of Gar's talents hidden for the time being. An asset like Gar could be a pivotal thing in a race for the position of the most powerful mage in history.

'Raven...Raven...' the words swam around his head as he clawed his way back to consciousness. His eyes opened slowly and he blinked to clear them. A blurry shape slowly took form and he realised it was the concerned face of Rabbet. The bland décor and antiseptic smell confirmed he was in a hospital somewhere.

'Sergeant Rabbet...Lucy, is she okay?' Raven groaned and tried to sit up. Rabbet gently put a hand on his shoulder and told him to lie still.

'Listen Raven, there's no easy way to say this so I'm just going to be straight with you. Lucy has gone. She wasn't in the apartment. There is no sign of her. But there's no burned residue either so…' Rabbet explained.

'Oh God, I remember now…' A look of horror spread across Raven's face.

'What do you remember?' Rabbet pulled a chair up to the bedside and sat down, 'Tell me as much as you can. Any little detail could help, no matter how useless it might seem. Any detail could prove helpful in finding her.'

'It's no good Rabbet. You don't understand; she *has* gone…she's gone!'

'You'd better explain, what do you mean she's gone?'

Raven struggled to sit up again and gasped as his burnt arm sent a jolt of pain through him that even the painkillers could not mask, 'Shit…the damn thing touched me. I remember now. I turned to send her away and the damn thing touched me. It felt as if acid was pouring all over my arm and then it burst into flames. The sprinklers came on and flooded the bloody place.'

Rabbet tried to stay calm but his agitation got the better of him, 'Raven what the hell do you mean she's gone!'

'Sorry Rabbet, my head's spinning. I'm just piecing it together. The sprinklers, yes they put the flames out and Lucy leapt at the guy. She knocked him down and he broke contact with me. The apartment was full of steam but I saw him get up and she grabbed hold of him and went for a killing-blow, I could see it in her face. The guy was as good as dead. Then…'

'Then what? What happened next Raven, tell me.'

'Then he started to turn to mist again. Lucy had grabbed him and…She was only inches away from me! I reached out for her ankle and my hand went right through it! Lucy went with him; before she could land the punch, they just disappeared, turned to smoke and just went. I suppose I passed out then. That is all I remember. Next thing I saw was your face.'

'If I didn't know you better Raven I'd say you were out of your mind. But this case doesn't surprise me anymore. Bats, people burning to death and nothing else touched, wait… did you say it was a guy? Not a bloody great bat, but a guy?'

'You heard right, a man. Just like you or me. Smaller than me, but slightly taller than Lucy. Rat-faced, and with one of the biggest damn tongues you will ever see. Scared the crap out of me I can tell you.'

'He went up in a cloud of smoke and Lucy disappeared with him. How the hell am I going to write a report up on this?' Rabbet groaned.

'What's happened to Lucy? Why didn't I grab the bastard? I should have snapped him in two. One minute he was a wraith, next minute he was solid. Rabbet, I've lost her.'

'I don't know what to say Raven. I just don't know what to say. I don't believe you could have done anymore than you did. I remember her saying she thought she could feel the presence of the thing and it seemed human. I think what you saw was a portal to another dimension or universe, something like that. However, I'm not going to say that to anyone but you Raven. Whatever it is Lucy can take care of herself; she has expected this for a long time. She knows what she has to do. Look, I've got to go. If I discover anything, you will be the first to know. That arm is going to take a lot of healing. You are lucky it's only third degree burns. The doctors reckon another few seconds and it would have charred you down to the bone. They think you'll be okay. Anyway, I shouldn't be telling you this. They'll explain it all in due time. Anything you need before I go?'

'Thanks, man. Yeah I almost pity the bastard when Lucy gets her hands on him. Another dimension? You had better keep that to yourself all right. You go Rabbet, I'm okay. I know you'll need a statement later, but how the hell I am going to explain what I saw….'

'Don't worry about that now, all in good time. Bye Raven, take care.'

Rabbet opened the door and started out when Raven called to him.

'One thing Rabbet…'

'Anything, what you need?' replied the sergeant.

'Bring that damn extinguisher in from the hallway and put it on the chair next to me,' replied Raven and he wasn't joking.

Lucy opened her eyes and realised she was blind. She tried to move but was bound tightly, her arms behind her back and attached to something on the wall that stuck into her. She slipped the Pyrolite mittens off her hands and felt her restraints. They were thick ropes that were tied around her wrists and through what felt like an iron hoop which projected from the damp stone wall and into her back. She was sitting and the cold of the stone floor penetrated the suit. She drew her legs beneath her and staggered to her feet, bright lights flashed across her vision and her head swam. She tottered for a moment and almost fell.

The memory of the fight in the apartment and her fall through the opening into the void came flooding back. Then she recalled waking up on grass, the smell of death in the air and suddenly a savage blow from nowhere knocking her out.

She stared into the blackness ahead of her and slowly but surely began to make out ghostly shapes. She wasn't blind! She was in an extremely dark room; a dim glow, from beneath what she imagined must be a door, gave a slight illumination. It was just enough for her to understand her predicament. It looked as if she was bound up in someone's basement. Someone who had thought nothing of hitting a defenceless woman with a club of some kind, she mused.

Lucy started to squirm and twist to get her hand into her hip pocket. She had hoped to reach her knife but her straining fingers closed around her mobile phone instead, she heard the sound of footsteps approaching and she sat back down on the ground, letting her head drop forward, resting her chin upon her chest. The mobile lay hidden within her hand and she thumbed it open, hearing it chirrup she felt for the key assigned to its video function.

Through her partially closed eyes, she saw the gleam of light beneath the door strengthen and then heard a rattle and the door swung open. What she saw caused her to give out a strangulated cry. The bat stood framed in the doorway.

'So, you are awake.'

Lucy opened her eyes and blinked, the 'bat' had spoken.

'Who are you? What is this place? Why am I tie...' she was interrupted by the man who held up his hand.

'Enough! Your questions are irrelevant. There will be questions and answers, all in good time. However, they shall be our questions, and your answers,' he said mockingly.

'Our?' asked Lucy.

Davvid Krell stepped to one side and Luther moved into the room, holding a lamp high above his head, 'Yes our questions. Then when they are adequately answered you will be reaped my young woman.'

'Reaped? You sure you don't mean raped?' She glared at them.

'Oh no, your soul will be harvested my dear. It will certainly give us a wondrous asset to put into our next creation, don't you agree Davvid?' Luther turned and asked.

'Yes, the souls from their world have proven to be incredible. Much, much better than anything we could find here,' replied Davvid.

Lucy looked at them in disbelief, 'What the hell are you two talking about?'

'From what I have seen of their world in the thirty years I was in the void; the little glimpses through gaps that opened and closed momentarily, I do not think they have evolved the art of magic, my dear boy. Oh they have many marvellous things there, but I do believe magic is not one of them,' explained Luther.

'Magic? You've got to be kidding me,' laughed Lucy, 'And what magic are you going to do with my soul?'

Davvid looked at Luther and smiled, 'Gar, come and meet our new friend.'

Lucy watched the door as she heard something come shuffling down the corridor; the shadows on the passage wall looked to be that of a young child until the thing entered the room. Then Lucy gasped as she saw the animated figure of clay stride towards her.

Barely taller than a child, featureless, yet human-shaped, the figure drew closer and Lucy realised that she was looking at something that was impossible to believe could exist. It was a golem.

Sarreg's mansion house had proved to be a much safer place for Davvid and Luther to return to, and much more comfortable. They had dragged Lucy up into the main room, which had now become their laboratory and sat her in a stout chair. She watched as they started working upon objects that lay upon the table. Her jaw dropped when Luther waved a hand in the air and a bowl rose from a nearby shelf and landed in his outstretched palm. He turned and scrutinized her face.

'You have no idea what power we can wield here, girl. Soon we shall be invincible. I even begin to wonder if we can travel to your world and use our powers there. Are you now beginning to believe in magic?' He asked.

Lucy, stunned by what she had seen, slowly replied, 'I've seen it but I still find it hard to believe. How...where?'

'Our world has a vigour which we tap into. Not everyone is attuned to it but those that are can manipulate that puissance. Some, like Davvid and I are masters of that energy, even fewer are capable of manipulating it on a vast scale by the use of a certain plant. You saw it in the glade. It was that which augmented our powers enough to tear through the fabric of space and time and allowed us into your world. I first used the plant over thirty years ago. But you remember that don't you?' Luther asked with his eyebrow raised mockingly.

'Thirty years ago,' she rasped the words out and twisted her arms that were bound to the chair, 'I saw a bat thirty years ago. It killed my father and then came for me. The feeling I had before you appeared was the same. Are you the bat?'

Luther Krell put his head back and roared with laughter, 'A bat Davvid, she thought me a bat!'

'The wings probably would appear bat-like to an uneducated person, Luther. I can quite imagine this one mistaking you for such a creature.' Davvid replied.

'Quite so,' he nodded to Davvid then turned back to Lucy, 'Yes, your father's soul proved to be one of my better reapings. His golem is surely the best I have ever made.'

'My father's soul?'

'Must I explain?' Luther sighed, 'So be it. The Rapture Bud not only allows me to travel to your world, it also acts as a siphon. When I place the stamen upon the prey, it reaps the soul from the body. It is transported back across the void and imprisoned in a magical tile that I have constructed to hold it. That tile's life force is what animates our golems. Oh, we do use souls from here as well, but they are vastly inferior. Add to that the inconvenience of the senate only allowing us to reap the dying or criminals for our work and you will understand our predicament,' he looked at Davvid and smiled. 'However, the senate does not know everything, eh, Davvid?'

His apprentice gave a chilling grin in return.

Luther continued, revelling in an opportunity to boast, 'The souls we steal from beneath their noses will not trouble them if they do not know. However, your world has a much higher quality and your father's was the best so far. I have high expectations of *you* though. I'm sure yours will excel.'

Lucy twisted and pulled at the ropes, they dug deep into her wrists and before too long the skin broke. Once again, her blood flowed from self-inflicted wounds; this time the reasoning behind the self-harm was different. This time it was not to satisfy a dark urge to bring pain upon herself, this time is was a means to an end. She wanted to break from her bonds and annihilate the two grinning figures before her. She screamed in rage as she struggled to free herself, knowing ultimately that her struggling was in vain.

Chapter 13

A time to vote

Pandemonium ruled the Senate until Sarreg entered with Wide, who was now restored to his original, towering shell. The shouting subsided immediately and the vast hall echoed to the sound of the Procurator's boots and the golem's heavy, hard clay feet.

Gasps broke from a number of the senators' lips as Sarreg reached the mayor's dais, stepped up to the ornate chair that stood upon it and sat down.

'Senators, senators, please be seated,' he shouted and magnanimously waved a laconic hand at the crowd. A murmur ran through them but one by one, people began to take their seats as Wide position itself behind the mayor's chair and folded his vast arms across his chest. 'My fellow members, it has been but a week since my dear friend Mayor Gorman took the life of his beloved wife and then his own. It pains me to be forced into the position that I now find myself due to the demise of a loyal and trustworthy friend. Oh, I know, I know, many of you here must have thought that the mayor and I were mortal enemies, far from it. We were lifelong brothers-in-arms; it served us to have people think we were anything but friends. Many secrets were divulged both to Mayor Gorman and me due to the fact that we appeared to be in opposition to each other, many secrets… by many people.' Sarreg looked around the room slowly and let his words sink in, he was pleased to note that quite a number of the senate could not meet his eye and he made a mental note of their faces.

'You may think it an insult that I now sit in the mayoral chair, but, fellow members, a document was given to me on the night of our beloved Mayor Gorman's death, a document which empowers me to act as substitute mayor until the senate can sit in its entirety. I now ask you if the senate has convened all its members here today so that a date may be set for an election. Although I am happy to carry on with the mayoral duties until such election takes place. Is the senate here in its entirety?' He asked, knowing full well that at least two members were missing, and they were safely ensconced in dungeons deep beneath Mayor Gorman's house, the house that Sarreg had decided he would procure as Gorman had no heirs.

A murmur rippled through the senate again and Sarreg looked on, amused, whilst deliberations took place amongst the members. Finally, one unfortunate soul was almost pushed off his seat and Sarreg realised that they had picked a member to act as speaker, probably one of the weaker members who had not been able to withstand the cajoling of the pack.

The old, tall and sallow-skinned senator wrung his hands and looked back at the seated members once before coughing and then approaching the dais. He opened his mouth to speak but left his jaw hanging open as Wide took a threatening step towards him.

'Do not be worried, Senator, Senator?' Sarreg asked and motioned to Wide to stop.

'Senator Casco, your worship,' replied the man, who was literally shaking in his boots.

Sarreg almost felt sorry for the poor old fool, 'Senator Casco. Ahh yes, a name I remember.' He peered at the man intently, though he had never heard the name before the effect was pleasing, the man almost collapsed beneath Sarreg's gaze.

'Procurator Sarreg, I have to tell…' Casco started to say but Sarreg stopped him by raising a hand.

'Senator, if you would be so kind as to use my proper title. Must I remind you? I am Mayor Sarreg until the senate's vote states that I am no longer required and a mayor is voted in.

Now are we a full senate? Can we decide on a date for the election?'

Casco coloured and coughed nervously; he turned to look at the rest of the senate but received no help from them. He sighed and continued, 'Mayor Sarreg, I apologize. Unfortunately, we do not have a full senate today. We are missing three senators. One is on a visit to the city of Delmare and will not return for a week, and of the other two, there is no sign. A date will not be able to be set today I am afraid to say.'

'Apology accepted. Hmm... that is a nuisance, Senator Casco. I had hoped to resolve this matter as soon as possible. Should you wish me to take the post of mayor for a full term it would be preferable to know as soon as possible. I do have other matters to attend to.'

'Understandable Mayor Sarreg, however, I believe we should know within the week who will be our new mayor. Once Senator Desit returns from Delmare I imagine the election can start.' Casco replied and moved back slightly.

'I thought you said three were missing? How can the election start if three are missing and only one is found?' asked Sarreg, tightly gripping the arms of the chair.

'Oh, perhaps you did not know. Senator Desit will be a candidate for the mayorship too. Moreover, as for the two other missing senators, well in extraordinary circumstances a senate comprised of the majority of members can act as a full senate. I think you will agree that we are indeed experiencing extraordinary circumstances?' answered Casco and wrung his hands even more as Sarreg's face darkened.

'I see. No, I did not know. Thank you for enlightening me. We shall have to wait for Desit then. Let us all hope he comes back to Fivewinds quickly and safely,' Sarreg replied and muttered quietly, 'But somehow I imagine that will not happen.'

'Seven golems in seven days. Luther we have excelled ourselves!' exclaimed Davvid as he patted Luther Krell on the shoulder.

'Yes, but seven souls reaped from our world are not worth two from the other world my friend. Oh they will suffice for now, but before we seek our revenge on Sarreg I would prefer to have a few 'special' golems too,' answered Luther, and for a moment Davvid felt sure his face had coloured as he thought of his own 'special' golem, Gar.

Then, as if Krell had read his mind, 'Yes, I know we also have Gar, a very, very special golem is he not, my young friend?'

Davvid chastised himself quietly, for imagining that he could hide things from his old master.

'Where is that boy with the clay? We still have a tile that can be installed into a golem. Where is the damn fool?'

'Vela is not known for his punctuality, but he is a fool as you say, Luther, and will not ask too many questions.' Davvid replied.

'If he asks even one question my dear boy then we will have need of yet more clay, for his soul will add to our compliment,' Luther responded with a snarl.

Davvid still found it strange on times to be addressing his old master who now wore the body of his torturer, Snape.

A soft tapping at the door to the laboratory announced Vela's arrival and Davvid strode over to open it, 'About time you young fool,' he said as the boy took off his cap and lowered his head.

'Forgive me Thaumaturgist Krell; I am late because I have been unable to locate enough clay. Thaumaturgist Descar has purchased the majority of my guardian's warehouse that is Master Jakob. Nearly all of the clay belongs to him now. What I could bring for you is below in the yard,' the boy explained as he gawked at the paraphernalia in the workshop.

Davvid hauled Vela into the room by his hair and dragged him to the window. He looked down into the yard and turned angrily to the boy, 'You bring me one barrow-load and expect to leave here with your life?' he asked and punched the boy in the face. He stumbled backwards and fell onto his rump, blood streaming from his nose.

Davvid began a hex but Luther put a hand on his arm.

'It will gain us nothing to kill the fool now; put him in the crypt with the girl. He may be of some use to us later.' Luther smiled and Davvid nodded in complete understanding, at least they had found another soul, if nothing else.

'We must speak with Descar. Find out his need for such a quantity of clay.' Luther said.

'I fear I already know the answer. It is his way of exacting revenge for his humiliation that he received on Lustre's Eve. Humiliation dished out by my hands,' explained Davvid.

'I see. Then Descar must be 'encouraged' to part with his clay. Perhaps we should invite him into our confidence? I wonder if he would like to further his position in society; let us go and ask.'

'Luther, the more people see you as Snape and wonder why I should count a Militiaman as a friend the more the risk that your identity will be discovered. Are you sure this is a wise thing to do?'

'My friend, whether they discover I am Luther Krell concerns me not. Snape lost himself in the ether. His body was an empty vessel that would have decayed and died. I merely used the opportunity to salvage some good from the man's stupidity in trying to do something, which only experienced mages like you, or I have the capability to control. There is nothing to fear; actually it should prove interesting to announce my return,' laughed Luther. 'Now let us take our little friend below and introduce him to our other 'guest'.'

Vela jumped to his feet, crashed into the desk, spinning

items everywhere and ran for the door but Davvid's hex was too quick, an iron-like grip pinned his arms to his sides and his feet felt as if the were glued to the floor.

Luther waved to one of the seven golems regimented against the far wall and it marched forward menacingly to stop in front of the petrified Vela.

'Take him to the dungeon,' he said and the golem picked the boy up as if he was a sack of feathers.

'Now my friend we shall see what Descar can offer us,' Luther smiled at Davvid and followed the golem out of the room, the howls of the terrified boy as he was carried into the bowels of the vast building echoed off the walls as the two mages made their way to the front door.

Business was brisk at The Uma Inn in Marin's Weir. It was the oldest establishment of its kind and attracted a clientele from near and far. Apart from being a well-known watering hole, it was also highly respected for its discretion and privacy. To some it was not just an inn, it was their place of business, whatever business that happened to be, even those that were not considered lawful, perhaps even more so for that fact alone. Situated in a private booth, head bowed close to his prospective client, Thaumaturgist Descar was deep in conversation when something made him halt in mid sentence. The room's hubbub had suddenly stopped; he looked up and almost fouled his leather pants.

'Hello Descar, not too busy to see an old friend, are you?' asked Davvid quietly but the room seemed filled with his voice.

Descar stood quickly and raised a hand to sign for his golem to protect him but realised it would be a futile gesture for it was suspended immobile a foot or two off the ground, held there by the hex of the smallest golem he had ever seen, Gar.

Memories of Lustre's Eve rose up in his mind as the sour

taste of bile rose up into his throat; the hand he was going to cast a hex with flew to it protectively.

'Oh, I trust your throat has completely recovered?' Davvid enquired and then looked at the booth's other occupant, a small pimple of a man who sat quivering silently, 'You can go.'

The man needed no further encouragement, he scrambled past Davvid and flew out of the inn's door; it was then that Descar spotted Davvid's other companion.

'Militiaman Snape?' Descar croaked and pointed at Davvid, 'This man, this man…'

'Descar, this man is my friend, and I am not Militiaman Snape; I unfortunately have to inhabit his body, for now. Allow me to re-introduce myself to you and everyone else,' said Luther and bowed slightly, 'I am Luther Krell.'

The room filled with gasps and murmurs, Descar collapsed back into his seat, 'But that's impossible. Luther Krell is *foreverdead*, we saw his corpse.'

'I assure you I am not *foreverdead*. Yes, you did see my corpse, but to repeat myself, I inhabit this body, for now,' Luther turned to Davvid then, 'We really must do something about that actually, it is not a body I consider worthy of my presence.'

Davvid nodded then turned to face the room, 'Be about your business, as Luther and I shall be about ours.'

The room gradually went back to its normal state of being, drinks were handed out, conversations continued once again, arguments and bartering resumed.

'What do you want with me?' whispered Descar, 'Haven't you humiliated me enough? Have you come to kill me?'

Davvid and Luther took the seats opposite Descar, 'Why should you imagine we should want to kill you?' asked Davvid, 'Oh, unless you believe that by purchasing most of the clay in Marin's Weir should merit your death. Somehow I don't think you did that for any other reason than to deprive me of it, am I correct?'

'Now, now Davvid, we must not pre-judge, perhaps Thaumaturgist Descar has an important project. He must have need of the clay. Surely, he would not want to incur your wrath again.' Luther's fingers formed a steeple and he peered over them across the table at the cowering figure before him, 'Would you?'

Descar put his hand to his mouth unwittingly then broke down, 'Thaumaturgist Krell,' he said and then looked at Davvid then at Luther, clearly confused.

'Carry on, my friend, you are correct. We are both magi, and both Krells,' smiled Luther.

Descar swallowed noisily, 'It's true. I heard that you had need of clay, a large amount of clay. I wanted… '

'Yes? You wanted?' asked Davvid patiently.

'I wanted retribution for Lustre's Eve. I thought by depriving you of the clay at least I would get some measure of satisfaction.'

'Ah, so you still wish to test my strength and patience…' sighed Davvid.

Descar held up his hands as if in supplication, 'No! I was a fool, I know. The clay is yours, please accept it as a gift from me, I beg you please take it, take it all.'

Luther put a calming hand on Davvid's arm; Davvid nodded, 'That is most generous of you Descar… Thaumaturgist Descar,' Davvid said.

'My friend, you will realise by now that, shall we say umm..'politics' in this region are in a state of flux. Davvid and Sarreg have become two opposite forces vying for a position of power that only one can command. I have no wish to seek this position myself, I am happy enough to carry on with my scientific studies and experiments. But you will appreciate that I do wish to see Davvid victorious and not that fat fool Sarreg.' Luther explained to Descar.

'I see; that is why you need the clay. It is for an army!' gasped Descar.

Luther smiled, 'Hardly an army, my friend. But enough golems of, shall we say, a certain standard, will suffice.'

Descar nodded, 'Yes, Thaumaturgist Luther Krell, your golems are indeed the most powerful that I have ever seen,' then he glanced at Gar, who still bore the scars of his fight with the militia. 'Of course yours too are truly incredible,' he blurted out quickly to Davvid in case he should offend him once more.

'Thank you; you are too kind,' Luther replied, 'but I should continue; Sarreg is even now in Fivewinds attempting to solicit support. If rumours I have heard are true he could even be attempting at wresting the mayorship away from Mayor Gorman. Therefore, as you can see we are now recruiting followers ourselves. When we prevail, anyone who has stood with us will be extremely well rewarded, extremely well. Anyone who stands against us will be…umm… very, very, sorry. Now think carefully my friend; where do you stand?'

Lucy heard the screaming and fought the urge to join in. The sound echoed down the passageway to her and slipped under the closed door like a wraith, she was sure it was a man's voice, a young man.

The door was kicked open and light filled the basement, she blinked and tried to focus on the two figures that entered. One was large, larger than a man and the outline in the doorway looked wrong somehow, crude, a facsimile of a human being, but not quite right. The other was a young boy and the wailing came from him. The large figure threw the boy into the room and he slid across the floor, almost crashing into her. She tried to fend him off but the ropes binding her to the iron hoop in the wall stopped any movement. She watched as he curled himself into a ball, almost into a foetal position and once again, she felt an urge to emulate him. A shuffling noise drew her attention back to the doorway as the golem turned to leave.

'Wait, I need water...' but the golem ignored her and left, closing the door behind itself. The room darkened once more.

'You ok, kid?' she asked.

Silence was her only answer, she asked again...

'Yes, I am now.' Replied the boy quietly.

'What's your name?'

'Vela, my name is Vela.'

'Hi, Vela, my name's Lucy.'

The boy started to move and she realised he was crawling to the door, 'You're not tied up!' she exclaimed.

'No, but we are locked in.' he answered as she heard him try the door.

'That doesn't matter, just come back here and help me free my hands,' she said. 'We'll worry about the door later.'

Vela bumped into her, 'Sorry.'

'No problem, kid. You're going to have to get closer to me than that.' She chortled, 'Now reach out and feel for my right hand pocket; there's something in it. Take it out.' She felt the boy rummage in her coverall suit, 'Um...no, Vela, that's my breast, nice try kid. Now put your hand in the damn pocket.'

'Sorry.' He said again.

'That's ok; I'll forgive you this time, next time I'll break your wrist. And stop saying sorry all the bloody time!'

'Sor...oh... I think I've found something!' Vela shouted.

'Shh... keep it down. Ok, is it like a flat tube?' Lucy asked.

'Yes, it is, feels like a knife. Shall I open it?'

'Sure but make sure you hold it carefully,' she instructed, 'and don't touch the blade!'

'Is it sharp?' There was a soft click, 'Oh... it's open' Vela said.

'Yes, it's ceramic; it'll cut you down to the bone as soon as look at you. So be damn careful when you slice through the ropes behind my back. I don't want anymore scars at this moment in time.' She told him and wondered at what she had just said.

When have I ever worried about cutting myself?

The blade barely touched the ropes and they fell away; Vela gasped in awe, 'It is a magic blade!'

'No Vela, just technology; an extremely sharp blade made from an almost unbreakable ceramic.' Lucy replied, massaging her wrists and then taking the lethal little knife from the boy. 'Right let's see about getting out of here. I have places to go, people to see and bastards to kill.'

A heavily laden wagon rumbled ponderously towards Luther and Davvid's new home, the home generously 'donated' by Sarreg. It was filled to bursting with Descar's clay. Descar himself sat alongside the grizzled old muleskinner who was prodding his unfortunate mule along with a stick. Flies buzzed hungrily around the raw and bleeding wounds that peppered the animal's rump then swarmed up towards the two men when the mule wearily brushed them away with its threadbare tail.

'God's curse on this,' swore Descar as he half swatted, half signed in the air in front of his face. The majority of the flies swirled away as if hit by a great hand and fell to the floor. The ones that survived Descar's hex returned to the relative safety of the mule's backside and its promise of food.

'Yarr, master. A pox on them damn flies. They do be a pain in the arse, especially for poor old Molly,' answered Jakob the muleskinner spitting a mouthful of brown liquid over the luckless animal's behind.

'Fool, if it was just the flies...'

Jakob looked quizzically at Descar and then shrugged, who knew what went through a Thaumaturgist's mind? They were a breed unto themselves.

At that particular moment, Descar's mind was seething with resentment. He was in no mood to be plagued by flies and despised the fact that not only had he been forced to give up his full supply of prime clay but had also been obliged to deliver it himself. The insult was almost unbearable, almost, but not quite, as he imagined what the consequences would be if he were foolish enough to go against his newfound 'friends'.

On nearing the grand house, Descar made an effort to calm his anger and even managed to smile and throw a cheery wave as Luther and Davvid exited the main door.

'Around the back, man; take it around the back. You will see where it needs to be unloaded.' Instructed Davvid, and Decsar's grin almost turned into a grimace as he swallowed his pride and nodded.

'When you have finished send your man back and come join us Descar.' Commanded Luther and for a moment a cold sweat broke out on Descar's face as he wondered what they wanted further from him. He watched as his two new friends turned their backs on him and re-entered the house.

'I do believe Descar would like to see both of us in wooden caskets.' Remarked Davvid as he closed the door behind him and followed Luther back into the house.

'More than probably so, however, the man is no fool. He knows that to betray us now would prove, ah…unfortunate?'

Davvid laughed quietly at the understatement.

'I think I shall have him work here for us now. Although he is not of our standard, his golems will suffice. I imagine Sarreg will have commandeered as many as possible and if we are to meet his challenge when it comes then numbers will most certainly count in the beginning. Our superior workmanship will show when the dross has been dealt with, and to combat dross why not use dross of our own?' Luther said.

'A valid point,' conceded Davvid and nodded, 'Numbers will help in the initial stages but our golems are vastly superior to anything that Sarreg may call up against us.'

The two men entered the laboratory and Davvid approached the window and gazed down at Descar and his driver as they manoeuvred the wagon beneath the apparatus for lifting the clay to their workplace. A smile flickered across Davvid's lips as Descar slipped and slid in the muddy grass below, oh how sweet it was to watch your enemies brought so low.

Lucy rummaged in her fatigue's zipped thigh pocket and pulled out her mobile, she flipped it open and the screen illuminated with a soft chirrup.

'Don't even ask...,' she said to Vela without looking up, 'Let's just say...it's magic.' She selected torch on the menu and then cast the small beam over the door. 'This should be easy enough, they're just common hinges. All we have to do is tap up the pins and we're outta here.'

She shone the torch around the bare room, then directed it at her trainers and sighed, 'Ok looks like we have to go with your footwear Vela,' she said as the beam fell across the sturdy leather boots the boy was wearing.

He looked down at his feet cocking his head to the side like a little dog, 'Go where with my boots?'

'We're going to escape my young friend; now take off one of your boots and give it to me.'

Vela mimicked a salute and tugged of his right boot then handed it to Lucy.

'Holy shit, don't you shower, kid?' she grimaced giving her mobile to the boy and then pinching her nose with her left hand whilst holding the boot away from her with her right.

Vela looked at her quizzically and opened his mouth.

'Doesn't matter, just hold that light up by here whilst I get these hinges off.' she interrupted him before he could ask the obvious question.

Lucy inserted the tip of her blade into the large pin holding the top hinge in place and started tapping the handle with Vela's boot; the solid leather heel made an excellent hammer and presently the pin began to move.

'It's working!' proclaimed Vela as he bounced up and down with excitement.

'Of course, now keep that damn light still, the pin is almost out.'

Another tap with the boot was enough and the pin shot out and dropped to the floor with a tinkle, both Lucy and Vela held their breath and listened at the door.

'One down, one more to go,' she whispered and began to assail the second pin with glee.

Before long the second pin succumbed too and flew out from the top of the lower hinge, this time Vela's hand snatched out and caught it.

'Nice catch, now give me a hand to get the door out of its frame.'

Both Lucy and Vela began wrestling the heavy door from the surrounding architecture; it groaned in protestation and then finally tilted in towards them.

The room filled with light as the corridor's illumination flooded in and both of them blinked until their eyes grew accustomed to the light. Carefully they shuffled the door to the side and leaned it against the wall; Lucy started to move to the open doorway but Vela grabbed her hand and pulled her back.

'Wait, it could be warded!' he said as he fumbled to put his boot back on. 'Here take this whilst I check.' He handed her back the mobile which she closed and dropped back into her pocket.

She watched the boy approach the open doorway with trepidation, 'What do you mean warded?'

Vela ran his hands around the framework of the doorway mumbling quietly to himself. If he heard Lucy then he did not acknowledge her, but she sensed that the boy's focus was entirely taken up with his task and other than dragging him away forcefully, she would not receive a reply from him.

Time protracted and she grew impatient but felt uneasy about disturbing Vela in his task. There was so much she didn't know about her situation and for the moment impelled herself to be insouciant and trust in her new found friend's ability.

'Friend Lucy, it is safe. They have left no glamours or wards against us. They bathe in their smugness and did not even consider we were capable of escaping!'

'Good, time to go and pee in their bath, friend Vela!' responded Lucy and stepped cautiously through the door.

The corridor was well lit, lamps guttered along its length and Lucy could smell the acrid fumes that permeated the air, 'Smells like kerosene,' she said. 'Well at least that's something I recognise. For a moment I expected then to be powered by little pixies with wands.'

In one direction the corridor sloped steadily downwards, doors similar to the one they had dismantled disappeared down into the gloom. The other direction seemed more hopeful, it led upwards. She motioned for Vela to follow and set off watchfully up the sloping corridor. Some doors they passed looked as if they hadn't been opened in eons, their hinges rusted solid. However, others showed signs of recent usage whilst from behind one or two they discerned the sound of movement and even sobbing. Although she wanted to open the cells and free whoever was imprisoned within Lucy restrained herself. For the moment, it was more important to gain freedom for Vela and her.

There must be some sort of authority in this kingdom I can appeal to. What those two men, if that is what they are, are doing cannot be lawful, she thought.

Minutes passed as they silently made their way upwards. Vela grabbed her arm once more and put a grubby finger to his lips, 'Shh… I hear something ahead.'

She froze and listened carefully. At first, she couldn't perceive any sound from before her, then, a muffled mumbling reached her ears. Someone or something was ahead of them. The corridor had a right-angled turn facing them, whatever was approaching was coming from around the corner, a wavering shadow played across the floor and Lucy crouched into a fighting stance. Vela seemed to slip into a trance-like state and a low mantra hissed from his lips.

Immediately the mumbling shadow stopped and Lucy witnessed a rapid fluttering in the penumbra upon the floor. Had Vela been heard? She worried.

The answer was mercurial as Vela was thrown back against the wall. He hung there, pinned like a butterfly as if in some mad entomologist's display.

Lucy stared incredulously at the boy for a second then turned to see a man step around the corner. He was covered in the residue of brown clay that flaked and dropped as he strode forward, a sneer spread across his face.

'So, I have delivered the clay and now the Krells send their apprentices to kill me. Am I so beneath their contempt they send amateurs to despatch me?

Then let it be so; *they* may have the better of me but you two will not.' Cried Descar and he gesticulated in the air in front of him then threw his open palm towards Lucy's face.

Without second thought Lucy stepped forward inside the man's hand, she was on automatic now and the heel of her right hand flew up crunching into Descar's nose, cracking the bone and cartilage and sending the splinters up into his brain. Blood fountained over her as he flew back to crash against the wall behind him. Lucy stood quivering, ready to throw another blow but it was unnecessary as Descar's lifeless body slid down the wall leaving a snail's trail of blood in its wake. Vela dropped too and sat bewildered on his haunches whilst Lucy breathed out and relaxed her combat stance, She sat down beside the boy, 'You ok?' she asked and handed the boy a green leather-bound book that had fallen from his clothing.

'Sorry Lucy, he sensed my incantation, I'm not very adept I'm afraid,' he stammered and took the book from her then inserted it into the waistband of his trousers.

'What is it with everyone here?' she groaned, 'Are you all Harry Potters?'

Vela looked at her questioningly and she shook her head, 'Doesn't matter now anyway,' and she nodded towards Descar's corpse.

'Is he dead?'

'If he isn't then he's going to have a bloody hell of a headache, but yeah. He's dead.' She replied and tried to wipe the blood from her face. 'Tell me Vela, what is this magic that everyone is using?'

'Not everyone, Lucy. Only a select few can wield thaumaturgy. I hoped I might be one, but now I'm not so sure.'

'But I don't understand, where I come from magic is smoke and mirrors. It is a parlour trick, a slight of hand. Here I've seen people manipulate inanimate objects, you have clay golems for the love of God! Krell told me he has my father's soul imprisoned in an earthenware tile. What is going on?'

'I don't really know Lucy. This started many, many years ago. There was no magic in our land and from what I have learned the people were happier without it. Then came the magi; no one knows where they came from but they were all powerful, much more adroit in the arts than they are now. The Krells are perhaps the strongest mages of our time but they are ants compared to the old ones.'

Lucy nodded, willing the boy to continue but he stood and

held his hand out to her, 'Lucy we must leave. Perhaps they will come looking for him.' He glanced at Descar's body.

'Ok, but when we are clear of this place I want to know all there is to know about Krell and his kind. Isn't there some authority here we can go to? Surely you must have a police force that can be informed about their atrocities?'

'No one in Marin's Weir, Lucy. The council here are as corrupt as those two upstairs.'

Vela stepped carefully over the rivulet of blood that ran from Descar's ruined face which was pooling and darkening on the cold stone floor. Fat flies had already begun gathering around the feast and the boy shivered involuntarily as he looked away. Large double doors stood ajar before the two escapees and a horse and cart stood outside to tempt them into the open. A large wicker basket filled with the last of the clay rose from the back of the cart to reveal a dishevelled individual enthusiastically picking his nose; he examined his grubby finger and then wiped it on his clay-covered trousers.

'Jakob!' hissed Vela hopping from one foot to the other, 'Jakob!'

The old man looked up at the Krells who were levitating the ultimate basket up to their laboratory and frowned. Vela sighed, reached down for a fragment of clay that lay nearby and threw it at the man. It hit him on the chest and he looked into the corridor. Vela put a finger to his lips and beckoned at Jakob to enter. The old man squinted at them and then realization dawned on his face like the first blush of sunrise and his mouth opened but by now Vela was bouncing up and down like a lunatic; he signalled the old fool to be quiet and pointed upwards towards the two magi. Jakob looked up and finally in a flash of comprehension gave a thumbs-up and climbed arthritically down from the cart.

'Vela,' he wheezed when he entered the corridor, 'whatever is the matter my boy?' then he hawked up a mouthful of phlegm, looked apologetically at Lucy and spat the green bolus of catarrh onto the floor, it landed close to Descar's body. 'Descar!'

'Keep your voice down Jakob, my friend. Descar tried to kill us. This is Lucy, she is not from these parts but she helped me,' Vela hesitated, looked at Lucy and she nodded to him, 'and she killed Descar. Lucy, this is Jakob, my friend and guardian. He and his wife have looked after me since my parents died.'

Jakob looked at the body, the pool of blood, then at Vela and finally turned his rheumy eyes onto Lucy, 'I never liked the man anyway,' he said, 'and I wondered where all the flies had gone, at least he's useful for something. Molly's arse will be grateful.'

Lucy looked at Vela and this time it was the boy's turn to say, 'Don't ask.'

Jakob scratched his stubbly chin, 'Bloody fortunate I got 'im to pay before coming in 'ere, innit?'

Vela nodded sagely, 'Always the best Jakob, you never know with these bastards if you'll ever get your cash if you don't get the money up front.'

'Nice to meet you Jakob, now talking about bastards,' butted in Lucy, 'where are those other two. You know, Jakob?'

'They be upstairs busying themselves with Descar's clay; fair angry he was too about it,' replied Jakob gawking at the corpse again. 'Reckon he don't care no-more now though, being *foreverdead* and all.'

'*Foreverdead*?'

'Yes friend Lucy, doubt he was prepared for his death, too late for him to do anything about it now,' explained Vela.

'I still don't understand what you mean by *foreverdead*.'

Vela rolled his eyes, 'He didn't have a vessel prepared for his soul, not even a tile. But he would have had to been desperate to use a tile. Who knows where he might have ended up being decanted.' Vela poked Descar's fly-encrusted body with his foot, 'Still, even a tile is better than this I merit.'

'So dead, doesn't have to be dead?'

'Yarr little lady, some people die but live on. Not for the likes of me though. Once this wretched body stops breathing I'll be worm-fodder,' moaned Jakob.

'Worm-fodder indeed, even the worms would flinch at the sight of your scabrous flesh. Best we just drop you into Dismal Swamp, you smell like it already,' bantered Vela.

Jakob squinted at Vela and spat on the ground, 'See you in the bloody swamp first you little shit.'

'Hey don't evil-eye me, dog's prick!'

'When you two have finished complimenting each other can we get out of here?' asked Lucy, 'Jakob, can you sneak us away in your cart?'

'Yarr, friend Lucy. Let me go first. If them magi aren't nearby I'll signal the two of yers. Run out and get under them blankets on the cart,' Jakob pointed to a bundle of rags piled into the cart's rear and then he shuffled out, glancing up towards the Krells' balcony. With obvious discomfort, he hauled himself up onto the cart's seat, looked at the balcony once more and then beckoned Lucy and Vela towards the rickety old vehicle. With trepidation, they left the cover of the passageway, leapt into the cart and covered themselves with the rank-smelling and clay-impregnated rags that Jakob proudly called blankets.

As Molly slowly pulled them away from Sarreg's mansion and the two men who had sequestrated it, Vela lifted up a corner of his covering and looked towards the window behind which they were constructing further abominations. He wondered if by continuing to dabble in thaumaturgy he too would become as corrupt and as heartless as all who seemed to practice the art. He let the blanket fall once more; it brought a dank darkness that matched his melancholy filled mood.

The coachman's eyelids carried the weight of two days worth of travel and they were drooping; tiredness and gravity overcame the man's resilience and as they finally closed, his stubbled chin wearily rested on his chest and he slept.

Desit's plush carriage continued on its way to Fivewinds, the two ebony stallions knowing the route well enough to have no need of guiding hands on the reins.

The coach made its sedately and opulent way along the river bank approaching the last bridge before the city with not a stride broken. Sun glinted off the burnished brass and the deep glow of the mahogany as it drew closer and closer to the darkened entrance of the covered wooden bridge, a bridge large enough to allow two such vehicles to pass side by side without hindrance. Even as the horses' hooves rapped out a staccato tattoo, like a demented drummer upon the creaking planks, neither the driver nor the passenger stirred. One of Desit's prerequisites to purchase of the carriage was that it be furnished with the finest springs available to carry his portly weight, and as such the transition from the baked ground to the wooden planks was indiscernible.

Another indiscernible item was nestling in the dark rafters of the bridge's roof. Inconspicuous and unmoving, the golem waited silently until the top of Desit's coach was beneath it, then with an agility that belied its great bulk, the creature lowered itself onto the vehicle as it passed below. Nevertheless, even the most careful of embarkation could not stop one of the best-sprung carriages in the land from settling lower and creaking slightly. Creaking enough to awaken Desit from his slumber and glance with a frown towards the curtained window at his side. He moved the silk drape slightly and perceived that they were within the framework of the ultimate bridge before Fivewinds. As the curtain dropped back into its previous position an arm the size of a tree branch, crudely formed from an ochre coloured clay or terracotta thrust in and grabbed Desit by his fleshy throat. He gripped the rough wrist with both hands but his attempts to remove the iron grip from his neck were fruitless and, if he could have gasped he would have as, he tried to pull air into his burning lungs. Desit, turning a deeper red than his usual wine induced floridity felt vertebrae crack in his neck, felt the impossible sinews within the clay wrist tighten and finally felt the pain reach an unbearable crescendo before darkness, more profound than the shadows within the bridge, claimed him.

Wide rifled through Senator Desit's clothes, removing the dead man's well-fed purse, his gold rings and an ornate dagger with a handle inlaid with green jade. Sarreg had taken pains to imprint upon the golem that Desit's death was to appear the result of a brigand attack, all too common an occurrence on the highways and byways nowadays. Next the golem eased around and approached the head of the sleeping coachman and as the vehicle approached the exit of the bridge Wide brought his fist down once upon the man's unprotected skull; one blow was enough. As the coach exited the wooden structure and the timpani of hoof-beats turned to dusty plodding the golem slipped off the rear of the vehicle and slid down the embankment and into the deep, swirling waters of the river. Wide would walk along the bottom of the river until reaching the city centre; only then and within cover of one of the many large stone-buttressed bridges within the city would he leave the water. He had entered the water the same way before Desit's murder, un-witnessed, silent and keeping his master Sarreg safe from any disparagement by his peers over the death of one of the senators who would have sought the position of mayor in direct competition to him.

'Please come to order, gentlemen, gentlemen, I beseech you. Sit and come to order,' the words of Senator Casco seemed to fall on deaf ears, so Sarreg nodded to Wide who strode from behind the mayoral dais, across the senate floor and slammed the bronze double doors to the hall shut, almost crashing them off their hinges. The double report of the sound echoed around the hall and subdued the bedlam that had ensued once the news of Senator Desit's demise had been announced to the senate. Immediately there had been shouts of 'assassin' but only from those who were hidden well enough from Sarreg. Although no assassin had been named everyone within the room seemed to have glanced his way after the outburst. Sarreg merely smiled patiently whilst the uproar continued, now he was becoming inflamed with a simmering anger. He raised his hands, 'Thank you gentlemen, may I have your attention?'

Silence reigned as no-one felt like incurring Sarreg's wrath, it seemed anyone who caused Sarreg discord tended to suffer from accidents or end up in extremely embarrassing positions, such as the two missing senators who had been found inflagrante delicto with a pair of pigs.

'I am a patient man,' he paused for effect and stared around, 'but as you know I am also a busy man, and therefore my patience is waning.'

A silence was his only response. Sarreg was pleased. He had them now.

'Therefore I wish to put it to the esteemed senate that due to the terrible murder and robbery of our beloved Senator Desit by vagabonds unknown. In addition, the unfortunate sexual preferences of Senator Crof and Halla, which I might add, I consider a thoroughly disgusting an unworthy behaviour by two elected officials of our council. It is with no sadness that I agree they should be stripped of all official duties and expunged from all senate records,' then he added with a sly smirk, 'They have already been stripped of everything else.' This solicited a titter or two from some of his fawning devotees.

'Perhaps it is time for us to formally choose a Mayor for our city, county and region. As you all know, my dear friend Roget Gorman, a mayor of outstanding wisdom and intelligence named me as a caretaker figure until a vote could be taken. Now is that time; I call for any candidates to step forward and join me on the mayoral dais and the balloting can begin, step up gentlemen, step up,' he flourished a wave towards the crowd of senators, none stepped forward, many took a step back.

'Am I to believe no one wants the venerated position of mayor?' he asked trying his best to appear astonished; the mask slipped subtly as a few of the senators tried to push Senator Casco towards the dais but the wiry old man twisted from the grip and moved back into the throng.

'I must say I am astounded and can only imagine that my humble term in office has proved to be adequate enough for you to warrant this simple servant of the state to remain in the position of mayor?' asked Sarreg with the piousness of a saint.

Two or three of his paid-for adherents burst into a well-timed and almost unrehearsed round of applause before one of them declared a vote of support should be instigated, another seconded it and so a vote was mandatory.

Yet another sycophant of Sarreg's, a narrow-faced individual with large bulbous eyes that gave him a fishlike expression, stepped forward, 'As there are no other candidates a written ballot is not needed, I suggest a show of hands. All those in favour of our dear friend Sarreg to remain mayor please raise your hand.'

After some hesitating, the remainder of the senate added their upraised hands to those of Sarreg's cronies, very few abstained and none dared vote no.

'My dear, dear friends, you embarrass me,' purred Sarreg like a cat who had just found the cream bowl with the top open, which was the case. Sarreg was now a formidable force within the council and furthermore had been voted in lawfully. What he could do in the name of the law and for the good of the state would not be questioned, and even if it was, Sarreg knew the inquirer would soon be convinced it was safer to simply agree to his wishes, 'How could I possibly turn down such a magnanimous gesture? Of course I will be your mayor, thank you, thank you, one and all!'

Sarreg nodded to Wide who opened the two large doors and the light shone in illuminating the dais and the city's new mayor with a sunbeam that vied with Sarreg's grin for the most radiance in the room.

He beckoned Senator Alayne, one of his followers, to him, 'Get me the young militiaman. Dainman I believe his name is.'

The man nodded and ran off. Sarreg stepped out into the bright sunlight with Wide ever vigilant at his side, 'What a wonderful day,' he said and laughed lustily as the senators filed out passed him. Some smiled and inclined their heads but the majority avoided his gaze and scuttled away as quickly as they could. Sarreg ignored them all.

'Sire, this is Garris Dainman,' his sycophantic new friend said and presented a lanky young man with a mop of unruly straw-coloured hair. Dainman drew himself upright and saluted Sarreg.

'Militiaman Garris Dainman, at ease my young fellow.'

'Sire, I am but Trooper Dainman, my superior officer is Militiaman Snape.'

'Yes, yes, Militiaman Snape,' replied Sarreg as if in deep contemplation, 'I think Snape carries too much weight on his shoulders for one man. In my capacity as Mayor of Fivewinds, I hereby promote you to Militiaman my young friend. You now have the same rank as your colleague Snape. I am sure the sharing of the workload will be welcomed. The man has not responded to a number of our pigeon messages. He must truly be a busy man in Marin's Weir.'

The young militiaman's face was ashen, his mouth dropped open and he stuttered, 'I... I... don't know what to say, sir.'

'Say nothing young man, say nothing. Now, as your first assignment I would like you to take a strong compliment of men to Marin's Weir to assist our friend Snape.'

'Marin's Weir?'

'Yes, and this is what I want you to do...' Sarreg put his arm around the newly promoted Garris Dainman and strolled away from the senate house explaining animatedly what assignment he needed the militia to carry out in his old hometown.

It was almost nightfall when Davvid and Luther finally succumbed to fatigue and decided to finish with their golem construction and retire to the inn for a refreshing ale and a meal. Another ten had now joined the seven golems. Of the seventeen, only fourteen contained the all-important hex-tiles, which would give them life. The three others and any remaining golems produced from the balance of the clay that lay heaped in the corner by the window would have to wait until the Krells had reaped further souls. Davvid pondered this as he washed the brown loam off his hands, 'We shall need more souls, Luther. Three are within easy reach but they will not be enough for this too,' he said and gestured to the pile of red clay yet to be formed into the golem frame.

'Yes, the boy Vela, the strange young woman and our friend Descar, where is the fellow? Didn't you instruct him to come to us when the delivery was completed?' asked Luther.

'Time flies like a drayk when I am in the thrall of magic; I have forgotten him,' explained Davvid.

Luther nodded in agreement.

Davvid, drying his hands on a rough-woven towel wandered to the small balcony and looked over. The horse and cart was gone but the doors below must have been left open as a glow filled the yard beneath him, 'Either the fool has gone or he is in the cellar. The doors are open.'

'Then we shall look for him on our way to the hostelry, come,' said Luther as he stepped out of the room to go down into the yard below.

Davvid sighed and closed the window then prepared to accompany his master, wishing that his own wings were healed enough for flight. He marvelled at how quick Luther had managed to grow his from the new body he now inhabited. Forced to walk for now, he used the stairs and followed his old master down to the lower floors.

By the time Davvid had exited the front door and walked around to the yard Luther had vanished.

'In here Davvid,' came a shout from within the passageway, through the two wooden and studded doors.

He followed the sound of Luther's voice and soon happened upon Descar's body and his master stooped over it as if in communion.

'A killing blow, masterfully executed. I warrant our two guests have absconded. Now we are three souls short.' Luther rose and kicked Descar's body viciously, 'A waste, even though he was an imbecile it smarts to see a useful soul wasted.'

Davvid continued deeper into the passageway until he reached the room in which the two had been held captive; he glanced inside and then returned to his old master, 'Nothing can be done Luther for now. I suggest we partake of some refreshments. The woman can't hide from us; she is too strange to wander the land un-noticed. I fancy a modest reward offered for her capture will soon procure her and the boy Vela.'

'The young woman, yes, but Vela is liked by the townspeople. It is one thing for him to disappear whilst out on an errand, it is entirely another matter to openly admit your interest in his whereabouts,' replied Luther thoughtfully.

'True, perhaps when we find her we shall find the boy too.'

Davvid closed and locked the doors behind him; Luther had already begun to approach the stables and the flock of drayks within. Of the three beasts inside the stalls, the two males were awake and preening whilst one, a pregnant female, lay sleeping. They saddled the males; Luther cuffed his across the beak as it angrily snapped at his hand, chastised, it lowered its head in subjugation and Luther climbed up onto its back. Davvid mounted his and using heels and simple hex commands they cajoled the beasts into the air and outside into the night.

The lights of Marin's Weir glowed softly on the near horizon and Davvid luxuriated in the flow of wind that whipped across his body as the drayk flew swiftly through the tenebrous sky. He carefully allowed the air to flow across his slightly open wings taking extreme care for should they open too much he knew the damage would be compounded. The circulation of the fresh air and the gentle flexing would help strengthen and repair the tattered skin but the bone damage was beyond repair. His flight — should he regain it — would always remain handicapped but whatever flying he managed was better than none at all.

Luther waved to him and pointed towards the ground, the outskirts of the town was beneath them. Davvid waved back and proceeded to coax his drayk to land near Jakob's warehouse and corral.

Jakob was locking up for the night; Molly was safely ensconced in her stall with an abundant amount of food and had been cleaned and pampered by Vela. As he clasped the padlock over the hasp of the warehouse door he made a mental note to treat his young charge, Vela to a little extra something next time he took his wife to the town market. The boy deserved a little pampering too on times. He scratched his chin and thought about the strange woman that had accompanied the boy. She appeared to have a good heart too, cleaning Molly's fly-bitten arse like that. He hoped they would be okay in the old ferry house.

He was about to amble down to The Uma Inn for a night-cap before going home to Mrs Jakob when the two drayks in his corral whickered and flapped agitatedly. A drayk's screeching call made him look up into the sky where he saw the two Krells guiding their mounts into his enclosure.

'Buggerit...' he swore, 'they can't bloody know can they?' and put on his best 'moronic' face and trudged over to them. 'Hello there young masters, what can I do for you?' he asked tugging the greasy wisp of hair on the top of his head that would have to serve as a forelock.

'Jakob, stable these drayks whilst we are in The Uma we'll collect them later,' instructed Davvid tossing the reigns over the fence posts to the old man.

'Yes sirs,' he replied. 'They will be safe outside with these other two. The warehouse has a mite infestation and you know what they do to drayks sir. Mites under their skin will make 'em buck you right out of the air they will y' know,' he continued, not wanting the beasts anywhere near his Molly.

'Yes man, yes, yes, that will do, just tie them securely. They've eaten and will soon settle down.' Davvid answered and began to walk towards the town.

Luther Krell passed Jakob and stopped, 'You didn't happen to see Vela and a young woman leave the mansion whilst you were there, did you Jakob?'

Jakob gave one of his best vacant stares and waited.

'Well man?' Luther insisted.

'Just thinking, sir,' answered Jakob, scratching his chin as if the stubble was infested with mites too, which was quite possible.

'Damn fool,' muttered Luther as he stormed off after

Davvid, 'A simple yes or no would have sufficed.'

'Yes I did see the two of 'em; I hid 'em in my bloody cart I did,' Jakob finally answered when he was certain both the mages were out of earshot. Then he made sure the two drayks were well secured, threw in a bale of hay for them to nestle in and decided to go straight home instead of visiting the inn.

Lucy darted to the side of the ferry-house door as her keen ears picked up the cautious footfalls as they approached from outside.

'Friend Lucy, it's only Vela,' a hushed whisper, from the other side of the rough-hewn door, made her relax from the combat stance in which she stood. The door opened, grating noisily on the dirt-ridden floor, and she grimaced as the boy slipped past her.

The smell of roast meat immediately brought a rush of saliva to Lucy's mouth and for the first time she realised that she was famished, 'Vela, you little beauty, you've been to the take-away?' She said, hungrily eyeing the bundle he had tucked under his arm.

The boy smiled, 'I won't even ask what take-away means, but by the look on your face I can tell you know what's in the cloth wrapper!'

'Enough with the talking; get the bloody thing open,' she said almost ripping the food parcel from beneath his arm.

Vela shook his head in disapproval, 'Greedy!'

'Greedy, my arse, I can't remember when I last ate or drank, have you got water here too?' she demanded, unfolding the cloth bundle and separating the little packages inside; a leather water-skin dropped out, 'Ahh, good.'

She pulled the cork out of the skin's neck and gulped the cool water down barely bothering to breath. Eventually satiated she flopped down onto the floor and sat crossed-legged whilst ripping apart the small packages. Vela sat beside her and sighed, 'Do all your people suffer from such bad manners?' He asked, then quaffed from the water-skin too.

'Bad manners?' she laughed. 'Where I come from you would have been knifed for a cigarette, let alone a bundle of delicious smelling chicken,' then she tore a piece of the white meat off the bone and crammed it into her mouth. She closed her eyes in ecstasy as she chewed the tender flesh and allowed the juices to run down her chin.

'I will never understand you friend Lucy,' said Vela shaking his head in bafflement, 'What is a cigarette?' Then, as Lucy looked towards him, her mouth half-full and opening to reply, he continued, 'and what is a chicken?'

Lucy stopped chewing and looked closely at the meat-covered bone she held in her hand; she sniffed it once and then looked back at Vela, her eyes narrowing.

Vela put the water-skin to his mouth and started to take another swig but burst out laughing. The water streamed out of his mouth and even his nose as he coughed and spluttered. When he ultimately calmed down and got his wheezing under control he looked up at her again, she was still frozen with the chicken-leg held halfway to her mouth, her expression darkening by the second.

'You should see your face!' he laughed and coughed once more.

'What is a chicken?' she said, 'Vela, tell me what this is and tell me now before you really see how bad my manners can get!'

'Sorry, Lucy, but your face…' he answered but she began to get up off her haunches so he quickly added, 'it's a chicken, it's a chicken, honestly.'

She sat back down, 'What does a chicken look like then?' she asked as she checked the chicken-leg again and started to raise it to her mouth once more.

'Well it has feathers, two wings, two legs… and a head like

a frog.'

Lucy closed her mouth and pointed the leg at him, 'Ever tried eating something like this through a different orifice?'

He smiled winningly at her, 'I don't know what you mean friend Lucy, but I can hazard a guess. Don't worry, it's only a chicken, there are no frog's heads involved.' Then he tore off a piece of the meat from the carcass and crammed it into his mouth, moaning with the delicious flavour, 'Mmm...divine.'

Together, they picked the chicken carcass clean, ate the baked potatoes, skin and all, then finished the water, 'Now I can think straight again,' Lucy sighed, shuffling back towards the wall of the ferry-house and leaning against it with her legs stretched out before her. Vela carefully folded the water-skin, squeezing it down as tightly as it would go. Then he wrapped everything up in the cloth, which the feast had arrived in and used it as a pillow as he reclined next to her. Within minutes, the boy had promptly dropped off to sleep. Shortly afterwards he was snoring softly, and Lucy felt her eye-lids droop as the steady cadence of his breathing lulled her into an almost hypnotic state; before long Lucy joined Vela in his slumber, and the pair passed the night in the old wooden building undisturbed.

A grey mist reached out tendrils of gloomy dampness over the millpond that languished up river from Marin's Weir. The ferry-house emerged from the vaporous haze like a ship through a fog as Lucy emerged from the haze of a good night's sleep. She yawned and nudged Vela; he snorted loudly and turned over. She poked him in the back with a rigid thumb and he squirmed then finally sat up rubbing his eyes. 'Good morning,' she said, stifling a yawn.

'Hello Lucy, sleep well?'

'Yes, I didn't imagine I could have slept as well as I did in a rat-hole like this,' Lucy replied, casting a critical eye over the interior of their overnight retreat.

A dilapidated ferryboat lay tipped upside-down looking like a giant turtle, but one with great holes eaten out of its shell, 'Wouldn't like to cross the river in that,' she remarked, pointing to the boat.

'That's not the current ferry; it's what's left of our old one. The one that took a trip over the weir. Steering a ferry across the Marin after spending a day in the Uma Inn isn't the best of ideas,' Vela rolled his eyes, 'They reckon the old ferryman is still walking the bottom of the river.'

'Nice, adds a little local colour I suppose,' was her dry reply.

'We can't stay here much longer,' Vela peered through a crack in the wooden planks of the wall behind him, 'Looks foggy outside but that won't stop the ferry. We'll be having company soon.'

'Well, I'm not going to get far dressed like this.'

'Truthfully, you do stick out like a drayk's penis,' replied Vela eyeing her critically.

'Oh…God I know I'm going to regret this…' Lucy sighed, 'What's a drayk?'

'Didn't you say the Krells brought you back from a forest?' Vela asked.

'From what I remember, it was a forest, but I wasn't conscious for very long after being dragged into this shithole of a world.'

'Then you were probably taken back to Sarreg's mansion on the back of the Krells' drayks. I don't imagine they would have carried you and thaumaturgists are usually too proud for carriages. Some, mind you, have their own wings.'

'So a drayk is like a horse?'

'If horses could fly, and had a set of murderous claws, and a pointy beak, then yes, it could be classed as a horse,' he sniggered.

'Sounds like a dragon.'

'Yes friend Lucy, its cry does sound like a dragon too.'

She looked at him expecting the punch-line but it never came, 'You're not playing around this time, are you?'

'No, Lucy, not this time.'

'Holy crap.'

'Yes, indeed, friend Lucy, holy crap.'

'Vela, let's get out of here. Can you find me some clothes?'

'That will be no problem. I have many friends in Marin's Weir,' then he brooded for a moment. 'Nevertheless they might become worried about me when I ask them for a woman's dress.'

'Forget a bloody dress; I want some sort of jacket and pants.'

'A good idea, to be disguised as a man will make you harder to be found, but your hair is too long for a male's.'

Lucy, delving into a pocket of her coveralls, withdrew the ceramic-bladed knife and handed it to the boy, 'You better make a good job of this or I'll be doing the cutting next and it won't be your hair.'

'I'm not sure I want the responsibility!' Vela moaned.

'You sissy, get cutting, and watch the ears!'

Lucy's hair fell; clumps of raven's wings collected on the floor around her feet and her throat tightened.

My hair is so much like my mother's, she thought, *smooth, shiny and raven-black. Raven…*

'What?' asked Vela as he finished.

'I didn't say anything.'

'I thought you said 'raven',' replied Vela frowning.

'Oh… perhaps I did, sorry.'

'Is raven your pet?'

She looked at Vela distractedly, 'My pet?'

He waited for her to collect her thoughts.

'No, Raven is… was, my friend, my boyfriend. The man I'll never be able to see again.'

'Ahh, now I understand.' Vela nodded wisely, 'He remains

in your world and you miss him.'

'Yes, Vela, I miss him.'

The boy stared thoughtfully at her until she asked him, 'What?'

'I believe it could be possible to bring him here.'

'What? I mean how?'

'Let's move, I'll tell you on our way to get your clothes,' he replied and his hand subconsciously felt for the little book he had secreted within the waistband of his trousers.

'Davvid, have you seen my journal?' Luther stopped rummaging through the detritus of tiles, papers and various objects on his desk and turned to his apprentice.

'Not for some time, Luther.' Davvid approached the desk and helped with the search.

'I seem to remember leaving it here when that fool boy came to tell us about the shortage of clay,' Krell stopped and frowned, 'Curse his soul, the simpleton has purloined it!'

'He's an ignorant loafer. I doubt he can read.'

'Yes but he may be savvy enough to try and sell it to another mage; that journal contains many secrets and formulae. Damn the child!' Krell's voice thundered.

'It can only be a matter of time; the blockhead will return to Marin's Weir, where else has he to go? Once he presents himself in town, our men will apprehend him, and that woman. I can't conceive how he will have time to find a customer for your journal.'

Luther Krell paced back and fore; his anger a simmering cauldron that threatened to boil over and Davvid did not want to be within the vicinity when it did.

'I trust you are right, my young friend.' His angry, shrew-like face sent a shiver down Davvid's spine, as once again the visage of Snape seemed to overcome the fact that inside that furious exterior resided his old master.

Luther, closing his eyes attempted to calm his exasperation and then returned to the desk and contemplated the three tiles that danced with a turbulent display of glyphs, 'At least we have another three souls,' he scooped up the terracotta squares like a hand of cards and flourished them before him.

'And so easily, and cheaply obtained; last night's visit to the inn was both refreshing and productive,' added Davvid.

'The benefits of being within easy reach of a sea-port are definitely a bonus. Certainly, the passage of wayfarers, wanderers and sailors makes the reaping of souls an easier prospect for us. Moreover, Marin's Weir is not a bottomless bag of resources. We have gleaned rather an excessive crop from our own little pasture; it bodes well to harvest from further afield,' agreed Luther.

'Faith! Marin's Weir contains nothing but dregs and windfalls,' Davvid's mind flew back to Tonn and the crippled boy's soul he had been obliged to reap.

Luther Krell approached the regiment of golems standing like stygian, frozen warriors awaiting a command to breathe life into them — which in fact they were — all except for the three devoid of hex-tiles. He prised open the jaws of the first of the vacant golems and inserted the tile; presently the texture of the hard-baked clay seemed to mutate. Its rigidity gave way to a more ductile appearance; he pressed a finger into the creature's chest and although there was a semblance of suppleness, he was pleased to feel the underlying temper of hidden strength. He repeated the procedure with the other two, satisfied that at least he had seventeen combatants ready for when the need arose, and he felt sure the time of need was inexorably drawing near.

'I feel a little more confident in our position now that these are completed,' Luther gestured towards the seventeen guardians, 'If we are fortunate enough to utilize the rest of the clay then so be it. Your little friend Gar could stand some repairs. Summon him Davvid and we can administer some restoration upon the poor creature.'

Davvid called Gar into the room with trepidation as he was unsure how much Luther knew about the golem's capabilities. Obviously, he had discovered that the child-like figure was capable of casting, but did he know to what extent?

However, he could not refuse the suggestion of renovation. In fact, it made good sense.

Luther ushered the golem towards the clay and set about working fragments of the ochre loamy material into the many gaps and cracks within Gar's frame.

The piece missing from the skull was manipulated and cajoled into place and finally there only remained the matter of the creature's left arm, which had been shattered off at the shoulder.

'I will have need of some stout willow, my boy, to complete the repairs. An entire arm and hand will need to be fashioned. I believe we have exhausted our supply up here but I am positive there are faggots of willow downstairs.'

Davvid surveyed the room with a quick glance; he was sure there had been a spare bundle of willow branches left over. He shrugged. Perhaps he was mistaken. 'Yes, there are plenty of bundles downstairs, I'll send a golem.'

'No, my dear boy, collect a bundle yourself. Do not leave the important choice to one of these brainless hulks. After all, Gar is one of a kind; does he not deserve the best?'

With misgivings rife in his mind, Davvid acquiesced and left Luther to refine the clay-work repairs whilst he departed to procure the lathes of willow.

Luther Krell waited until Davvid's footfalls faded and then he prised open Gar's jaws, 'Now... let's see what we have here...'

The mound of freshly dug earth in the courtyard drew

Davvid's eyes like a pin to a magnet. Six feet below the rich soil, Descar was completing his last good deed. He was feeding the worms.

'Pity,' he sighed, 'I would have liked to finish him myself. Still, Sarreg will more than suffice my desire for retribution; perhaps I should add his harridan of a wife to my list of revenge too?' Then he thought of Mari and the possibility that she would grow to despise him.

As he entered the stables to collect the willow he was a troubled man; the image of Mari had come to him unbidden and from nowhere. Why he should suddenly feel compassion towards her he could not understand; perhaps it was the vision of the lonely grave and the knowledge that all too easily, it could have contained his corpse and not Descar's, if it hadn't been for Mari Sarreg.

The three drayks raised their dreadful heads and watched him greedily as he collected the wood, 'Your breakfast will have to wait,' one of the males, snapped its beak at him and he tumbled the beast onto its backside with a quickly flourished spell. Its two companions shied away, not wanting the same treatment, 'Carry on like that and you'll have none.' The drayk whimpered, almost as if it had understood the man.

Breakfast was also on the minds of Lucy and Vela as they sauntered along the walkway of the town's main street. Lucy was dressed in patched leather trousers, the colour of which was debatable. Both of them had argued over their shade, Vela insisting they were dark green and Lucy that they were grey. Her woollen jacket was high-buttoned and unmistakably dark red and closely matched the hat she had sat on her shorn head at a jaunty angle. Vela had made sure she had rubbed some river mud into her face to disguise her 'feminine features', he had said, but she suspected a major reason was the fun he had in persuading her to rub the smelly stuff over herself. She covered her trainers too, and now at his suggestion swaggered as she walked, but felt like she was impersonating a drunken sailor.

'All I need is a parrot on my shoulder and I'd fit in on any boat around here. Ohh, excuse me.' She stepped aside as a portly, well-dressed gent raised his cane at them.

Vela shook his head as she stood there in the mud and seemed to deliberately barge into the fat man.

'Why do you need a parrot?' Vela asked, lost by her remark.

'Never mind, let's go and eat. You sure no-one will recognise these clothes?' she looked down at herself again.

'Doubt it; I didn't steal them from the same house. And I've patched the trousers, pity I couldn't match the green though.'

'Grey…'

'Okay, grey,' he conceded graciously.

'Yes, like Krell's journal, that you 'liberated', Vela if you fail as a mage at least you have an excellent career ahead as a thief. Do you really think you can summon Raven here or perhaps even send me back?'

The boy patted the book concealed in his waistband, 'Lucy, everything is here, All of Krell's little secrets. I have read some of them and from what I understand; he has found a way to contact your world. Strange thing is… his notes suggest that somehow a link has been established to a particular area of your land, because of you.'

'Why me?'

Vela hesitated and she gave him a stern look.

He held up his hands, 'Okay, okay, but you won't like this. You told me your father was killed a long time ago by a bat; the bat you thought could have been Davvid Krell but in fact Luther admitted to you it was he and not his apprentice?'

'Yes, he babbled on about a plant of some kind which allowed him to travel between the two worlds. It was him I saw back on Earth. He killed my father and did this to me.' She held up her hand and showed the burned knuckle to the boy.

'Yes, that is the key. Part of you was bonded somehow to Krell. He entered the ether and the bond drew him to where you were. Perhaps that will be the answer to your problem, perchance I can send you back, or call your friend.'

'But there is no key for me on Earth. Krell pinpointed me through the fact that part of me *was* bonded to him when he murdered my father. What bond do I have?'

'Your bond is your love for your friend Raven. Do you love him enough though I wonder?'

She cast her eyes down, unable to look Vela in the face, 'I see,' Lucy barely whispered, 'Vela, when my father died, something happened to me. I didn't allow love into my life again. I didn't want to be hurt like that ever again. My mother died young, unable to continue without him. But by then I had grown a shell around me and nothing or no-one was allowed in. I felt sorry for her but I didn't feel the anguish that I felt before. I was fourteen.'

'A young age to become so embittered,' Vela reflected.

'It wasn't embitterment; it was a method of survival. I could not stand that sort of pain again. This was a survival tool also,' she rolled her sleeve up and showed the boy the network of scars on her arm, 'another form of pain, but one which I could endure. Nobody came close to being allowed within my shell. Until a gothic idiot decided to 'save' me one night in a bar brawl, and almost got killed for his trouble.'

'Raven?'

'Yes, Raven. He has been my co-star, my friend and my lover since. However, do I love him enough? I can't answer that Vela.'

'If you decide to go into the ether then an answer will be supplied to you I suspect Lucy. Should your love prevail I believe you will find your way. Raven will be as an anchor for you, but otherwise where you will wander...'

'I'm no magician Vela, will it work for me?'

'If I come with you perhaps it will.'

'But if I get back to Raven and my own world and you are with me how do you get home then?'

'Umm… not sure…'

'Not sure?'

Vela fidgeted, 'Not sure…'

'Great.'

'Well, I'm only just a novice mage you know.'

'What does the journal say?' She enquired.

'Hmm… a bit vague there. I think once the plant's stamen has finished trying to mate with my mouth, giving up because I'm not a plant, it withdraws and I get pulled back too.'

'Seems logical.'

They arrived at the entrance to The Uma, 'Let's leave it there for now Vela. I do not want the thought of rotted meat and plant's tongues rattling around my head whilst eating breakfast. By the way, how're we going to pay for this food?'

Vela produced a leather purse from up his sleeve with the grace of a master conjuror pulling out a rabbit.

'Where did you get that?' she demanded as he tossed the fat purse up and down, causing the coins within to jingle.

He looked back up the street towards the portly gent who hadn't realised yet that he had recently contributed to the Lucy and Vela breakfast fund.

'Oh no…' she moaned and grabbed Vela's arm and dragged him into the inn before the fat man checked on his lightened pocket.

The inn smelled of stale beer and freshly baked bread. Vela and Lucy could not have asked for a more welcoming smell. They sat at a booth near the door and glanced around the smoky interior. Standing near the open hearth, warming his behind was a militiaman. He looked across at them, his hand strayed to the sabre, which dangled from his belt. He nodded.

Vela inclined his head in response and Lucy touched her hat. 'Is he some sort of cop?'

'Cop?'

'Law enforcement, he looks military or police. The leather uniform is neat, a few too many buckles perhaps,' she explained.

'He's a militiaman. Could be classed as a 'cop' but if he's like most of our law enforcers then he's corrupt; as dirty as your face, friend Lucy.'

'Thanks; no good telling him about the Krells then?'

'He's probably working for them.'

'Shit,' she lamented, 'Let's hope we can eat first before I have to knock him out.'

'Only knock him out? You must be gaining some serenity from being in my company.'

'Shh… someone is coming over, you speak to her. If I open my mouth, she will know I'm no sailor. Just don't order me any frogs, and gain serenity from you? Like shit…'

'You two gentlemen ready?' a lanky young girl, her ginger hair, which was bundled up on her head, threatened to fall over her face any moment. She licked a stub of a pencil and held a scrap of paper ready to take their order.

'What's the special this morning?'

'We got fresh bass, baked with leeks and potatoes,' she glanced towards the innkeeper behind the bar, 'but the fish smells a little too much of ammonia to be called fresh, I'd go with the eggs, bacon and fried bread. I baked the bread myself; it's good.'

'We'll go with your recommendation, give us two jugs of warm mead too, please,' and Vela slipped a small silver coin into her hand.

'Why, thank you sir,' she blushed and tried to curtsy but only managed to dislodge her precarious bun of ginger hair.

Lucy and Vela watched her go, 'I think you made a

conquest there, you dog.'

'Why am I a dog?'

'Jeez, questions, questions, questions,' she grumbled, 'It's just a saying Vela. Seen those two behind you? They seem pretty interested in us, no don't turn.'

He rolled his eyes at her, 'Questions, questions,' and mimicked her voice causing her to smile. He clumsily reached for one of the knives on their table and knocked it onto the floor. Vela reached down for it and glanced around to where she had indicated with a slight inclination of her head.

Vela wiped the knife on his jacket and returned it to the table, 'Hmm… I can't be sure, but those seem to be familiar. The militiaman *could* be one of Krell's cronies but I'm almost positive the other two *are*. We're lucky they aren't golem-handlers.'

'Golems aren't so tough,' she cracked her knuckles and Vela's eyes were drawn to the calluses. 'Takes years of punching a 'makiwara' to get those, and before you ask, it's a wooden board covered in straw and driven into the ground…'

'I know what a 'nakiwara' is,' scoffed the boy.

'Okay, cool, we'll call it a 'nakiwara' then, just to please you.'

He looked at her quizzically, knowing somehow he had made a mistake but he would not ask her how. 'Good,' he said.

'Food's coming,' Lucy licked her lips in anticipation.

'There we are gentlemen, please be careful, the dishes are hot,' the young girl placed the two enormous plates she had held with a thick, almost white towel onto the table before them. By the time she had returned with a basket of warm bread and the two jugs of mead they were ravenously stuffing the breakfasts into their mouths. She beamed a smile at them, obviously pleased that the two 'gentlemen' appreciated her cuisine. As she turned away from Lucy's table, a movement from the other two men caught her eye and she approached them wondering why all her customers couldn't be as polite as the fine young men she had just served.

'Two more ales, girl, and some of your bread and cheese,' the younger of the two ordered gruffly. She nodded and tried not to look at his face. A livid scar ran from high up on his forehead, down across his left eye and curved under his left ear. His left eye was a milky pool of bluish white, but his other, the good one, glittered malevolently as he gripped her hand. 'Can't you look me in the face?' He dragged her hand up to the scar and held it there as she tried to pull it away.

'Leave the girl alone, Miko. You are drawing attention to us,' his partner said and glanced in the direction of the militiaman.

Miko brought her palm down to his mouth and licked it lavishly. 'Pieter, you worry too much. Mmm the taste of youthful virginity.' The girl pulled her hand away, wiping the saliva onto her apron and ran into the kitchen.

Pieter shrugged at the militiaman and made a whirling sign with his finger next to his temple.

'Are you suggesting to that trooper I'm mad, Pieter?'

The older man, pulling his long grey hair into a ponytail and binding it with a leather thong, paused and turned to Miko, 'But you *are* fucking mad.'

The single eye blazed with hatred, but Miko was no fool. Although Pieter was twice his age, and his thin frame suggested a certain frailty he knew that beneath his baggy clothes there was a whipcord of a body. The old man had fought in the 'Saffron War' and anyone who had returned from that far-away land of yellow-skinned savages could be considered almost immortal. Miko did not intend to ever take on the veteran in a fair fight. If the time ever came when they would part company acrimoniously, then a dark night, an exposed back and a sharp knife would be Miko's preferred method of settling things.

Pieter tied off the thong, for a moment he thought Miko would actually make a move on him, there and then. The time would come, he knew, he just hoped he would see it coming.

Miko slapped Pieter playfully on the back, 'Only you can say that to me and not leak his breakfast out through his opened guts, you old fool.'

'Of course, we are friends.'

'Yes, we are truly friends,' agreed Miko nodding wisely.

Pieter turned his attention to the two customers in the booth near the door, 'It's definitely Vela, so the other must be the girl.'

Miko acknowledged him with a grunt.

'We'll finish our food and drink whilst they eat their last breakfast. You stay with them and I'll get the Krells,' instructed the old mercenary.

Miko turned his mutilated face towards Pieter, 'Why not just kill them and take their bodies to the mages. It would be a lot easier.'

Pieter did not survive the horrors of war by being impatient so he smiled slowly, 'For one, we have our 'friend' the militiaman over there who might object to us turning this place into an abattoir. Two, the Krells are paying for them to be delivered alive. And three, why do all the work yourself when someone else is willing to do it for you?'

Miko's face was a picture of disappointment, 'Ah…'

The food and ale arrived but their attendant this time was the grumpy innkeeper who thumped the tray down onto their table slopping some of the beer over the bread.

Miko looked around for the girl, 'Bloody waitress didn't come back.'

Pieter sighed, 'Perhaps it was something you said?'

Chapter 14

Return to the void

Lucy's apartment looked like a rhino had taken up residence, but its only occupant now was Raven. The film studio's doctor had changed the dressing on Raven's left arm and gave one more exasperated try, 'Look, the arm is healing well enough. It's time to leave here. The damn place needs a good sorting out; get some cleaners in and go to a good hotel. Spoil yourself.'

Raven ushered the doctor out of the door, 'Thanks doc, I'll take your advice on board.' The doctor opened his mouth and Raven slammed the door.

Kicking the empty pizza box out of the way, he slumped onto the sofa and switched on the television. Channel after channel failed to keep his attention resulting in him choosing a blank-screened radio station. As the room filled with Nights in White Satin, he reached under the sofa and withdrew the katana.

'The soul of the samurai,' the words slipped out from between his lips as quietly as the blade left the 'saya' or scabbard. He turned the sword with a smooth flick of his wrist and the subdued lighting of the room danced along its length. This was not the rubber prop from the film-set but his favoured weapon in his big collection. Three thousand layers of metal, forged with a precision, which gave the blade its shape. The pierced guard or 'tsuba' featured a coiled snake swallowing its own tail, whilst the curved blade went from a fairly thick back to a razor sharp edge, giving the weapon strength, flexibility and above all, the keenest of cutting edge.

Raven's katana was said to have been made between the late 14th century and the early 15th. He now knew it could possibly be a Muramasa, although there was no signature to suggest it was, but because of the history that was known about the blade, he believed it was possible. The weapon had taken lives, many lives. Katanas produced by the master Muramasa had a reputation for violence and bloodshed, whilst those made by the master craftsman Masamune were considered weapons of peace.

He had acquired the sword at an auction where it was mistakenly identified as a WW2 Japanese army officer's Shin-Gunto. After sending the weapon to a restorer in Portland, Oregon, he was surprised to receive an excited telephone call, early one morning, from the restorer. He was informed that immediately on seeing the blade the restorer had realised it was no mass-produced sword made for the many officers of His Imperial Emperor Hirohito. It had a much, much older provenance. The expert hazarded an estimated date of 1550 and speculated that it was possibly a Muramasa.

Raven remembered the restorer's words, 'It is said that a Muramasa blade always has something evil about it, and once it leaves its scabbard, it never returns to it with out first seeing blood.'

He had been captivated with the idea of owning a sword with such a dark history. Raven gleaned every possible piece of information from the restorer who, when renewing the grip, recognised the file markings that were cut into the tang; the upper part of the weapon that was never touched, as it was meant to show how the blade-steel was aging. The restorer photographed the tang then renewed the grip and lovingly polished the blade.

Raven felt the hairs raise on the back of his neck when the myth the restorer told him about came to mind again, 'Raven, legend tells of what happened when two swords made by Muramasa and Masamune were held in a stream carrying fallen leaves. While those leaves touching the Muramasa blade were cut in two, those coming towards the Masamune suddenly changed course and went around the blade without touching it.'

He had never used the blade in anger. But Raven knew, if the katana had been in his hand the day Lucy was spirited away by the phantom visitor, he would not have hesitated in trying to separate the thing's head from its body.

At the thought of Lucy a lump rose in his throat. The Moody Blues chorus reached its crescendo with, 'and I love you, oh how I love you...' and he lightly touched the blade to his palm. He let the metal taste his blood, before wiping off the crimson with a piece of lint cloth, and returned the satiated weapon to slumber once more within its scabbard.

'So, we need to fast for three days and fill our mouths with minced-down human flesh. Then we lie down next to a flower which only blossoms once every thirty years?' Lucy looked at Vela incredulously, 'Jeez, it couldn't be something simple like a teleporter, and I'd just have to say 'beam me up, Scotty...''

'Sorry, Lucy. Perhaps on your world it would be so, but here it is as I explained,' he shrugged. 'Perhaps we will not need to fast and any rotten meat would do. Mages adhere to the rules because they want to return with a soul. We do not; perhaps for us the rules can be bent.'

They had prolonged their breakfast as long as they could before attracting too much attention. Lucy had watched one of the two at the other table rise and leave. He was tall and gaunt. A long, grey ponytail swished back and fore as he had stridden past. His lined face carried the weight of his years well and his crooked smile softened the hardness of his blue eyes. As he had opened the door to leave Lucy noticed the blanket roll he had strapped across his back slide down and for a moment she felt sure she had glimpsed the pommel of a sword, a pommel very much like one she had seen before.

They had purchased a mortar and pestle from an

alchemist's and Vela was now taking them to a butcher's shop, where they hoped to find a meat substitute for the human-flesh. Lucy put a hand on Vela's arm, 'Don't slow down or turn, but I'm sure we are being followed.'

He steered her towards a window. Behind the glass was a display of various cuts of meat. Slabs of bloodied steak lay on the red-stained marble alongside haunches of what looked like venison, rabbits still in their skins and an assortment of fowls. Vela pretended to examine the display but he was peering at the reflection of their stalker in the glass, 'Looks like it's our friend from the inn.'

'The militiaman?'

'No, the scar-faced man. His partner left before us,' he replied.

'Yes,' Lucy squinted into the window pane, 'you're right. He is definitely following us. He's just pulled back around the corner, out of sight.'

'It could be just a common thief. There are enough of them in the town, but…'

'But?' she prompted him.

'I think they recognised us. Scar-face will follow us while the old man gets the Krells.'

'Probably makes sense. We could get him somewhere quiet and find out.'

Vela looked into the shop, 'I think we should get the meat and try losing him. We don't need to draw inquisitive eyes if we can help it. That militiaman warming his arse pretended not to be interested in the comings and goings but he was watching everything, mark my words.'

'Okay, I'll wait here. You go in and buy the meat,' she said

'Try not to get into any trouble, friend Lucy.'

'I'll be all right. Just don't go buying any frogs.'

Miko adjusted the two short, double-edged blades that sat in their oiled leather sheaths sitting either side of his waist. Pieter and he had passed many an hour arguing over whether they were long daggers or short swords. He favoured the short sword description, but Pieter revelled in calling them cutlery, masquerading as weapons.

Miko's lips curled back to reveal his brown-stained teeth. He wondered what the old man would think of them when one day they were sticking out of his back.

He peeked around the corner again; one of his quarries was entering the shop. The other, the one Pieter suggested was a woman, was staring into the window and pointing at something on display. He hoped the strangely dressed sailor was a woman in disguise.

He toyed with the idea of perhaps finding out first, before Pieter and the Krells arrived. It would be a pity to drag them all the way here for the wrong person.

Rummaging through a pocket in his leather waistcoat, he eventually found the plug of chewing tobacco he was searching for and bit off a mouthful. Within minutes, the yellow stain on his teeth had deepened and his mouth was filled with a sticky volume of saliva and ground tobacco leaf. He turned and spat.

The boots the gob narrowly missed were shiny, and almost the same shade of brown as the sticky mess that splattered minute drops over their toes. He looked up at their owner.

'Ah…' Miko muttered.

'Ah, indeed,' the militiaman from the inn fingered the hilt of his sabre then looked down at his boots, 'I hope you have a clean kerchief.'

Miko sighed and moved a hand towards the handle of one of his swords.

'Oh dear,' the militiaman murmured, 'it's going to be like that, is it?' and he moved to one side.

Miko's hand froze as he saw the other five troopers

standing behind the first. 'Just getting my kerchief out,' and his hand moved from the sword's handle to a pocket.

The rag he pulled out caused the militiaman to grimace, 'Put it away,' he tilted his head and surveyed the rogue's waistcoat, 'Take that off, it will have to do,' he pointed to the leather jacket.

Miko took a deep breath, and then he took off his waistcoat, dropped to his knees and wiped the tiny drops of spit off the shiny boots.

One or two of the militiaman's backup sniggered and Miko felt his face redden, but commonsense overcame his anger and he forced a smile as he stood up. 'Sorry about that. You were on my blind side,' he said and pointed to his ravaged face.

'No damage done,' replied the man with the shiny boots then looked at Miko's blades, 'Nice pair of knives.'

'They're short swords.'

'Look like knives to me,' and the militiaman smoothly drew his sabre from its scabbard. The curved blade scintillated in the sun then whistled as he swept it through the air just missing the tip of Miko's nose, 'Now this is a sword.'

Miko could feel his forced grin turn to a snarl; he weighed the odds again. His patience was thin at the best of times but now daylight was beaming through its wafer transparency. If he did not move soon he'd throw caution to the wind and cut this buffoon, he just knew he would.

'Why are you loitering here?'

'I was just leaving. Stopped to chew me a plug of baccy is all.'

The militiaman nodded sagely, 'Then leave.'

Miko touched his forehead, turned on his heel and walked away.

Garris Dainman sheathed his sword and explained to his five men, 'That is a dangerous fellow. Do not ever turn your back on him and if you have to have a conversation with the rogue keep your back to a wall and a hand on your sword.' The five men nodded solemnly. He pointed at the smallest of the five, 'Edward?'

'Yes sir.'

'They were outside the butchers. Take a look, see if they have gone inside. If they spot you just stroll past and go around the corner. If they are there signal us by brushing your hand through your hair. Now go.'

'Yes sir, brush my hair, yes sir.'

Dainman watched as the youthful militiaman trooper, doing his best to act nonchalantly, walked around the corner and approached the butcher's window. He was not surprised when the young man turned towards him and shook his head. During the confrontation with the scar-faced brigand, Vela and his friend had made good their escape.

'Liver and lungs, nice.'

'Easier to mash up and good and smelly too,' Vela stuck his nose into the paper containing the offal.

'Oh, it's the meat that's smelling?' she laughed, 'Thought it was you.'

'Yes, friend Lucy. Very funny,' and he poked his tongue out at her.

'Well. At least we've lost our tail,' she replied and looked surreptitiously over her shoulder.

Vela turned to look at his backside and then touched her on her behind, 'I never realised we had any tails.'

'Not that sort. I meant our pursuer.'

'Our pursuer had a tail!' he exclaimed as she spun around to slap him.

She saw the mischievous look on his face and grumbled, 'You are heading for a bruising my fine friend.'

'No friend Lucy, we are heading for Jakob's stables,' his smile was infectious and she could not help but laugh and give him a hug.

'Hey!'

'Oops, sorry, I forgot I was supposed to be a man.'

'Okay, just don't kiss me,' he snorted.

'Fat chance,' she laughed. 'Tell me again about our visit to Jakob's?'

'According to the journal the plant is in a woods many leagues from here. It would take us a number of days to walk there. If Jakob has some horses or even a drayk or two we can get there within hours. Whatever we do, it will be safer out of the town. There are too many who know me here and money is always money. It buys the betrayal of friends and the deaths of enemies.'

'And pizzas and McDonald's.'

'Yes, true,' Vela replied with raised eyebrows.

'Can we survive out in the wilds?'

'It's possible, but boring,' Vela scowled, 'Sooner or later we will have to confront the Krells. Unless we leave the country, and I'm not sure I want to do that. I'd prefer to kill the Krells, or be killed by them.'

'Hmm… that's a possibility too.'

'Look, if we can get you back to your world, friend Lucy, perhaps I can disappear for a while until they get fed-up.'

'You hope.'

'Yes, I hope,' Vela didn't look convinced.

Jakob was pitch forking the dung into a wooden wheelbarrow when the two friends hailed him. He creaked upright and waved, 'Welcome back.'

'Hi there you old fart,' yelled Vela.

'Have some respect, will you?' Lucy pushed him, 'That old fart got us away from the Krells, remember?'

'Of course I remember, Lucy,' Vela looked at her in confusion, 'but if we don't trade insults Jakob will think something is wrong.'

Lucy shook her head, 'I don't think I'll ever understand your customs.'

'Lucy and Vela,' Jakob gave a toothless grin then sniffed the air, 'Vela, you shit yer pants again?'

'See what I mean?' he turned to Lucy, eyebrows raised.

'It's the meat,' Vela wafted the bag under Jakob's nose.

'The butcher fooled you again, Vela, that's dog-shit. Not meat.'

'Yes, yes, Jakob. Now tell me old friend. Do you have any horses stabled with you at present?'

'Pleasantries over with so soon?' Jakob looked abashed, 'No horses, my friend. But there are two drayks that are begging to be filched.'

'Even better!'

'Wait, Vela, Jakob. Are these drayks the flying dragon-like horse with beaks and claws and things?'' Lucy demanded.

'Yes, of course, what other drayks do there be?' enquired Jakob and then continued, 'Unless you are speaking of draykons. But they do be much too large to stable here and I doubt much you could handle one between you.'

'Crap, so drayks are baby dragons?' She asked.

'Baby draykons,' clarified Vela, 'Draykons must be like the dragons in your land Lucy. I can't handle one, Jakob is right. But we can doubtlessly ride the drayks, once you've punched them a few times.'

'Punch them?' enquired Lucy.

'Yes, they need dominating or you'll end up losing a finger or if they're hungry enough, an arm.'

'Great.' Lucy shook her head.

'Fear not little Lucy, they do be well fed. Old Jakob looks to the beasts in his care well,' the old man said proudly. 'Until they be pinched, of course.'

Vela patted the old man on the arm, 'Time we left, Jakob.'

'Okay Vela,' he indicated they should follow. The three entered the barn. Molly looked up from her bucket of oats and gave them a welcoming whinny. Lucy reached over and smoothed the animal.

'Molly is looking happier.'

'Aye, she is happiest when her stomach is full and the flies don't be eating her arse.'

Jakob pulled down some leather harnesses off the wall and handed them to Vela. He paused and looked at the boy, 'Do you have a weapon?'

'No, only this,' and he tapped his head.

'Yes, that do be good, but this be better as a distance weapon,' and he handed the boy, who was struggling with the leather traces, a small recurved bow and a quiver of arrows.

Lucy stepped up and took the bow from him, 'Wow, nice,' she said as she raised the weapon and drew the string back to her cheek. 'Good draw, about thirty inches. What's it made from, bamboo and some sort of horn?'

'Water buffalo horn,' answered Jakob.

'Lovely weapon. Know how to use it Vela?'

The boy puffed out his cheeks, 'Of course I do.'

'Good,' and she slung the quiver over her shoulder then unclipped the bowstring. Taking an arrow from the quiver, she looked down its length and examined the tip. 'A bodkin, armour piercing. You didn't go hunting rabbits with this.'

Jakob just winked at her, 'This way, your mounts wait.'

He led them through the old barn. Sunlight casting beams across the straw-covered floor, dust spiralling up like smoke where they strode. He opened a door at the rear of the storage area, its rusted hinges complaining raucously. It opened out onto the corral where two drayks were penned and lying amongst bundles of hay. Lucy thought they looked like enormous chickens roosting amongst the straw, she half expected to find giants eggs beneath them when they stood up.

'Don't forget, if they challenge you, cuff them quickly. You must dominate them or they will dominate you,' Vela reminded Lucy as he strode towards the two beasts.

In unison, the two animals rose and flapped their great wings then folded them, eyeing the approaching humans with distrust. Vela made a soft cooing noise, which seemed to placate one of the drayks. The other followed Lucy's every move.

'I don't think this one likes me,' she moaned.

Vela gently fitted the harness on his drayk and fastened the reins around its beak. With the leather strapping acting as a muzzle, he felt content enough to pat the animal on its head, the drayk made a soft purring noise.

'Females are always the gentlest,' Vela acknowledged.

'I guess mine is a male?'

'You guessed right,' replied the boy as he approached the second drayk.

The animal turned its angry gaze on Vela, 'Okay, its attention is on me, give it a damn good slap.'

Lucy stepped forward and gave the beast a short, twisting punch to the side of its head. The drayk squawked once as its eyes rolled up into its head and then the animal collapsed to the floor.

Vela looked at the unconscious animal, then at Jakob and finally at Lucy who held up her hands in despair, 'Sorry, I get carried away sometimes.'

Jakob said, 'I do believe you won't have any trouble at all with them there beasts no more,' and he pointed to the female drayk that cowered away from them, her eyes rolling in fear. 'I'll get some water.'

'Well at least I can harness it with out any problems, come on give me a hand. Lift up its head,' instructed Vela.

By the time the pair had finished, the old man had returned with a leaky pail of water. Vela took it from his gnarled hand

and threw the whole contents of the pail over the unconscious drayk's head. The animal cawed like a giant crow and shook itself, spraying water everywhere and staggered to its clawed feet. Then it turned its baleful glare on Lucy and lowering its head made a quiet mewling sound quite akin to what she thought a kitten sounded like.

'I think he's subdued now,' observed Vela.

Jakob looked around the back of the big animal, 'Aye, he's really subdued now, he's gone and crapped himself he has.'

Lucy felt sorry for the beast and approached it carefully, her hand held out for the drayk to just sniff, she hoped.

After a few moments of indecision, the male drayk finally acquiesced and snuffled her hand then its dark blue tongue emerged from its beak and licked her.

'Well, I never seen no drayk do that before. Seems you might have made a friend, little lady,' Jakob watched them in awe.

Vela climbed up onto the female drayk and motioned Lucy to mount her animal. The drayk was docile and she climbed up onto its back with very little effort. The boy showed her how to manipulate the reins and the best way to guide the animals with knees and heels.

'We don't need to do any fancy flying so very little magic will be necessary.'

'Good,' she replied, 'Because I don't know any.'

They reined the drayks around and waved goodbye to Jakob. Then both riders dug their heels into their animal's flanks and held tight as with a whirlwind of wing beats they rose into the air.

As they circled and gained height, they heard old Jakob shout, 'Safe travels and be careful.'

Vela waved to the old man then wheeling his drayk around, called to Lucy, 'Okay friend Lucy, follow me. Time to go for a picnic in the woods!'

Rubbing the stubble of his salt and pepper coloured beard, Pieter approached Sarreg's old mansion house. He observed he was being scrutinised by two figures standing on a small balcony. Occasionally he questioned himself on his partnership with Miko. Since teaming up with the dubious character the work he seemed to get had gradually deteriorated in quality but had increased in quantity. He did not like the disparity but his financial situation brooked no other choice at the moment; he was flat broke, again.

'Hmm...the Krells seemed to have settled in well,' he mumbled to no one in particular but his brindled pony whinnied softly as if in agreement. Pieter patted the lathered neck of his mount and urged it forwards with a gentle squeeze of his knees. 'Press on, Chaco, press on. I feel their gaze too, my friend. But press on.' The pony snorted, shook its head negatively but moved ahead just the same. Once again, Pieter wondered what he was doing, and what he had got himself into.

'I imagine he brings us news of Vela and the woman,' remarked Davvid.

Luther Krell contemplated the sweat-covered animal and the dishevelled character upon its back, 'He's ridden hard to get here. The news he carries must be of importance. Call him up.'

Luther wandered over to the group of golems. Casting a critical eye over them, as if inspecting a squad of soldiers, he heard Davvid call down to the mercenary. Davvid instructed him to leave his pony with a handler at the stable and to proceed up to their laboratory with all haste.

Of the seventeen colossal figures, Luther selected one in particular. Fluttering a curlicue of complicated hand-signals before the behemoth's face, he was pleased to see the golem step forward almost eagerly. He remembered the soul within this one very well. It had come from a strange location in the alternative world. The man had been incarcerated like an animal within a cage made from iron-bars. Luther imagined he must have committed some heinous crime to warrant solitary imprisonment like that. The parallel world seemed a less harsher environment than here though. Sarreg's dungeons were infinitely more shocking than the cage, but so was this world in its entirety. He reached down and inspected the golem's capacious hands. They were broad, axe-like and rugged. 'You shall be known as...Axe,' he said, 'My safety is your prime goal in life.' For a moment, Luther believed that Axe had dipped its head slightly as if accepting the name and the responsibility, but he then shrugged; golems were automatons only, you could not attribute emotions to them.

A respectful tap on the doorframe drew Luther from his pondering, 'Enter.'

Pieter stepped into the room, his face glistening with sweat. The ride from Marin's Weir had been hard for both him and his pony Chaco.

'What news do you bring mercenary?' Demanded Davvid brusquely.

'Good news, sires,' Pieter touched his forehead slightly, 'We have found the child and the woman.'

Luther approached the old man, 'And you did not bring them?'

Pieter shook his head, 'I do not think they will be favourable to being asked to accompany us here, sires.'

'Fool, do not *ask* them. *Make* them come,' snarled Davvid and Pieter stiffened.

'Wait until he explains, Davvid. There is more, is there not?' asked Luther.

The grey ponytail slipped onto Pieter's shoulder as he bowed slightly, 'Yes sire, there is more,' and he cast a chiding glance in Davvid's direction. 'The boy is no complication. I can

subdue him immediately and transport him like an old rug.
The woman could be a different matter. I observed the way she
comports herself. She is disguised as a man, and by her light
step and demeanour I would suggest that her lineage is that of
a warrior.'

Davvid chuckled, 'A warrior?'

Pieter raised an eyebrow, 'Sire, a woman may be a
warrior,' he paused, 'Just as a man may be an old biddy.'

Luther had to hold Davvid's arm down as the younger
man flew into a rage, 'Your insult will not go unanswered,
knave,' He ranted.

'I meant no offence, surely you did not believe I would call
you an old biddy, sire?'

Luther fought to hold back a smile, he appreciated the fact
that the old mercenary had spirit, but he knew that Davvid
was not a force to sport with, no matter how quick the old
man's blade might be. And he eyed the rolled blanket
concealing the adventurer's curved sword.

'Enough of this. Do you truly believe the woman to be a
danger?' enquired Luther as he released a simmering Davvid
from his grip.

The mercenary rolled up his left sleeve. A vicious gouge,
covered with cicatrices of pink shiny skin, contrasted with the
tanned bark-like texture of his arm, 'This is a little gift from an
oriental lady during The Saffron Wars. My colleague was not
as lucky, her sword took his eye. Between us, we were unable
to vanquish her. When she offered us a truce neither of us felt
the desire to decline, as galling as it felt at the time.'

'Obviously you had no mages with you,' surmised Luther.

He turned the sleeve back down, 'Our mages were
slaughtered by arrows before we even knew we were under
attack. We foot soldiers were offered the honour to die by the
sword. Many of our companions did. My colleague and I
were... fortunate.'

'You have a suggestion?' asked Luther.

'There is yet more.'

'Continue, man, continue,' Davvid prompted.

'Whilst keeping a vigil on the two, I noticed others expressing an interest in them also.'

'And who would that be?'

'A militiaman, and a ranked militiaman too. He was alone in the inn. But... let's say my bones tell me there were others nearby,' replied Pieter, 'and they also tell me that perchance he was not just observing the pair, but was keeping watch on whoever else showed interest in them.'

Luther and Davvid exchanged glances, and then Luther spoke, 'Sarreg...'

'Procurator Sarreg?' exclaimed Pieter and indicated the mansion with a sweep of his hand.

'Yes, knave... that Sarreg. Shall we say... there rests an unfortunate disagreement between my young associate, Davvid and our odious procurator,' explained Luther.

'Ah...' nodded Pieter.

'Ah... indeed,' agreed Luther, 'and therefore if a disagreement exists between Davvid and him, then it exists for me too. Moreover, the militiaman was watching you pair of fools. They would know nothing of Vela and the woman.'

Pieter tried to look concerned; knowing now that this was yet another shit commission. Procurator Sarreg would be yet another man he might have just made an enemy of. The list was long and forever growing.

Luther's lips grew thin, a gash across Snape's rat-like face, 'Is that all?'

'Yes, sire,' replied Pieter. 'My associate is following them. He has been instructed to stay close, but to also keep out of their sight.'

'I trust he retains the tile I furnished you?' Luther Krell frowned.

'He has, sire.'

'Good, good,' and he turned to Davvid smiling, 'Then let's pay our two friends a visit.' He addressed Pieter, 'Your mount can remain here. We have drayks in our stables.'

'Your command, sire,' Pieter clenched his right fist to his chest.

Luther beckoned Axe to his side. Pieter winced; he hated golems and considered them unnatural bastards.

'Davvid, bring Gar. He could prove useful,' instructed Luther.

Davvid, with a bare flick of his fingers called the small creature to his side.

Pieter frowned, 'A golem child?'

Davvid laughed, 'Think so?' Then with an almost imperceptible movement, ordered Gar to restrain the mercenary. As the creature signed Pieter realised something was afoot. With a litheness, which made a mockery of his elderly appearance, he twisted and drew his sword from the pack-roll across his back.

He was quick, but not quick enough. The golem completed the hex and Pieter's body became as rigid as one of the inanimate golems standing frozen across the room from him.

Davvid approached the man and examined the curved blade, 'A beautiful sword. It looks foreign. Not much use to you now though. Is it?' Then he prised the mercenary's fingers apart and took the weapon from his grasp. He hefted the sword and finally held the tip near his victim's eye. 'Remember? I told you your insult would not go unanswered.'

'Davvid, he has his uses. To deplete our resources now would be a mistake. You have made your point. Release him, please,' ordered Luther Krell.

Long seconds passed then Davvid took the sword point away from Pieter's unblinking eye. He held the weapon by the furthest point of its handle and raised it up until the pommel was eye-level with the old man. 'Here's your sword back,' he said and dropped it. The point impaled the wooden floor with a dull thud and the blade vibrated like a plucked string. Davvid nodded to Gar and Pieter was released.

The mercenary looked down, the blade was uncomfortably close to his soft, leather boot, 'Your accuracy is commendable,' he commented as he pulled the blade from the floor and stowed it back in his pack-roll.

Davvid smiled, 'Wasn't as if I aimed.'

They stood toe to toe, a vein in Pieter's jaw throbbed.

Luther pushed them aside and walked out of the room. Axe almost bowled them all over as he followed his master, 'Come on you two,' called the mage from the hall.

'This is the place!' Vela waved and pointed down.

'About time,' she called back, and then mumbled, 'I need a pee...'

The two riders circled the coppice until Vela, referring to the journal, was sure the opening below them was the correct spot. He signalled her to descend, and both drayks plummeted like hawks to the ground. On alighting from her mount Lucy threw the reins to Vela, 'Grab these a minute, I've gotta go powder my nose.'

Vela slipped from the back of his drayk and pulled both animals towards a tree. He flung the reins around the trunk and tethered them. Rummaging in his pack, he drew out two large bones. They were bloodied and still had pieces of sinew and gristle attached. The drayks snapped their beaks in anticipation. 'See what treats Vela has for his favourite drayks?' he bantered as he showed the animals their rewards for not tipping their passengers off in mid-air. Both drayks slavered and dropped their heads in deference, 'I see you still remember Lucy's lesson in manners,' and he tossed the bones to them.

'Back,' Lucy cried as she approached the tree.

The boy studied her nose searchingly.

'What?' she asked and rubbed it.

'Nothing,' he sighed, as confused as ever.

'Okay, where's this triffid?' she asked eagerly.

'Lucy, please do not confound me anymore!'

'Oops… sorry Vela,' she tousled his hair, 'The plant, where's the plant?'

Vela pulled out the green leather journal and thumbed through the dog-eared pages. He ran a dirty finger down the yellowed leaves until he found what he was looking for, 'Ah…' he looked around the glade, and then up at the sky. 'This way,' he pointed and set off. Lucy trotted behind him.

It wasn't too long before Lucy could smell the Rapture Bud, 'Holy crap, is that the bloody plant I can smell?'

The boy nodded, 'Yes we are close now, and phew you're right. It stinks.'

Lucy grimaced, 'And you're going to put rotting meat in your mouth to attract the stinking thing's stamen into it? Rather you than me, mate.'

'It's the only way the journal says it works,' the boy shrugged. 'Look, there it is!'

A purplish looking flower was growing near a decaying tree trunk. Its leaves, like brown sacks, protected the pulpy flesh-like petals. A rock offered it protection from the elements. There was no need for any protection from animals; nothing would find this particular shrub pleasant to eat.

They approached the thing with awe. Both held their hands over their mouths and noses as they circled around the plant. As Vela drew nearer, the bud seems to quiver in anticipation.

'I think it smells the rotten meat,' he said through his hand.

'Either that or your pants,' replied Lucy.

He gave her a disparaging look and sat down near the

flower. He patted the grass beside him, 'Come sit here. Lucy, you must decide on your actions when, or if, we get to your world. Are you going to try and remain there or persuade your friend Raven to return here with us?'

She was a long time answering, 'I'm not sure Vela. Now that I know who was responsible for my father's death I want to avenge him. However, I also want to return to my old life and Raven. It is strange.' She examined the thin scars on her arms, 'Life and love is all the more precious when you are close to losing them. I won't know what I'll do until the time for a decision is upon me.'

The boy nodded in understanding.

Lucy helped him empty his pack and wrinkled her nose at the rotten meat when she opened its paper wrapping. The plant shook fervently, 'Patience, patience,' she yowled and started to grind the offal with the mortar and pestle.

'Do you feel the magic in the air?' asked Vela as if mesmerised.

'I just feel sick,' Lucy looked from the pestle towards the boy and he saw her face had a slight green tinge to it.

'Here, let me,' Vela held out a hand and Lucy passed him the offending vessel and its contents.

'Oh, it's almost done,' he noticed and finished off the mixing of the disgusting concoction.

'Yuck, I feel all done too.'

Eventually he finished pounding and grinding and lifted the mortar high above the pestle. The slurry attached to it dropped back into the container and the Rapture Bud throbbed excitedly.

'I think we are ready,' he held out a hand to her.

She scrambled closer to him, they were both adjacent to the plant now and watched as its flower turned towards them. Vela, lying down with his head as near to the bud as he could position it, opened his mouth and scooped a handful of pulverised meat into his palm. He looked at Lucy and smiled sickly, 'Okay?'

'Okay,' she affirmed.

'Whilst in the ether, whatever happens, don't let go of my hand. If you decide to stay with your friend, then upon entering your world, you must let me go,' Vela warned.

'I understand my friend,' and she kissed his forehead, 'I won't let go unless I must stay there, don't worry.'

He nodded, 'If you do stay, then this is goodbye, friend Lucy. I will miss you,' he kissed her on the cheek and scraped the foul-smelling paste into his mouth. For a moment he thought he would gag it up again but then a potent tremor ran through him as he experienced a terrific surge of magical energy. Vela glanced at Lucy but he could tell by her expression that she had felt nothing.

'I'll miss you too, Vela,' and then she pointed towards the flower, 'Look!'

The petals had opened wide and the thick stamen was progressing towards the boy. Vela reclined once more and closed his eyes. The energy flow was unbearable and he quivered uncontrollably. Lucy watched the stamen reach over and enter the boy's open mouth. His eyes rolled up into his head until all she could see was white. Then amazingly, his body seemed to flicker and fade before her eyes. Her hand, gripped so tightly by Vela that her knuckles cracked, wavered in and out of her perception. Finally, darkness rippled over her and dragged her away.

Vela felt the stamen enter his mouth, questing for the carpel or pistil, its female equivalent that the boy had fooled the plant into believing he was. The power exuded by the Rapture Bud was dragging his mind into the void and he held Lucy's hand in a death-grip as he lost consciousness.

When he awoke, he was sure that their transference into

the ether had been unsuccessful and that night had fallen. A few stars twinkled overhead. He looked around and realised that a small number of stars twinkled everywhere, not just overhead but to his side and below. He looked down at his body and felt a moment of panic when he could not discern it. However, the journal had prepared him for this eventuality and he calmed his fears. He could feel Lucy's hand in his own but again there was no sight of his friend. Vela scrutinised the small points of light; they were doorways into Lucy's world, he knew. But which was the one to take her to her lover Raven? Vela realised he had no idea; it would have to be Lucy who decided. He squeezed her hand and hoped she would remember his instructions.

Lucy was far less calm than Vela. Even though this was the second time for her to travel the void, during the first voyage she had lost sense of awareness due to being completely panic struck. Now she was merely frightened. She understood that the twinkling spots of light that showed themselves on every plane of the complete blackness surrounding her, were not stars but openings to her Earth. She felt Vela's hand squeeze hers but she could not see him. She could not even see her own body. Lucy tried to calm herself and returned Vela's signal. She knew she had to concentrate now and think of only one thing... Raven.

After an unknown passage of time, she felt one speckle of light attract her attention. It looked like a single pixel on a black computer monitor but she fixed it with her mind's eye and concentrated... Raven.

More time passed, she wondered if they had been in the void for minutes or days. Vela was unsure of the flow of time in the void. Krell's notes were vague on the subject, but one thing they both understood, back on Vela's world the plant would eventually remove its stamen from the boy's mouth and drag him back. She thought the pinpoint of light she had accepted as her goal had grown. Depth perception was an impossibility she realised. The light could be thousands of miles away or just within reach of her fingers, *if I have any fingers in this place*, she thought.

Vela must have spotted the star expanding too. She felt him signalling frantically now, so she fixed it in her mind and imagined it expanding. It did, rapidly...

Raven would not sleep in her bed, he couldn't. The scent of her on the sheets drove him crazy, so he slept on the couch, covered by his long, black, leather coat. Raven had switched off the television and was on the brink of sleep. Sleep that had evaded him for days and days — since her disappearance — he could not recall how many. The malt whisky had been a good memory neutralizer.

The edge of somnolence inveigled him to step over the boundary between awareness and drunken unconsciousness and finally he accepted the invitation. His eyes closed.

When his eyes opened an hour later, he could not remember where he was. He rubbed them tiredly, and as the darkened room swam into view, his recollection returned. He moaned softly and looked at the luminous hands of his watch; he had slept just an hour. The hairs rose on the back of his neck as the reason why he had woken so soon dawned on him. Something in the shadows was moving, and whatever it happened to be was darker than the surrounding area.

A slight movement of air rolled past his cheek as the deepening shadow seemed to pull the atmosphere of the room into it. Raven drew his black coat on and rolled quietly off the couch onto the floor. He reached his left hand under the couch and felt the reassuring warmth of the wooden scabbard or saya, which contained his katana. Soundlessly he drew it towards him, his thumb feeling the guard or tsuba and gently pushing it up to release the blade from its sanctuary.

The shadow exploded silently. Blackness, far more profound than the room, filled one corner, and within it he felt sure he glimpsed stars. It was an ephemeral glance though because unexpectedly an entity occluded the view into the depths and Raven surmised that something was coming through the rift. He hoped it was the bat as he rolled to his feet and drew the katana in one fluid movement.

The blade flashed high above his head, ready to strike and the scabbard was presented horizontally across his body in defence.

A figure stepped through, followed by another and Raven swept the blade down.

Lucy's heart was pounding, even though she understood that corporeally she was still in the alternative world. The reason for her excitement was the vision appearing before her. The tiny light had grown into a doorway and that doorway opened out onto her lounge and Raven asleep on her couch. She watched avidly as the portal opened, Raven was awake. She stepped through and Vela was pulled along behind her.

Vela had desperately tried to communicate to Lucy that the plant's stamen had begun to show signs of withdrawing from his mouth, but she had not understood. Now she pulled him through into a strange room, and as he watched her smoky form coalesce, a glittering blade flashed down and cut straight through her.

The attacker, expecting at least some resistance, stumbled forward, and ended up between the two, and face to face with Vela. He could not shout a warning as his jaws were locked onto the wriggling stamen, and it was a battle he was losing.

Vela noticed the man's scabbard held across his chest and with his spare hand grabbed for it. It was pure reflex, Vela had no idea if the few seconds that had passed were enough for him to attain an adequate tangible form, they were, and his fingers wrapped around the wood. This, to his surprise, immediately burst into flame.

Lucy turned towards them and reached out for Raven but Vela screamed through his clenched teeth and shook his head madly. He could tell she did not understand his warning. He threw himself backwards with all his might, dragging Lucy and Raven with him into the dark abyss.

Chapter 15

The King's Man

Sarreg heaved himself onto the girl. An ugly beached whale of blubber crushing a beautiful mermaid. The strange oceanographic analogy slipped into the girl's mind as the Mayor did his best to slip into her. A loud knocking at the door put paid to any chance of him succeeding and she drew a long breath as he rolled off her.

'This had better be of the utmost importance,' he bellowed, drawing his robe around him. He signalled to Wide to open the door and the golem obliged. Standing outside, an embarrassing expression on his face stood a shivering Alayne.

'Sire, I know you instructed me to not disturb you, but...'

'Yes, but?'

'A pigeon has arrived from Marin's Weir, and you told me to tell you immediately we received news from Dainman.'

Sarreg looked at the girl whose colour had returned to normal and lamented, 'Yes, I did. Let me dress. I will be with you once I am clothed,' and looked at Wide who closed the door.

Senator Alayne's thin frame continued shaking even when the door closed on him and he could no longer see Mayor Sarreg and his golem. Nevertheless, within a minute or two the door to the room opened and Wide stepped out, looked up and down the corridor of the inn, and then stood to one side, thereby allowing the mayor to leave the room. Alayne caught a glimpse of the beautiful young woman on the bed who was placing a handful of coins into her purse. She looked up and saw him gawking. He blushed when she winked at him, but he also thought she looked terribly relieved. He might have just annoyed his new benefactor but he had a feeling he had also just made a new friend.

Sarreg climbed into the coach. Its previous owner, Senator Desit no longer had need of such a luxury, and therefore he had sequestrated it and was putting it to good use. The well-sprung vehicle sagged to one side as Wide clambered up to sit next to the coachman who seemed decidedly uncomfortable. The mayor beckoned Alayne to enter and moved over to give the skinny man room. As he did so a flash caught Alayne's eye, and for a moment he imagined that tucked into the enormous cummerbund around Sarreg's waist resided a dagger. It was quite a beautiful dagger. One with a large green stone, a stone that looked very much like jade. Alayne's shivering started again, the jade stone was identical to the one that Senator Desit had in his dagger.

'Are you cold, man?' demanded Sarreg brusquely, 'Each time I see you I wonder if you are feverish. You don't have some sort of ailment do you?' his eyes narrowed.

'No sire,' Alayne mopped his forehead with his sleeve; a cold sweat had broken out on his brow, 'I tend to feel the cold a lot.'

Sarreg felt that something had just happened, the man seemed positively petrified, but he could not fathom out why.

'You should dress warmer man,' he advised. 'Now, give me the message, if you will,' then he rapped the window frame with his knuckles and called out, 'Coachman, to my abode.'

Alayne fumbled in his woollen coat, he was dressed warm enough. He knew that, but fear can make you sweat and shiver too. He hoped Sarreg would not get suspicious, he also hoped he didn't see him ogle the bejewelled dagger tucked barely out of sight at his ample waist. Then he wondered how many people knew of Desit's dagger, he had a horrible feeling that not many did.

'Take your time,' Sarreg complained and Alayne jumped, he had daydreamt for a moment and had completely forgotten what he was searching for. The slip of paper rustled as his fingers closed around it and he let out a long gasp of relief.

'Sorry,' he said as he handed the thin rice-paper over to the mayor.

Sarreg took the flimsy material from him and scanned its contents. A cruel smile formed as his lips moved silently whilst he read the words, 'Good news from Dainman. Davvid could be breaking cover soon. Seems like someone has upset him and he is prepared to risk spending more time away from the sanctuary of my mansion to hunt him,' then his eyes narrowed and his face became grey.

'Are you unwell, Mayor Sarreg?'

Sarreg shook his head, both in reply to the man and in disbelief as he read the final part of the message.

'Snape may be dead. Dainman has heard that he was in Davvid Krell's company when he died.'

'Oh... the poor man,' Alayne wished he could have sounded more sincere but Snape had not been a man he had particularly liked.

'The more remarkable news is that an old friend of mine may have returned from the dead.'

Alayne looked at the mayor and raised his eyebrows sceptically.

Sarreg saw his disbelief, 'Oh yes dear Alayne. Luther Krell, perhaps the most formidable thaumaturgist that ever was has returned.'

Alayne's mouth now opened as his incredulity increased dizzily, 'I thought he was *foreverdead*!'

'So did everyone. I want you to raise all of my followers, all of them. Make sure they bring as many golems as they own. Sequestrate whatever number of draykons and drayks required to transport us all to Marin's Weir. Matters there need to be settled for once and for all.'

Vela felt the plant's stamen snatch away from his mouth and the obsidian vagueness that he had fallen through changed to a swirling green and blue. His eyes fluttered open, the blue resolved into the sky above him, and the green became the leaves of the leather-leaf trees around the glade. He was back. But with whom?

The boy's right hand gripped Lucy's and the left held a wooden scabbard. The scabbard was scorched and he coughed as the acrid smoke caught his breath. Someone on the end of the scabbard coughed too.

'What the fuck?'

Vela released his grip on both Lucy and the scabbard and rolled away quickly, 'Friend Raven?'

Raven staggered to his feet, the scabbard still held in his left hand, but, more importantly to Vela... the katana was still in his right. 'What the fuck?' Raven repeated.

Still lying prone, Lucy moaned and opened her eyes, 'Raven... you silly sod. Give me a hand up.'

The tall man looked as if he had been kicked between the legs. He gasped, 'Lucy?'

'Yes, bloody Lucy, now help me up!'

Raven dropped the katana and scabbard. He launched himself on top of her and grabbed her in a bear-hug, knocking all the wind out of her body. He gasped again, this time he *was* kicked between the legs, or rather, kneed, as she tried to get him off.

'You're crushing me, you lump!'

He rolled onto his side, and although obviously in some discomfort, managed to laugh like a fool, 'It *is* you! I thought...'

'Don't say 'I thought you were dead'. Please do not say that. It reminds me of that bloody film with the guy named Snake something.'

'But what... how...' he pointed at Vela, 'Who?'

She sat up and put a muddy finger to his lips. 'Shh... Let

me explain a few things.'

Raven did not think he could have been shocked anymore. An hour spent sitting with Lucy and Vela flew, whilst they explained the situation and the build-up to their flight between the worlds to get her back home. He cursed vehemently when he understood that by slashing at Lucy with the katana he had spurred Vela into dragging her, and him, back into the void. He was grateful that he had been premature in his attack though, she had not materialised enough. The blade had tasted fresh air only. Vela had frowned when Raven returned the katana to its scabbard, but not before he had touched it to his thumb and let a dribble of blood smear the weapon.

'It's a ninja thing,' Lucy rolled her eyes at Vela, who by now knew better than to ask questions anymore.

They left the clearing as dusk began to settle. The sky changing from a deep pink to a purple glow studded with stars. 'That's Orion,' Raven pointed to an area of the sky.

'So?' Lucy stopped and looked towards the heavens.

'Well, it's the same constellation as we see on *our* Earth.'

'Oh, didn't think of that,' she turned to Vela, 'That's a thought, Vela what's the date?'

'Date?'

'Time of year.'

'Oh, it's vernal equinox,' he explained.

'That means springtime, Luce,' interjected Raven.

She gave him a glance, 'I'm not thick. What year, Vela?'

'Ah, sorry,' the boy replied, 'It's vernal equinox 2000.'

'That is so weird,' she shook her head, 'Why 2000? What happened 2000 years ago?'

'Everyone knows that, friend Lucy,' he looked as if he was admonishing a child, 'It was the first Lustre, of course.'

'And what exactly was the first Lustre?'

The boy shook his head in disbelief, 'When the great flame lit the sky!'

Lucy and Raven exchanged awestruck glances, 'This is getting weirder,' she said and Raven nodded in agreement.

Vela shrugged, 'I thought everyone knew.'

'We do, but we don't call it Lustre. We call it Christmas, because it is the birthday of Jesus Christ.'

'Who is Jesus Christ?' the boy enquired.

The two drayks had settled down for the night and bickered when the three returned to where they were tethered.

'What the hell are those?' Raven's hand went to his sword's handle instinctively. Lucy grabbed his wrist and forced him to keep from withdrawing the blade.

'They are our mounts. Keep that katana sheathed, I don't want you fainting from loss of blood. That damn myth of yours... *the soul of the samurai and my blade must see blood before it can return to its scabbard,*' she mimicked his voice and Vela burst out laughing.

Raven gave the boy a one-fingered salute that Vela just shrugged to, 'It's not a myth, it's a code by which men of honour lived by,' but Raven knew his words were wasted on her.

It was confirmed when she replied, 'If it only has to *see* blood why don't you carry a photograph of the last nose-bleed you had?'

He turned to Vela, 'Would it be much trouble for you to send me back?'

As Vela got ready to explain the complications Lucy threw her arms around Raven, 'Oh you big baby,' then she grabbed his hair and pulled his mouth down onto hers.

Vela coughed and went over to the drayks and began to calm them down. Then he busily set about building a fire and making a campsite for the night.

After a few moments Lucy and Raven strolled in, arm in arm. She hunkered down by the little flames that crackled and sparked as the dry branches caught, 'I'm starving, wish we had a chicken to cook over this.'

Vela gave her some more branches to add to the fire, 'I'll go see what I can do.'

She watched him take the bow and quiver from drayk's webbing and trot off into the trees, 'Be careful!' she shouted as he waved once and disappeared into the woods.

'Nice kid,' Raven commented and sat beside her.

'Certainly saved *my* arse,' she slipped her arms through his and hugged into his side.

Raven watched the sparks swirl and rise up into the dark sky on the invisible thermals of the campfire, 'Three magi arrived on Lustre's Day and thaumaturgy was brought into the world, Vela said. A bit of a coincidence don't you think?'

'I don't want to think about it Rave. It is hard enough to imagine that there could be an infinity of other worlds out there. Let alone ones where the three wise men were magicians that flew down on a space ship, and Jesus never became the saviour. It's too much Raven. My poor old brain is in a big enough mess as it is; I don't need to clutter it anymore with, 'what ifs…''

'What about this Krell guy, we going to pay him a visit?'

She smiled at him, 'Don't think we have to worry about that. He is so far up his own arse with his bloody ego he will come looking for us. He'll probably bring his little friend Davvid Krell too.'

'His friend or his son?'

'His apprentice from what the boy says. This Luther Krell is the bat I saw killing my dad. Davvid is carrying on his tradition. We'll get both of the bastards.'

'What about these Gollums? Thought he was that slimy thing in Lord of the Rings.'

'Raven you can be so thick on times,' she remarked, 'They are called golems. They make them from clay on a wooden sort of frame. Then, through a means I just can get my head around, they capture the essence of someone onto a tile. That tile is put into the golem and they have a ready made, heavyweight, bouncer. Big and strong.'

'Yeah, but still a lump of clay.'

'It's not *just* clay, Raven. They are tough buggers. Oh, I can take one down, but I bet there aren't many on this world that can. Unless they have one of their own of course.'

He raised the sheathed blade up, 'Shouldn't be a problem for this.'

She nodded, 'That'll cut through one like butter, as long as the mage's magic doesn't affect you in any way. It didn't do anything to me but Vela couldn't combat it.'

'Well if it didn't cause you any problems then shouldn't hurt me too much either,' he growled.

She looked silently into the flames and shivered.

'What's the matter?' he asked, concerned.

'I don't know, this place, Vela, us,' she replied and put her head on his arm. 'The Krells aren't the only ones who can use magic. Others here do the same sort of shit. They leech off the people, mostly the weak, the poor, and the ones who cannot fight back. I would like to think when we returned to our own world we wouldn't have anymore 'bats' coming through to bloody haunt us.'

'Didn't Vela say that only the Krells knew about that stinking plant though? If we sort those two out then all our problems are over.'

'Yes, only the Krells,' she whispered, 'and of course, Vela.'

'Ah...'

'Ah... indeed...'

The fox crept downwind of the rabbit, drooling with anticipation of the kill and a stomach full of fresh meat. Its ears flattened and it sniffed the air as it tracked across another spoor. Perhaps an additional hunter was stalking its prey. It growled quietly, deep within its throat; a driblet of saliva dripped off its chin and landed on its paw. The animal moved forward. Hunger was a powerful motivator, even when danger warned it to seek another victim. The trees thinned a little and its jaw shook in excitement as it spied the fat rabbit cropping the grass, totally unaware of its stalker.

Vela nocked an arrow into the small bow and sighted on the big rabbit, it would be more than enough for the three of them. His stomach rumbled as he pulled back the string to his cheek.

With excellent hearing and the keenest sense of smell amongst the many predators within the woods, the fox was high on the food chain but it knew his opponent was just as well equipped but he could not yet see him. He prepared to leap; the rabbit was too much a temptation.

The boy held his breath, brought the point of the arrow inline with the rabbit's ample chest and let fly… just as the boar flew from the bushes at his side and bowled him over.

The arrow missed by a few inches and thudded into a tree. The rabbit dashed away from the commotion made by Vela and the boar and ran straight into the fox's jaws. A quick shake and a snap resulted in a small scream, which died rapidly, cut-off by the fox's grip around the rabbit's throat. It did not bode well to advertise your kill in these woods. The fox glanced at the boar and the boy locked in mortal combat and a satisfaction swept over it. Its senses had been correct. The boar had also been tracking the rabbit, until it caught scent of a larger, more fulsome prey… Vela.

It gripped the dead rabbit well, and turned, its den would be a comfortable place tonight.

Vela's sleeve tore and the boar stepped back with it in its jaws. It worried the piece of cloth for a second or two before realising there was no meat in it. The animal grunted and looked up at the boy lying before it. Vela slowly put a hand into his pocket and gripped the smooth handle of Lucy's knife, all embarrassment he had previously felt about lifting it from her faded. The bow would be no good at this range, now it was the knife and his brains against a pair of deadly tusks and a mouthful of rotten teeth. The boar pawed the ground, Vela's sleeve hung from one of its tusks and it was annoyed, it shook its head and Vela cast his hex.

The material whipped up over the animal's eyes and knotted tight. The boar was confounded and for a moment stood perplexed. Vela withdrew Lucy's knife and flicked open the blade as he rolled quickly towards the animal. As the boar decided at last to move, Vela thrust the blade into its stomach. It slid in with hardly any effort, the blade was so sharp. Even the boar took a second to understand it had been impaled. When Vela drew the knife down its belly, opening its intestines onto the grass, it squealed in pain and astonishment, and then wavered, its legs wobbling. He withdrew the blade and scrambled away as the animal grunted and collapsed.

'Something's coming,' Raven stood up as the two drayks both turned towards the wood. He watched them sniff the air, open, and close their beak-like mouths, 'Dunno what, but they're excited about it, anyway.'

'Hey, friends Lucy and Raven!' Vela called as he stepped out from the line of trees. Raven saw him struggling to drag an object towards them and ran to help.

'Shit, what you got here?' Raven grabbed one of the boar's legs and between them, they carried it to the campfire, 'You're not going to believe this Lucy, he's caught a bloody pig!'

'It's not a bloody pig, friend Raven. It is a wild boar. Well it was wild when I gutted it. Now its supper.'

'Nice one, Vela,' Lucy searched her pockets for her knife.

'Here,' he handed her the weapon, 'I, umm... borrowed it.'

'No sweat. Just as well you did, by the looks of things,' she indicated the gaping wound in the animal's belly, 'I told you it was sharp, didn't I?'

She started skinning the animal and Vela threw the unusable pieces to the drayks. The two mounts snatched them up greedily and ate with gusto. Raven added more wood to the fire whilst Lucy speared a generous sized steak with a small branch and balanced it over the flames. Within a minute or two, the campsite was filled with the delicious aroma of roasting boar.

'I do love a barbeque,' Raven commented then licked his lips, 'I don't suppose you brought any beer too, did you, Vela?'

Miko contemplated smashing the tile and just jumping on the next ship that was due to leave Marin's Weir on the evening's tide. The militiaman's games had cost him any chance he had of following the two friends. He knew the Krells would be unforgiving, and better to leave Pieter with the problem than to have to confront it himself. He was just about to put his plan into action and make his way surreptitiously onboard a sailing vessel when a pair of circling drayks caught his eye. He was unsure... but there was a good possibility their riders were the two fugitives. Miko turned away from the docks and made off at an easy lope towards Jakob's warehouse, hoping he would yet be able to salvage things.

'Arr, you do be a good girl, and tomorrow I'll bring you a nice apple, so I will,' Jakob patted Molly's neck and she nuzzled him in return. 'Settle down now then, see you on the morrow.'

He closed the pen's gate and limped towards the warehouse's main door, took one last look around and then slid the large wooden bolt and pulled the door open. It opened forcefully and for a moment, he thought the wind had caught it, but only for a moment. The fist that caught him a fierce blow just below his left eye convinced him otherwise and he staggered back and landed on his rump. As his eyes fought to focus on his attacker he heard him chuckle.

'Okay, old man, where have they gone?'

Jakob let his head loll to one side as he feigned unconsciousness. He had determined that anyone capable of hitting an old man like that would not qualm at doing who knows what to a young boy and a woman. His pretence was short-lived however as a boot struck him in his arthritic hip. He yelled out in pain and tried to roll away.

'Not as senseless as it seems eh?' laughed Jakob's assailant.

'What the bloody 'ell you want!' Jakob cried holding his injured hip.

'One more chance then I'll start on you with these,' replied the man and he drew two mean-looking knives from their sheaths.

Jakob looked past his assailant in the hope someone was within earshot. The track leading up to his warehouse was devoid of any traffic and the main road was too far for his voice to carry. The ruffian stepped closer to him and tapped the edges of his weapons together, the sound made the old man wince.

'You be speaking 'bout the two lads that hired my drayks?'

'Two *lads*, eh?' he stooped closer to Jakob and pressed the point of one of his weapons into the old man's hip.

Jakob gasped in pain, 'Okay, okay, one was a woman. They done hired my drayks for to go to Fivewinds. Reckon they be there for a few days.'

Miko studied the old man for a few moments. It didn't seem as if he was lying but he was unsure. At least he had a link now to their whereabouts. Perhaps if he remained here with the old fool the Krells could interrogate him when they arrived.

'Get into one of your stalls and quit whimpering. We'll

wait for some friends and see what they think of your story,' he said and prodded Jakob towards an empty pen.

Jakob crawled into the straw-laden stall and collapsed. The pain in his face was nothing in comparison to the profound misery coming from his hip. He hoped Vela and Lucy would get back before his attacker's friends arrived. Perhaps the two of them would be able to conquer him. If they arrived too late then they would have to confront who knows how many. Jakob nestled himself into the hay and cursed his age and infirmity, knowing that if only he had been forty years younger he would have made mincemeat of the bastard. His guard sat opposite him and grinned.

The old man watched as Miko sheathed one of his knives and then unrolled his blanket bundle. A wine bottle and leather package fell out. He reclined onto the woollen cloth and opened the leather pack and Jakob's nose twitched when he caught the smell of the local inn's famous bread. The mercenary cut a hunk of bread off the loaf and crammed it into his mouth, and then delving deeper into the pack found a slab of cheese and bit into it. Jakob's mouth watered. He hadn't eaten since mid-day and his stomach rumbled. Miko glanced at him when the sound of the old man's stomach rumbled again but he didn't offer any food. Instead, he uncorked the wine with his yellowed teeth and took a long swig. Red wine flowed down his chin and ran onto the front of his vest, adding yet another stain to the soiled garment.

'Hungry, old man?'

Jakob eyed his attacker suspiciously. He was hungry but did not want to admit it so he clamped his jaws shut and left the question unanswered.

'I take that as no then. Good, because you weren't getting any grub from me you old goat,' retorted Miko.

Jakob nodded knowingly to himself, he knew that was coming.

Miko stowed away his gear but left the blanket on the floor. He wiped his blade along his trouser leg and stood up. Next he wandered around the warehouse until he found what he was looking for; a coil of rope. He returned to Jakob and indicated that the old man should turn around. Reluctantly, Jakob did. Miko looped the rope around the older man's shoulders and pulled it tight. Then pulled him to an upright wooden post and threw the rope around that too. Within a minute, he had trussed the old man up like a chicken ready for the oven.

'Now I can get some sleep without worrying about you, you old fool.'

Jakob struggled slightly to test his restraints, they would not be easy to escape from he realised, 'So, *you* can sleep but what about me?' he moaned, 'I can't sleep sitting up like this, my bones are old.'

'Then stay awake,' snarled Miko, 'But waken me and you will be very sorry you did,' then he pulled his blanket over him and dropped off to sleep.

Some time later Molly snorted softly and Jakob raised his head slowly. His neck felt as stiff as the old bow he had given Vela, and as curved. His assailant was snoring sonorously, and Jakob wondered if it was his snoring or Molly's fretfulness that had disturbed him as she shook her head and stomped the ground.

Then another sound impinged on his awareness, the call of a drayk. Vela and Lucy were back!

Yet again, the old man tested his bonds and found them unforgiving. He had barely managed to loosen them enough from around his wrists to allow his circulation to flow. Escape would be impossible but perhaps he could warn his two friends. Holding his breath he listened carefully as two drayks alighted in his corral. He hoped they would approach the warehouse quietly. If they could enter and see him bound before the ruffian awoke they might have a chance to over-power him, he would still be drowsy. On the other hand, should he shout a warning to them so they could enter already prepared, but then the assailant would awaken too and perhaps extract revenge upon his old body before the two could intervene. He was torn between the two choices.

Low voices could be heard outside and then footfalls, they were at the rear door! He glanced at the sleeping mercenary again and decided to shout out a warning.

'Vela, Lucy, there is someone here, be careful!' Jakob shouted, and Miko woke up then jumped to his feet. He glanced around, his one eye red from sleep. Drawing his two weapons, he crouched ready for attack. 'Now prepare yourself for a beating, rogue,' mocked Jakob.

Miko snarled and lashed out with his foot, giving the old man's head a glancing blow.

The rear door burst open and a massive golem strode into the warehouse. It made straight for Miko who launched a flurry of blows against it with his short-swords. The blades skittered across its vast chest and chips of clay flew off but it ignored them and scooped the man up in a powerful bear-hug. Miko gasped as his arms where pinned to his sides and the wind was driven from his body. The bones of his rib-cage creaked and red spots began to fill his vision.

In a last desperate effort he butted the creature on its irregular nose and was awarded with a gash across his forehead, which spurted blood that ran down into his eye, blinding him.

'That will do, Axe,' Miko heard the voice as darkness reached for him, 'Drop him, he is one of ours.' Then all pressure was released and he collapsed to his knees in front of the enormous clay figure. His breath came in great wheezing gulps as he tried to get oxygen into his lungs.

A moment or two later a strong hand went under his arm

and helped him to his feet. His head cleared and he wiped his watering eye with the back of a grubby hand. Pieter stood before him with a smile on his face, 'See, short swords just don't do the trick.'

Miko pushed him away roughly and glared at the golem. Deep score marks were across its chest but the damage was minimal, he had to admit to himself that Pieter was probably right. To take on a monster such as that would need a heavier weapon, a much heavier weapon.

Two more men came into his field of view and he recognised them as the Krells. The older of the two called the golem named Axe to his side and it was then he noticed the child-like figure of Gar, 'What...' he began to ask but Pieter stopped him with a warning hand.

'Best if you don't ask.'

'Report, where are the two we seek?' Davvid Krell demanded brusquely.

Miko baulked at the abrupt tone of Davvid's voice but another glance at Pieter told him not to enrage the man, 'The old man hired them some drayks. He told me they would be away for days but his lie has just been exposed. He thought you were they. It is possible they must be due back anytime.'

'So, you lost them?' Davvid sneered.

'No, not really. I was prevented from following them by a militiaman and his five troopers.'

Davvid turned to Luther, 'Sarreg's men.'

'Yes, not a worry for now. We shall deal with Vela and the woman first before concerning ourselves with the militia. Then I think we shall have to pay our fat friend a visit,' Luther smiled.

Luther approached Jakob and stooped down near him. The old man's head was lowered and his breathing was heavy. The mage paused for a moment, then placed a hand under Jakob's chin, and raised his head up. A bruise bore testament to Miko's earlier attack and a red scuffmark showed where the more recent kick had landed.

'Ah Jakob, you old ruffian, forever being the thorn in someone's shoe. When are you going to understand your days of soldiering are long, long past?'

Jakob's eyes opened slowly, 'And what do you know of my soldiering?'

'Oh, I know enough. Jakob Gawen, servant to the King,' replied Luther with a knowing smile.

'The days of Kings are long past too. How do you know me?'

'Gentlemen, let me introduce you to a King's man, a paladin,' he glowered at Miko, 'A man who would not betray his friends to escape a beating. Even if his bones were brittle and his frame wracked with ague such as they are, he would hold his tongue.'

'That old cod-fish a paladin?' sneered Miko.

Luther freed Jakob's bonds with a cursory wave of his hand then helped him up.

'Jakob served the King decades before the Saffron War. He trained many of the men that fought the yellow skins. He probably would have gone with them too, if not for this,' and he lifted Jakob's right hand up and opened his fingers, all except his index and middle, which were missing.

Pieter stepped forward, 'The forks? Just how old are you Jakob?' he turned to Miko, 'He must have served on *The Gazelle* to have that done to him.'

Jakob pulled his hands away from Luther and scrutinised the mage's face, 'Who are you?'

'Oh course you don't recognise me. I bear Militiaman's Snape's form, but you are speaking to Luther Krell.'

Jakob stepped back and gasped, 'You butcher!'

'Come, come, Jakob. You are alive… are you not? Many of your ship-mates lived, did they not?'

'And many more did *not* live. Including my King!' spat

Jakob and stepped forward, Axe restrained him.

'All things pass, including monarchies, including us...' Luther replied.

Miko looked at Luther Krell; confusion reigned supreme upon his scarred face, 'What was *The Gazelle*?'

'Have you no inclination of your country's history?' enquired Luther, '*The Gazelle* was King Roan's flagship. When his decree to curb the use of magic instigated the mages' revolt, and his men were overwhelmed, he fled Fivewinds and put out to sea on *The Gazelle*.'

'His men were *not* overwhelmed, they were slaughtered. The majority of them were crushed in their barracks by witchcraft,' Jakob interrupted.

'Witchcraft? Sorcery perhaps, but not witchcraft, you know no woman wields magic. And we did what we had to do, Jakob.'

The old man sneered, 'What you had to do,' he turned to Miko, 'They pulled the stone parapets down on sleeping men. They dropped golems onto *The Gazelle* from a dozen draykons. They stayed well away from the fight themselves though; no thaumaturgist dirtied his hands that day, though they *were* soaked in blood. Any soldier left alive was made an example of. Swordsmen lost their hands. Archers lost their fingers. King Roan lost his life.'

'The monarchy ended and the senate began. The examples we made that day curbed any future rebellion.'

'Rebellion?' Jakob gasped, 'You were the bastard rebels, not us.'

'And who placed Roan in his position of power? Who gave him the right to censure our thaumaturgic art? We gave the people the chance to choose who should rule,' Luther answered angrily.

'Mages did. Mages gave the people the choice. But show me a position of office not held by a mage or one of his toadies,' Jacob retorted.

'We are the obvious choice...' and Luther shrugged his shoulders, 'But enough. What's gone has gone.' He frowned at Miko, 'Torturing this man will not bring forth answers. Torture his friends... now that is a different matter.'

'The *paladin*,' Miko used the name like a swearword, 'has no friends here.'

Luther shook his head slowly, 'He has one,' and then he walked around the warehouse towards the stall that contained Molly.

Chapter 16

'If this wasn't so Goddamn cool I'd be shitting myself, but this rocks man!' yelled Raven excitedly in Lucy's ear. He clung to her, his arms wrapped around her waist and his knees firmly clamped onto the drayk's flanks.

'Don't shout, you silly sod. I'm not deaf and your big gob is right next to my ear.'

He snuffled her ear and poked his tongue in, 'And it's a gorgeous ear too,' he murmured and laughed when she squirmed.

'Don't do that! You know it sends shivers up my spine.'

'Yes, of course I do. That's why I did it,' he kissed her neck.

'Wasn't last night enough for you, bloody oaf?' she squirmed again.

'That was last night,' he waved a hand around, 'This is the morning, and what a great morning it is too.'

She shrugged him away, 'You're embarrassing the kid,' and she waved at Vela.

Vela smiled shyly back at the two, 'Not far now.'

Lucy looked over the drayk's head and recognised Marin's Weir in the distance as the taller houses broke through the early morning mist. The sun had risen and already its golden rays had broken through in places, splashing the town with swathes of colour. Jakob's warehouse came into view. Lucy nudged the drayk with her left knee and pulled the reins gently. The animal snickered softly and she patted its neck as it turned slowly to the left and descended. Vela followed them as they spiralled down towards the corral. Suddenly he whistled and gestured to the three drayks already tethered in the compound below.

Lucy nodded and then pointed them out to Raven, 'Looks like we've got company.'

'Great, things just keep on getting better. Can I use the katana?'

'You're just like a big kid, Raven,' she scolded him, 'Make sure you don't stick me with the bloody thing.'

'There's only one thing I'll stick you with Luce...'

She shrugged him off as he tried to squeeze her again, 'Get your act together Raven. These people mean business. Their golems are bloody tough so do not let them grab you. Keep them at a distance.'

The two drayks fluttered down around the back of the warehouse. She decided not to land in the corral and disturb the three animals there; although they did turn and look at the new arrivals they did not give a challenging call.

Vela stepped up to Lucy and unlatched his bow, bending the weapon with his knee he nocked the bowstring into place and selected an arrow from his quiver.

'At least three in there with Jakob. If they're after us they might have golems. I can use this on a man but it won't do much damage to one of those monsters,' the boy explained.

'Yeah, we know, Vela. When we go in, Raven and I will go for the clay-heads, you take out the mages, or whoever makes a move on us, okay?'

'Okay, friend Lucy.'

Raven gripped Lucy's arm, 'What the fuck is that noise?'

The piercing cry and shouting coming from within the barn made her shiver, 'No idea but someone is getting hurt, let's do it Rave.'

Raven kicked open the rear door to the warehouse and stepped in, 'Holy shit...' he gasped as he saw his first golem. Vela appeared at Raven's shoulder and sighted the bow on Luther Krell. Axe stepped away from Molly, its blood-soaked fingers flexing. Raven's eyes narrowed when they saw the marks on the animal's back. For some reason the golem had been digging its finger's into the animal's flesh. It was Molly that they had heard screaming and Jakob's raised voice.

Luther raised a hand towards Vela and Raven but the boy let fly with the arrow. Molly's screaming was nothing compared to Luther Krell's as the arrow flew across the barn, pierced his hand, and pinned it to the wooden beam that ran up into the roof.

Davvid shouted to Gar and then ran over to Luther and supported the mage as his legs buckled. The little golem stood steadfastly between the Krells and Raven and cast a hex at the big man, Raven looked at the golem quizzically 'Don't think it will work on me little fella,' he said and drew the katana in one swift move up to his right, and then brought it down diagonally across Gar's neck. The golem's head flew off and tumbled to the ground to roll to the feet of Pieter who looked at Raven with respect.

Axe lumbered towards the two, arms outstretched. Raven brought the katana up to his left shoulder and gripped it with both hands as the golem drew near, 'Watch those two, Vela.''

The boy had already fitted another arrow to the bow and now drew it taut. 'Don't move guys, Vela can be a might twitchy,' said Raven sliding his right foot forward and bending his knees slightly as the golem closed on him. 'Best you back off, big guy,' he warned as the golem came within the katana's range and didn't stop. He brought the blade flashing down and took the giant's right leg off at the knee. It collapsed at his feet but still scrabbled towards him until Raven lopped off its head as well, 'Bah... this is too easy!'

Luther pushed Davvid away and shouted at him, 'Get them!'

Davvid grabbed Jakob and pulled him towards him, holding him in the line of fire. He signed a hex and Raven laughed, 'Doesn't work on me pal.'

Davvid smiled and turned to the two mercenaries, 'Now earn your pay. The boy won't interfere.'

As Miko drew his weapons Raven whispered to Vela, 'Okay kid, shoot the bastard with one eye,' he waited and then, 'Umm, anytime today kid.' Then glanced over at the boy who stood frozen like a marble statue, 'Shit,' he groaned.

The main door to the warehouse flew open and Lucy dived in sweeping Miko off his feet and causing him to lose one of his short swords as he fell heavily, 'That's evened it up a bit,' she said, throwing a leg-lock around his neck and gripping his other sword-arm tightly. As he struggled, she tightened her legs until he gasped for breath, his eyes rolling up into his head, 'Don't take too long though, honey, we got company coming up the main road,' she warned.

'Shouldn't take long,' Raven eyed Pieter, 'Want to leave while you can, pal?'

Pieter reached behind his back and withdrew the sword from his blanket-roll; it was a close match for Raven's katana. He stepped into a defensive stance, blade held out, and point facing Raven, 'I think not, do *you* want to leave?'

Raven raised an eyebrow, admiring the blade, which could have almost been a katana too. In addition, the old man seemed to know how to use it.

'Too late for that, my friend. The blade is drawn, now it waits for blood,' he answered.

Pieter nodded, '*Ken ore, ya mo tsuki…*'

Raven gasped, 'With swords broken and without an arrow.'

'You understand The Yellow's language,' Pieter stated as he began to circle the room, the blade held unwaveringly in front of him, 'You look too young to have seen the Saffron Wars.'

'Don't know what the Saffron Wars was, pal but I do understand some Japanese *and* a little Chinese,' Raven manoeuvred for space, he didn't want the grey-haired mercenary to box him into a tight corner.

'Rave, what the hell are you talking about?' demanded Lucy as Miko finally passed out and dropped his sword.

'He just quoted an old samurai saying. It's an honour thing, Luce. You fight until the last arrow has flown, till all swords are broken, or until one dies or surrenders.'

'This samurai bullshit is going to get you killed you idiot. Vela shoot the old sod in the chest.'

'Vela is slightly incapacitated at the moment, Lucy,' Raven answered not daring to take his eyes off Pieter. He watched the stealthy movements of the mercenary, the way he placed his feet, the angle he held his sword. Raven knew he was facing a person who had been trained in some form of Kendo. The sword his opponent wielded was no wooden bokken though, but had to be a variation of his katana, and it was well looked after. The large hurricane-lamp, high in the ceiling, gleamed in the reflection of the curved, oiled blade as Pieter stepped forward, and Raven recognised it as an okuri-ashi or gliding motion. The mercenary's blade slowly rose upwards to shoulder height, into the jodan, or high stance. Raven moved slightly forward and to his right and mimicked Pieter's stance, both swords held high created an arch of glittering razor-sharp metal.

The silence that fell upon the warehouse was eerie as the two men stared into each other's eyes. Then Pieter moved, his body uncoiled like a spring as he quickly stepped forward and closed the gap between them, his sword flashed down towards Raven's head.

Lucy gasped as she thought Raven had left his parry too late but the big man cried out, 'Kiai!' and flowed to his right as his sword blurred to intercept Pieter's attack. The clash of the two blades rang through the warehouse and incandescent sparks flew from their point of impact and ran down Raven's katana as Pieter stepped past, his blade sliding down to stop at

Raven's tsuba. Raven rolled his katana around and Pieter's weapon flew away from the guard. He carried the sweeping action onwards until his katana streaked towards the old man's unprotected back. But Pieter was no fool, his own weapon, carried by the momentum, swept up over and behind his head and hung vertical. The two blades thundered into each other again and lightning sparked from their encounter once more. Pieter pivoted on the ball of his left foot and swung his right leg around swiftly, aiming to sweep Raven's legs from beneath him, but the big man had seen the move coming and jumped back just in time.

They circled each other warily. Both men acknowledging the other's moves as being nothing other than professional. Two samurai, from two different worlds, and two different times, both bonded by their sense of honour. Raven nodded to Pieter and the old man nodded back as he changed stance, left leg forward, knees slightly bent and his sword held horizontal over his head. The tip pointing at Raven's chest. Raven slid his right foot forward slightly and with the pommel of the katana level with his navel tipped the point up towards Pieter's face. Yet again, the two stared into each other's eyes as they waited for an opening and built up their Ki, or inner energy, life force, so that the attack would be unstoppable. This time Raven moved first, he pushed off with his right leg and lunged forward. The tip of his blade accelerated towards Pieter's throat as the mercenary brought his curved blade down and turned side on to the attack. Raven's katana was flicked away and he spun continuing around to his right, ducking as he did so. Pieter's weapon streaked through the air where Raven's head had just been, but now he stood side on to his opponent and his sword was slow to come up to parry the sweeping slice of Raven's katana as it whistled through the air and cut through Pieter's leather jacket at shoulder height. A spurt of crimson blood flew from the neat gash in the leather and Pieter grunted in surprise.

They moved apart and contemplated each other. Raven glanced down at his blade, which was filmed with red. With a sharp twist of his wrist, he flicked the blood from the blade; it splattered against the partitioning of one of the stalls, a broken line of scarlet that soaked into the old wood.

'Leave, my sword is quenched, take your honour with you intact,' Raven offered.

Pieter pulled the leather thong from his grey ponytail and tied it quickly around his right upper arm, never taking his eyes from Raven's face, 'But *my* sword still thirsts,' he smiled.

Luther Krell had snapped the arrow shaft and pulled his hand free; he sank to the floor and nursed the bloodied hand to his chest. Davvid looked to him for counsel but the mage was in too much pain to offer any. Davvid started to raise a hand.

'Don't even think about it, bat boy...' Lucy warned and tossed one of Miko's swords into the air and deftly caught it by the blade. She stood ready to throw it the mage.

He sneered, 'And if you miss?' he manoeuvred Jakob around to a more shielding position.

'I don't usually, but I'm willing to chance it. Are you?'

He dropped his hand to his side and pulled Jakob in closer to him, just as the crash of blades sounded again and everyone's eyes flew back to the duel between the two swordsmen.

Raven watched the mercenary carefully wondering how he would attack next. High, low, or a thrust?

The answer was soon to follow as Pieter sped in to attack, his sword held low. As if in slow motion Raven watched as the dust and small particles of straw kicked up by the mercenary's soft boots rose into the air as he charged forward. His sword slashed towards Raven's legs. Raven stepped back, lowered his blade to protect his lower limbs, just as Pieter twisted violently, and unexpectedly turned the low sweep into an upward spiralling thrust for his face. His katana flew up but a second too slow and Pieter's sword flashed past his face and the guard smashed into his jaw. He felt warm liquid flow down his chin and tasted the coppery flavour of blood in his mouth as he locked Pieter's sword-arm to his shoulder with his left hand. He felt the mercenary clamp a vice-like grip on his own right hand and they stood face to face for a moment each cancelling out the other's struggle. Then Raven smashed his forehead into the mercenary's face, breaking both their holds and causing the man to stagger back blood streaming from his nose. Pieter fell backwards as Raven moved forwards with his katana coming up for a killing blow. Instead of the old man collapsing onto his rear end, he palmed the ground with his left hand and twisted in the air to land back on his feet, his sword thrust low, aimed at Raven's stomach. The katana was yet again too slow to be able to parry the thrust and Raven had to side step. The sword ripped through his leather coat and he felt a sting as it skimmed over his midriff. Pieter was slightly off balance and dazed by the blow to his nose and unable to stop his forward movement, which meant once again his back was exposed to Raven's blade. This time it was his turn to be too slow with an overhead parry and the whistling arc of metal tore through his leather jerkin high up near his left shoulder blade. Once again, blood spurted up from the wound and the old man roared as he spun around sweeping low for Raven's legs. His sword bit into the fleshy mound of Raven's left thigh and he gripped the wound and stepped back, swearing vehemently.

Both men were panting now, perspiration streamed down their faces and mingled with the blood. Pieter flicked the blood from his blade and smiled at Raven when it splattered across the line of his own which was slowly drying on the wooden partition, 'Now both our blades are slaked of their thirst,' he coughed and spat out a mouthful of blood.

'Then why don't you boys kiss and make up?' Lucy growled.

'Your woman gives good advice. I have no desire to slay an honourable warrior,' Pieter said but still fixing Raven with his unwavering stare.

Raven sighed, 'She's not my woman, she's my girlfriend and I wouldn't annoy her if I were you.' Then he lowered his sword, swept it out to the right and bowed to Pieter, keeping his eyes on the man all the time. He felt a feeling of camaraderie when the old mercenary did the same and looked away from Raven's face. Pieter watched quizzically as Luther Krell pulled a small earthenware tile from his sleeve and flourished a sign upon it.

Jakob saw the movement too and thrust Davvid aside whilst yelling a warning, 'Krell is casting!'

Lucy, twisting around in one fluid movement, hefted the short-sword at Davvid's head, it spun end over flashing end and then the heavy pommel struck the man fully in the face. He dropped like a stone as Jakob swung an arthritic fist into Luther Krell's face.

In the same instance, most of the rear of the warehouse's wooden wall splintered and smashed open as Luther's seventeen golems battered their way in.

With Davvid unconscious, Vela was set free and he gawked at the chaos unfolding before him, 'Lucy, Raven... what shall I do? We can't fight this many!'

Lucy ran over to Jakob and pulled him off Luther, she struck the mage with her elbow and he folded like a wet rag to the floor, 'Vela, shoot the damn lamp out, we're leaving, there's more coming up the main road. Get out the back door, quickly!'

She hesitated for a moment, torn between giving Krell the

coup de grace and helping Jakob. The decision was taken out of her hands as the first of the golems reached for her. She caught its hand and pulled it towards her and upwards then thrust her elbow under the joint and cracked it. The arm fractured then came away. If it had been a human, the excruciating pain would have stopped it but the animated clay monster did not flinch, it just threw a pile-driving blow to her head with its other arm. Lucy ducked beneath the blow and swept the golem's legs from under it with her arm. It clattered to the floor and she followed it down and dealt it a crushing blow to the skull.

Jakob pulled her to one side as another giant reached for her. Its outstretched arm flew away as a flash of metal cut through it. She looked up and Pieter offered her a hand, 'Yes, I agree, it's time to leave. Mind if I come with you?' His grizzled tanned face split into a smile.

As she sprung to her feet, aided by the mercenary, Vela's arrow demolished the lamp and darkness filled the barn with even more chaos. Pieter and Lucy hand in hand stumbled towards Raven and Vela who were fighting a retreating battle against the encroaching golems, whilst Jakob freed Molly and encouraged her to leave with a slap on her rump. Raven's sword hissed like a demented snake and bits of terracotta flew like shrapnel. Pieter spun around, in one swift movement swept his blade upwards, and beheaded a golem that stumbled from the darkness towards them. Then they were through and Lucy grabbed Vela, 'Let's get out, come on quick, out, out!' She dragged them to the rear door that was now hanging off its hinges.

The front of the warehouse shook as the doors burst open and a compliment of militiamen stormed in with sabres drawn and torches held high. The flickering torches danced a macabre fandango of shadows on the ruined walls of the barn as the golems turned their attentions to the new arrivals. The clatter of steel on clay combined with the screams of pain as some of the less fortunate militiamen were torn limb from limb. From behind his men, Militiaman Dainman pointed at the Krells, 'Two men seize those mages, you others form a defensive wall, hold back those golems… now!'

Lucy and Raven took one last look at the hellish scene of severed limbs, flesh and clay, blood and smashed terracotta mingling with the straw covered floor, turned, and left.

'Is there anywhere safe we can hide?' She asked.

'Why bloody well hide, Lucy?' Raven looked at her with an astounded expression as she dragged him away from the warehouse, 'We were kicking their damn asses!'

'Kicking their asses… yeah right, Rave,' she sighed, 'We took a few of them down but we were slightly outnumbered don't you think?'

They ran into the fringe of the woods and Jakob stopped them, 'We can go to my house, the old woman won't like it, but…' He shrugged and breathed a sigh of relief as he saw Molly cantering away towards his home.

'Won't they come looking for us there?'

Jakob shook his head, 'Them there militiamen will take care of the Krells. Don't see why they'd want anything from us.'

She looked at him, undecided.

Pieter touched her arm, 'I noticed their leader at the inn, and I fear he has had you under watch since you entered the town. Perchance he knew the Krells were hunting you… as he was hunting the Krells.'

'And as you were hunting us, too.'

Pieter shrugged, 'Nothing personal was meant, it was merely employment. Poverty brings strange bedfellows.'

'He did accept my truce, Lucy,' Raven stepped between them, 'and I believe him to be a man of honour. Man's character is his fate. Herakleitos said that, amongst other things.'

'Christ on a crutch, Rave,' she snarled at him, 'This bloody honour code thing of yours, and your Greek philosophy, I'm sick of it. Where is the honour in robbing a man of his life, and then stealing his soul too? Where does honour belong in watching someone burn from the inside out, so that you can steal their life-force just to add it to their fucking clay monsters? What honour did my father feel? I'd rather be poor than share a bed with the Krells.'

'Your father fell prey to them?' Pieter asked.

Lucy's dark look answered him.

'I have dishonoured myself,' Pieter stated and swiftly pulled his sword from his pack and deftly spun it around to offer the handle to Lucy whilst he knelt before her, 'I am ronin. My family is no more, my clan is no more, I am the last. Should you wish to command me I am at your service. Should you wish my life as some recompense for your father, then death by your hand would restore my honour.'

'You're just as bad as that idiot,' she glared from Pieter to Raven, then pushed his sword back, 'Put that away before you poke someone's eye out.'

'As you command me,' Pieter said solemnly and stood up, returning the sword to its place behind his back, 'Friend Lucy.'

'Crap, another... friend this, friend that.' She glanced at Vela and Jakob.

Raven smiled and slapped Pieter on the back, 'Welcome aboard Pieter. If ronin means the same here as in my world then you'll be master-less no more,' then he held up a hand to hide his other one and pointed at Lucy, 'But now you'll have a mistress instead who'll break your bloody balls... I should know,' he whispered.

Pieter just shrugged as if what would be would be.

'So, do we spoil my old woman's day and go to my house?' asked Jakob.

'I would rather not, Jakob,' she shook her head, 'It's too risky. We know the Krells want us and perhaps the militia do too. We need to find somewhere else.'

Vela tugged at Lucy's sleeve, 'Remember you asked if there was any authority, any police we could go to?'

She nodded, 'Yes, go on.'

'Marin's Weir is run by corrupt officials; they turn a blind eye to The Krells and their like. However, Fivewinds is a major city. It is the capital city, the senate sits there and Mayor Roget Gorman is their appointed legislator. He is the mayor of Fivewinds, we could petition him to impeach the two criminals and bring them to justice. But we'd have to get to Fivewinds and get to see him ourselves. I'm not saying there isn't corruption within the government there too, but we would have a public hearing if our petition was granted.'

'That could be done,' interrupted Pieter, 'There's a ship sailing on this evening's tide. Its first port of call is Fivewinds. We could be there in less than two days; all we have to do is embark without being seen.'

'I'll go home friends. My wife does worry something terrible. I'll go home, but you all take care. Just because Fivewinds has a senate doesn't mean it isn't as rotten with thieves as the Weir. I'm too old to fight anyway, I'd just be a sack 'o bones for you to look after,' Jakob's rheumy eyes watered as he bid his farewells.

Pieter bowed low, one leg held straight before him and his right hand held over his heart, 'I salute you, Paladin Gawen, King's man, good health and good speed.'

The old man struggled to reciprocate but Pieter stopped him, 'You need not bow before me, Jakob. I do not merit your respect.'

Lucy, Raven and Vela all bid their goodbyes; Lucy kissed the old man on his leathery cheek, the rasp of his stubble grating her face, 'Don't stay at your house Jakob, please, just in case someone does come visit you. Take your wife away from here.'

He nodded once, put a gnarled hand to her cheek and then with an extravagant genuflection, which must have cost him a deal of pain, he bowed before them all and then made his way along the tree line until he disappeared from their sight.

'A fine old man,' acknowledged Raven.

'Yes, friend Raven, and a secret man too. In all the time I have stayed beneath his roof, I never knew he was a paladin. I only knew him as Jakob the mule-skinner,' Vela shook his head.

Lucy put her arm around the boy, 'Don't worry, kid, he'll be okay.'

'I hope you're right, Lucy, I really do.'

I hope so too Vela, she thought as the ragged band of misfit friends made their stealthy way through the outskirts of the woods and down to the river and the promise of a boat to Fivewinds.

Miko's eye fluttered open and he blinked it rapidly whilst trying to focus on the rotund object that lay close to his face. The tears from the dusty grit made his vision waver until finally, the object swam into view and he saw it was the head of a soldier. The soldier's eyes were closed and his bloodied mouth open in a silent scream. Miko pushed himself upright and the head rolled away, the man's body was nowhere to be seen. He felt about for his swords as he stared around at the slaughter, which encompassed him. Limbs, both flesh and clay, lay strewn about the place like discarded toys from some child's tantrum. Four golems, two of which were badly battered and cracked, stood like sculptured nightmares. Drenched in blood, pieces of unidentifiable human flesh hung from them like ribbons and Miko felt his stomach heave.

Behind them lay the two figures of the mages, either dead or knocked senseless. He no longer cared. *He* was alive and that was all that mattered. Keeping a close watch on the golems, he slowly backed away from them and exited the warehouse. As he was about to turn a hand gripped his ankle and he yelped in dismay.

'Help me,' a blood-soaked face stared up at him as he wrenched his leg free from Militiaman Dainman's grip.

A smile spread across Miko's cruel mouth and his yellow teeth gave him an almost feral look, 'My friend the militiaman.'

Dainman coughed up a gobbet of blood, which sprayed onto the mercenary's boot. Miko's grin spread even wider. He glanced around quickly, 'Of course I'll help you, militiaman, but there is the matter of my dirty boot. Perhaps you could clean it for me first?'

Militiaman Dainman's left hand was crushed and his right arm almost wrenched from his shoulder socket but he attempted to move the ruined hand onto Miko's boot although the pain drew curses from him.

'No, no...' admonished Miko, 'You'll make it worse. Perhaps if you lick it off?'

'I can pay you,' groaned Dainman, 'Help me please.'

'Yes, yes all in good time,' Miko nodded, enjoying himself immensely, 'First the boot. Then you can pay me.'

The militiaman struggled painfully to prop himself up and then glanced imploringly at Miko.

'Go on!'

As Dainman's tongue cleaned the blood and dust off Miko's boot the mercenary drew his short sword and thrust it down into the base of the man's skull. Dainman grunted quietly, almost a sigh, as if grateful for the release from the pain he was in.

'There, what use was your sabre against my short-sword then, eh?' Miko laughed and kicked the dead man out of his way and left the barn.

The three draykons and accompanying drayks, which

were circling to land, stopped him in his tracks.

Two crossbow bolts thudded into the dusty earth at his feet. Miko, dropping his sword, raised his hands swearing softly as the contingent of Sarreg's forces landed.

'I hope they didn't see that,' he groaned quietly as the group of militiamen, golem-handlers and golems approached; Sarreg brought up the rear, flanked by Wide and Alayne.

'Quick they're inside. I did what I could to help the militia but their golems were too strong. There was nothing more I could do; I've come out to call for help!' Miko grovelled to the militia as Sarreg pushed his way to the front.

'The Krells?' puffed Sarreg, his red face beaded with sweat, 'Do you mean the Krells?'

'Yes sir, they're inside, but there are still four golems protecting them. I barely got out with my life. I did my best to help your gallant men, but...' Miko, let his voice break, quite pleased with his performance.

Sarreg nodded and put a reassuring hand on the mercenary's shoulder, 'You've done well, Miko, protecting our little deal. The Krells didn't guess you were working for me, what about your colleague?'

Miko shuddered, 'It is an abattoir in there sire, I don't think poor Pieter stood a chance.'

'Then your purse does not need to be shared,' and Sarreg dropped a heavy leather pouch into Miko's hand.

'Thank you, sire.'

Sarreg smiled and waved two of his militia over, 'This is the mercenary I spoke of. Escort him to safety then report back to me.'

Miko retrieved his sword and sheathed it on his left hip, opposite its twin on his right. The two burly men saluted Sarreg and escorted the mercenary towards the main road and away from the slaughterhouse.

Sarreg watched the three leave and his grin turned to a

sneer, 'Let's finish our business with the Krells now,' he patted Wide's bulky arm and the party of men and golems entered Jakob's warehouse.

'Abattoir isn't a strong enough word for this!' Gasped Sarreg, as he pulled a scented, lace-edged handkerchief from his sleeve, and held it to his nose. The warmth of the noonday sun had turned the wooden structure into an oven. A tepid breeze belched out from the main door like an out-breathe from hell itself. Sarreg fought back a desire to splatter the dark-stained floor with his breakfast. He stayed in the relative freshness of the doorway as his men and their golems entered. A furious, but brief battle developed between the last four golems guarding the supine figures of the Krells and Sarreg's contingent. Then the two mages were dragged out unconscious and dumped at his feet.

'Where is the other one?' Sarreg demanded as he turned Davvid over with his foot, 'This is Davvid Krell but where is Luther? Alayne, bring some men to aid Militiaman Snape. Treat him well, this man is a hero, we were miss-informed, he is alive.'

Alayne beckoned two militiamen to him and instructed them put the unconscious Luther Krell onto a litter, 'Mayor, where would you like me to take Militiaman Snape?'

'Transport him to my mansion. Take a healer with you. For security make sure you have handlers and their golems accompany you too. Luther Krell is still at large; he could even be at my old home. If he is, do not confront him until we join you there,' instructed Sarreg. He motioned Alayne away with a cursory movement of his hand, then lowered his bulk to the ground and slapped Davvid's face with the back of his flabby hand.

As Alayne moved away, he glanced back and saw Sarreg draw a dagger from beneath his cloak, it was the jewelled weapon he had seen before… it was definitely Senator Desit's.

'Time to wake up, Davvid.'

Sarreg, turning his head sideways like an enquiring dog examined the bruise on the mage's forehead. It was dark red and full of blood, the skin was tight and shining. He pushed the point of his dagger into its centre and the pressure of the blood caused a small fountain to spurt out over the blade. Davvid moaned and raised a hand, Wide stamped down on it hard, 'Now, now, Davvid. Careful, do not annoy Wide. He might pull off your arm if you do.'

Davvid blinked, 'Sarreg!'

'Yes, my boy. Sarreg,' he replied gleefully, 'So nice to see you again.'

Davvid's head twisted around and he gasped, 'Is everyone dead?' his eyes widened as he surveyed the body-parts strewn around the barn's interior, 'Luther...'

'He wasn't here; your master deserted you, young Davvid. There were just two survivors, you and Militiaman Snape.'

Davvid paused and frowned, 'Snape?'

Sarreg noticed his expression, 'Yes... Snape.'

For a moment Sarreg thought the young mage was choking, and then he scowled, as he understood, Davvid Krell was laughing at him.

The healer, bending over Luther Krell's bed, opened a small bottle of ammonium carbonate and waved it under the unconscious mage's nose, 'Militiaman Snape... can you hear me?' he asked as Krell groaned quietly and turned his head away from the pungent aroma. The healer tried again and Krell slapped the man's hand away, coughing and choking. 'It's going to be all right Militiaman Snape; we've got you away from the Krells. You are safe now.'

Luther Krell raised his right hand to his head; the linen bandage, which bound it, brought memories flying back as the movement caused the damaged limb to ache. As he struggled to sit up, the healer attending him put a supporting arm around his shoulders in an effort to assist him.

'I can manage. Where are we?'

'We're in Mayor Sarreg's mansion, Militiaman Snape. He instructed us to bring you here whilst he and his men searched for Luther Krell. Unfortunately he escaped, but we do have Davvid Krell in custody.'

The healer watched in confusion as his patient doubled over on the edge of the bed, holding his sides as if in terrible pain. It was only when he reached out to help he understood that the man was not in pain. As Luther Krell stood up, and the healer saw his laughing face, the mage cast a hex, which threw the healer back towards the open fire that was burning in the bedroom's large fireplace. Luther grinned as the healer's eyes watched him pick up the iron poker from beside the soot-stained hearth. Luther studied the terrified man for a moment and then pounded the poker into the healer's skull until the man's eyes glazed over and then he returned the bent poker to the fireplace.

'My name is not Snape...'

Luther smoothed down his leather jerkin and blood came away on his hand. He opened the oak garderobe and withdrew a fresh one, discarded the bloodied jerkin and shrugged to put on the new one. He chose a navy-blue cloak and flung it across his shoulders then dragged the healer's body into the large closet and closed the door.

The corridor outside the bedroom was empty but Luther heard the low murmurings of a discussion on the floor below. There were people in his laboratory. Although he knew it was more prudent to put as much distance between him and the mansion the temptation to see who was rummaging through his secrets was a powerful motivation to stay. Walking lightly down the stairs, he began to understand their conversation and he did not like their comments.

The two golem-handlers rummaging through the desk in Luther's laboratory were bickering over the contents as Luther strolled in. The two large golems moved towards him and he smiled as he recognised them as creatures he had constructed many years previously and therefore had a fail-safe hex built into their being. A fail-safe he now activated with the slightest of hand signal.

'Gentlemen, making yourselves at home I see?'

They stepped back from the desk, hastily secreting their plunder in pockets and up sleeves. Luther was impressed with their sleight of hand.

'Militiaman Snape,' the braver of the two, a young thin man with a face full of freckles and a greasy rat-tailed mop of hair which he fingered constantly stepped forward, 'It's good to see you up and about. We were just examining Krell's desk for evidence.' His partner, an older man with heavy jowls and the complexion of a chronic drunkard, fidgeted nervously too.

'Ah… yes, so I see,' Luther folded his arms, 'and *did* you find any evidence in *my* desk?'

The smile of the younger man's face wavered and the finger twirling the greasy lock of hair froze, 'I don't understand… *your* desk?' He looked at his colleague who shrugged and then glanced towards the doorway. 'And where is Tomas the healer?'

Luther motioned a signal to the two golems, 'Yes, *my* desk, and let me take you to join your friend Tomas.' The golems moved towards the two men who signed frantically in an attempt to regain control of them. They were unsuccessful and soon enveloped in the monsters' tightening and hard embrace. By the time the two handlers were bundled into the oak garderobe, they had truly 'joined' Tomas.

'This place is beginning to feel like my second home,' Lucy sighed as she squirmed around trying to find a comfortable spot on the ferry house floor.

Raven strode around the vast shed kicking up the debris with his boots, 'Looks like it too.'

She turned a withering gaze his way, 'You better not have turned my flat into an industrial tip.'

Rolling his eyes, he walked over to her and dropped down onto his haunches, 'As if I would.'

'Yeah, right.'

The door opened and Vela entered followed by Pieter who was toting a burlap sack. They sat down near Lucy and Raven. Pieter drew the cord from around the sack's neck and the unmistakable aroma of roast chicken filled the air.

Lucy licked her lips and grinned, 'Mmm… I'm getting feelings of dé·jà vu.'

Raven raised his eyebrows. 'Oh yes?'

She pulled a face at him, 'Vela and I hid out here earlier. He stole us some food.'

Lucy pulled the sack away from Pieter, 'I'll be mother.'

Pieter tilted his head quizzically but Vela put a hand on his arm, 'Don't worry about it Pieter. She does not come from here. I don't understand her most of the time either.'

Raven mumbled, 'Glad it's not just me then.'

Lucy ripped the first chicken into portions and handed them around. She waited for Raven to get a good mouthful of his and then asked, 'Well, what do you think of their frogkens, Rave?' she paused for her question to hit home and then continued; 'Doesn't it taste like chicken?'

Her reward was a mouthful of partially masticated meat that sprayed over her red woollen jacket. She looked down at the mess, took off her hat and wiped herself down.

'It's not fucking chicken?' he coughed, the last remnants causing her to flinch as they struck her face, 'And what the hell has happened to your hair?'

'Yes, it's chicken you idiot, and how the hell do you expect me to blend in here dressed as I was?' then she looked him up and down and frowned, 'Crap, you don't exactly blend in either do you?'

'No, way...' he reached up to his long hair; 'You're not getting your hands on this.'

'Nah, that's okay, but your coat isn't. I don't think a Matrix leather coat works here somehow.'

'You know it's not a bloody Matrix coat, its Goth,' he pointed a greasy finger at her, 'and I'm not giving it up.'

Vela reached into the sack, withdrew a large brown hooded cloak, and handed it to Raven, 'There is no need to discard your fine coat, friend Raven. I have *procured* this for you. It should suffice, should it not?'

Raven shook the garment out and then raised it to his nose, 'Stinks of bloody chicken though,' he threw it over his shoulders and raised the hood, 'But it does do the job, I think.'

'Makes you look like a monk, but at least you don't stick out like a sore thumb,' she said.

'Ahem... as long as you don't expect me to become celibate, I'll wear it.'

She reached over, grabbed him and drew him close for a long, lingering kiss, 'Ooh... a lecherous monk!'

Pieter looked at Vela, 'I think we should look around outside,' and he inclined his head towards the two lovers, 'And what is a monk?'

Vela shrugged and grinned, 'We are just getting some air, should you need us, friend Lucy and Raven.'

Lucy raised a hand and waved them off without lifting her face from Raven's.

Chapter 17

The old mercenary and the young boy closed the ferry-house door behind them quietly and without conferring walked down the slipway to the weir's edge. The late afternoon sun had almost disappeared behind the tree line on the far bank. Rays of gold threaded their way through the branches and glinted off the ripples on the water. A flock of waterfowl scattered at their approach, peddling furiously upon the water's surface until reaching take-off velocity and then rose into the air. Their discordant warning calls echoing around the weir.

'I like this time of day,' Pieter said and he eased his long frame down onto the wooden deck of the slipway. His legs dangled over the clear water and he leaned forward and spat, 'For your souls.' He said quietly.

'Do you believe that?' asked Vela.

Pieter shrugged,'Until someone proves it means nothing… I suppose I do.'

Vela studied him carefully, 'How did you survive and get back?'

'The Saffron Wars?'

'Yes.'

Pieter looked up at the darkening sky and sighed, 'I was wounded and helped by a yellow-skin woman. She hid me for four months until it was safe to make for their coast and then she assisted me in stealing a small skiff. Three days drifting almost finished me off but I was picked up by one of our ships. The men who had served with me all died.'

'Why didn't she turn you in?'

Pieter hesitated, 'I saved her life,' he looked into Vela's

face, 'I killed the man who was raping her. He was one of my own men.'

'Oh…' Vela nodded, 'It was an honourable thing to do. The war was not meant to be waged upon women and children.'

'Yes, but it *was*. And we call *them* barbarians…' He snarled, 'Bloody mages. There would not have been any war if it were not for them.'

'At least you showed one of them that we are not all savages, as they thought.'

Pieter shook his head slowly, 'For what it was worth. When I pulled away from the beach a patrol broke through the surrounding forest and captured her,' he looked into the boy's face, 'They executed her on the beach in front of me. They took her head, and I rowed away.'

'But what could you have done?'

'I could have died.' Pieter stated flatly.

'So, the mages started the war?' Asked Vela.

'Initially we were there to trade. You do not have to sail halfway around the world just to start a war. We can do that just across our own channel if we wanted. But the mages saw an almost unlimited supply of souls for their golems. The land of the yellow-skins is beyond measure, and their peoples are millions upon millions. Before long the mages lost all control and started reaping, any trade agreement was swiftly forgotten. Soon the majority of our ships were full of hex-tiles, that was when they attacked. Almost all the fleet was destroyed. Although they had no mages, their ships could spew fire; we were out-manoeuvred and out-numbered.'

'The woman, if you *had* died, would that have *saved* her?' The boy asked.

Pieter gave Vela a wane smile, 'No, but it would have saved *me*…'

A crescent moon hung like a silver sickle above their heads by the time Lucy and Raven joined them on the wooden jetty. Both the boy and the old man were lying on their backs looking up at the velvet tapestry strewn with more stars than Lucy or Raven had ever seen. They stretched out next to the two of them, 'That's some night sky, how come there are so many stars?' she asked.

'Bet they're the same number as we see on Earth,' Raven explained, 'It's just we have so much light pollution we don't get to see so much anymore. He pointed skywards, 'Look at that, The Milky Way. Our galaxy, about two, to four hundred billion stars, some with planets swirling around them. Somewhat scary eh Luce?'

'So can you tell where we are Raven?'

'Not really, only that we're in the northern hemisphere. There is the big dipper, follow the pointer stars in its bowl and voilà! There's Polaris, the north star.' Raven drew her attention to the brightest star in the sky.

'Never took you to be another Patrick Moore, Raven.'

He turned his gaze on her and smiled, 'There's a lot you don't know about me, Lucy.'

She entwined her fingers in his, 'Touché.'

Pieter sat up and coughed politely, 'Before you two start again, I think you should know that the tide is almost full. We need to get to the docks and board ship.'

Lucy stood up and wrapped a bundle of light-coloured cloth around a rock that Raven handed her. Then, as if shedding chains and manacles, she threw the rock enveloped in her Pyrolite suit as far out into the weir as possible. It sent up a spout of water. Gurgling faintly, it submerged, leaving ever-expanding interference rings and popping bubbles to mark its passage from existence and her neurosis.

'Never thought I'd ever see you out of that damn suit,' Raven said.

'You saw me enough of me tonight, didn't you my dirty

little monk?' she teased.

He looped her arm in his and dragged her away whispering, 'Stop embarrassing me in front of those two, will you?'

'Oh shush, don't mind them.' She turned and grinned at Vela and Pieter.

The four friends left the weir and followed the river on its bubbling and gurgling way downstream towards the town and its docks and their ship.

Chapter 18

The Altair

Alayne held the small water-skin over Davvid's bloody mouth and dribbled some of the cool water over the mage's lips. He shook his head in dismay at what he had witnessed. Sarreg had lost all sense of dignity and restraint when Davvid had explained that they had allowed Snape to leave and that Luther Krell now inhabited the unfortunate militiaman's body. His anger overflowed when Davvid laughed again and Wide had stepped forward at Sarreg's command and had beaten the mage unconscious. Now re-grouping outside of Sarreg's old mansion Alayne had the opportunity to tend to Davvid's wounds, as best he could.

'Don't waste water on him,' Sarreg snarled.

'But... but... he's badly hurt,' stuttered Alayne, 'He could die.'

'Not could, Alayne,' Sarreg replied, 'He *will* die. When the time is right, he *will* die.' He reached over and hit the water-skin out of Alayne's hand and in doing so allowed his robe to fall open. Alayne's eyes fell upon the green-gemmed dagger secured in the fat man's waistband and more than ever he felt sure that Sarreg had been responsible for Senator Desit's death, but he kept quiet whilst Sarreg continued. 'Now come with me, leave him there. I want to reclaim my home, and if Luther is there I shall claim his life too.'

Alayne gently lowered Davvid's head to the ground and followed Sarreg towards the imposing mansion. The company of militiamen milling around and murmuring suddenly became still and silent as the two approached. Wide turned his sightless gaze upon the men and Alayne noticed some of them flinch.

'Men, as Dainman was unfortunately killed and Snape, the poor man, has been usurped of his body by that madman Luther Krell, I hereby appoint Alayne as Master Militiaman. He is now your commanding officer.'

Alayne stared at Sarreg open-mouthed, 'But I know nothing of military procedures!'

As the murmuring commenced again amongst the company of men Sarreg gripped Alayne by the arm, 'Neither do I! Nevertheless, someone has to lead these men and I have enough to do. Now lead them.'

'Yes sir…' replied Alayne as he watched the dissent grow in the ranks of his newly assigned force. With a determination he never realised he had he approached the militiamen, 'Golem-handlers forward, at the double.'

There was hesitation for a moment and then the first man moved away from the group, his golem following. Before long, five handlers and their charges stood before him.

'Men, you all know Luther Krell is a master thaumaturgist. If he is inside the mansion, he is either incapacitated and we can proceed with no conflict, or on the other hand, if he awakened then we can presume that our men that accompanied him are dead. They would not have known that Krell possessed their leader, Snape. They would have been defenceless. You men must lead the attack; your golems will be our pathfinders. If Krell has left any nasty surprises for us they will bear the brunt of the damage,' he looked past them, 'Bowmen, step forward next.'

Ten troopers, equipped with crossbows and quivers full of quarrels, moved a pace or two forwards.

'If Krell is there and decides to cast he will be in line of sight of you men. When the attack begins, do not stay bunched. Spread out and be ready. If he appears fire continuously, he must not be allowed to cast. Do you understand?'

They nodded, some even said, 'Yes sir.'

'See?' said Sarreg, slapping Alayne's back, 'I knew you were a leader of men.'

Alayne fought not to shrug off the fat mayor's hand and replied, 'Yes Mayor,' then started towards the front of the mansion, waving his men forward.

Of the five golem-handlers, none could be called a mage, and therefore would not have the 'sight' or the proficiency to spot any magical booby trap set by Luther. Anyone could be trained to handle golems and cast basic hexes, but the art of thaumaturgy required knowledge of magic that very few people possessed. Therefore, not bravado or heroism motivated the five to move ahead with their golems marching line abreast, as the first wave of attack. It was ignorance.

All went well until the ten reached the massive front door, as one of the handlers instructed his charge to try the handle, which it found locked, a grating sound made them look up. High above them large blocks of masonry on the castellated wall were moving. Suddenly the first piece reached the point of no return and overbalanced then crashed to the ground crushing two of the golems beneath its weight. The handlers dashed closer to the building and pressed themselves to the cold stonework in an attempt to put themselves inside the range of the falling masonry. The golems remained in the open and soon another of the clay giants fell foul to a large block of granite.

'Get them to smash down the door!' shouted Alayne in desperation.

The two remaining golems began battering at the wooden door, following the instructions from their handlers. The bowmen, having moved up into firing positions, scanned the windows and roof for a target but found none. A shriek drew their attention to one of the golem-handlers that was pressed against the mansion wall. The man was becoming enveloped in the stonework, half of his body seemed to have been absorbed by the structure against which he was pressing. The granite surrounding him glowed purple and flowed like liquid as he was inexorably drawn into its depths. His screaming stopped as his face was finally sucked into the wall, his hands clutched at air for a few seconds before finally becoming still, frozen like a pair of predator's claws reaching for their prey. Forever preserved in stone.

Another handler cried for help as he too began to be absorbed by the hex Luther Krell had cast upon the walls of the mansion. The handler standing next to him pulled at his jacket in an effort to extricate him but drew back in horror as that same jacket began to harden beneath his grip. He stepped back a pace too far. Another gigantic block crashed to the ground, crushing the unfortunate man beneath it. The door splintered and cracked beneath the onslaught of blows rained upon it by the two remaining golems. A large enough crack appeared for one of the golems to insert its crude hand and tear the wooden planking apart. Its handler reached in and slipped the bolt. The battered door swung inwards, its upper hinge giving way and allowing it to lean crazily against the inner wall.

As the handler turned towards the men outside and waved for them to come forward, a sound from within the hallway caused him to stiffen with trepidation. His golem pushed its way in and was immediately pole-axed by two other golems from inside. One of them grabbed the handler's face and dragged him in. His muffled screams motivated his golem into action once again and it attempted to get up from the floor. Krell's two attacked it. One held the handler as the other brought its foot down on the struggling golem's chest and stamped until its framework cracked and disintegrated. The terrified man struggled and pummelled at the golem's hard clay chest. It lifted the man up, looked quizzically at its victim's bulging eyes that stared through the coarse clay fingers and then tightened its grip on the handler's face. A muffled gasp and a gout of blood spurted through its clay fingers, which ended with a bubbling gurgle as the golem let the man fall to the floor, choking on his own blood, his face crushed in on itself. A fusillade of crossbow bolts peppered the doorway. Some embedded themselves in the woodwork; others skittered off one golem's torso. One wedged into a small crack on the other creature's chest and the golem ripped it out contemptuously, crushed it between his two hands and then the two walked back inside. The last golem-handler's nerve broke and he sprinted away from the building leaving his charge standing near the doorway. A final block of masonry tumbled down and thudded into the ground a few feet behind the terrified man.

Sarreg watched as the handler rejoined the main force, 'Well that went extremely well.'

Alayne shrugged, 'We need more men and golems.'

'Impossible. We have more than enough,' Sarreg replied, 'Luther Krell is only one man.'

'But he *is* Luther Krell,' Alayne answered, 'and he has at least two golems, if not more.'

'His golems can be handled by Wide. You and your men keep him occupied,' he waved to the bowmen, 'You men come with me,' and he strode off towards the rear of the building.

'Keep him occupied,' mumbled Alayne quietly as he left Sarreg and went to rally his men.

Raven's heavy leather boots beat a rhythmic tattoo upon the wooden decking of Marin's Weir pier as the band of friends made their way down its length to where a ship was taking on cargo. Huge wooden-framed cranes, powered by golem strength alone, hoisted bundles and crates from the dockside into the cargo area of a medium sized brigantine. Men climbing the two masts of the ship busied themselves preparing for departure, their voices bouncing and echoing off the wooden buildings that lined the pier. Pieter motioned them to stop and then he went ahead alone and negotiated their passage to Fivewinds with the captain. Within a few minutes, he returned.

'*The Altair* is basically a cargo vessel but she does have a couple of cabins for passengers. One is already taken but I have acquired the other for Lucy and Raven, unfortunately our money is insufficient for us all, therefore, Captain Foyle will allow Vela and me to work our passage.'

Vela grimaced, 'Why me?'

Pieter shrugged, 'Lucy is a lady and Raven is somewhat… strange.'

Lucy laughed and looked at Raven.

Raven glowered at her, 'And when did *you* become a lady Luce?'

She punched him playfully on the arm that deadened it for quite a while as they walked up the swaying gangplank and aboard the vessel.

Pieter moved closer to Raven and rested a hand on his arm, 'Raven, I have informed the captain that you are a haruspex and that Lucy is your serf. It should give you a certain degree of authority and will keep the majority of people away from you.'

'What?' Raven stopped for a moment, 'What the hell is a haruspex? Hey, I'm hetero, man. Don't go spreading any stupid rumours about me all right?'

Pieter shook his head, 'I think you misunderstand, my friend. You are a haruspex. You are a seer. You see omens and bring good luck. It is an important profession.'

'Ah… I see… the monk's robe and all. Now I get it.'

Pieter was about to ask Raven what a monk was when the captain approached them and singled Raven out, 'I wonder if yer would perform a divination before we leave port, Seer Raven?' he linked arms with Raven and drew him aft towards the helm and the large, multi-spoke ship's wheel.

Raven looked around helplessly as the captain, a dapper old man, dressed in a worn, dark blue uniform with tattered gold braid ushered him towards the binnacle and its nearby heavy oak table. Lucy shrugged when his eyes fell upon her and she mouthed silently, 'Just go with it!'

He rolled his eyes at her and mouthed in return, 'No shit!'

A gnarled old sailor, carrying a tethered goat on his shoulders, climbed the steps up to the table and dropped the bleating animal onto it. He tugged a piece of his unkempt hair at the captain and backed away a step or two. The captain walked to the balustrade dividing the raised wheel-deck from the rest of the ship, put both his callused hands upon it, and then shouted, 'Stop yer work boys. Seer Raven has done us the favour of a divination. Then for supper tonight we'll be having spicy goat my lads, spicy goat.'

Realisation dawned on Raven and he groaned as the captain returned to the table and nodded towards the animal. Raven stood uncomfortably before the ship's compliment and the expectant captain. The captain stretched the goat's head over the table's edge and smiled helpfully. Raven looked at Lucy once again and she moved to his side.

'Do it Rave,' she said, 'We don't have any choice. Do it and do it quick, so the poor thing won't feel it.'

He nodded, then in one quick motion flipped his robe aside, drew the katana and brought it down in a flashing arc. The captain stumbled back with the goat's head in his hand whilst a fountain of blood spewed over the table, balustrade and onto the deck below causing the men gathered there to jump aside.

The captain blinked in astonishment, 'I've never seen it done that way before.'

Raven nodded, 'We do it differently where I come from.'

'Do you need a knife to extract the liver or will your...

sword… do?'

Raven groaned quietly, 'No it's okay. I can manage.' He slit open the animal's belly. Its intestines spilled out onto the deck. He flicked the blood off the katana, sheathed it and then gritted his teeth before plunging his hand into the goat's body. The animal quivered beneath his questing hand, dying autonomic reflexes firing one last time. It was enough to make him jump. He almost pulled his hand out in response but contained his shock and felt inside the warm carcass until he found the required organ. The captain and his crew waited expectantly whilst Raven put the goat liver on the table, 'I need more light Captain Foyle.' He said.

'You man, bring a light here.' The captain shouted down to one of his men near a lantern. He unhooked it and ran up to Raven doffing his woollen cap.

'Hold it up for me, please.'

The young sailor looked at his captain who affirmed Raven's command with a slight nod of his head.

Raven began to delve within the liver's interior, his fingers stained dark red by the blood. He picked at pieces, held them up to the light, and mumbled a few times.

Lucy moved closer to see what he was doing. 'You almost look as if you know what you're doing, baby.'

'Shut up, I'm concentrating,' he answered sarcastically.

A few minutes later, he stood up and smiled, 'Excellent news, the voyage will be swift and profitable. The wife of one of your men will have a son. The future looks promising for all of your crew and for yourself, Captain Foyle.'

The captain, duly impressed, clapped Raven heartily on the back, 'Fortunate news indeed, Seer Raven, most fortunate. I thank you for your divinations,' he glanced down at the pieces of liver on the table, 'Please continue.'

'Ahem, that's all I see, I'm afraid, captain.'

'Yes, yes, of course,' he nodded, 'But, please, eat… seal the divination, please.'

Lucy coughed and fought back a giggle.

'Ahh… eat… well, yes, obviously,' Raven stuttered.

The captain, crew and Raven's friends all watched in anticipation as he finally picked up a small portion that didn't have any grisly bits showing and popped it into his mouth. He smiled sickly and swallowed.

The captain clapped his hands and the crew joined in, Lucy took her hand away from her mouth and applauded too, 'Well done, lover, well done.'

'Mmmfff…' replied Raven who was too scared to open *his* mouth.

Captain Foyle moved to the balustrade and bellowed down to the crew, 'Ok men, to yer stations, make ready to cast off. Cook, get yer fat gut up here and collect the goat. I want the stew hot and spicy tonight; it will go down well with the firkin of rum I am going to open in celebration of Seer Raven's telling tonight. Now get yer fingers out of yer arses and get moving.'

The crew cheered at the mention of rum and burst into motion, some climbed up into the rigging like monkeys whilst others raised the gangplank and pushed off the dock with long poles, the ship was underway.

With the meal over, and an ample amount of rum in their stomachs, Lucy and Raven took leave of the captain's table and made their way below.

'Somehow I don't think that old seadog believed I was your serf.' She whispered as they walked down the corridor to their room.

'Yeah, I saw him scrutinising you more than once,' Raven replied, 'He either thinks I'm not as celibate as a seer should be and you are my lady friend in disguise, or that you are a feminine-looking boy and I'm as queer as a three pound note.'

They passed the other passenger room and Lucy stopped

to listen, 'I wonder who our other guests are. Didn't see them come aboard or take food. Bet you the bloody room is empty and old Captain Foyle didn't want the guys to have it. He prefers to keep his workers in their places.'

He pulled her away, 'Rubbish, just because they want some privacy you have to think up a conspiracy theory.'

She poked her tongue out at him, the silver stud on it catching the yellow light of the lantern and he pulled her to him and kissed her.

Lucy broke away from his grip and skipped to their room, opened the door and cocked a finger at him, 'Come on, I'll be Roger the cabin boy and you can be the naughty pirate.'

'Great, can I make you walk the plank?'

She smiled and pulled him into the room, 'We'll see... we'll see,' and then closed the door behind them.

A minute passed and the door to the other room opened quietly. The interior of the cabin was pitch-black. A hand reached up to extinguish the light in the walkway and as it guttered and went out a shadowy figure made its way along the passageway and up the stairs to the deck.

Vela snored quietly, curled up like a cat on a large coil of rough plaited rope. A heavy woollen blanket partially covered him and Pieter gently pulled it up over the boy, covering him completely. He mumbled a few words in his sleep as Pieter walked away and prepared for his round of night watch. When four hours had passed, he would awaken the boy for his turn and then *he* could repose until dawn. Pieter raised a hand to the helmsman on the poop deck, who in turn waved in acknowledgment. Then he made his way forward to the forecastle, checking hatches and crates secured to the decking by ropes and netting. The hiss of the water combined with the creaking wood and flapping sails instilled calmness in the old mercenary that he had not felt for a long, long time. He breathed in the cool night air, relishing the salty ozone and flecks of frothy spume thrown up by the capricious wind that stung his cheeks. Rounding a large tarpaulin, which covered a high stack of crates, he noticed one edge fluttering in the wind, its undone length of rope whipping across the deck. He stamped down on the line and brought it under control. Then bent over to pick it up and secure the tarpaulin. As he stood up with the rope in his hand a noise from behind made him turn, a flash of silver swept down towards his head and he stepped back raising his hand with the rope in it to protect himself. A glancing blow to his arm sent a flash of pain through it and he lost his balance crashing into the low railing behind him. A shadowy figure snapped a kick to his chest and Pieter fell backwards over the railing and into the dark waters that rushed by below.

Miko returned the short-sword to its sheath on his hip and smiled cruelly, 'I always knew you were too old for these games my friend,' he said quietly and then began to return below to complete his next task. He would kill the large man with the girl and then capture her. The boy Vela was not a problem, when he found him he would either kill or capture him too, Miko did not mind.

He reached the doorway to below-decks and before entering acknowledged the hesitant wave that the helmsman gave him, who probably wondering who Miko was, and how he had managed to get onto deck unseen. Miko crept down the dark passageway, passed his door and reached the one to Lucy and Raven's room. He put an ear to the rough wood and listened. Muffled sounds came from within along with the intermittent bouts of laughter. He was pleased they were busily occupied and at their ease. He would perhaps be able to enter unobserved. Although he was not particularly worried about waking the ship's compliment he preferred to finish his assignment before explaining to the captain what he had done. The papers he carried from Sarreg were not carte blanche to do whatever he felt necessary, but they did give him a certain leeway. The gold pieces in his fat purse would prove an added advantage too. He drew a short sword and held it ready in his right hand as he gently turned the doorknob with his left. There was no resistance, the door was unlocked and he pushed it open slowly. A single candle on a small shelf near the bed guttered noisily in the draught caused by his entrance. The mound of dark blankets on the bed stopped moving as Lucy and Raven grasped that something was amiss. Wasting no time, he rushed to the bed and as Raven's head appeared from beneath the coverings he crashed the heavy handle of his sword down on his unprotected head. Raven grunted softly and collapsed back down onto Lucy who struggled fruitlessly to extricate herself from beneath him. Miko threw back the blankets and placed the tip of his blade beneath Lucy's chin and a finger to his lips.

'I'd prefer to present you to Sarreg in one piece, but make any noise and I'll have to make do with just your head,' he said softly, his single eye glittering malevolently in the candlelight, 'Understand bitch?'

She could not nod her head so answered quietly, 'Yes, I understand.'

Miko suddenly pulled Raven off her by his hair, the unconscious man rolled off the bed and landed heavily on the floor leaving Lucy spread-eagled on her back. Miko's eye traversed her body and he licked his lips, 'Hmm... well you *can* make a sound. A little moaning won't hurt,' he said as he pushed the sword point closer to her throat and struggled to slip off his jacket. Lucy closed her eyes and turned her head away even though the blade drew a small line of blood from her throat. He smiled, 'Yes, close your eyes if you must. Pretend I'm your friend if you wish.'

A guttural laugh came from deep down in Lucy's throat and Miko's smile petrified on his face as she replied, 'Oh, I'll close my eyes you freak. That way I'll get my night-vision, quicker than you,' and she chopped his hand away and blew out the candle.

Wide crashed through the ruined door of Sarreg's mansion. Its heavy clay feet crushing the remains of golem and human that lay in his path. The dark recesses of its eyes flashed with red and it made for the stairway to the upper floor. On reaching the landing the two golems under Luther Krell's command attacked Wide. One went low and tackled Wide around the legs making it stumble, whilst the other body-checked the big golem, finally resulting in Wide over balancing and crashing to the floor. The second golem collapsed on top of Wide and attempted to hold the bigger golem down whilst the first assailant rained blows upon Wide's head.

Sharp splinters of clay flew from the impact of the golem's fists. They came from the attacker and from Wide, but more so from the attacking golem which wasn't as resilient or as well made as Wide. The second golem was thrown back across the room by Wide's sweeping arm. It crashed against the wall, a large crack ran horizontally across its chest and it tumbled to the floor. The other golem continued its battering upon the giant golem's head but not for long.

When Alayne had deemed it was safe to enter, he ushered his men forward and followed them up the stairs. Wide was just getting to its feet, the first golem was decapitated on the floor by his side. The other was near the wall and struggling to get up, a large crack across the middle of its chest flexed open and closed as it moved. Wide aimed a twisting punch to the golem's chest and the creature staggered then cracked in half and folded to the floor.

Alayne indicated left and right to his men and they split up to search for Luther. He beckoned Wide to his side and followed the group that had taken the right. Room after room proved to be empty and finally the two groups arrived at Sarreg's basement. They tried each and every door. Behind a couple, they discovered the remains of people Luther had used for his work. Little remained of them, barely husks or desiccated shells. Finally, they reached the end of a darkened corridor and a door, which showed no means for opening, no handle, or hinge was discernable.

Alayne pointed to the door and said to Wide, 'Open it.'

The huge golem crashed into the woodwork and splintered it. It reached a hand into the broken wood and tore pieces out until a big enough gap was made for them to pass through. Inside was another room, the farthest wall had collapsed exposing a tunnel strewn with broken masonry. The dust around its entrance showed that someone had recently used the area.

'Looks like our man's in there,' pointed Alayne, and Wide crouched and entered the tunnel, followed by Alayne and his men.

Luther Krell scrambled over the last of the debris and saw light at last filtering down from the well. Davvid had recounted the tale of Sarreg's secret passageway and now Luther was grateful for his apprentice's story. Whilst his two golems were creating a diversion he would scale the rungs set into the wall of the well and climb out. A short distance away was the stable and a number of drayks. He would sneak in, take one, and be long gone before his pursuers understood the ruse. He climbed up the wall of the well. Reaching the top, he hooked his hands over the rough stone of the lip and pulled himself higher, put a knee on the edge and stiffened.

'At last, Militiaman Snape,' said Sarreg, 'Oh, excuse me. I should say Luther Krell, should I not?'

Luther's lips peeled back in a snarl as he saw the bloated figure of Sarreg only paces away and surrounded by about a dozen men with crossbows. His arms quivered as he supported his weight and he looked back down the well, in the darkness below he saw movement. Looking back towards Sarreg, he started to incant a hex as the fat man in an almost casual manner waved his hand and said, 'Fire!'

Alayne heard a cry. The sound of something crashing against the interior of the well made him step back quickly as a shadowy shape careened down. It hit the floor with a sickening thud. Luther Krell moaned in pain and struggled feebly against the netting Sarreg's men had fired over him. He had lost his precarious hold on the well's rim. Only his rebounding off the interior wall had saved him from certain death by slowing his rate of fall.

Sarreg's voice echoed down to him, 'Alayne, are you there?'

He stepped tentatively around the smashed body and called up, 'Yes sir, I'm here... sir, Luther Krell is captured.'

'I should hope so,' replied Sarreg, 'He should have half a dozen nets over him. Nevertheless, just to make sure, when you come up, bind him firmly. Especially his hands.'

Alayne enquired, 'His hands?'

'Are you deaf?'

'No, sir.'

'Then do it, and be quick. I do not want him casting. We can deal with Davvid next. I want to see his face when his master is dropped into his lap,' the well echoed with manic laughter as Sarreg walked away.

Alayne looked at his men, 'Step forward someone and bind him. I'd rather one of you volunteer than have to order any of you.'

None of them moved, they shuffled nervously and one or two seemed to take more interest on what was going on behind him than what he had just said.

He asked again, 'Will anyone volunteer?'

A strange ripping noise rang around the tunnel and one of

the men pointed past Alayne, 'I don't think it will be necessary now sir.'

Alayne looked around and Wide stepped out carrying Luther Krell in his arms like a trussed chicken. The golem had twisted and torn the netting, and now had it holding the man like a strait-jacket. Drops of thick blood dripped down the ropes and tendrils of skin that hung from the mage who was unconscious and breathing heavily. Alayne twisted away and vomited copiously.

He waved to his men, 'Wrap him in something and take him up to Sarreg.'

Miko swept the short-sword around blindly, connecting with only air. A soft laugh came from his right and he spun towards it. A stabbing blow caught him in the throat and he dropped his sword and grabbed his neck with both hands. Heaving for breath Miko held his damaged larynx and dropped to his knees. He dragged in a deep breath and tried to pierce the dark to find his attacker but could not see Lucy in the gloom. He sensed she was near, perhaps now in front of him and he surged forward. Lucy caught his outstretched arm, ducked beneath it, and then twisting it, she stood up. Miko's arm locked at the elbow and she pulled down on it hard. The bone snapped and he howled in rage. Lucy stepped back and her foot touched his fallen sword. She lithely stooped down to retrieve it, 'You are one noisy bastard,' she said and thrust the blade up through his chin. It pierced the roof of his mouth and ultimately entered his brain. Soundlessly he crumpled to the floor, with Lucy still holding the dagger. She felt the warm stickiness of his blood run down her arm and she grabbed the blanket to wipe it off. Next, she felt on the bedside shelf for the candle and the small container of primitive matches. Striking one, she saw that Raven was stirring and so quickly lit the candle and carried it over to where he lay.

'Take your time,' she said to him softly, 'He gave you a nasty damn blow to your head.'

'What the hell happened?' He asked feeling the lump on his head that was swelling up.

'Our old pal Miko fancied a ménage à trios. I talked him out of it.'

Raven pulled himself upright and stood swaying, 'Well he's certainly not going to answer back, that's for sure. *Now* what do we do with him?'

Lucy began wrapping the body in the blanket, 'Let's get him on deck before anyone starts waking. A quick heave over the side and all our problems are solved.'

He shook his head, 'And when Captain Birdseye notices him missing tomorrow?'

'Nothing to do with us. We didn't even know who was in the other room. Poor bugger must have fallen overboard, shit happens.'

'Remind me never to fall out with you,' he replied and grabbed the heavier end of the bundle.

Lucy looked at him askance, 'Why ever would you fall out with me... we are the perfect couple. Aren't we?'

'I suppose so. We have a lot in common. Both of us like our film work, martial arts, pizzas and curry. Oh... and yes, killing people and chucking them into the sea. The perfect couple...' He said sarcastically.

'Stop moaning and open the door.'

'You open the bloody door; I've got the heavy end, and I'm wounded.'

Lucy fluttered her eyelashes, 'Poor baby,' and she opened the door and checked outside. 'All clear, let's move it.'

Between them, they carried the cumbersome body down the corridor and to the steps leading up onto the deck. At the top, she motioned him to stop and peeked around the doorframe. The helmsman would see them so she ducked back in, 'I'll have to go and distract him.'

'That should be easy,' he smiled.

'Shit.' She said, looking down at her naked body and then capered back to her cabin to get dressed.

Two minutes later, she returned fully clothed and squeezed past Raven and his burden.

'Hurry up, I'm bloody frozen,' he said, his teeth chattering.

She looked down at *his* naked body and giggled, 'Yes I can see,' then sauntered onto deck and made her way to the man at the helm.

It was not long before she had the man walking to the stern and explaining some part of the ship's rudder to her. Raven, seeing his opportunity, manhandled Miko's corpse up onto his shoulder and walked quickly to the ship's side. He grunted and tipped the body over the side then glanced around quickly and returned to his cabin.

Lucy heard the splash and so did the helmsman. He turned around just as Raven disappeared down the hatchway.

'Was that a fish jumping?' she asked and immediately felt stupid. *It sounded more like a bloody body falling into the water than a fish,* she thought.

The man shrugged and walked to the side and looked over, 'Someone has fallen overboard!' He said and started tugging on a rope that hung down the side of the ship, 'Quick, boy, help pull him up.'

Oh crap, Lucy thought as she helped the man heave on the coarse rope, *now we are going to be right in the shit when they find a bloody great knife sticking out of Miko's head.*

Vela's face appeared from beneath the woollen blanket and he looked at the two of them bleary-eyed, 'What's happened?'

'Someone's fallen overboard,' she answered, 'Give us a hand, Vela.'

The boy jumped to his feet and the three of them hauled on the rope, foot by foot it came aboard. Before long, she could feel it become sodden in her hands as the last few feet that had been close to the water reached them. Then a hand appeared and gripped the wooden railing before her. Lucy stiffened, *I do not believe this. He had a fucking knife through his chin and up into his brain!* She thought.

Another hand appeared and then Pieter's soaking wet head came into view and he coughed and spluttered as he dragged himself back on board.

'Pieter!' she gasped then looked over the side into the dark sea, 'What the hell were you doing down there?'

He lay on the deck and heaved up seawater, wiped his mouth with the back of his hand and struggled to his feet. He looked at the helmsman and then at Lucy, 'Sorry, I lost my balance trying to tie down that tarpaulin.'

The helmsman gave a look, which said, *landlubber* and took the rope from his hand and made fast the tarpaulin then returned to his duty behind the wheel.

Lucy took Pieter by his arm and helped him down below. She told Vela to start his shift and then guided the old mercenary to her cabin. Raven was fully dressed by the time they entered and he looked Pieter up and down.

'Raining?'

Lucy dropped Pieter onto the bed, 'Better get those clothes off, Pieter, and get into bed. You don't look too good. So what happened?'

Shivering he stepped out of his jacket and turning his back to her pulled off his trousers. Raven put a quilt over the old man's shoulders and he wrapped it around himself gratefully and climbed onto the bed. He still shivered violently and Lucy added more blankets.

'Miko, the bastard. He is on board. I did not hear him. He pushed me overboard. I was lucky to have held onto the rope. I've been dragged through the water for what seemed ages.'

Lucy rubbed the man's torso and nodded to Raven, 'Get

rubbing, we need to get his circulation going,' she smiled at Pieter, 'Forget Miko. He's gone for a long swim. Though for a moment back there I did think we hadn't got rid of him as easy as I had thought.'

He nodded in understanding, 'You thought I was he?'

'For a second, yes.'

'You're lucky she didn't throw you back in,' said Raven.

Pieter smiled, 'Yes I suppose I am a poor catch.'

Lucy smiled back, 'Oh, I don't know. We could have caught worse.'

Davvid's eyes were stuck closed with blood and gummy tears. As he fought to open them, his head banged rhythmically against a stone wall. His blood was pooled in his head, and his chest was constricted making his breathing difficult. He deduced he was being carried, probably over a golem's shoulder. He screwed his eyes tight and then fought to open them once again. A glimmer of light was his reward as one of his eyelids fluttered open and he looked into the face of his master, Luther, who was suspended from Wide's other shoulder. He seemed to be in worse condition than Davvid. Some kind of netting encompassed him and it was covered in mud and what looked like blood. His clothing was torn and where the flesh beneath was exposed he could see abrasions and cuts. Luther's breathing was laboured, and as Davvid's other eye opened, he could see in more detail that his master's nose was broken. Congealed blood covered it, blocking his nostrils. His mouth was hanging open and frothy spittle hung from it like a spider's thread. Davvid craned his head around slowly and the world spun. He blinked rapidly and managed to focus again as blurred figures swam into view. Militiamen and Senator Alayne were walking behind them in deep conversation. Suddenly a hand grabbed him by the hair and twisted his head around.

'Davvid, awake again, I see,' Sarreg said then turned Davvid's head towards Wide's other passenger, 'Look, your master has joined us.'

'He's dying,' Davvid said and coughed uncontrollably.

'Yes, I hope so,' Sarreg replied, 'and *you* don't sound so good either. But it would be nice if the two of you survive so we may give you both a fair trial in Fivewinds...' He smiled, 'and then execute you.'

Wide stopped and unceremoniously dumped Davvid and Luther onto the ground. Davvid rolled and broke his fall with him arms but Luther dropped like a sack of potatoes and laid there, his breath ragged. Alayne, kneeling down, sprinkled some water on the mage's face and then handed the small water-skin to Davvid who guzzled the liquid down noisily.

'Take your time Davvid, or you'll bring it all back up.'

'Thank you,' he replied and returned the skin.

'Don't waste your time and water on them,' Sarreg said, turning towards the corral where the great draykons and the lesser drayks were tied, 'Get the mounts ready, we'll fly to Fivewinds straightaway.'

'Wouldn't you prefer to fly in the morning?' Asked Alayne.

Sarreg sighed, 'Alayne, make me repeat myself once more and I'll instruct Wide to clean your ears out, and you've seen the size of his fingers, haven't you?'

'Yes sir, sorry sir.'

Sarreg waved him away and Alayne went gladly. The draykons were in a state of readiness as their handlers had stayed with them. Animals of this size needed constant watching. If left to their own devices first they would have killed and eaten their smaller cousins, the drayks, and then they would have turned on each other. However, they had been well fed and watered during their sojourn at Marin's Weir. The scattered bones of various large animals, horses, cows and some Alayne wondered about lay in the corral. He approached the squad of men there and checked their status and that of the animals. He was relieved to find out that all they had to do was climb the wooden ladders onto the draykons and take flight. He told Sarreg and within minutes the whole entourage had boarded and was in flight.

Strapped next to Luther on one side of the framework of a draykon, Davvid sprinkled water from the skin Alayne had slipped him onto a torn piece of cloth. Gently he wiped the encrusted blood from the mage's face and nose and looked at Alayne who sat the other side of Luther, 'Thank you,' he said.

'Just don't let Mayor Sarreg see it,' Alayne said and looked over the draykon's humped back to where the mayor sat on the opposite side.

Davvid nodded then jumped when Luther groaned and gripped his hand.

'Master!' he whispered, 'We are not safe. Try to keep your voice low, Sarreg sits opposite us.'

Luther's head rose slowly, one eye was bloodshot and puffy; his nose looked broken and his lips were split, yet he managed to smile, 'We fall on hard times, young novitiate,' then he rested a hand on Davvid's, 'But I must not call you that. You are a mage in your own right, my friend.'

'We are on our way to Fivewinds. Sarreg means to put us on trial then have us killed.'

'Then we have a chance young Davvid, we have a chance.'

The Altair had made excellent time during the night and all through the following day. Questions were asked about Miko's 'accident' by the captain, but as no sign of foul play could be seen and the watch had not witnessed anything, then the log showed that he had fallen overboard. An unfortunate accident. As the sun began to set at the end of their full day at sea and evening drew close again, so did their destination. Captain Foyle joined Lucy and Raven at the bow and pointed to the large bay the ship was entering, 'The estuary leading up to the port of Fivewinds. A few more hours and yer voyage will be over. We'll be crossing the channel for foreign ports on the morrow's tide should yer finish yer business and have a wish to travel.'

'Thank you captain. Should the opportunity arise we might do that,' replied Raven.

Foyle touched his cap and left them to shout orders to his men as the coast-line gradually crept up on the ship and the wind began to drop.

'Rave, take a look over there.' Lucy pointed over the port side, 'Doesn't this seem a little familiar to you?'

He put his hands on the railing to his left and looked over, 'What?' he said looking around quizzically.

'The coastline,' Lucy pointed now and he followed the line of her finger.

'What about it?'

'This is going to sound stupid but it reminds me of somewhere,' she said, 'Look, that's an island over there. I think its Sheppey and I'm almost sure we're coming up on Warden's Point Radar Station. I've sailed here with Ridley; he has a yacht over the other side of the estuary at Alexandra Yacht Club. Raven, we're sailing up The Wash. Fivewinds is London!'

'There's nothing on the island though.'

'Of course not, they haven't got radar here. This world is bloody medieval isn't it?'

'Yeah, I know. I didn't mean that,' he said, 'Its just there's nothing there at all. No buildings, no light, nothing.'

'Probably just farm land I suppose. I wonder what London looks like?'

'Well, we'll find out soon enough. Should be far enough up the Thames shortly and there's still enough light,' he looked up at the evening sky, 'We must have come from around Southampton or Portsmouth area then.'

'Weird, so damn weird,' Lucy shook her head in wonderment.

Vela strolled up to the pair and rested his arms on the railing too, 'Shouldn't be long now my friends.'

'What's the name of this place, Vela?' she swept her hand around to encompass the whole shoreline.

'That piece of land?'

'No, the whole island. All of this,' again she indicated the whole portside shoreline, and then turned and pointed to the other shore too, 'The lot, what is this island called?'

'Oh, now I understand, friend Lucy. This is Angleland, and there,' he pointed up river, 'is Fivewinds. Our largest city, our capital.'

Lucy and Raven looked to where the boy was pointing; a soft glow illuminated the sky, the streetlights of the great city welcoming *The Altair* and its cargo.

The streetlights which they had gazed at from the ship shone on the poor and the crippled, rummaging through the waste and spoils. Rubbish thrown from the lighted windows of the well-off and more fortunate citizens of the city. On a hillside stood the brightly lit townhouse of one of these fortunate citizens, who was also a member of the senate, and who was also chairing a clandestine meeting of disgruntled senators. He tapped his wine-glass with a silver fruit knife, 'Gentlemen, gentlemen, we are getting nowhere,' said Senator Casco to his guests, 'We have far too little time to discuss this matter. Mayor Sarreg will return from Marin's Weir soon. If we are to stand against him we must be sure that we are in the majority.'

'If we are not?' asked someone from the far end of the long dining table.

Casco peered down the table's length at the tall man, standing and pointing towards him with his smoking pipe, 'Senator Ferris?'

'Yes.'

'Ah, Senator Ferris, if we are not then I fear we may go the way of those that have already stood against our... ahem, illustrious mayor.'

Another of the senators interjected, 'There is no proof that Sarreg had a hand in Crof's and Halla's...' he paused as if searching for the correct word, 'let us say unfortunate set of circumstances. And there is certainly no proof that he had anything at all to do with Senator Desit's death. I am Senator Tiernan, by the way.'

'I see you Senator Tiernan and I apologise to Senator Ferris. It is not that I did not know him, rather it is my old age I am afraid. My eyesight is not as it was,' he explained, 'However, as you say my dear fellow, there is indeed no proof at all. Therefore we must be sure of our facts and our strength before attempting to oust the man from the strong position he has entrenched himself in. Do you not think it fortunate for Sarreg that the three main obstacles to his appointment of mayor befell to importune misfortune just before the senate's vote?'

'It is one thing to be fortunate and benefit from another's misfortune. It is quite another to have been the instigator of it. However, unless we have hard proof then even if we are in the majority it will be difficult to lever the man from his position. He has settled into the mayor's seat, and may I say, his home, very easily,' replied Tiernan.

'There also remains the question, who will put himself forward as contender for the mayorship?' asked Casco.

An immediate discussion swept around the table like a tidal wave as the pros and cons of senators were argued. Casco shook his head sadly at the display of back-biting and bickering that confronted him. He rose slowly and pushed back his heavy chair backwards with his legs, its wooden feet scraped loudly on the tiled floor and one by one the arguing senators composed themselves as he left the table and walked to the door. Senator Ferris stood up and intercepted him, trailing a cloud of blue smoke.

'Are you leaving Senator Casco?' he asked.

Casco coughed and waved the smoke away from his face, 'I see no more reason to stay my friend,' he pointed to the men around the table, 'How can we confront Sarreg when we have no discipline ourselves? I fear we shall be encumbered with our mayor for a long, long time. Now I grow tired, if you'll excuse me I shall retire to my bed. When you have finished with your, ahem... deliberations my servant will let you out.'

Ferris held the old man gently by the arm, 'Senator Casco, forgive us. You are right as usual. Please, come back to the table. This unruliness must stop,' he glowered at the other senators.

Casco hesitated, then with a last longing look at the doorway, returned to the table and retook his seat. Senator Ferris drew his own chair next to the old man but before sitting down he tapped the highly polished table with his knife. Senator Casco winced with each tap.

'Gentlemen, if you please, a little silence for a moment,' Ferris said and waited for the murmuring to die down. 'It should be obvious to everyone here that the candidate to challenge for the mayoral seat needs to be above reproach and be a steadfast beacon for us all. Therefore I would like to nominate our illustrious friend Senator Casco. Shall we have a vote? Perhaps just a show of hands will suffice; all those in favour raise their hands please.'

As Casco struggled to rise and protest, nearly everyone in the room raised their hand in favour. By the time Casco was on his feet the room resounded with applause and his protestations could not be heard. He put a finger to his lips to plead for quiet but he had to wait until the ebullient senators one by one ceased their hearty enthusiasm and let him speak.

'My friends, I am overwhelmed by your generosity and

your faith in my capacity to take up the mantle of mayorship, but colleagues, fellow senators, I am *far* too old and frail for such a demanding position. Oh, I know you might think me a coward and afraid to confront Sarreg, but this is not the case.'

Many of the senators nodded in understanding but Casco didn't give them the chance to interrupt him.

'I *will* confront him; however, I *will not* stand against him as mayor. We shall have to decide on a younger man for this, and personally I would prefer to see the seat occupied by someone other than a mage.' This last comment caused a ripple of consternation amongst the senators and once again Casco raised a wrinkled hand to his lips in an attempt to bring the meeting to order.

'Shh… quiet a moment, please,' Ferris said and motioned them to be seated, 'Let our friend continue.'

'I know one or two of you are budding mages but do you not see the evil behind this practice?' He paused a moment and bowed his head, 'Many of you older senators will remember when the monarchy was the ruling body of this proud nation of ours. Many of you, like I, served the King,' some of the older senators shifted in their seats at the mention of the old monarchy and Casco smiled at them.

'Is it so bad to admit your past allegiance? Friends, I am not saying that a return to a sovereign power or a totalitarian government is the answer but think, when the mages led the revolt against King Roan they made certain pledges. Pledges that there would be a fair voting system for the people. For the first time everyone would have a say in their future. The people would decide who would be elected to the senate. The mages assured us that they would step down once the revolution had succeeded and normality was returned to our island, but they were deceitful my friends, deceitful…' he coughed and Senator Ferris passed the old man a glass of water. Casco sipped from the crystal glass and dabbed his thin lips with a handkerchief before continuing.

'Oh I know superficially it might seem as if those appointed to the senate are voted in fairly and on the whole I would say many of us are in our posts legitimately, but look at our history. Whilst we on the senate are placed here by our citizens the position of mayor has nearly always been selected by our senators; now, someone name me a mayor who has not also been a mage?'

A thickset man with a florid face and heavy jowls raised a hand and then said loudly, 'Mayor De Fillipo!'

'Yes, Senator Tobias, Mayor De Fillipo. If my old brain remembers correctly he was the first mayor elected after the revolution. And, once again if my memory serves me right, he served in office for the grand total of six days. Didn't he get trampled by a horse?'

Tobias nodded, 'Your memory is still keen Senator Casco. Yes he fell under a horse.'

Casco laughed quietly, 'Yes, yes. The strange thing was that the poor man's body was found in his bedroom.'

The room fell silent, and then Ferris spoke up, 'I haven't heard that before. How do you know Senator Casco?'

'A friend of mine sought sanctuary and De Fillipo, who was a kind man, offered him it. He was the one who found the body,' Casco twisted around and looked towards the door, then shouted, 'You can come in now.'

The door opened and a cloaked figure with a hood covering its head entered the room. It shuffled slowly towards the table, a gnarled hand reached out from beneath the cape and grasped the back of a chair to pull it out and a number of senators gasped when they saw it was missing two fingers.

'Gentlemen, this is a dear friend of mine, Paladin Gawen.'

Jakob pulled back the hood and unbuttoned his cloak; beneath it he wore a uniform of studded leather armour which even though was worn had been kept in pristine condition. At his side was a leather-handled dirk and high up on the left hand sleeve of his jerkin was a badge.

'Good evening senators, I be a bloody surprise to yer all, I bet eh?' Jakob cackled.

Ferris shook his head in amazement, 'I never thought I'd see the day a King's man would dare show his face in Fivewinds again,' he said then took a closer look at Jakob's badge, 'Noblesse d'épée. You were truly close to the King, a knight of the sword, no less.'

Casco put a hand on Jakob's shoulder, 'Yes, a true nobleman, a true knight and a true friend. Swords were not your preferred weapon though my friend, as your missing fingers so readily proclaim. But pray tell my colleagues about De Fillipo's death.'

A sadness crept over Jakob's face as he told the meeting of how he had heard a disturbance in Mayor De Fillipo's room and had rushed to his aid only to find he had arrived too late. The mayor's body lay crushed and broken upon the bedroom floor. The window smashed and its frame almost torn out. Of the attacker there was no sign but Jakob had known only a golem could have inflicted such damage upon a human body. He recounted how he had run downstairs and burst out of the front door in a raging frenzy, desperate to get his hands on the perpetrator of the terrible crime, not even thinking what the consequences would be if he had indeed confronted the golem. On returning to the house sometime later he was dismayed to find the building over-run by militia and their golems.

'I could not stay in Fivewinds anymore. That night I stole a horse and over the following days I made my way cross country to finally end my days in Marin's Weir. It was weeks later I heard that De Fillipo's body was found in the stables and his death was said to be have caused by a horse. A bloody horse indeed. De Fillipo never went anywhere near horses. My poor old friend was scared of the damn things.'

Senator Tobias snorted, 'We are expected to believe the words of an aged royalist?'

Jakob was on his feet surprisingly swiftly considering his age and arthritic condition and the dirk which appeared in his left hand was also swift, 'Make no mistake. I can't draw a bowstring anymore because of these,' he held up his right hand and showed Tobias the stumps of his two missing fingers, 'But I am still able to pin your loose tongue to the wall with this,' the dirk flashed as he drew back his arm.

'Now, now Jakob, he doesn't know any better. He does not know you like I. Put that away and continue with the news that you bring us,' said Casco as he rested his hand on the old paladin's arm.

Jakob stared at Tobias whose florid colouring had paled to a sickly grey and hesitated momentarily before returning the dirk to its scabbard with a fancy twirl of his fingers. He leaned in close to Casco and whispered in his ear, 'Thank you old friend. I don't think I could have hit his fat arse let alone his tongue, my fingers are not as nimble as they once were.'

Casco laughed gently and whispered back, 'You old rogue I saw your hand twirl the dagger. You could still castrate a fly on the wall if you so desired.'

The old paladin winked at his friend and sat back down, saying, 'An apology would be acceptable.'

Casco narrowed his eyes at Jakob who raised a hairy eyebrow in return. Then he looked down the table to where Senator Tobias was still quaking in his soft leather boots and waited patiently.

'I am sorry for doubting your word, paladin.'

Jakob nodded sagely, 'Yer apology is accepted, senator.'

'Now if we can continue?' asked Senator Ferris as he struck a flint and taper to light his pipe which had gone out, 'I, for one, would like to know the rest of the story.'

'There is nothing much more I can add to what happened

to Mayor De Fillipo. All I would say is that he was a good and kind man. He took me in when I returned from the wrecking of *The Antelope*, my hand still raw and bloody from the mages' message. I was one of the lucky ones. Not many lived to carry the message home.'

He paused and cleared his throat. 'You have been discussing our present mayor and the fact he is a mage. The man that took De Fillipo's place was also a mage. It is time our senate was purged of such filth.'

'So, gentlemen, as I was saying, whether we like it or not, we have merely accepted one tyrant over another since the king was deposed,' Casco said, 'Whilst merchants, businessmen, anyone who can afford golems continue to provide a market for the thaumaturgists they will forever pull the strings, and we, the puppets, will dance to their merry tune.'

Ferris tapped his pipe on the table, 'Hear, hear. Well spoken senator. Just look at the number of golems we have working in our dockyard for example. There must be hundreds there alone, and whose livelihood are they taking?' he emphasized his point by aiming his pipe at everyone sitting at the table. 'The common-man, that's who. The citizens you see begging on corners in any part of this fair city that you care to examine.'

Murmurs of agreement came from the senators and Casco waited patiently for them to finish before asking Jakob for the important news that had him sequestrate a drayk and fly with all haste to Fivewinds with the information.

'Mayor Sarreg has arrested two mages. One, perhaps the greatest mage of our time, Luther Krell, and the other his apprentice, Davvid Krell. Who I may say is every bit as devious and evil as his master.'

'Luther Krell was pronounced *foreverdead*, wasn't he?' Asked Tiernan from the far end of the table.

'Yes he was, and Davvid Krell inherited everything his

master left behind, including his unfulfilled promises. That is what brought Sarreg to our city, his vendetta with the apprentice,' explained Casco.

Jakob nodded in agreement, 'Luther Krell, through some wizardry, vanquished even foreverdeath. Unfortunately, to return to the land of the living he required a body. Militiaman Snape was the unwilling donor. Sarreg wants to make an example of them. His intention is to put them on trial before the senate and then when they are found guilty, have them publicly executed.'

Senator Ferris took the pipe from his mouth, blew a cloud of blue smoke across the table and commented, 'And is that such a bad thing? Will it not mean two less potential mayors should our esteemed Mayor Sarreg meet with an untimely death?'

'Make no mistake, I have no qualms about Sarreg killing these two. They have terrorized Marin's Weir for long enough. However, wouldn't it be an even better outcome if all three managed to kill each other?' Casco asked.

Ferris frowned, 'I do not see how we,' he waved a hand around the senators at the table, 'can influence this outcome.'

'We cannot, but we can make sure Sarreg and the Krells are given an equal opportunity to destroy themselves. When our mayor insists that the trial be held with the Krells either guarded or incarcerated we vote against his decision. Until proof of their guilt is shown we can deem them to be innocent. Then we stand back and watch the fur fly,' Casco explained.

'There is another string to our bow too,' Jakob reminded Senator Casco.

Casco hesitated and looked around the table, 'You all may think we are mad when we speak of this, and already my dear friend has had his word questioned tonight. But, if this man believes in what I am about to tell you, then I believe it too, unconditionally.'

'Tell us, tell us!' exclaimed Ferris excitedly, 'The suspense is unbearable.'

Jakob looked towards Casco who nodded, 'There are strangers in Fivewinds tonight who could well be the catalyst of change for our senate, our lives, even our whole world. Certainly they will aid us in overthrowing the rule of the mages.'

'Are they foreigners?' asked Ferris.

'In a way you could call them foreigners I suppose,' replied Jakob, 'But to be more accurate I would describe them as not of this world.'

The room fell silent.

Jakob stared from senator to senator until finally his eyes rested on Casco who shrugged.

Then Ferris cleared his throat. 'When you say they are not of this world, then where are they from?'

'I'm not really sure,' replied Jakob, 'But I imagine they are visitors from another world. I think the word best to describe the strangers is... alien.'

Ferris mouthed the word silently then said, 'A strange word indeed but perhaps fitting for them. What do they...' his question was interupted by a loud rapping at the door to the room and then it burst open and one of Casco's servants rushed in.

'I beg your pardon Senator Casco,' he glanced around the room, 'and senators.'

'What is it?' asked Casco.

'Sir, you instructed us to keep watch for Mayor Sarreg's return. Young Coleen, the cook's assistant, has just returned with news. Mayor Sarreg has just arrived at his mansion. He was accompanied by a force of militia and golems. He also has two mages in custody.'

A cacophony of chairs being pushed back from the table resounded throughout the room as the meeting broke up.

Senator after senator bade their swift goodbyes to Casco and as he clasped each and everyone's hand in salutation he repeated the same instruction, 'When the time comes, you must stand fast and vote against Sarreg. We must be in the majority, we must.'

Finally the last of the group tendered his goodbye and closed the door behind him leaving Senator Casco and Paladin Gawen in deep discussion. Then, after a few minutes more they too rose. Two old comrades once more re-united and ready for battle albeit with poor eyesight, frail muscles and aching bones.

'Time for a night-cap Jakob, and then to bed. Tomorrow is going to be a hard day for us all,' Casco said, patting the old paladin's back.

'Ahh... a nice glass of rum would warm me old bones before bed, indeed it would,' Jakob replied licking his lips. Then he stopped and looked at Casco, 'And when do we give them the rest of the news, my old friend?'

'Not yet Jakob, not yet,' Casco shook his head, 'We must not play our hand too early in the game. First we must be sure Sarreg is deposed, then, when it is safe, we shall tell the senate that all those years ago you were commissioned with the safe keeping of the king's young daughter and that an heir to the throne of Angleland still lives.'

Chapter 19

In London's fair city

Lucy, Raven and Vela gazed over the side of *The Altair* as the ship was manoeuvred carefully alongside the dock by small tugs powered by a number of primitively constructed golems. Large mechanical cranes, like vast wooden giants crawled their way along the quay-side as they to and fro-ed between various cargo vessels berthed within their grasp. Lights from huge lanterns strung upon cables hoisted high above the dockyard made shadows dance drunkenly upon the many warehouses and walkways. All around the noise of frenetic work echoed between the buildings and out over the water. Lucy wrinkled her nose as the pungent stench of old fish wafted up in the light breeze, 'Bloody hell, what a stink!' she said putting a hand to her mouth.

'Ammonia from the rotting fish, they haven't got refrigerated cargo holds to keep them fresh,' said Raven, 'They probably salt most of them at sea and store them in barrels,' he pointed to a crane hauling a net-full of barrels from the hold of a trawler.

'Those are barrels of Bacalhau da Noruega,' explained Vela, 'It's excellent cooked with potatoes and grated cheese.'

Lucy laughed, 'You're a thief, a mage and now a cordon bleu cook?'

He smiled, 'I like my food but I prefer someone else does the cooking and I've never eaten a cordon bleu, whatever fish that is, friend Lucy.'

'It's not a fish, kid,' Raven said, 'That's interesting though. Bacalhau da Noruega, dried codfish, from Norway. Seems like some places have the same name as our world. History is certainly weird and wonderful here.'

Pieter joined them, hauling a coil of rope behind him. He dropped it near the ship's railing and unwound a quantity then hefted it over onto the dock-side. Then he wound the other end around the capstan and called Raven and Vela to him.

'Can you help please my friends?' he handed the two a pair of wooden handles and showed them how to insert the thicker ends into the holes in the rim of the wooden, drum-shaped capstan. When all three were fitted they started to push the capstan around and the excess rope was turned onto it like a gigantic fishing reel. Slowly, but surely *The Altair* drew closer to the dockside until after a few minutes they felt a slight bump and the boat ground to a stop. Other members of the crew secured bow and stern lines and then the gangplank was run out onto the quay. They stowed the handles and Raven helped Pieter secure the rope. Captain Foyle shouted a few last orders to his men and then approached the group of friends. He offered Raven a small leather purse and smiled, 'For your services and the good fortune you have brought us. One of the fastest voyages the old girl has made and no problems with weather or pirates.'

Raven looked embarrassed, 'Honestly, it's not necessary. You have done enough by allowing us passage on your good vessel.'

Foyle pressed the purse into Raven's hand, 'I won't hear any more of it. Please accept this small token of my thanks.'

Reluctantly the big man accepted the gift and bowed slightly, 'Thank you.'

'So where are you making for now?' asked the captain.

Raven looked at Pieter and Vela, then Vela stepped forward and answered, 'First we shall find an inn for the night, Captain Foyle. Then tomorrow we will petition to see the senate. My master, Seer Raven has business with them.'

Foyle nodded his head wisely, 'Yes, yes, the senate has need of your foresight. Times are... unfortunate, at the moment for the state,' he looked around as if worried about being overheard, 'Since poor Mayor Gorman's suicide the senate has been very troubled. I can't say I care much for the new mayor. His name is Sarreg.'

'Yes,' replied Vela, 'We have heard of him.' He thanked the captain for the safe passage and then with the rest of the group descended the shaky gangplank to the quayside and the crowds of men and golems busily going about their business.

For Lucy and Raven the walk through the city at night was like a step back in time to the Dickensian era of London. Guttering lamps shone with a sickly yellow glow on open sewers flowing with the excrement of human and animal waste. The smell wafting up was almost enough to make them vomit. More than once the men, even young Vela, were accosted by garishly painted women hoping to find business and they had to forcibly push them off. Vela made sure that Raven's and his purses were carefully hidden deep within their clothing as pick-pockets were also rife.

A man, his legs lopped off high above the knees pushed towards them a wooden trolley with brass castors fixed beneath. His hands were leather-bound and he used them as paddles to propel himself to Raven's side.

'Spare a coin, Master Seer, spare a coin for a poor soldier ruined in the war against the yellow fiends.' His hand grasped Raven's leg and held on tightly. Raven fumbled deep within his cloak, reaching into his trouser pocket for a coin or two but Vela gripped his arm and shook his head.

'Don't friend Raven,' he drew his attention to the darkened doorways and alleys surrounding them, 'Show mercy to this man and we will never reach our destination. Many eyes are upon us now. If they think us soft and vulnerable our money will soon be taken from us, and perhaps even our lives.'

Pieter nodded, ''Tis so. This unfortunate man is but a baited hook, if we bite, the line will soon be pulled taut.' He reached a hand around to his pack and unsheathed his sword, the flashing blade was enough of a warning for the crippled beggar who dropped his hand from Raven's leg and backed away into the darkness.

'Nice place,' Lucy said, 'I think it's about time I got myself one of those,' she inclined her head towards Pieter's sword.

'You would have to cross the world to get one like this, Lucy,' smiled Pieter.

Raven laughed, 'She'd have to cross dimensions to get one like this though,' and he pulled aside his cloak so that his katana was easily available.

She cracked her knuckles loudly, 'Guess I'll make do with these as usual then.'

'Seems to have worked well enough up to now,' Raven put an arm around her then spoke to Vela, 'Okay kid, where's this inn? I need a crap, some grub and a bed. It better not be too far or the first of those three is going to be added to this open sewer right here, right now.'

'That won't be necessary, the inn is close now. A few more minutes.'

Lucy wiped imaginary sweat from her forehead, 'Thank fuck for that. I had terrible visions of your big, hairy, white arse scaring the hell out of the population and polluting this fair city.'

'Har... har...' Raven answered back and lifted her off her feet with the arm he had around her then carried her closer to the sewer, 'Now, if we are talking pollution, I bet dropping you in there will certainly poison the environment.'

She squealed and wriggled, knowing full well he wouldn't dare drop her in, and if she wanted to, it wouldn't take much to break his hold on her and turn the tables. Then he would be the one floundering in the gutter. But she liked it when the two of them could participate in some tomfoolery together. No-one else had ever been able to get as close to her as Raven and whenever given the chance, she made the most of it.

A group of men appeared from a side street accompanied by their golems and Raven put Lucy back on her feet and let his hand rest on the pommel of his katana. Vela motioned to the group of friends to be calm, 'They are only dock workers and their charges, finishing for the night. There is no need for alarm.'

Lucy eyed the clay creatures with unbridled animosity, 'Those damn things give me the creeps. Look at this place,' she waved a hand around the squalid square they had entered, 'There is no progress here. The city, in fact everywhere that I've seen, has stagnated. Magic has made life too easy for those who wield it and too hard for those who don't.'

Raven nodded in agreement, 'Just look at the dockyard. No railway to transport goods away from the port. The cranes could be clockwork for all we know; they certainly aren't power-driven. Science hasn't flourished because it's just too easy to make one of those clay things and tell it to do all the work for you. Why should people strive to do anything? They can sit back on their arses, and have a never tiring, uncomplaining slave do it all for you.'

She pulled Vela closer to her, 'Vela, does each one of those things,' she pointed to the group of golems who were a few paces ahead now and going in the same direction as them, 'contain one of those hex-tiles, or whatever you call it, to power it?'

He nodded, 'Yes, otherwise it would just be a terracotta statue.'

Lucy's eyes flashed, 'Krell has killed hundreds then, to perpetuate the supply of these 'uncomplaining slaves' as you call them Rave…'

'Not just the Krells, Lucy,' Vela answered, 'Golems have been made since the first mages arrived, about two thousand years ago. Krell has made an enormous amount but some existed before he ever drew breath, and some are made by other mages. However, Luther Krell's, and now Davvid's, are the only ones with souls taken from *your* world.'

She stopped and looked angrily at the boy, 'And *you* would like to become a mage yourself after knowing what it entails?'

'Sometimes you have to become the equal of the thing you hate… to overcome it.'

'Bullshit, if you did that then *you* are no better than the thing you hate,' she snarled at him.

Vela turned his gaze on her and for a moment she saw a depth in him she hadn't noticed before, 'Then *you* will no longer be seeking vengeance for your father's death?'

She opened her mouth to answer and found she could not. Grasping Raven's arm she turned her back on the boy and continued across the square with Raven in tow.

'Perhaps I should not have said that,' Vela said to Pieter.

'Revenge is a terrible thing my young friend. You think it will heal the wounds and bring peace to the soul, but that is a falsehood. An old soldier once told me, 'Before seeking vengeance, first dig two graves.'' Pieter patted the boy's back and set off after Lucy and Raven.

To the east of the inn that Lucy and friends were making for, stood a grand house. Outside of the old city walls, set within its own grounds, languished the sprawling mansion of the deceased Mayor Gorman, now however belonging to Mayor Sarreg. Made from ragstone pilfered from the defensive walls that once circumvented all of Fivewinds City it was one of the rare edifices that could be fortified independently of the city's militia, and withstand an assault by even the most capable of adversaries. It was more akin to a castle than a house. The cook's assistant had been diligent; her report of Sarreg's return was both accurate and rapid. It had reached the clandestine meeting of senators within an hour of his homecoming. With the draykons and drayks stabled for the night, the handlers, militia and most of the mayor's entourage were busy eating supper before retiring. However, not all of Sarreg's men were eating. Alayne and a select few, with their compliment of golems, were gathered together policing the Krells whilst the mayor busied himself by having a hot bath and then an ample supper.

Luther and Davvid were securely strapped into stout chairs. Healers working under Alayne's instructions had attended to their wounds. Sarreg had shown no interest in them other than they should be tightly bound and allowed no possibility to cast hexes or sign.

Alayne sat at a substantial mahogany desk. Its surface covered in green-tooled draykon leather and littered with papers, through which he was sifting. His stomach growled and he patted it as if trying to cosset it into silence. He looked up at the guards and they averted their eyes. The golems stared into space, unmoving, uncaring, and never hungry. As if reading his mind, Luther spoke, 'Is he trying to starve us to death before our *fair* trail and our *fair* execution?'

'We are every bit as hungry as you two,' answered Alayne, 'When the mayor is ready I imagine he will allow us all to eat, including you and Davvid.'

'My bindings chafe, would you loosen them for me?' asked Luther.

'Mayor Sarreg said you would ask,' replied Alayne with a smile.

Luther shrugged as best as he could under the circumstances, 'One hand at a time would not be a lot to ask, surely?'

'So that you could cast a hex and paralyse everyone in the room?' Alayne said, shaking his head, 'Now *that* would be a lot to ask.'

'You give me more credit than I am due. Many call me

Master Thaumaturgist, which does not mean I am capable of controlling everyone in here,' he smiled and then added, 'Perhaps one, maybe two, but not everyone.'

Alayne shivered involuntarily as the mage's smile cut into him like a knife.

The door opened and Mayor Sarreg bowled into the room followed by Wide. A wine stain blotched his white lacy shirt and he belched alcoholic fumes into Alayne's face as he drew up close and asked, 'Have they said anything?'

Alayne shook his head, 'Davvid has slept most of the time, Luther,' he looked at the mage, 'Luther has kept his own council.'

'Hmm... no tricks Luther?' Sarreg said as he walked around the chairs inspecting their restraints. He paused by the side of Davvid and slapped him across the head. Davvid's eyes flew open and he stared angrily at the mayor, 'Wake up, you might miss something.'

'I'll miss *you* when you are dead, fat tub of drayk shit.' Retorted Davvid.

Sarreg bunched his podgy fist and drew it back then thought twice about it, 'No why should I waste my energy on you. You are already dead,' he looked at Luther then, 'and so are you,' then he waved the guards and their golems out and said to Alayne, 'Take them to the kitchens for food. Wide will watch these two until you come back. I'm tired, tomorrow we have much to do and I need my rest.'

Alayne lingered for a moment and then nodded and left.

'Wide, if either of these two tries to move, render *both* of them unconscious,' then Sarreg yawned and left too.

A grin broke across Luther's face as he heard Sarreg's heavy footfall gradually recede. He waited a few minutes to be sure then spoke, 'Wide, come stand here before me.'

'Luther are you mad?' whispered Davvid, 'It's been instructed to strike us should we move.'

He laughed, 'Davvid, you forget. Wide is my creation.'

Davvid whispered again, 'Yes, but it is indentured to Sarreg!'

'But it answers to me, don't you Wide?'

As if in reply the golem strode purposefully across the room and stood in front of Luther's chair and looked down at its creator.

'Wide, I want you to carefully remove the binding around my right arm. Do not destroy it because you must replace it when you have finished,' commanded Luther as Davvid craned his neck around to try to watch.

With a grace which was in contradiction to his size and bulk, Wide knelt by Luther's side and his enormous fingers delicately unstrapped the leather belting that fixed the mage's arm and hand to the chair. Luther flexed his fingers and shook his hand to get the circulation flowing again as Wide moved around to stand in front of him once more. Once the pins and needles had faded and all feelings returned, Luther began to weave intricate signs in the air and murmur quietly as the golem stood transfixed by the incantation. Moments passed and finally Luther dropped his hand back down on the arm of the chair, 'Wide, if you have understood your warrant acknowledge it now please.' Seconds passed, Davvid fidgeted and tried in vain to see what was transpiring behind him and then he heard Luther laugh quietly as Wide's empty eye sockets flared red, 'Good my clay friend, very good,' said Luther. 'Now replace the binding as it was and then return to your position in the room. We don't want them to find out our little surprise too soon now do we?'

As the golem secured Luther to the chair Davvid asked, 'What have you commanded it to do and how can such a complicated warrant be instructed by voice only?'

'As I have said on many occasions, Wide is my masterpiece, unique,' he looked down at the clay monster as it carefully looped the leather strapping through a number of brass buckles and tightened them down. Luther's expression was almost that of a proud father watching his son's first faltering steps. He continued, 'Wide's tile can be modified in situ by my voice only. For a more complicated set of instructions, such as those it has now received, I need to be able to be able to gesture too. That is why I had it release me temporarily. Now, as I said to you yesterday, we have a chance, but it has become a very, very good chance.'

The Welcomed Stranger was a grandiose coaching house, half-timbered with the spaces filled with wattle-and-daub, painted white. Standing three stories high it overlooked the surrounding terrace of houses like a mother hen over its chicks. The upper floors projected out slightly in jetties supported by wooden horizontal beams. Well-lit windows welcomed Lucy and Raven and as they drew closer, the sound of pipe and drum filtered out along with the delicious smell of roasting meat.

'Look at that!' said Lucy, 'Looks almost Tudor in style with its white paint and dark wood façade.'

'Who cares?' he shrugged, 'As long as it has a toilet, I really need to take a dump.'

'Philistine,' she answered.

'Oh, so only Philistines need to crap then I suppose?'

'Can we drop this bloody subject of crapping?' she sighed, 'I'm more interested in having a nice warm bath and getting some of that delicious meat inside me,' she closed her eyes and breathed in deeply. When she opened them, Raven was grinning at her.

She looked quizzically at him for a moment and then thumped his arm, 'I was talking about food you idiot.'

Pieter and Vela caught up with them, 'Good, this is a clean and friendly place. You will enjoy the food here too. It's owned by an old friend of mine,' the old mercenary said as they approached the front door.

As Pieter pushed down on the big wooden latchkey and swung the door open, a wave of warm air swirled out carrying the raucous sounds of laughter, singing and music along with a mouth-watering smell of food. Someone from inside the large room shouted for them to either get inside or bugger off and close the door, and so the four friends entered. Vela closed it behind him. Lucy pulled Pieter to her and whispered something in his ear. He nodded and looked at Raven.

'Friend Raven, go across the bar to that doorway,' he nodded in the direction, 'Beyond it, across the courtyard you will find the latrines.'

Raven puffed his cheeks out and replied, 'Thank fuck for that!' Then he pushed his way through the crowd and disappeared outside.

'Will he be all right on his own?' Lucy asked.

Pieter gave a tight strange smile, 'I would prefer not to go with him.'

Lucy laughed, 'No! I don't mean that.'

'Ah…' said a relieved Pieter.

'I was just worried; you know what he's like. If there's trouble, Raven will find it.'

Pieter surveyed the room, 'Looks peaceful enough. Mostly travellers and some workers from the dockyard.' He waved at a friendly-looking man bearing a long red beard held in check with plaits and little leather thongs, 'That's Ivor, our host, and a good friend.'

Lucy nodded at the innkeeper and said, 'Oh dockers?' she looked around, 'I don't see any golems.'

'The owner prefers not to have any in his establishment, that looks delicious…' he pointed towards the open fireplace. It had a large boar turning on a spit over the leaping flames. A small terrier was running inside an enclosed wheel that, through pulleys and straps, turned the boar's carcass around so it would not burn. 'The golems are probably out back in the courtyard,' replied Pieter and then he looked at Lucy and Vela.

All three said, 'Raven!' at the same time.

Raven closed the door behind him and walked across the dimly lit inner courtyard to a group of wooden buildings lined up along the opposite wall. Halfway across he noticed the collection of statues in one of the many alcoves and paused momentarily, then shrugged and entered a vacant toilet. He looked at the crude wooden box inside and groaned, 'Great, a box with a hole in it. Very hygienic.'

On the wall was a sconce with a half-melted candle and a small box with crude matches. He struck a match, it flared and spattered fragments of incandescent sparks onto his cloak and he swore then lit the candle and closed the door.

In the gloom of the claustrophobic toilet he unbuckled his belt and dropped his trousers, trying not to sit down he manoeuvred himself over the hole. A few moments later, he sighed with relief, stood up, and looked around for toilet paper. There was none. 'I don't believe this!'

A hammering came from outside and Raven pushed a hand against the door, 'Someone's in here!' he shouted and then thought and continued, 'Hey, any paper in one of the other toilets?'

Laughter answered him and he heard Lucy say, 'See? I told you he'd get into trouble.'

He raised his eyes to the wooden ceiling and swore quietly to himself, took a deep breath and let it out slowly. Then he asked, 'Can you please check the other toilets for paper?'

Vela answered him this time, 'What do you need paper for, friend Raven?'

Raven closed his eyes and shook his head slowly as quiet giggling filtered through from outside, 'To wipe my bloody arse. Now if you've all had your fun, get me some paper!'

'There is no paper,' Vela replied, 'Look around; there should be a bucket in there somewhere.'

He looked right and left and in the far left corner, there was indeed a bucket. Trying to hold his trousers up with one hand, he shuffled over and looked down into it. The bucket was full of water and poking up from it was a stick. He withdrew it and a saw a sponge attached to the end; it dripped water over the floor as he studied it. 'I've found the toilet brush.'

The sound of murmuring came from outside then Lucy said, 'Um… Vela just told me it isn't the toilet brush. It's salt-water and the sponge is for wiping your arse,' the last words came out with a guffaw of laughter.

It was going to be a nice day. The dawn sky was almost cloudless. Even though the sun had yet to gain much altitude in the early morning air, there was still a pleasant warmness that Sarreg felt as he stood before the open window of his bedroom and he inhaled deeply. Below his window, congregated around the marble fountain that threw jewels of water up from the mouths of nymphs and sea-creatures, were the militia and their prisoners. Sarreg rubbed his hands together happily and went down to join them.

Luther and Davvid were trust like chickens again, ready for the oven. Not only were their arms and hands bound, but this time Sarreg had them wrapped in hessian sacking too. It would be impossible for either of them to sign hexes or cast spells. The mayor took it upon himself to give the mages' bonds a final check before signalling the carriages he had waiting, forward. His own transport was the luxurious mahogany and brass coach, which he had appropriated when taking office. The one Alayne and his men climbed into was little more than a wooden flatbed wagon with vertical posts at each corner. Strung across these posts was a crude canvas roof with rolled up edges which, when unfurled, could provide the passengers with makeshift walls and privacy. The seating arrangements were even grimmer, as they were simply planks of wood nailed to a framework than ran down each side of the wagon. Positioned in parallel files alongside the mages who were tethered by lengths of rope to the wagon's rear, stood two lines of golems. They would be walking the distance to the senate hall. Finally, Wide brought up the rear as Sarreg wanted the huge golem to be the last failsafe should Luther and Davvid somehow slip their restraints.

Sarreg, wheezing loudly climbed the steps into his carriage and it squeaked and dipped in response to his ascension into the cool interior of the vehicle. He pulled the little half-door closed, poked his head out for one last look and told the driver to proceed.

Circumnavigating the ornamental fountain, the caravan made its stately way down the long private roadway towards the iron gates set into the estate's surrounding wall. The crunch of gravel under the plodding hooves of the horses soon turned into a rhythmic clip clop as the crushed granite surface changed to cobblestones. A pair of golems guarding the gate pulled back the retaining bolts and swung them open on oiled hinges. When the procession had traversed past them and only Wide was left to pass through, the golem paused for a moment, and unseen by the coach's passengers, it flourished a sign before the two guarding golems. A shiver ran through both of the clay creatures and Wide continued on its way. Behind the huge creature, the golems at the gate pulled the two halves together, rammed the bolt home. Instead of standing guard once more, they waited for the caravan to gain a little distance, and then began to follow it.

Luther, looking back had seen the little exchange between Wide and the golems on the gate, and allowed himself a satisfied smile. Davvid saw his master's expression and raised a questioning eyebrow.

'It has begun my young friend, Wide has carried out his first conversion,' explained Luther.

'I still don't understand. What sort of conversion are you talking about?'

'A great amount of golems have been created over the years by me, as you know. However, what you do *not* know is that nearly all of them have the capability to break their original instructions given to them by their owners and handlers. They will then accept new orders from me, or from someone who I have designated. Davvid, you thought your little golem, Gar, was the only golem to use magic. It is not, Wide will be casting hexes upon every golem that we encounter, if they are creatures that I have created then they will quietly follow us until I have need of them.'

'How many do you think we will have by the time we get to the senate?'

The rope tied around Luther's wrist jerked almost pulling him off his feet as he was about to reply, and his smile turned into a snarl as he looked towards the two carriages and his mortal enemies, 'More than enough,' he replied.

Lucy stretched luxuriously in the four-poster bed. There had been no need to pull down the heavy curtains from the tester above it, which was there to keep out draughts, because the fire in the blackened iron grate had been kept lit all night and the room had been warm and cosy. The terrier from the barroom snuffled her face and she smoothed its wiry coat and patted its head.

'If that pox-ridden dog has given me fleas I'll skin the bloody thing,' yawned Raven and throwing back the blankets stepped out of bed.

'More like you gave poor little Sheba the damn fleas,' she kissed the little dog's muzzle, 'Didn't he girl?'

'I can't believe you made Ivor free that stupid mongrel and give it to you last night.'

'The poor thing was roasting alongside that bloody boar,' she smacked her lips, 'Mmm… that roast boar was lovely though, wasn't it?'

Raven pulled on his trousers and stood up, 'Yeah, it was delicious,' he buckled up his belt and looked at her, 'They say roast dog is tasty too.'

She threw her pillow at him and Sheba jumped off the bed and nipped his leg, 'Ow! Okay, okay pull your rottweiler off.'

'Sheba, come here girl,' she laughed, 'She does look a little like a rottweiler, now you come to mention it. But a very small one.'

'Are you getting up?' he asked, pouring a jug-full of water into a heavy china basin and then splashing it over his face. He picked up the open-razor off the chest-of-drawers and eyed it nervously.

'Yeah, want me to do that for you?'

He looked at her with a cynical expression, 'I can cut my own throat thank you.'

She poked her tongue out at him and jumped out of bed, 'Just don't ask me to call you an ambulance.'

Ten minutes later they had washed, dressed and were ready to go down for breakfast. Lucy fixed a small length of leather lead to Sheba's collar and went to collect Vela and Pieter whilst Raven rolled up their paltry belongings, including his long leather coat, into a blanket roll and slung it over his shoulders. He looked at himself in the mirror. The long, hooded cloak was positively non-gothic but it did suit him well, 'Looking cool. Seer Raven. Looking cool,' he said quietly.

Lucy knocked on Vela and Pieter's door and a moment later it opened and Vela invited her in. Sheba jumped up and down barking frantically at the boy and he knelt down and picked the dog up. It licked his face enthusiastically and he laughed and tried to turn his head away but the dog would not give up and continued. Lucy let the two battle it out and went over to Pieter who was examining something in the light from the window.

'Hi Pieter,' she said.

The old mercenary turned, touched his forehead in a little salute and smiled, 'Good morning, friend Lucy. Did you sleep well?'

She yawned and put her hand to her mouth, 'Oh, excuse me. Yes, I did…' she smiled, 'eventually…'

Pieter laughed and she noticed a cylindrical tube in his other hand with what appeared to be a fuse sticking out from its top. She held out her hand and Pieter placed the device into it, 'Take care, don't go too near the fire,' he said, indicating the flickering embers in the grate.

'Is this what I think it is?' she asked turning it over in her hand and then smelling it; 'It is, isn't it? I can smell the sulphur. It's a firework!'

He shrugged, 'I don't know the term, firework, but it's a good description. It is fire, but contained within this leather tube. When you light the end it burns quickly and then bursts into flame, very noisily.'

'So, do you make them?'

This time *he* laughed, 'No, no. I have no idea how you make them and I doubt anyone in Angleland knows either. This is a…' He took it from her and searched for the correct word, 'a souvenir from Cina.'

'It's more of a bomb or grenade then than a firework,' Lucy replied, 'Cina? Was that where you fought in the Saffron Wars?'

For a moment, Pieter seemed to be somewhere else. Lucy studied the man's face and for a brief instant felt she could see the devils that haunted him play across it. She felt a kinship with the old mercenary then, for similar devils had visited her on many occasions.

'Yes, that was the place. This toy,' he tossed the little grenade up in the air and deftly caught it without taking his eyes from hers, 'was nothing compared to what we encountered.'

'I can imagine. If you visited, where I think you visited, then the natives had much more than that. Rockets, grenades, big tubes which threw out massive iron balls?' she watched his expression change.

'How can this be possible?' he frowned, 'You cannot have seen the Saffron Wars. First you are too young. Second, if what I have been told is true, you are not even of this world.'

'Oh it's true Pieter,' she replied, 'But some things run parallel to my world. Some things do not. We do not have magic, we do not have golems, but we do have gunpowder, and the Chinese discovered it. We haven't had the Saffron Wars, however... Yet...'

'Then you are lucky.'

'I suppose so, but in my world if we did have a similar sort of war it wouldn't be settled with katanas and gunpowder. We have the capability of destroying the whole globe. I know it might seem strange to you Pieter, but you are the lucky ones.'

'But how is this possible?' he looked dumbfounded, 'You have said yourself that you have no magic. How can you create such devastation without it?'

Lucy thought long and hard before answering, 'I was mistaken Pieter, we do have magic but none that you would recognise. Our magic we call science. Our magicians or thaumaturgists, as you call them here; we call scientists where I come from. They don't capture the essence of people in clay monstrosities but they can split something far smaller than the eye can see and in doing so unleash a power that can make even the sun look dim.'

Pieter struggled to comprehend and then finally said, 'And

you would wish to return to this world?'

For a moment, Lucy was lost for words and then said, 'To be honest? I don't really know.'

Pieter opened his mouth to reply just as a knock came to the door and he put the grenade down and walked over to open it.

'Hi Pieter,' said Raven as he entered. The mercenary smiled and closed the door as Raven checked out Vela and his new best friend, Sheba.

'Watch out for fleas,' Raven warned the boy.

'Yeah, don't let Raven anywhere near you,' shouted Lucy from the window.

He pulled a face at her then crouched down and patted the dog's head, 'We all ready for breakfast? There's an incredible smell of bacon and eggs coming from downstairs.' He said.

Lucy didn't think it possible after the supper they had eaten the previous night but, at the mention of bacon and eggs, her mouth watered and she picked up the grenade from the table beneath the window, 'Mind if I keep this for a while?' she asked Pieter who raised his shoulders, 'Why not? I have another in my pack.'

Ivor slapped Pieter cordially on the back when the group entered the barroom. A couple of travellers sat at a window seat, heartily polishing off large platters of the bacon and eggs Lucy had smelled, even up in Pieter's room.

Pieter tugged Ivor's beard and ordered breakfast for them all. The jovial innkeeper pulled his head from Pieter's grasp, 'Don't make me throw you around the room. My beard only gets touched by my sweetheart,' he said as his spouse, a large, happy-looking woman with grey hair tied up into a bun, swept into the room carrying a tray full of steaming food.

Elbowing Ivor playfully, Pieter said, 'Does your wife know?'

'I heard that Pieter you old rogue!' Ivor's wife said, 'Now

get your bum settled down somewhere. Bacon, eggs, tomatoes and toast for everyone and I don't want to see anything left when I come to collect the plates.'

'Yes Phoebe, darling. You're wasted on a man like Ivor, you should have married me.' Pieter said.

Phoebe put the tray down and fussed with her hair, 'Oh. Don't you start on me you old fool. Ivor is bad enough, I don't need you teasing me as well,' then with a whirl of her ample skirts she scampered back into the kitchen with the laughter from Ivor and Pieter ringing in her reddening ears.

It did not take long for the four friends and Sheba to finish off the tray of food. Ivor had brought them tankards of mead and a bowl of water for the dog to wash it all down and soon they were all leaning back, replete. Lucy patted her stomach, 'Oh that feels better, now I'm ready for anything.'

Standing up Pieter replied, 'Good, because once we enter the senate hall, anything can happen.' He clasped hands with Ivor who declined any payment for the food and rooms. Lucy kissed Ivor on the cheek whilst Raven and Vela waved from the doorway. As she was about to leave the inn Ivor shouted, 'Don't forget our bargain young Lucy.'

Outside Raven linked arms with her and asked, 'What was all that about? What bargain?'

She glanced down at Sheba and then back up into Raven's face, 'I promised him you'd turn the boar on the spit tonight.'

'What!'

'Well how else did you think I could persuade him to let me have Sheba?'

Chapter 20

The Senate

The hubbub from the petty quarrels, and squabbles, brought by the citizens for resolution by the senate, penetrated through the oak door. The howls of derision and bouts of laughter crept into the semicircular apse, which stood far back in the senate hall where Senator Casco and Paladin Jakob Gawen sat opposite each other across a marble-topped table. An almost empty crystal decanter of fortified wine was before them and each held a glass up for a toast, 'Let's make this the last one Jakob or I'll collapse before Mayor Sarreg can knock me out,' Casco said, raising the glass.

Jakob frowned, 'Bloody mage will have to go through me first, yer know that don't ya!'

'We're alone old friend. You can stop the barnyard accent. It is your turn to propose a toast. It's the last one so make it the best.'

The old paladin grinned, wagged a gnarled finger, 'I have to keep in character. It's served me well for most of my life.'

Casco nodded in understanding. Jakob might have been mutilated and set free all those years ago as an example, but there were many who would have liked to have gone a little further and finished the job.

Jakob stood up and clinked his glass against Casco's, ''Tis better to ignite a candle than to stand in perpetual darkness, even if in doing so we are consumed by its flame.'

Casco's watery eyes glittered and he blinked the tears away and drank the last of the glass' contents, then threw the delicate crystal into the empty fireplace, where it exploded into a myriad fragments. Seconds later Jakob's glass joined its twin in a crashing tinkle of sound and flying pieces, 'There... they will never carry a better toast than that,' the paladin stated.

Senator Casco linked arms with Jakob and the two old friends left the sanctuary of the high vaulted apse and entered the furore of the senate's debating chamber. Petitioners still queued noisily for their turn to present whatever case had brought them to the monumental chamber. Their voices rebounded off the enormous circular ceiling, which was buttressed and supported by thick columns of fluted marble, as the senator who had heard the case, handed down his adjudication on another petitioner. Whether or not the decision was agreeable to the man was a mute subject as there was no appeal, and the senate guards escorted him away immediately after the decision.

Scribes, sitting high up in the circle embankment of the hall busily wrote down the outcome of the petition. The scratching of pens on the sheaves of paper lost in the pandemonium, as the next claimant and his opponent jostled for attention.

'Still the same I see,' Jakob had to put his mouth next to Casco's ear to make sure the old senator would hear, 'Very much like the cattle market, only the livestock is missing.'

It was Casco's turn to lean his head in close as he replied, 'That is insulting, old friend,' then he laughed, 'The cattle would object if they heard your disparaging remarks about them.' He lead Jakob up through the tiered seating of white marble benches that ran in expanding circles, as the higher they climbed, the wider they became. At last, they came to a space, directly in front of the huge, open bronze doors, a space that had been kept free for him and the paladin, on the third tier up. High enough to be seen, and easily enough reached by any golem assassin should their stand against Sarreg prove to push the man over the edge of all propriety. Casco mentioned it to Jakob quietly. The old fighter raised his bushy eyebrows and shrugged as if to say, *what would be would be.*

Casco raised his head slightly as the aroma of pipe smoke

wafted by and he looked around to see Senator Ferris working his way through the throng towards him. He raised a hand in welcome and Ferris clasped it and sat down beside them.

'Ready for the fray?' Ferris asked as he tapped his pipe out on the tiled floor leaving an ugly stain of brown nicotine on the pristine white surface.

Casco knew it was futile to waste his frown on the senator but he could not stop himself and, as he imagined, the man did not even flinch, 'As ready as we shall ever be.'

'Well Senator Tobias is on form this morning,' Ferris pointed towards the lower tier of seating to where Tobias was standing. He was passing judgement on a case involving a dispute over grazing rights. Tobias's face was gradually turning darker hues of purple and he paced back and fore between the two antagonists. The toga -style linen cloak that he wore over his usual woollen tunic, masked his heavyset features, but his fleshy jowls could be seen shaking in rage even from their position. 'Both men have valid arguments and Tobias is by far the worse man to have in such a position. I wait in trepidation for his ruling.'

However, the ruling was not to be. A movement at the entrance caught Casco's eye and he nudged Jakob and Ferris as the forum's boisterous and disorderly manner suddenly began to peter out, 'The main act has arrived,' Casco said.

Sarreg stood framed in the doorway with an air of imperious authority, waiting for the multitude inside to afford him the silence he felt he deserved. The sun at his back cast a substantial shadow across the floor. It pointed like a sundial's gnomon to the seating opposite the doorway and as he lumbered further into the room, his shadow seemed to reach for Senator Casco and Jakob. He stopped. The room quietened and then positively stilled as if everyone was holding their breath as another gigantic shadow joined Sarreg. Wide pounded its way to Sarreg's side, its hard clay feet resonating loudly in the new found muteness of the room.

'My fellow senators, friends!' Sarreg enjoyed the echoing boom of his voice in the quietness, 'It is so good to be back amongst you all. Moreover, I have not returned alone. You will all be pleased to know that I have apprehended the two despicable malefactors, Luther and Davvid Krell,' he raised a chubby finger and Alayne entered with the militia and their golems, towing the two mages on lengths of rough braided rope. Both mages looked footsore and tired but Luther's face also demonstrated an air of calm indifference.

Casco rose unsteadily to his feet, his reedy voice faltered slightly as he called out, 'Welcome back Mayor Sarreg,' then he raised a hand in the direction of Tobias, 'This session of the senate will now conclude Senator Tobias, all petitioners are asked to leave. We shall continue on the morrow.'

Tobias hardly had to bother ushering the remaining appellants out of the senate, even his two grazing rights claimants were more than eager to get away from the storm that was brewing.

Sarreg trudged up the first tier and took his mayoral seat, Wide positioned itself near his left side. Without looking behind him Sarreg replied, 'Thank you Senator Casco, it warms my heart to receive your welcome.' He beckoned Alayne forward. 'Alayne, if you would be so kind as to bring the prisoners forward and have them kneel before the senate.'

'Yes mayor,' Alayne motioned Luther, Davvid to advance, and they did, however, neither of them dropped to their knees.

'Kneel before the senate you pair of murderers,' snarled Sarreg.

The two mages stood defiantly.

As Sarreg struggled to his feet, his temper flaring, a polite cough from behind him caused him to pause.

'Ahem… if I might make a comment?' Senator Casco said, raising a hand.

With narrowed eyes Sarreg stared at Casco and then smiled magnanimously, 'Why, of course Senator Casco, comment if you so wish.'

'Thank you mayor,' he looked at the two mages, 'If I may be so bold. I can't see the reasoning behind trussing these two men in such a manner. They have only been *accused* of crimes. They have *not* been found guilty of any crime, as far as I understand. Therefore, shouldn't they be allowed the courtesy of being tried as innocent men, until they are proven guilty?' he waved an arm around, 'There are enough militiamen and golems here to afford protection. Isn't that enough Mayor Sarreg?'

Casco watched Sarreg's fists bunch and then he saw the mayor consciously try to control his anger before replying through gritted teeth, 'Senator Casco you have not seen what these men can do. I have.'

'Correct, we haven't seen what these men do or in fact what they have been accused of doing. Therefore we are obliged to treat them with the common courtesy we would expect for ourselves.'

'But these are The Krells! They are masters in the art of thaumaturgy and are an extreme danger to everyone one of us here.'

Casco shook his head slowly, 'That is yet to be proven. I am not entirely satisfied.'

'*You* are not satisfied... *you*?' Sarreg's lips curled back in a sneer, 'and who exactly are *you*?'

Casco swallowed, then drew himself up straight, 'I am a member of the senate and as such I demand a ruling here,' then he pointed at Luther, 'Mayor Sarreg, you accuse these men of being murderers, of being criminals, of being a danger to us all here. You even state that one of them is Luther Krell, whom we all know was declared *foreverdead*, many, many years ago. *I* see before me Davvid Krell and Militiaman Snape. Who do *you* see

Mayor Sarreg?'

The mayor spluttered and look around for support, a few of the senators loyal to him tried not to be caught in his sights, finally his gaze fell upon Alayne, 'Alayne, tell that old fool about Luther Krell stealing Snape's body, tell him, tell him.'

A wave of hope had been washing over Alayne as he had listened to Casco's speech and he had watched the senators nod in agreement to his words. Though Sarreg had not seen it yet, Alayne had a premonition that the senate were ready to turn on the mayor, and perhaps, go as far as to oust him from his position. He took a deep breath and made the most dangerous decision of his life.

'Look at that,' Lucy said and pointed to the people rushing out of the senate, some tripping over themselves to vacate the place as quickly as possible.

'Must be something big going on,' Pieter commented, 'Usually they don't finish much before dinner-time. I wonder if we will be allowed in. Sometimes they have closed sessions.'

'That's just great. I thought senates were elected by the people, for the people. But this one kicks you out when dinner is ready or they decide to have a closed session,' Lucy replied.

Vela raised his shoulders, 'I'm not even sure if they *are* elected by the people, Lucy. If you have the money, it has been said you can buy a seat on the senate. But to be the mayor you can forget it, unless you are a mage.'

'Have you noticed anything else weird?' she asked.

Pieter nodded, 'Yes, but I didn't think it was worth mentioning.'

'I saw them too,' Vela added.

'What?' demanded Raven, looking around, 'What... what?'

'The golems,' she flicked her head left and right, 'There are bloody loads of them.'

He looked around the square. In alleyways, doorways and

in groups on corners, there congregated a multitude of golems. He pursed his lips, 'Oh yeah the golems. I saw them too but didn't think to mention them either.'

'Shouldn't they have handlers?' asked Lucy.

'Yes, they should,' Vela replied.

'Well we've come this far. May as well go across the square and try to get in,' Raven suggested.

Lucy cracked her knuckles and stepped forward but Raven held her arm, 'Wait, you just going to crash in there? What's the plan?'

She gave him a wry-looking smile and said, 'We just crash in there, that's the plan,' then she handed Sheba's lead to Vela, shrugged off Raven's hand and strode purposefully towards the two militiamen guarding the doorway to the senate.

Raven watched her go and shook his head. He adjusted the katana in its saya to make sure it would clear its scabbard easily. Pieter moved up to stand at his right shoulder and Raven noticed that the old mercenary had dropped his bedroll and his own sword was now strapped vertically down his back. He watched as Pieter pulled his grey ponytail tight and wrapped a leather thong around it then tied it off tight.

Pieter glanced at him and shrugged, 'Don't want it to get in the way.'

Vela checked the little bow Jakob had gifted him. He pulled the string back and the bow arced smoothly, he nodded sagely as if he had handled bows all his young life.

Then he bent down and slipped Sheba's leash, 'Better if you stay here a while girl,' he said. Then without needing to say anything further, the three walked after Lucy.

As she approached the wide granite stairs, which led up to the double bronze doors, Lucy could see something of the interior. There seemed to be a number of people stood in the middle of the hall, but the majority of occupants were seated in row upon row of tiered marble benches. *Like a Roman amphitheatre waiting for the gladiators to arrive,* she thought, *well, here we are.*

The nearest guard to her stepped forward and held out a hand as if to stop her. She grabbed the man's little finger with her right hand and twisted. He yelled in surprise and dropped to one knee and with her left; she chopped down on his exposed neck with the hard edge of her open palm. His eyes closed and he dropped backwards, she held onto his hand until he reached the floor. A shadow to her left warned her that the second guard was near and she swept around with her leg catching him off balance. He watched his short, stabbing sword spiral from his hand as he scrabbled for balance then crashed onto his backside on the floor. Lucy pointed a finger at him, 'Stay down.'

In reply, the guard corkscrewed his legs around and whipped himself onto his feet with the momentum. Then, he crouched into a martial arts type stance. She cocked her head to one side and dropped into a fighting stance too, 'Hmm... cool move, don't recognise the stance though,' she mused.

The guard did not answer but spun around trying to swipe her legs; she skipped easily above the attack and then saw him turn the swipe into a reverse roundhouse kick, which was aimed for her head. She stepped inside the swinging arc of his leg and then snapped a punch into his groin. The man gasped and collapsed to the floor, his hands clutching his testicles, and his legs drawn up in a position of protection that was far too slow to be of any use.

The three friends looked at the guard whose face was now red and who had seemed to have stopped breathing. Raven grimaced, 'Ouch, that's gotta hurt.'

Lucy held her hands up, 'I did tell him to stay down.'

Raven knelt beside the guard, 'Well. He's still breathing, but in short sobbing gasps.'

'Come on we're wasting time,' she pulled Raven away,

'Pieter's right, something's going on, let's sneak in whilst we can.'

Not many of the senators bothered to pay any attention to Lucy and friends as they quietly sidled around the inner wall and took position overlooking the scenario on the senate floor. She gripped Raven's wrist tightly as she recognised the two mages bound, but defiant, in front of the mayor and senators. Raven put his hand over hers and whispered, 'Before you go wading in, listen to what's going on. Look's like they've been arrested.' He felt the pent up energy in her as her grip tightened, 'Just let it play out first, Luce. This could be to our advantage.' She finally relaxed her grip on him and nodded.

Further up in the seating, Jakob nudged Casco gently and looked towards Lucy and friends, 'They've arrived,' he turned back to watch Sarreg interrogate Alayne, 'Now what is Sarreg trying to get Alayne to say?'

Casco muttered, 'I have a feeling it's not what he expects.'

Sarreg brought his fat fist down on the seat next to him and bellowed, 'Speak up Alayne. Tell them what's happened!'

Alayne cleared his throat, 'I would like to request a boon Mayor Sarreg.'

Sarreg looked dumbfounded, 'What!' The word exploded from his mouth, 'You fool. Now is not the time for boons, favours or requests. I want you to confirm that Snape's body has been sequestered by Luther Krell, who has in fact murder our militiaman.'

However, Alayne would not be cowed, 'Do you deny me a boon, Mayor?' asked Alayne, 'I will of course tell the senate about Militiaman Snape, but first. Your honour, will you respond? Is my request denied?'

The mayor's expression changed subtlety as he imagined the game Alayne was playing. Sarreg deduced the senator was manoeuvring for a more powerful position before confirming

Luther and Davvid's culpability, and so he acquiesced.

'I will grant your boon.'

Alayne's hands twisted nervously behind his back as he said, 'I would like to borrow your dagger, Mayor Sarreg.'

Sarreg's mouth fell open, 'My dagger?' He had expected some request for promotion, again he asked, 'My dagger?'

'If I may.'

Sarreg smiled and shrugged, 'If that is all you want my young friend, then certainly,' he reached into the folds of his robe, withdrew the bejewelled weapon, and handed it to Wide. With the barest hand movement, he instructed the golem to take it to Alayne.

The golem's big hand almost hid the dagger as it approached Alayne. Then it held out its fist and placed the weapon into Alayne's hand. Instead of returning to Sarreg, however, it moved a pace away and stood near Luther Krell.

Alayne approached the senate, 'Senators, you've seen this dagger presented to me by Wide, who in turn was given it by Mayor Sarreg. I ask you to examine it closely, please.' He handed it to Senator Tobias who turned the weapon over and over in his hands, looked confounded and then past it on to the senator sitting next to him.

'Is there a point to this Alayne?' demanded Sarreg.

'Certainly Mayor Sarreg.'

The dagger passed through a number of pairs of hands before Casco stood up and said, 'May I see it please?'

Senator Ferris reached down and collected it for him and his eyes tightened for a second before handing it on, 'I recognise this.'

Casco's hand shook as the dagger was finally laid to rest in it. He bony fingers traced the intricate workings inlaid into the jade covered handle and he murmured, 'I know this dagger too.' He raised his eyes, 'Where did you get this from Mayor?'

Sarreg raised his shoulders, 'It's just a dagger. Perhaps it was in Mayor Gorman's house. I cannot remember. Senator Casco, what has this to do with anything?'

Casco handed the weapon to Jakob at his side and then looked towards the nearest guard to Sarreg and dipped his head slightly. The guard motioned to the others in the forum and then approached the mayor as Casco replied, 'It is not *just* a dagger, Sarreg. It could not have been found in Mayor Gorman's mansion either. It belonged to Senator Desit, I should know. It was a gift from me to him.'

Sarreg's face darkened, 'You insult me senator. I am Mayor Sarreg and should be addressed so. Furthermore, I have no idea what you are talking about. That dagger could have belonged to anyone.'

Casco raised a hand, 'Guard, please restrain Mayor Sarreg. I accuse him of the murder of Senator Desit, and I imagine his hand has been in the trouble that has befallen Senators Crof and Halla too.'

A clamour of remarks followed as number of senators rose to their feet culminating with someone shouting out the name of the deceased Mayor Gorman.

'Please sit down. Mayor Gorman's death will be investigated too,' announced Casco.

As the guard placed his hand on Sarreg's shoulder, the mayor flourished a sign towards Wide and shouted to the militia to protect him.

Alayne halted the militia with a hissed command, 'He is no longer your superior, hold fast.' They did.

Sarreg tried to shrug off the guard's grip but more arrived to restrain him, however, he smiled when Wide started moving, 'To me, Wide. Stop these fools.'

The golem ignored Sarreg and approached Luther Krell who spoke to it briefly, much to Sarreg's chagrin. Wide gripped the hessian sacking which enclosed Luther and tore it apart, its tattered remnants hung from the mage like the drooping branches of a leather-leaf tree. The ropes and leather binding beneath broke as if made of smoke and suddenly Luther Krell was free, 'Free Davvid,' he told Wide and then he walked to the entrance as he massaged his wrists to return some kind of circulation into them.

'What the fuck!' Lucy pointed towards Luther, 'The bastard's free.'

'Hold back a sec', let the guards handle him,' Raven put a hand on her shoulder.

Vela shook his head, 'If they can, friend Raven. Luther and Davvid are more powerful than people think. Look,' he pointed towards Wide, 'I think he's just taken control of that golem of Sarreg's.'

'Can he do that?' she asked.

Vela patted the journal he had stolen from Luther, 'He mentions it in here. When he makes a golem he inserts a secret command into it.'

She watched the golem free Davvid next as Luther reached the door and waved a flurry of hand signals towards the square outside.

'I don't like the look of this,' she moaned, 'Look at the creep. If what you say is correct the bastard is calling in reinforcements.'

The sound of a sword being unsheathed made the three turn and look at Pieter, 'I believe you are right, Lucy,' he said, 'I shall secure the doors. Someone please entertain the clay giant.'

Lucy smiled, 'Now we're cooking with gas,' she put a hand over Vela's mouth, 'Shh, it's just another weird saying from my weird world.'

All around the senate floor people began to realise things were getting out of control, Sarreg now had three guards attending him and, as fat and heavy as he was, he was finally man-handled into his seat by them, as he watched in dumbfounded amazement whilst Wide disobeyed him and released the two Krells.

Alayne, with Sarreg secured, turned to face Davvid, 'I can't allow the two of you to escape. You must see that?' he cried and waved his men forward. 'Allow yourselves to be tried fairly. Sarreg is finished, Davvid. Do not carry on with this madness!'

'Alayne, you were kind to Luther and me, therefore, I'll give you a chance. Leave now, we are not attempting to escape. Luther has other plans for the senate and I shall assist him in fulfilling them.'

Shaking his head, Alayne backed away from the mage as his militiamen and their golems approached Davvid.

Shrugging off the torn remnants of the hessian sacking, Davvid backed away from the encircling militiamen. He flexed his shoulders and with unconcealed joy and pride unfurled his wings. They stretched behind and above him beating once or twice sending small swirls of dust up into the air. The militiamen faltered and stopped but the eight golems they controlled reached out to ensnare him. Davvid cast a hex.

Up in the third tier-seating circle Casco gasped, 'This could be a bloodbath,' he faced Senator Ferris, 'Call in the guards.'

Ferris stood and called out above the noise, 'Guards, protect the senate.' Without even knowing it, he popped his pipe into his mouth and puffed noisily before realising it was out. Lighting it he made his way down towards the senate floor, 'I'm going down for a closer look, Senator Casco.'

Casco mumbled, 'Bloody fool,' then asked Jakob, 'Will you follow him down and keep him out of trouble?'

Jakob drew his dirk and cackled, 'It will be a pleasure.'

'I have a feeling I've just made things worse,' Casco said to himself, as he watched the old paladin scamper after Ferris, all thoughts of arthritic pain either forgotten or put to one side.

The few guards within the senate drew their swords and ran to assist the militiamen as Davvid's hex hit the golems. An invisible hand struck them forcefully. The weaker made golems fractured and lost limbs or large fragments of torso but all were swept back, and tumbled end over end, to fetch up sprawled beneath the first circle of seating.

Luther, his tattered restraints looking like a vagabond's cape writhing around him as he returned to Davvid's side, said, 'Your wings are healing well.'

'I can't wait to fly again, Luther,' Davvid admitted, 'But first. Shall we show the senate how things will be from now on?'

As Luther Krell smiled, a heavy, rhythmic drumming sound began to vibrate through the vaulted hall, 'I think they are about to find out. Our army has just arrived.' He swung around and gazed out of the forum. The square below the senate steps was filling with figures. They converged from all corners, all alleyways and all adjoining streets that opened onto the rectangle. They swarmed up the capacious stairs before the senate like an army of ants. Luther's army was a force fabricated from clay and the life force ripped from untold numbers of unwilling human beings.

'How could there be so many and so fast!' exclaimed Davvid.

'After Wide signed to the first few golems it became exponential, they in turn signed others. However, I have to admit I had forgotten just how many I had made.'

Two of the braver militiamen rushed Davvid from the side; Luther raised a hand and with a laconic twirl knocked them off their feet, 'Wide, come here and protect us.'

The massive golem lumbered up to them and planted its

clay legs apart its huge arms hung loosely at its sides but the hands bunched into hard fists.

Pieter reached the open bronze doors just as the initial influx of Luther's golem army entered. The senate guards who had reached the entrance moments before him fought bravely, as two valiant senators struggled to close the doors on the multitude climbing the steps towards them. Pieter scythed off the head of one crude clay figure that had swept a guard up in a bone-cracking embrace. It keeled over backwards and shattered upon striking the floor. The guard rolled clear and holding his ribs clambered to his feet, as yet another golem reached for him. Pieter's sword-arm drew back to slice into it, but was beaten to the blow by Raven's katana as it cleaved through the golem's torso. For a split-second, it stood there, then the upper half slewed away from the bottom and both segments crashed to the floor.

The guards, rallied by Raven and Pieter's intervention laid into the other golems with renewed energy as the two friends joined the senators pushing against the bronze doors.

As all four began to close the gap in the entrance, Luther noticed the dark shadow of the doors creep across the floor and he spun on his heel, cursing, 'Wide, stop them. That entrance must be kept open.' The golem swivelled, a militiaman who had gotten too close had his sword and hand crushed, then Wide stalked towards the group of four, struggling against the weight of golems pushing to get in. With their backs turned to the main room, Raven and Pieter did not see the giant looming up on them. The first thing Raven knew of its presence was when he was lifted off his feet and a crushing band of pain circled his chest, pinning his arms to his side. He crashed his head back, connecting with the solid clay projection that was Wide's nose, almost knocking himself out in the process. The golem did not even flinch.

Vela sighted along the arrow and held his breath. Luther Krell's face was twisted in fierce determination as he cast hexes left and right, throwing guards, militiamen and any golem that had recovered from Davvid's spell back to the floor. The arrow's point centred on Luther's throat and as Vela quietly exhaled, he let fly. Flashing across the crowded floor, the arrow ran straight and true until the last moment when a golem's swinging arm deflected it, sending the projectile whistling passed the mage's face. With a snarl, Luther wheeled around and identified Vela as his assailant. Whilst the boy desperately tried to fit another arrow to his bow, the mage bunched his unbandaged and undamaged left fist, and then thrust it outwards towards Vela, opening it at the last moment. Everything in the hex's path flew apart. Golems fragmented, militiamen and guards hardly had time to scream before being ripped apart. Only the huge marble column, by which he was standing, saved Vela and the senators, who were behind it as the spell hit. It vibrated and groaned but held fast. Those unfortunates standing *out* of its protective shadow, smashed into the wall, shattering bones and flesh. Vela ducked his head out quickly to see Luther Krell double over with the after effects of the raging hex. Davvid stooped by his side and the boy saw the master mage say something to his apprentice. Davvid's eyes flicked up to where Vela stood transfixed and then he too threw a hex at the boy. Without thinking about it, Vela raised his own hand and muttered a spell he had studied in Krell's journal. A purple flare of energy coruscated between Davvid and Vela as the two spells collided and burst apart. The unleashed energy backlash threw both of them head over heels. Vela, blown back by the force landed awkwardly and lay stunned amidst a jumble of bodies and pieces of golem heaped up against the wall. Davvid, keeping his footing, but staggering backwards off balance, ended up lurching into the arms of two militiamen who desperately tried to pin his arms whilst calling for assistance.

Raven's vision dimmed as he struggled for breath. He did not see the small figure advance on his captor from behind, and with a well-aimed kick, catch the large golem behind the knee which caused it to topple and drop him. Raven gulped in a huge lungful of air and watched as Lucy shook her head at him.

'Stop messing around, will you?' she said.

He coughed and rubbed his chest and then his eyes widened as the big golem got to its feet. Lucy watched as Wide turned its attention onto her, its empty eye sockets flashed an angry red, but she just folded her arms and stood her ground. The golem closed the gap between them quickly and as it was about to reach out for her she whipped her right hand out with a swiftness born from years of dojo practice and put her index finger high up onto Wide's chest.

From behind him Raven heard Pieter yell out as the door he was trying to close was pushed open by the ever growing phalanx of clay bodies pressing from outside.

He dragged his eyes away from Lucy's fight with Wide and jumping to his feet rushed to help Pieter who was furiously hacking away at the golems trying to enter through the one door. The right door, the nearest to Raven, had been closed and secured by the senators and the golems were being funnelled through the one Pieter defended, but he was slowly being pushed back. Sweeping his katana downwards, Raven lopped off both arms of one golem that had almost grabbed hold of the old mercenary. For a moment, the clay figure just stood there as if not knowing what to do, Raven did not give it time to decide as his blade swept back up and cleaved through its middle, and yet another pile of shattered terracotta was added to the forum floor. Side by side, Raven and Pieter defended the door, but as quick as they despatched a golem with either of their swords, another took its place, as inexorably the pair of them were pushed back.

Lucy had taken a chance, her finger rested on Wide's chest and the golem had stopped. Gradually the huge giant's head moved downwards as if to look at Lucy's finger that pointed towards his chest. When its chin was almost fully lowered she flicked her finger up and hit Wide's nose, the way her father had used to do thirty years in her past, in another world and in another life. The golem visibly quivered and when its head raised once more the flames within its eye sockets had gone.

'Daddy,' the word sobbed its way out as if dredged from within her heart and in response Wide reached up slowly and pointed its finger at her chest. Sobbing uncontrollably now Lucy looked down at the thick terracotta digit and a second later, it slowly raised and flicked her under her nose. She leapt forward and embraced the massive figure, which gently swept her up in its arms. Her tears dropping onto the golem's great shoulders turned the clay a deeper red and her mind flew back to all the times she had spilled her own blood in an attempt to ease the pain trapped inside her.

'Now crush her, Wide,' Luther Krell said as he panted for breath, his face drained from the exertion of his last hex.

The golem looked over Lucy's head towards the mage, and then inclining its head, stared down into her face. With her eyes cascading tears down her dirty cheeks she scrutinized Wide's vacant sockets as if searching for her father's ensnared soul.

'Put me down, Daddy and help Raven and Pieter. They can't hold the door any longer.'

Luther's face twisted in unbridled hatred, 'Obey me, Wide. Kill her,' and he initiated a hex.

Wide lowered Lucy gently to the ground, looked once again at Luther, then turned on its heel, and strode purposefully to the door through which at least a score of golems now were clambering to enter. As Luther rose his right hand, which was covered with a bloodied and dirty bandage, to cast on Lucy, her lips twisted into a sneer, 'Don't forget, your shitty magic won't hurt me.'

He raised an eyebrow and laughed, 'I know, but *this* will, when I drop it on your meddlesome head,' and he directed the hex towards a jumble of golem pieces and marble debris. As he raised his hand, the conglomeration of hexed material rose in the air and he moved it higher and towards her.

Jakob had steered Senator Ferris away from the worse of the fracas. Now on seeing Lucy's predicament, he had to leave the man to his own devices as he pushed his way to the mage in an attempt to stop him crushing the girl beneath the imminent avalanche of rubble. Knowing he would never reach the mage in time Jakob drew back his dirk and aimed for Luther's bandaged hand. The blade leapt from his rugged old fingers as if embodied with a life of its own. Over and over it spun until piercing the outstretched hand and knocking it sideways with its momentum. A ghastly wail rose up from Luther as once more blood gushed down his already ruined hand and he gazed at it in astonishment. The rubble, no longer under his control, collapsed thunderously to the floor, great waves of cloudy dust billowed up blinding and choking all within its perimeter.

Jakob mumbled quietly, 'Still got the touch...', then coughed and spluttered as the encroaching cloud rolled over him. For a brief instant, he thought he saw Ferris stumble his way towards Lucy and then he too was enveloped in the murky atmosphere.

Lucy stepped cautiously forward. Somewhere in the swirling sirocco stood her father's torturer, for now she knew that although he had been torn from her side that terrible day in 1969, he had not been killed outright. Luther Krell had stolen his soul, life force, the ethereal essence unique to each individual, from him for the base purpose of animating a being, crafted from an inanimate material... clay. Now the time had come for payment, and Lucy was ready to present the mage with the bill, and collect compensation for all those he had abused.

A figure stumbled out from cloud waving a hand, which she thought held some sort of weapon. Sparks cascaded from it and, as he drew closer, she leapt on him and grabbed the man's hand and swept it around into an arm-lock. Then she elbowed him smartly in the solar plexus. He grunted and dropped to his knees and Lucy wrestled the weapon out of his hand. It was a pipe.

Raven and Pieter did not have time to react to the huge figure of Wide as it bowled its way into the forum entrance toppling men, golems and the two friends on its way passed. With its arms full of struggling golems, Wide kicked its way through the open door, launched itself forward into the crush of clay bodies that pressed to gain entry to the senate. Raven sprang to his feet, lashing out with his katana he knocked back the only golem that now impeded the door's progress, heaved the bronze form into its framework, and slammed home the heavy-duty bolt. A constant drumfire of reverberations shook the door as wave after wave of golem bodies crashed against the bronze entranceway, but the doors stood firm.

'Come on, let's find Lucy,' Raven said to Pieter as he helped the old mercenary get to his feet. With their hands waving away the dusty air, they moved deeper into the coiling miasma of haze. Within a few paces, both men became separated and lost in their own world of grey swirling cloud.

Neither saw Luther Krell slink past holding his bloodied right hand and muttering a hex as his wild, maddened eyes sought a view through the dust to see the senate's entrance.

Lucy helped Senator Ferris to get his breath back, 'I'm really sorry, Senator. For a moment I thought you were attacking me.'

Ferris sucked in great gulps of dust-laden air and coughed. His ashen face caused not just by the fine particles of powder but also by his shock at being assaulted, turned painfully towards her and he shook his head as if to say it did not matter. Then his eyes widened and he pointed over her shoulder towards the doorway as a gap in the obscurity showed Luther escaping.

As Lucy swivelled, responding to Ferris's expression, she saw Luther begin to cast his hex, and watched in horror whilst the weighty bolt vibrated in its socket. The pressure from the golems outside had jammed it tight, but Luther's mad anger was taking its toll and reluctantly it began to move. Lucy looked around for something to throw and realising she was clutching Ferris's pipe drew her hand back. It would not damage the mage in any way, but at least it might distract him for a moment, but then she paused.

Reaching inside her jerkin, she fumbled around until her fingers closed upon the smooth cylinder that was Pieter's grenade. Drawing it out, she blew onto the pipe's bowl, and was rewarded with a flurry of sparks and a deep glow within its depths. She tilted the grenade and lit the fuse. Spitting like an angry snake the fuse took light and burned rapidly down, far more rapidly than she had anticipated and, gasping in surprise, she launched the grenade towards Luther as the gap in the dust cloud began to close over and the mage was lost from view.

Luther knew his strength was waning. The beating by Sarreg and company, the forced march to the senate and the thaumaturgical energy he had expended was taking its payment from his body, and he tottered, but the large bolt was moving slowly. Soon the doors would burst open and the senate would be flooded by his creations. Something struck the back of his head and he felt it drop into the tattered hessian sacking that hung from his shoulders. It hissed and spluttered and he frowned as he hooked his hand around to extricate it. As he twisted and turned to reach behind him his concentration on the doorway lapsed and the huge bolt stopped moving. A smell of burning reached his nostrils and frantically he tried to struggle out of the sacking. A huge hand smashed into his back, lifting him off the floor and smashing him face-first into the bronze doors. His ears, for a split second, had registered an enormous boom, and then nothing. His collision with the doorway was soundless, but excruciatingly painful as bones broke and skin split. He tumbled to the floor and through a red haze, saw flames leap up all around him as he realised he was on fire.

The sound of the explosion echoed around the senate room and for a moment, everyone froze. Lucy had expected something of the kind, but yet again, was startled by the grenade's reaction. She understood it would be more potent than the firework she had mistaken it for, but as her ears rang from the deafening explosion, all comparisons with squibs or bangers were swiftly discounted.

That was more like a stick of bloody dynamite, she thought, *I hope Luther was within its range.*

As the dust began to settle and her hearing returned to normal her hoped-for result was confirmed, as staggering towards her, was the blazing figure of the frenzied mage. Flames ate hungrily at his clothes, and where they had consumed the tattered remnants away, they licked across his blackened flesh. The smell of char wafted from him as giggling madly he limped forward. One ankle was patently broken as his left foot was almost twisted backwards. However, his hatred seemed to have overcome any pain he was experiencing, as unremittingly, he hobbled forward. Tendrils of purple energy corkscrewed and writhed over his burning body and Lucy wondered if it was only his prodigious magical power that kept him upright.

'Doesn't that guy know when he's beat?' asked Raven as he stepped next to her and pointed towards Luther with his sword.

Lucy took the katana from him and replied, 'Perhaps he needs more persuasion,' as she swept the blade up over her head and ran forward.

'I'll make it easier for *you*, than you did for my father,' she snarled as the katana flashed down onto Luther's left shoulder. It sliced effortlessly through the mage's torso and exited just above his right hip. A combination of blood and purple energy spewed from the two halves of his body as they plummeted to the dust-strewn floor. Remarkably, his eyes locked onto hers for a moment before glazing over, and finally Luther Krell went to a place from where even *his* magical prowess would not be able to free him.

Lucy flicked the blood from Raven's katana and handed it back to him. He gazed around the shocked senate and knew it would not be needed again, and so sheathed it.

Looking at the bronze doors he said, 'Listen!'

'What? I don't hear anything,' she replied.

'Yeah, that's just it, we can't hear anything. The golems have stopped trying to get in.'

Pieter joined them, helping a battered but intact Vela along with him. Vela blanched at the sight of the dismembered body of the mage, 'Well, it looks as if he's really dead this time,' he said.

'I bloody hope so too,' replied Lucy.

'I think his golems will have stopped now. They were obeying his command. Now that he's dead perhaps they'll go back to their owners,' Vela surmised.

'We can find out easily enough,' Lucy said as she pulled Raven with her and walked up to the entrance. She put her hand on the heavy bolt and Raven helped her pull it back. The doors creaked open. Golem fragments, piled waist high, collapsed into the room and they jumped back to avoid them. Outside in the square clay figures stood rigid like statues. 'Looks as if they won't be going back to their owners after all. Perhaps he didn't program them to revert to their previous instructions…'

'Lucy, look…' Raven knelt down by the mutilated remains of Wide. Both its arms were sheared off, the right at the elbow, and the left high up near the shoulder. One leg remained but great fissures were spread across it and ran up its torso, 'It helped. When we were pushed back from the door. It fought its way through and held them back for us.'

'I know, Rave…' She said as tears sprang to her eyes again, 'Wide was the golem that Luther imprisoned my father's soul in.'

As if hearing its name the golem stirred and its head grated towards Lucy; fragments of terracotta dropped from it as the damage it had sustained caused the cracked surface to loose coherency.

'It's still alive!' gasped Raven moving back, his hand reaching for his sword.

'Don't, Raven,' she said laying a hand on his arm, 'It freed itself.'

Although the golem had no eyes, Lucy knew it was looking at her, as it slowly opened its mouth and revealed the hex-tile within. She bent down close to the prostrate giant and smoothed the debris from its forehead, and as she placed a kiss upon its head, she withdrew the tile from its mouth.

When she stood up all that remained on the floor was a broken statue. In her hand, the tile felt as heavy as the world. On its surface glyphs and strange symbolic figures swirled in agitated dances in dimensions that made her eyes ache.

With a long, shuddering sigh, she broke the tile between her small but tough hands, 'Go now Daddy, time for you to rest. Mommy is waiting for you; give her my love.'

As she wished her father goodbye, a wisp of ethereal mist seeped out from the broken tile with the gossamer quality of the finest cobweb, and pirouetted in the air. It spun before the group of friends as if in jubilation before being caught by the wind and then melted away to nothing.

All three, Raven, Vela and Pieter surrounded Lucy and hugged her whilst she sobbed uncontrollably. The little group of four were too deeply entrenched in their own sadness to notice the renewal of an altercation from within the forum, but as a shadowy shape rushed passed them and leapt into the sky each recognised the figure of Davvid Krell and understood he had slipped the custody of his guards and had made good his escape. Watching the young mage gain altitude with great beats of his leathery wings, all four felt the bitter taste in their mouths of a job unfinished. However, Jakob chased out after the runaway and squinting up into the sky at the ever-diminishing figure, he reached out for Vela, 'Give me my bow for a moment, young Vela, and pick me a true arrow.'

Vela handed the old paladin the weapon and chose an arrow at random, 'All your arrows are true you old fart. And if you get within twenty paces of him I'll muck out Molly's crap whenever you ask me to.'

Without taking his eyes off his target, Jakob took the bow from the boy and held it in his right hand. The two missing fingers did little to inconvenience him as he notched the arrow and drew it back to his cheek with his left, and unmutilated, hand.

'It's a deal, and if I miss you can have all the treasure I've saved,' then he let fly.

The arrow soared upwards towards the escaping Davvid,

but seemed a little high. However, on the next down beat of his wings, Davvid rose a fraction upwards and the arrow struck him in the back. He arched in the air and one wing folded. In a spiralling fall, he crashed towards the ground but fell far beyond their view behind the row of roofs near the dockyard.

Jakob handed the bow back to the boy and then stuck the two stumps of his fingers up in the air to where the young mage had fallen, 'You silly buggers cut off the wrong fingers. I'm left handed,' he cackled as Vela bemoaned the fact he could be called upon to clean out Molly's shit anytime Jakob felt like. Nevertheless, his face did light up when Sheba bounded up the steps and leapt into his arms, licking the chalky, white dust from the boy's face.

Senator Ferris called them from the doorway, 'Jakob, can you bring your friends inside please? Senator Casco would like you to address the senate. He says you have some important news about our guests?'

'What's this all about now?' Lucy asked Raven quietly.

He raised his eyebrows, 'Your guess is as good as mine.'

Brushing off the dust before entering, the four speculated on what news there could be awaiting. Raven hoped it was a knighthood. He had always fancied himself as Sir Raven. Lucy surmised it was probably a prison sentence for the damage caused to the once beautiful senate building.

'We didn't start it!' he retorted.

As she stepped around the charred corpse of Luther she replied, 'But we certainly finished it.'

Casco waited until his old friend rejoined him and then standing up he raised both hands for silence, 'Healers, attend the wounded. Militiamen and guards, attend to the dead. As our illustrious mayor is under arrest for murder and other acts of violence against his fellow senators, and ultimately the state itself, I ask the members for permission to act as temporary mayor until such time as another is voted into office. All in favour please raise their hand.' The room filled with raised hands and raised voices, all giving their support to the old senator. 'Are there any not in favour?' Not one dissenting hand was raised. 'Thank you all for your faith in me.'

A burst of applause filled the senate and Jakob clapped Casco on his back making clouds of white dust puff up from the old senator's toga-style robes.

'Can we tell them now?' Jakob asked eagerly.

Shaking his head slowly Casco whispered to his friend, 'Don't you think we've had enough excitement for today?'

Jakob looked downhearted and scratched his stubbly chin, 'I was just beginning to enjoy myself.'

'When are you going to act your age you old rapscallion?'

'Ha... if I acted my age I'd be bloody six foot under. Let's tell them, go on, and tell them.'

Knowing he would get no peace, acting-Mayor Casco waved for silence once again, 'Some of you know I have some important news to announce. Although I would have preferred to wait until tomorrow to explain,' He frowned at Jakob, 'some people do not have the patience to wait.' Many of the senators laughed quietly knowing whom Casco was referring to but all waited anxiously for Casco's revelations.

Raven nudged Lucy, 'Here we go, arise, Sir Raven.'

She elbowed him back, 'Or off with his head!'

Casco continued, 'We have among us today two strangers. Two strangers who have assisted with the salvation of this austere house from the menace of rogue mages, and their desire to enslave our citizens, and us in much the same way they have enslaved the spirits reaped for use in their creations.' He whispered something to Jakob and the old paladin replied softly. Casco waved the four friends forward, 'Come closer, Lucy and Raven. These two are the ones of which I speak. They are not only from far away, but, if I understand correctly they are from another world.'

The senate resounded with the awestruck mutterings of disbelief.

'Oh, I doubted too,' Casco nodded, 'But have you not seen with your own eyes? These two could not be affected by magic directly. Luther Krell was unable to use his powers upon them.' Many of the senators clapped in agreement.

Casco looked down on Lucy and Raven, 'We owe you much. Therefore, this senate offers you both a boon. Choose what you wish.'

Raven hopped up and down like a child before receiving his Christmas presents, 'See? I told you so. Let's ask for something cool. I've always wanted a mansion house and a bit of land,' he turned to her, a questioning expression on his face, 'I wonder who owns Cornwall?'

She rolled her eyes at him in despair, 'I give up,' she sighed, 'What good is Cornwall to you here, if we decide to go back to our Earth?'

He frowned, 'Oh… yeah,' then added, 'If you want to go back, I suppose.'

She looked at him in surprise, 'You'd consider staying?'

Raven shrugged, 'I suppose. Herakleitos once said, 'No man can cross the same river twice, because neither the man nor the river is the same'. Things have changed Lucy. We are different now. I'd never be a knight in our world and no way would I be allowed to walk around with this on my hip,' he patted the katana.

'Bloody Herakleitos!' she moaned.

Lucy turned her attention towards Casco, 'Mayor, senators and gentlemen. Thank you for your offer. My…'friend' and I gratefully accept it,' she glanced once at Raven's beaming face and then carried on, 'Our boon would be to request the immediate cessation of all golem production, and the dismantling of all existing golems. Plus the destruction of the tiles which trap the life-force of their unwilling victims.'

The room fell silent, only the strangled gargling sound from deep within Raven's chest broke the stillness.

Casco cleared his throat, 'A difficult boon to fulfill. As strangers to our laws and customs I can understand your misconceptions about our golems but please appreciate that golems have been produced since the first mages arose, more than two thousand years ago. They only contain the life-force, as you describe it, of willing donors or criminals. The stealing of souls from people is *never* condoned and your experience with Luther Krell visiting your own world will be impossible to reproduce. That terrible part of our history is just that, history. Golems play a major part in our economy. To ask this boon is to condemn us all to hardship, and for many, financial ruin. I beg you to reconsider.'

Lucy extricated her mobile phone from her pocket and strode up to where Casco and Jakob stood. She opened it and thumbed the video button, and pressed play.

'This is magic from my world. And this is what your mages think of your laws regarding the reaping of souls, life-force, whatever you want to call the thing they rip from the poor people they abuse. This is what *you* are defending,' and the video started playing.

'Must I explain?' Luther sighed, 'So be it. The Rapture Bud not only allows me to travel to your world, it also acts as a siphon. When I place the stamen upon the prey it reaps the soul from the body. It gets transported back across the void and imprisoned in a magical tile that I have constructed to hold it. That tile's life force is what animates our golems. Oh, we do use souls from here as well, but they are vastly inferior. Add to that the inconvenience of the senate only allowing us to reap the dying or criminals for our work and you will understand our predicament,' he looked at Davvid and smiled, 'However, the senate does not know everything, eh, Davvid?'

His apprentice gave a chilling grin in return.

Luther continued, 'The souls we steal from beneath their noses will not trouble them if they do not know. However, your world has a much higher quality and your father's was the best so far. I have high expectations of you though. I'm sure yours will excel.'

She closed the phone and returned it to her pocket and folded her arms, a stern look crossed her face as she waited for Casco's response.

'In my old age I had hoped to spend my time sitting in the back of the senate, listening to my esteemed members debate passionately the implications of land usage or taxes, perhaps something as controversial as voting for women. However, I did not think I would find myself facing a decision as difficult or as controversial as this. Nevertheless, from what I have witnessed today, I can only conclude that the power mages hold is ultimately perverting and sinister. Have we not witnessed the way it can twist even the most benign mind into the thralls of megalomania and omnipotence?' he smiled at Lucy, 'Even though I will go down in the annuls of our history as the mayor, albeit temporary one, who instigated the biggest crash in our country's economy by granting you your boon. It will be done. Your boon is granted. From henceforth golem productions is illegal. Each and every golem is to be freed of their hex-tile and that tile is to be destroyed.'

Lucy put her arms around the old man's neck and kissed him on the cheek as he chuckled gleefully and whispered, 'But granting your boon does have its advantages!'

She stood back and pouted playfully, 'Naughty!'

As Lucy returned to Raven, who looked as if he had found a penny and lost a pound, she heard Casco cough and call for attention.

'The last order of the day before we conclude and bring to close what has been what must be the most eventful few hours in our history, is to do with our future leader. We have already discussed the necessity of selecting a younger person for the post, and preferably a non-mage this time,' he brought Jakob closer to his side. 'Most of you know Paladin Gawen's story, and therefore I will not repeat it. However, none of you know that when he escaped the sinking of *The Antelope* with his fingers missing, but his life intact, he also took something, or rather *someone* else with him.'

Jakob reached inside his studded leather top and pulled out a leather thong upon which dangled a ring, he snapped the cord and dropped it into Casco's hand.

'Jakob was entrusted with the safety of the King's daughter.'

For a moment, it was if the senate had fallen into the chaos of battle, again, as senators argued over the statement Casco had dropped on them like another grenade.

'Please, please, let me continue. I grow very tired my friends and my afternoon nap is long overdue,' he smiled gently as the room came to order, 'It is true. The King had a daughter that only a select few knew about. Jakob was one of those few. She was born out of wedlock and to a commoner. The King would have announced her one day but felt the time was not right as there was much unrest amongst the people. Unrest instigated by none other than the mages, I might add.' He paused for breath and lifted the ring up to show the room.

'This is the King's sigil. It was given for safekeeping to Paladin Gawen whilst the Princess was growing up. When circumstances allowed, we, Jakob and I, were to produce her before the senate, and offer our citizens the chance to decide if she should attain a position *in* the senate, perhaps that of Mayor. However, it was not to be. As she grew older, she fell in love with a young soldier in Marin's Weir. Unfortunately, he was killed in the line of duty and she was left alone and with child,' Casco looked at his feet and shook his head sadly, 'Misfortune paid another visit to the Princess nine months later, when, during childbirth, she too passed on. Her son survived however, and it is he, today, Jakob and I wish to present to the senate,' Casco searched the crowd of dusty up-turned faces until he found the one he looked for and his teary eyes filled as he said, 'Please, join us Prince Vela, and retrieve your father's ring of office.'

Chapter 21

The Duke of Cornwall

Two drayks wheeled and swooped in the fresh air of the summer morning. The passengers of one whooped and cheered as the single passenger on the other somehow managed to coerce his mount into doing a complete loop whilst he gripped onto the saddle framework with his hands and knees.

'Come on Lucy,' shouted Raven excitedly in her ear, 'Let's land. I want to try that too. You can stay on the ground if you don't trust my driving.'

'Listen, I can be a little mad on times, perhaps even stupid. But there's no way I'm going to do that, and furthermore neither are you… Sir Raven,' she shouted back and his face beamed when she called him by his title, 'If Pieter wants to break his stupid old neck that is up to him, and Sheba is getting air-sick enough as it is,' she patted the little dog's head that poked out from the leather harness in front of her. 'Another thing, I'm not staying in this world on my own. Even if I am the Duchess of Cornwall, and will have suitors coming to call on me. Probably gagging to put a ring on my finger and get me into their bed. Hmm… that is a thought. Let me land then and you can give it a try,' she teased as he dug his fingers into her backside.

'No way. José… that ass is all mine,' he laughed, 'Keep on flying. I want to see what this estate Vela has bestowed upon us is like. Who would have guessed that little runt was royalty eh? Thief, mage, cook and Prince. Great c.v.'

As they flew over the coastline, and the sea appeared below them, a shimmering blue expanse of white capped waves, she reached into her jacket and pulled out an old green journal and threw it away from her. It tumbled end over end, leaves of paper falling out and fluttering to the sea like dying birds.

'Strike out mage from that c.v. of his,' she said quietly as the remains of Luther Krell's journal struck the sea's surface and with the next crashing wave sank down into its depths.

Many miles away, but upon the same white capped sea, the sailors on a small ketch-rigged fishing smack stowed the last of their catch below in salted barrels, whilst others turned the ship towards their homeport of Fivewinds. The change in tack provoked an opposite list, which resulted in the sleeping man below, to roll painfully onto his broken wing. He groaned in his sleep and the young cabin boy at his side dipped the rag he was holding into the bucket of tepid water, wrung it out and placed it on the man's fevered brow. The ship's captain had refused to return to port when they had fished the man from the sea, just off the coast of the large estuary that led up to the city of Fivewinds. So what if he was a mage? If he had been any good he would not have been floating, half dead in the water, the captain had decided... and kept to his schedule. If the man survived, then all well and good. If he did not...he did not.

As the fishing smack ran before the rising wind, the captain examined the glowering sky. Black clouds billowed up on the horizon behind them and threatened a storm. In the dark and cramped cabin below decks the cabin boy lit the small stub of a candle as the sparse light from above faded, and pulled out the small brown leather-covered book he had found hidden inside the man's boot, and opened it. He turned the book around and around as he tried to make sense of the words and hieroglyphics that filled its damp pages. A muttering escaped from the lips of the unconscious man, and if the boy had dragged his eyes away from the pages, he would have perhaps wondered at the strange tendrils of purple mist that wound their sinuous way up from the man's body.

Epilogue

<u>London 2006</u>

'I've got a can of lager if you wanna swap, but it better be more than just a mouthful this time. Pull the paper down. Lemme see how much ya got left in the bottle.'

The woman looked at the battered lager can that the old man proffered forward and sniffing, wiped a filthy and threadbare sleeve across her grubby face. She only managed to spread the mucus that streamed from her broken nose even further across her scowling countenance.

'That there lager looks empty. How do I know there's sommit in it?'

As if imploring the stars that twinkled down on them from the hard winter sky the old man raised his eyes upwards to the heavens, 'Jesus, you are one mistrusting bitch. Look!' He shook the can up and down and the sound of the trapped liquid within filled the doorway in which the two homeless tramps had pitched their cardboard houses for the night. 'Can ya hear that? Now let me see how much stuff ya got in that bottle, or bugger it. I'll drink the lager instead and ya can get stuffed.'

She ran her white-coated tongue over her dried and cracked lips. The lager would quench her thirst but the buzz from it would be less than what she'd receive from the remains of the methylated spirits. She cradled the bottle to her chest like a child. When the old man fingered the ring pull on the can, as if preparing to open it, the temptation and her thirst proved too much for her and she nodded. She pulled down the brown paper bag from around the bottle. 'There, it's got about three or four swallows left in it, all right?'

The old man squinted and leaned forward in an attempt to verify her claim. The streetlight offered poor illumination but it was enough. 'More like two, perhaps three at most,' he rubbed his straggly beard, 'I dunno, what else ya got to add to it?'

'You can have this too,' she plucked a partially smoked cigarette from behind one of her grimy ears and held it up for him to inspect.

'I dunno, seems like a poor deal to me. That all ya got?'

'It's been a quiet day,' she said glumly, then looked at with a sly smile on her tired face, 'You can cuddle up to me tonight. I'll keep you warm, I will.'

He laughed and hawked up a bolus of phlegm and with practised accuracy spat it into the gutter, 'Keep me warm indeed. Yer skin and bones, woman. It'd be me keeping *yer* arse warm and not t'other way round.'

'I ain't had any complaints before.' She replied haughtily and brushed a hand through the tangled bird's nest that was her hair.

'Yeah, well p'raps some of yer mates ain't as particular as me.'

'Shit, I didn't realise you were royalty and such, excuse me!' She started to get up, 'I'll find another spot for tonight and one without a bloody prince in it.'

The old man grabbed the hem of her worn coat and pulled her back, 'Now, now. Don't go all feisty on me. Ok, it's a deal. The meths, the ciggy and you sleep in my sack with me. All right?'

She sat back down, 'Yes, sleep. That's all.'

He shook his head, 'Woman, it's too fucking cold for anything else. I don't even wanna take it out for a pee, let alone have it poking around *your* old bones.'

'Ok, hand over the lager and I'll give you the meths and the ciggy.'

Like a pair of fighting cocks warily circling and waiting for an opening, the two carried out the swap. The bottle and cigarette left her dirt encrusted right hand as the battered lager can was grasped by her left. The exchange was done.

As the can hissed and the woman slobbered the spume and lager into her mouth the old man tipped the meths bottle to his lips and swallowed greedily.

'Three, I said it was more like three. Didn't I?' He moaned, 'It was almost two and a half but I took smaller mouthfuls, so it was three.'

'I can't help it if you got a big gob,' she said and watched him warily in case he decided to make a lunge for the remains of the lager, 'You ain't gonna light that cigarette now are you? I don't want be next to you if you do.'

'Nah, I'll keep it for breakfast,' he stretched out on his cardboard mattress and pulled a heavy blanket over himself, then patted the ground beside him. 'Come on then, princess. Your prince awaits.'

She giggled and for a moment the light played a trick with her face and eyes and the old man saw a glimpse of what she had been before reaching the depths of despair and poverty in which they both now dwelled.

D.I. Rabbet ducked under the blue and white 'Police Do Not Cross' tape and hesitated before going into the doorway. The smell was one he recognised. The heavy tarpaulin covering the two bodies did little to contain the acrid odour of char. He swivelled around and beckoned his young sergeant forward.

'Ok, Taylor, prepare yourself. This isn't going to be pretty.'

The young sergeant raised an eyebrow, 'I *have* seen corpses before, Boss. A couple of rummies who've been drinking meths and dropped off to sleep with a lighted cigarette isn't exactly rare on this beat.'

Rabbet nodded, 'True, unfortunately it happens all too often. But from what I've already been told this isn't the case here. And from what my old nose tells me, I think I know what's happened too.' He tapped the side of his nose with a finger. 'And call me 'Boss or Guv' once more and you'll be sorry. I've worked damn hard to be entitled to be called Inspector, so you can bloody well use that.'

'Yes, sir.'

The two men moved closer to the tarpaulin and Taylor frowned, 'That's weird, sir.'

'What is?'

'Just doesn't seem to be any fire damage to the doorway.' Taylor bent over and gripped the edge of the tarpaulin and before Rabbet could reply the young sergeant pulled the heavy sheet away. 'Holy crap! What the hell's happened here!'

Rabbet was impressed. Taylor had taken it better than he imagined he would have done. Although looking slightly green the youngster had recovered quickly from the initial shock.

'I said it wasn't going to be pretty.'

'I know, sir. But I've never seen anything like this before. Look at her face! She was terrified. Whatever burnt them both must have been ferocious, like a flame-thrower or napalm, I dunno. If it wasn't for the fact that there's three legs remaining and her head, it could be just one body.'

'No it's definitely two. We've canvassed and a couple of vagrants heard the screaming. They knew the victims.'

'Did they see what happened, sir?'

Rabbet paused then looked at Taylor, 'Yes, they did.'

'And? Was it some sort of vigilante thing? Did they get doused in something and set alight?' Taylor examined the floor and doorway again, 'But nothing else it burnt, just them.'

'No, it wasn't any of those things.' Rabbet sighed, 'I almost wish it was.'

Taylor dropped the tarpaulin back over the grisly remains, 'So what does your nose tell you, sir? And what did the witnesses see?'

D.I. Rabbet's lips tightened as if the words he wanted to say were better left unsaid, but finally he answered the young sergeant.

'My nose tells me its S.H.C. and the two vagrants saw a figure with the two deceased in the doorway.'

'You mean, spontaneous human combustion?'

'Yes.'

'Weren't you involved in something a few years back that was similar?'

'Yes, in '99. We had two people go missing too. We never found them.'

Taylor nodded, 'I heard rumours.'

Rabbet sighed again, 'I bet you did.'

'Can the vagrants ID the figure?' asked Taylor.

'Yes, for what it's worth.' Replied Rabbet.

'So?'

Rabbet hesitated, he really didn't want to say it.

'Sir?'

'They saw a giant bat.'

Taylor laughed, 'You're kidding, right?'

Rabbet didn't answer.

'You're not kidding, sir, are you?'

D.I. Rabbet shook his head slowly, 'No, Taylor, I'm not. The bat is back.'

About The Author

Bob Lock is a Gower born Welshman, married with two grown-up children and two grand-children. After taking early retirement he now spends his time writing.

Find more info on Bob's site at : www.scifi-tales.com

One Small Step

Chapter 1 starts with the famous speech by Neil Armstrong during the first moon landing. The more common version of the text is used here, although space enthusiasts may argue about the missing 'a' in this sentence.

In the 2005 book *First Man: The Life of Neil A. Armstrong*, Armstrong told Hansen that others have pointed out that he can often be heard dropping the vowels from his speech in radio transmissions.

"It doesn't sound like there was time for the word to be there," Armstrong said in the book. "On the other hand, I didn't intentionally make an inane statement, and ... certainly the 'a' was intended, because that's the only way the statement makes any sense.

"So I would hope that history would grant me leeway for dropping the syllable and understand that it was certainly intended, even if it wasn't said — although it might actually have been."

Other SD Books Available

The Midnight Hour by Neil Davies
14 Tales Of Dark Imagination
ISBN : 978-0-9555185-0-8

Coming Soon

Dead Ends : *A collection of dark fiction*
short stories by various authors

The Postmodern Mariner by Rhys Hughes
A book of implausible adventures

Past Sins by Dave Cook
A supernatural tale of horror and revenge

Kangazang! by Terry Cooper
Epic space adventure with plenty of humour

Against The Darkness by John L. Probert
A collection of supernatural detective stories

Screaming Dreams
www.screamingdreams.com

Printed in the United Kingdom
by Lightning Source UK Ltd.
118380UK00001B/1-39